The Rex Stout Library

REX STOUT

Some Buried Caesar

&

The Golden Spiders

Introduction to Some Buried Caesar
by Diane Mott Davidson

Introduction to The Golden Spiders
by Linda Barnes

BANTAM BOOKS

SOME BURIED CAESAR / THE GOLDEN SPIDERS
A Bantam Book / October 2008

Some Buried Caesar is published by arrangement with the
author's estate.
The Golden Spiders is published by arrangement with
Viking Penguin.

Published by
Bantam Dell
A Division of Random House, Inc.
New York, New York

Cover art and design by Daniel Pelavin

Bantam Books and the rooster colophon are registered trademarks
of Random House, Inc.

ISBN 978-0-553-38567-0

These titles were individually published by Bantam Books.

Printed in the United States of America
Published simultaneously in Canada

www.bantamdell.com

OPM 10 9 8 7 6 5 4 3 2 1

Some Buried Caesar

Introduction

What some people will do for publicity. In the realm of food, you can make a Guinness record–defying submarine sandwich or pepperoni pizza. Or, in the case of Thomas Pratt, owner of a string of 1930s-vintage fast-food restaurants known as pratterias, you can propose to barbecue a prizewinning bull. To spend $45,000 on a piece of beef that will serve only 100 people, explains the enterprising Pratt to an unamused Nero Wolfe and a goggling Archie Goodwin, is not only an efficient way to spend money that would otherwise go to ineffectual newspaper advertising, it also makes *psychological* sense:

Look here. Do you realize what a stir it will make that the senior grand champion Guernsey bull of the United States is being barbecued and served in chunks and slices to a gathering of epicures? And by whom? By Tom Pratt of the famous pratterias! Let alone the publicity, do you know what the result will be? For weeks and months every customer that eats a roast beef sandwich in a pratteria will have a sneaking unconscious feeling that he's chewing a piece of Hickory Caesar

Introduction

Grindon! That's what I mean when I say psychology.

But psychology has a tendency to run amuck, as do both people and sedans. Stranded at the Pratt house in upstate New York owing to an unforeseen encounter between their car and a tree, the immense, unflappable Nero Wolfe and his smart-mouth assistant, Archie Goodwin, have to remake both housing and transportation plans on their expedition to exhibit Wolfe's orchids at the fair in nearby Crowfield. In the process, they land in the middle of a not-so-neighborly altercation between Guernsey League officials, longtime stockmen, and Pratt. Infuriated at Pratt's plan for Hickory Caesar Grindon, the stockmen cajole, threaten, insult, and even propose a dangerous wager in order to save Caesar. So heated is their conflict that a character from the sixties might observe, "Hey! Don't have a cow, man."

But of course that is the point: despite the many remonstrances, the cow will be had. And this being the thirties rather than the sixties, the demonstration ends there. The various characters skulk off concocting complicated designs to fulfill their passions: amorous, financial, and bovine. There is the female golf champion ("one of those," Archie uncharitably observes), formerly engaged to one of the feuding neighbors, who in *his* turn is now smitten with a Pratt houseguest, who has in *her* turn begun to lavish her attentions on an unreluctant Archie. The female golf champion is willing to pay Archie the cost of lunch to keep the houseguest away from her brother, Jimmy Pratt. (And the cost of the lunch for two people in 1938? Two dollars, which will not quite get you a cup of cappuccino in 1994, much less a biscotto to go with it.) There is the big-boned stockman who, after his herd was virtually destroyed by anthrax, sold Caesar to Tom Pratt, but only with great sadness ("I was up all night the day he was dropped—he sucked these fingers when he was only six hours old."). And there is the love-smitten, bet-proffering neighbor, also an expert stockman. He is accompanied by a suspicious-looking city slicker friend, who persists in presenting himself as the model of sartorial perfection in a Crawnley suit and Monteith tie, despite the fact that this is, after all, the country.

Unfortunately, the country is immune to neither bizarre couture nor evil. When first one and then another murder occurs, Nero Wolfe diverts himself from attending to his precious orchids (prizewinning albinos) and rouses himself (but not much) to apply logic and observation, and some sleight of hand, to the solution. When pursuit of the murderer leads him out to the Crowfield fair, Nero Wolfe fortifies himself with regular trips to the Methodist tent, where the followers of John Wesley are making quite a name (and a pretty penny) for themselves with their excellent chicken fricassee and dumplings. Archie manages to maintain, albeit tenuously, his love interest, while fooling the smarter-than-expected rural police, who suspect he is hiding evidence. Despite his quick hand, quick brain, and even quicker mouth, Archie ends up in the Crowfield County jail, where he amuses himself by forming the Crowfield County Prisoners' Union, complete with a much-disputed list of demands.

The solution to this delightfully complicated plot comes at last, and just in time for Nero's and Archie's safe deliverance from the perils of upstate New York.

Introduction

For those still hungering for a barbecue at book's end, I offer a recipe for beans to go with your ribs. Serve them with potato salad, rolls, corn, coleslaw, and rich, fudgy, homemade brownies—all essential components of a true all-American barbecue. While Archie would undoubtedly refer to a side dish as "a cute number sitting on the bench," and refer the cooking of beans to Fritz, I found the best recipe for a bean dish from Tom and Enid Schantz of the Rue Morgue mystery bookstore in Boulder, Colorado. Enjoy, and don't let anybody give you any bull.

RUE MORGUE BEANS WITH BACON

8 slices bacon
1 15-ounce can pinto beans, drained
1 15-ounce can kidney beans, drained
1 15-ounce can garbanzo beans, drained
1 28-ounce can baked beans, including sauce (recommended brand: B & M)
4 cups onions, quartered and thinly sliced (about 2 large onions)
½ cup dark corn syrup
¼ cup cider vinegar
1 tsp. dry mustard

Cook bacon, drain, and cut into 1-inch slices. Combine bacon and rest of ingredients in Dutch oven on top of stove. Simmer uncovered for 2 hours, stirring every 15 minutes, until sauce is slightly reduced and onions are completely cooked. Serves 8.

—Diane Mott Davidson

Chapter 1

That sunny September day was full of surprises. The first one came when, after my swift realization that the sedan was still right side up and the windshield and windows intact, I switched off the ignition and turned to look at the back seat. I didn't suppose the shock of the collision would have hurled him to the floor, knowing as I did that when the car was in motion he always had his feet braced and kept a firm grip on the strap; what I expected was the ordeal of facing a glare of fury that would top all records; what I saw was him sitting there calmly on the seat with his massive round face wearing a look of relief—if I knew his face, and I certainly knew Nero Wolfe's face. I stared at him in astonishment.

He murmured, "Thank God," as if it came from his heart.

I demanded, "What?"

"I said thank God." He let go of the strap and wiggled a finger at me. "It has happened, and here we are. I presume you know, since I've told you, that my distrust and hatred of vehicles in motion is partly based on my plerophory that their apparent submission to control is illusory and that they may at their pleasure, and sooner or later will, act on whim. Very well, this one has, and we are intact. Thank God the whim was not a deadlier one."

"Whim hell. Do you know what happened?"

"Certainly. I said, whim. Go ahead."

"What do you mean, go ahead?"

"I mean go on. Start the confounded thing going again."

I opened the door and got out and walked around to the front to take a look. It was a mess. After a careful examination I went back to the other side of the car and opened the rear door and looked in at him and made my report.

"It was quite a whim. I'd like to get it on record what happened, since I've been driving your cars nine years and this is the first time I've ever stopped before I was ready to. That was a good tire, so they must have run it over glass at the garage where I left it last night, or maybe I did myself, though I don't think so. Anyway, I was going 55 when the tire blew out. She left the road, but I didn't lose the wheel, and I was braking and had her headed up and would have made it if it hadn't been for that damn tree. Now the fender is smashed into the rubber and a knuckle is busted and the radiator's ripped open."

"How long will it take you to fix it?"

"I can't fix it. If I had a nail I wouldn't even bother to bite it, I'd swallow it whole."

"Who can fix it?"

"Men with tools in a garage."

"It isn't in a garage."

"Right."

He closed his eyes and sat. Pretty soon he opened them again and sighed. "Where are we?"

"Two hundred and thirty-seven miles northeast of Times Square. Eighteen miles southwest of Crowfield, where the North Atlantic Exposition is held every year, beginning on the second Monday in September and lasting—"

"Archie." His eyes were narrowed at me. "Please save the jocularity. What are we going to do?"

I admit I was touched. Nero Wolfe asking me what to do! "I don't know about you," I said, "but I'm going to kill myself. I was reading in the paper the other day how a Jap always commits suicide when he fails his emperor, and no Jap has anything on me. They call it seppuku. Maybe you think they call it hara-kiri, but they don't or at least rarely. They call it seppuku."

He merely repeated, "What are we going to do?"

"We're going to flag a car and get a lift. Preferably to Crowfield, where we have reservations at a hotel."

"Would you drive it?"

"Drive what?"

"The car we flag."

"I don't imagine he would let me after he sees what I've done to this one."

Wolfe compressed his lips. "I won't ride with a strange driver."

"I'll go to Crowfield alone and rent a car and come back for you."

"That would take two hours. No."

I shrugged. "We passed a house about a mile back. I'll bum a ride there or walk, and phone to Crowfield for a car."

"While I sit here, waiting, helplessly, in this disabled demon."

"Right."

He shook his head. "No."

"You won't do that?"

"No."

I stepped back around the rear of the car to survey the surroundings, near and far. It was a nice September day, and the hills and dales of upstate New York looked sleepy and satisfied in the sun. The road we were on was a secondary highway, not a main drag, and nothing had passed by since I had bumped the tree. A hundred yards ahead it curved to the right, dipping down behind some trees. I couldn't see the house we had passed a mile or so back, on account of another curve. Across the road was a gentle slope of meadow which got steeper further up where the meadow turned into woods. I turned. In that direction was a board fence painted white, a smooth green pasture, and a lot of trees; and beyond the trees were some bigger ones, and the top of a house. There was no drive leading that way, so I figured that there would be one further along the road, around the curve.

Wolfe yelled to ask what the devil I was doing, and I stepped back to the car door.

"Well," I said, "I don't see a garage anywhere. There's a house across there among those big trees. Going around by the road it would probably be a mile or more, but cutting across that pasture would be only maybe 400 yards. If you don't want to sit here helpless, I will, I'm armed, and you go hunt a phone. That house over there is closest."

Away off somewhere, a dog barked. Wolfe looked at me. "That was a dog barking."

"Yes, sir."

"Probably attached to that house. I'm in no humor to contend with a loose dog. We'll go together. But I won't climb that fence."

"You won't need to. There's a gate back a little way."

He sighed, and bent over to take a look at the crates, one on the floor and one on the seat beside him, which held the potted orchid plants. In view of the whim we had had, it was a good thing they had been secured so they couldn't slide around. Then he started to clamber out, and I stepped back to make room for him outdoors, room being a thing he required more than his share of. He took a good stretch, his applewood walking stick pointing like a sword at the sky as he did so, and turned all the way around, scowling at the hills and dales, while I got the doors of the car locked, and then followed me along the edge of the ditch to the place where we could cross to the gate.

It was after we had passed through, just as I got the gate closed behind us, that I heard the guy yelling. I looked across the pasture in the direction of the house, and there he was, sitting on top of the fence on the other side. He must have just climbed up. He was yelling at us to go back where we came from. At that distance I couldn't tell for sure whether it was a rifle or a shotgun he had with the butt against his shoulder. He wasn't exactly aiming it at us, but intentions seemed to be along that line. Wolfe had gone on ahead while I was shutting the gate, and I trotted up to him and grabbed his arm.

"Hold on a minute. If that's a bughouse and that's one of the inmates, he may take us for woodchucks or wild turkeys—"

Wolfe snorted. "The man's a fool. It's only a cow pasture." Being a good detective, he produced his evidence by pointing to a brown circular heap near our feet. Then he glared toward the menace on the fence, bellowed "Shut up!" and went on. I followed. The guy kept yelling and waving the gun, and we kept to our course, but I admit I wasn't liking it, because I could see now it was a shotgun and he might easily be the kind of a nut that would pepper us.

There was an enormous boulder, sloping up to maybe 3 feet above the ground, about exactly in the middle of the pasture, and we were a little to the right of that when the second surprise arrived in the series I spoke of. My attention was pretty thoroughly concentrated on the nut with the shotgun, still perched on the fence and yelling louder than ever, when I felt Wolfe's fingers gripping my elbow and heard his sudden sharp command:

"Stop! Don't move!"

I stopped dead, with him beside me. I thought he had discovered something psychological about the bird on the fence, but he said without looking at me, "Stand perfectly still. Move your head slowly, very slowly, to the right."

For an instant I thought the nut with the gun had something contagious and Wolfe had caught it, but I did as I was told, and there was the second surprise. Off maybe 200 feet to the right, walking slowly toward us with his head up, was a bull bigger than I had supposed bulls came. He was dark red with white patches, with a big white triangle on his face, and he was walking easy and slow, wiggling his head a little as if he was nervous, or as if he was trying to shake a fly off of his horns. Of a sudden he stopped and stood, looking at us with his neck curved.

I heard Wolfe's voice, not loud, at the back of my head, "It would be better if that fool would quit yelling. Do you know the technique of bulls? Did you ever see a bull fight?"

I moved my lips enough to get it out: "No, sir."

Wolfe grunted. "Stand still. You moved your finger then, and his neck muscles tightened. How fast can you run?"

"I can beat that bull to that fence. Don't think I can't. But you can't."

"I know very well I can't. Twenty years ago I was an athlete. This almost convinces me . . . but that can wait. Ah, he's pawing. His head's down. If he should start . . . it's that confounded yelling. Now . . . back off slowly, away from me. Keep facing him. When you are 10 feet from me, swerve toward the fence. He will begin to move when you do. As long as he follows slowly, keep backing and facing him. When he starts his rush, turn and run—"

I never got a chance to follow directions. I didn't move, and I'm sure Wolfe didn't, so it must have been our friend on the fence—maybe he jumped off into the pasture. Anyhow, the bull curved his neck and started on the jump; and if it was the other guy he was headed for, that didn't help any, because we were in line with him and we came first. He started the way an avalanche ends. Possibly if we had stood still he would have passed by, about 3 feet to my right, but either it was asking too much of human nature to expect me to stand there, or I'm not human. I have since maintained that it flashed through my mind that if I moved it would attract him to me and away from

Nero Wolfe, but there's no use continuing that argument here. There's no question but what I moved, without any preliminary backing. And there's no question, whoever he started for originally, about his being attracted by my movement. I could hear him behind me. I could damn near feel him. Also I was dimly aware of shouts and a blotch of something red above the fence near the spot I was aimed at. There it was—the fence. I didn't do any braking for it, but took it at full speed, doing a vault with my hands reaching for its top, and one of my hands missed and I tumbled, landing flat on the other side, sprawling and rolling. I sat up and panted and heard a voice above me:

"Beautiful! I wouldn't have missed that for anything."

I looked up and saw two girls, one in a white dress and red jacket, the other in a yellow shirt and slacks. I snarled at them, "Shall I do it again?" The nut with the shotgun came loping up making loud demands, and I told him to shut up, and scrambled to my feet. The fence was 10 yards away. Limping to it, I took a look. The bull was slowly walking along, a hundred feet off, wiggling his head. In the middle of the pasture was an ornamental statue. It was Nero Wolfe, with his arms folded, his stick hanging from a wrist, standing motionless on the rounded peak of the boulder. It was the first time I had ever seen him in any such position as that, and I stood and stared because I had never fully realized what a remarkable looking object he really was. He didn't actually look undignified, but there was something pathetic about it, he stood so still, not moving at all.

I called to him, "Okay, boss?"

He called back, "Tell that man with the gun I want to speak to him when I get out of here! Tell him to get someone to pen that bull!"

I turned. The guy didn't look like a bull penner. He looked more scared than mad, and he looked small and skinny in his overalls and denim shirt. His face was weathered and his nose was cockeyed. He had followed me to the fence, and now demanded:

"Who air you fellows? Why didn't you go back when I hollered at you? Where the hell—"

"Hold it, mister. Introductions can wait. Can you put that bull in a pen?"

"No, I can't. And I want to tell you—"

"Is there someone here who can?"

"No, they ain't. They've gone off to the fair. They'll be back in an hour maybe. And I want to tell you—"

"Tell me later. Do you expect him to stand on that rock with his arms folded for an hour?"

"I don't expect nothin'. He can sit down, can't he? But anyhow, I want him out of there right now. I'm guarding that bull."

"Good for you. From what? From me?"

"From anybody. Looky, if you think you're kidding . . ."

I gave him up and turned to the pasture and called: "He's guarding the bull! He wants you out of there right now! He can't pen the bull and no one else can! Somebody will be here in an hour!"

"Archie!" Wolfe bellowed like thunder. "When once I get—"

"No, honest to God, I'm telling you straight! I don't like the bull any better than you do!"

Silence. Then: "It will be an hour before anyone comes?"

"That's what he says."

"Then you'll have to do it! Can you hear me?"

"Yes."

"Good. Climb back into the pasture and get the bull's attention. When he moves, walk back in the other direction, keeping within a few feet of the fence. Was that a woman wearing that red thing?"

"Yes. Woman or girl." I looked around. "She seems to be gone."

"Find her and borrow the red thing, and have it with you. When the bull starts a rush go back over the fence. Proceed along it until you're away from him, then get back in the pasture and repeat. Take him to the other end of the pasture and keep him there until I am out. He won't leave you for me at such a distance if you keep him busy. Let him get the idea he really has a chance of getting you."

"Sure."

"What?"

"I said sure!"

"All right, go ahead. Be careful. Don't slip on the grass."

When I had asked the girl if I should do it again, I had thought it was pure sarcasm, but now . . . I looked around for her. The one in yellow slacks was there, sitting up on the fence, but not the other one. I opened my mouth to request information, but the answer came before I got it out, from another quarter. There was the sound of a car's engine humming in second, and I saw the car bouncing along a lane beyond some trees, headed toward the fence down a ways. It stopped with its nose almost touching the fence, and the girl in the red jacket leaned out and yelled at me:

"Come and open the gate!"

I trotted toward her, limping a little from my right knee which I had banged on the fence, but the other guy, using a sort of hop, skip and jump, beat me to it. When I got there he was standing beside the car, waving the gun around and reciting rules and statutes about gates and bulls.

The girl told him impatiently, "Don't be silly, Dave. There's no sense leaving him perched on that rock." She switched to me. "Open the gate, and if you want to come along, get in. Dave'll shut it."

I moved. Dave moved too and squeaked, "Leave that gate alone! By gammer, I'll shoot! My orders from Mr. Pratt was if anybody opens a gate or climbs in that pasture, shoot!"

"Baloney," said the girl. "You've already disobeyed orders. Why didn't you shoot when they opened the other gate? You'll be court-martialed. Why don't you shoot now? Go ahead and blow him off that rock. Let's see you." She got impatient again, to me, and scornful: "Do you want your friend rescued or not?"

I unhooked the gate and swung it open. The bull, quite a distance away, turned to face us with his head cocked sidewise. Dave was sputtering and flourishing the gun, but it was obvious he could be ignored. As the car passed through—it was a big shiny yellow Wethersill convertible with the top down—I hopped in, and the girl called to Dave to get the gate shut in a hurry. The bull, still at a distance, tossed his head and then lowered it and began pawing. Chunks of sod flew back under his belly.

I said, "Stop a minute," and pulled the hand brake. "What makes you think this will work?"

"I don't know. We can try it, can't we? Are you scared?"

"Yes. Take off that red thing."

"Oh, that's just superstition."

"I'm superstitious. Take it off." I grabbed the collar of it and she wriggled out and I stuck it behind us. Then I reached under my coat to my holster and pulled out my automatic.

She looked at it. "What are you, a spy or something? Don't be silly. Do you think you could stop that bull with that thing?"

"I could try."

"You'd better not, unless you're prepared to cough up $45,000."

"Cough what?"

"$45,000. That's not just a bull, it's Hickory Caesar Grindon. Put that thing away and release the brake."

I looked at her a second and said, "Turn around and get out of here. I'll follow instructions and tease him down to the other end along the fence."

"No." She shifted to first and fed gas. "Why should you have all the fun?" The car moved, and she went into second. We jolted and swayed. "I wonder how fast I ought to go? I've never saved a man's life before. It looks from here as if I've picked a funny one to start on. Should I blow the horn? What do you think? Look at him!"

The bull was playing rocking horse. His hind end would go down and then bob up in the air while he lowered his front, with his tail sticking up and his head tossing. He was facing our way. As we passed him about 30 yards to the left the girl said, "Look at him! He's a high school bull!" The car came up from a hole and nearly bounced me out. I growled, "Watch where you're going," and kept my head turned toward the bull. He looked as if he could have picked the car up and carried it on his horns the way an Indian woman carries a jug. We were approaching the boulder. She pulled up alongside, missing it by half an inch, came to a stop, and sang out, "Taxi?"

As Wolfe stepped carefully down from the peak of the boulder I got out and held the door open. I didn't offer to take his elbow to steady him because I saw by the look on his face that it would only be lighting a fuse. He got to the edge of the boulder and stood there with his feet at the level of the running board.

The girl asked, "Dr. Livingstone, I presume?"

Wolfe's lips twitched a little. "Miss Stanley? How do you do. My name is Nero Wolfe."

Her eyes widened. "Good lord! Not *the* Nero Wolfe?"

"Well . . . the one in the Manhattan telephone book."

"Then I did pick a funny one! Get in."

As he grunted his way into the convertible he observed, "You did a lot of bouncing. I dislike bouncing."

She laughed. "I'll take it easy. Anyway, it's better than being bounced by a bull, don't you think?" I had climbed to the back of the seat, since Wolfe's presence left no room below, and she started off, swinging to the left. I had noticed that she had good strong wrists and fingers, and with the jacket off her arms were bare and I could see the rippling of her forearm muscles as she steered expertly to avoid hummocks and holes. I glanced at the bull and saw he had got tired of playing rocking horse and was standing with his head up and his tail down, registering disdain. He looked bigger than ever. The girl was telling Wolfe, "Stanley would be a nice name, but mine is Caroline Pratt. Excuse me, I didn't see that hole. I'm nothing like as famous as you are, but I've been Metropolitan golf champion for two years. This place seems to be collecting champions. You're a champion detective, and Hickory Caesar Grindon is a National champion bull, and I'm a golf champion . . ."

I thought, so that accounts for the wrists and arms, she's one of those. When we got to the gate Dave opened it, and closed it against our tail as we went through. She eased it along under the trees, with overhanging branches trying to scrape me off, and finally emerged onto a wide graveled space in front of a big new concrete building with four garage doors at one end, where she stopped. Dave had come hopping along behind us, still lugging the gun, and the girl in yellow slacks was sauntering our way. I vaulted over the side of the car to the gravel. The golf champion was inquiring of Wolfe if she could drop him somewhere, but he already had his door open and was lifting his bulk to descend, so she got out. Dave bustled up to Wolfe and began to make demands in a loud voice, but Wolfe gave him an awful look and told him, "Sir, you are open to prosecution for attempted murder! I don't mean the gun, I mean jumping off that fence!" Then Wolfe walked around the rear of the car and confronted his rescuer and bowed to her:

"Thank you, Miss Pratt, for having intelligence and for using it."

"Don't mention it. It was a pleasure."

He grimaced. "Is that bull your property?"

"No, he belongs to my uncle. Thomas Pratt." She waved a hand. "This is his place. He'll be here shortly. Meanwhile . . . if I can do anything . . . do you want some beer?"

"No thanks. I do want beer, but God knows when I'll drink beer again. We had an accident. Mr. Goodwin was unable to restrain our car—I beg your pardon. Miss Pratt, this is Mr. Goodwin."

She politely put her hand out and I took it. Wolfe was repeating, "Mr. Goodwin was unable to restrain our car from crashing into a tree. After inspecting the damage he claimed he had run it over glass. He then persuaded me to trespass in that pasture. It was I, not he, who first saw the bull after it had emerged from behind the thicket. He boasted complete ignorance of the way a bull will act—"

I had known when I saw his face as we approached the boulder that he was going to be childish, but he might at least have saved it for privacy. I put in brusquely:

"Could I use a telephone?"

"You interrupted Mr. Wolfe." She was reproving me. "If he wants to explain—"

"I'll show you the phone." It was a voice behind me, and I turned. The girl in yellow slacks was there close. I realized with surprise that her head came clear to my chin or above, and she was blonde but not at all faded, and her dark blue eyes were not quite open, and one corner of her lips was up with her smile.

"Come on, Escamillo," she said, "I'll show you the phone."

I told her, "Much obliged," and started off with
her.

She brushed against me as we walked and said,
"I'm Lily Rowan."

"Nice name." I grinned down at her. "I'm Escamillo Goodwin."

Chapter 2

Wolfe's voice came through the open door, "What time is it?"

After glancing at my wrist watch where it lay on the glass shelf I walked out of the bathroom, holding my forearm steady and level so the iodine would dry where I had dabbed it on. Stopping in front of the big upholstered chair he was occupying, I told him:

"3:26. I supposed the beer would buck you up. It's one of your lowest points when you haven't even got enough joy of life to pull your watch out of your pocket."

"Joy of life?" He groaned. "With our car demolished, and those plants in it being suffocated . . ."

"They're not being suffocated. I left the window open a crack on both sides." I tilted the arm, watching the iodine, and then let it hang. "Certainly joy of life! Did we get hurt when we had a front blowout? No. Did the bull get us? No. We ran into nice people who gave us a swell room with bath to wash up and served you with cold beer and me with iodine. And I repeat, if you still think I should have persuaded one of those

Crowfield garages to come and get us and the car, go down and try it yourself. They thought I was crazy to expect it, with the exposition on. This Mr. Pratt will be back any minute, with a big sedan, and his niece says she'll take us and the luggage and the plants to Crowfield. I phoned the hotel, and they promised to hold our room until ten tonight. Naturally there's a mob yelling for beds."

I had got my sleeves rolled down and buttoned, and reached for my coat. "How's the beer?"

"The beer is good." Wolfe shuddered, and muttered, "A mob yelling for beds." He looked around. "This is a remarkably pleasant room . . . large and airy, good windows . . . I think perhaps I should have modern casements installed in my room at home. Two excellent beds—did you try one of the beds?"

I looked at him suspiciously. "No."

"They are first class. When did you say the garage will send for the car?"

I said patiently, "Tomorrow by noon."

"Good." He sighed. "I thought I didn't like new houses, but this one is very pleasant. Of course that was the architect. Do you know where the money came from to build it? Miss Pratt told me. Her uncle operates a chain of popular restaurants in New York —hundreds of them. He calls them pratterias. Did you ever see one?"

"Sure." I had my pants down, inspecting the knee. "I've had lunch in them often."

"Indeed. How is the food?"

"So-so. Depends on your standard." I looked up. "If what you have in mind is flushing a dinner here to avoid a restaurant meal, pratteria grub is irrelevant and immaterial. The cook downstairs is *ipso facto*. Incidentally, I'm glad to learn they're called pratterias because Pratt owns them. I always supposed it was because they're places where you can sit on your prat and eat."

Wolfe grunted. "I presume one ignorance cancels another. I never heard 'prat' before, and you don't know the meaning of *ipso facto*. Unless 'prat' is your invention—"

"No. Shakespeare used it. I've looked it up. I never invent unless—"

There was a knock on the door, and I said come in. A specimen entered wearing dirty flannel pants and a shiny starched white coat, with grease on the side of his face. He stood in the doorway and mumbled something about Mr. Pratt having arrived and we could go downstairs when we felt like it. Wolfe told him we would be down at once and he went off.

I observed, "Mr. Pratt must be a widower."

"No," said Wolfe, making ready to elevate himself. "He has never married. Miss Pratt told me. Are you going to comb your hair?"

We had to hunt for them. A woman in the lower hall with an apron on shook her head when we asked her, and we went into the dining room and out again, and through a big living room and another one with a piano in it before we finally found them out on a flagged terrace shaded with awnings. The two girls were off to one side with a young man, having highballs. Nearer to us, at a table, were two guys working their chins and fluttering papers from a brief case at each other. One, young and neat, looked like a slick bond salesman; the other, middle-aged or a little

past, had brown hair that was turning gray, narrow
temples and a wide jaw. Wolfe stopped, then in a minute approached nearer and stopped again. They
looked up at him and the other one frowned and said:

"Oh, you're the fellows."

"Mr. Pratt?" Wolfe bowed faintly. "My name is
Wolfe."

The younger man stood up. The other just kept on
frowning. "So my niece told me. Of course I've heard
of you, but I don't care if you're President Roosevelt,
you had no business in that pasture when my man
ordered you out. What did you want in there?"

"Nothing."

"What did you go in there for?"

Wolfe compressed his lips, then loosened them to
ask, "Did your niece tell you what I told her?"

"Yes."

"Do you think she lied?"

"Why . . . no."

"Do you think I lied?"

"Er . . . no."

Wolfe shrugged. "Then it remains only to thank
you for your hospitality—your telephone, your accommodations, your refreshment. The beer especially is
appreciated. Your niece has kindly offered to take us
to Crowfield in your car . . . if you will permit that?"

"I suppose so." The lummox was still frowning. He
leaned back with his thumbs in his armpits. "No, Mr.
Wolfe, I don't think you lied, but I'd still like to ask a
question or two. You see, you're a detective, and you
might have been hired . . . God knows what lengths
they'll go to. I'm being pested half to death. I went
over to Crowfield with my nephew today to take a
look at the exposition, and they hounded me out of the

place. I had to come home to get away from them. I'll ask a straight question: did you enter that particular pasture because you knew that bull was in it?"

Wolfe stared. "No, sir."

"Did you come to this part of the country in an effort to do something about that bull?"

"No, sir. I came to exhibit orchids at the North Atlantic Exposition."

"Your choosing that pasture was pure accident?"

"We didn't choose it. It was a question of geometry. It was the shortest way to this house." After a pause Wolfe added bitterly, "So we thought."

Pratt nodded. Then he glanced at his watch, jerked himself up and turned to the man with the brief case, who was stowing papers away. "All right, Pavey, you might as well make the 6 o'clock from Albany. Tell Jameson there's no reason in God's world why the unit should drop below twenty-eight four. Why shouldn't people be as hungry this September as any other September? Remember what I said, no more Fairbanks pies . . ." He went on a while about dish breakage percentages and new leases in Brooklyn and so forth, and shouted a last minute thought about the lettuce market after Pavey had disappeared around the corner of the house. Then our host asked abruptly if Wolfe would like a highball, and Wolfe said no thanks he preferred beer but doubtless Mr. Goodwin would enjoy a highball. Pratt yelled "Bert!" at the top of his voice, and Greasy-face showed up from inside the house and got orders. As we sat down the trio from the other end came over, carrying their drinks.

"May we?" Miss Pratt asked her uncle. "Jimmy

wants to meet the guests. Mr. Wolfe, Mr. Goodwin, this is my brother."

I stood to acknowledge, and became aware that Wolfe was playing a deep and desperate game when I saw that instead of apologizing for not raising his poundage, as was customary, he stood too. Then we sat again, with Lily the blonde doing a languid drape on a canvas swing and a beautiful calf protruding from one leg of her yellow slacks.

Pratt was talking. "Of course I've heard of you," he was telling Wolfe. "Privately too, once or twice. My friend Pete Hutchinson told me that you turned him down a couple of years ago on a little inquiry he undertook regarding his wife."

Wolfe nodded. "I like to interfere with natural processes as little as possible."

"Suit yourself." Pratt took a gulp of highball. "That's my motto. It's your business, and you're the one to run it. For instance, I understand you're a fancy eater. Now I'm in the food business, and what I believe in is mass feeding. Last week we served a daily average of 42,392 lunches in Greater New York at an average cost to the consumer of twenty-three and seventeen-hundredths cents. What I claim—how many times have you eaten in a pratteria?"

"I . . ." Wolfe held it while he poured beer. "I never have."

"Never?"

"I always eat at home."

"Oh." Pratt eyed him. "Of course some home cooking is all right. But most of the fancy stuff . . . one of my publicity stunts was when I got a group of fifty people from the Social Register into a pratteria and served them from the list. They gobbled it up and they raved. What I've built my success on is, first, quality, second, publicity." He had two fingers up.

"An unbeatable combination," Wolfe murmured. I could have kicked him. He was positively licking the guy's boots. He even went on, "Your niece was telling me something of your phenomenal career."

"Yes?" He glanced at her. "Your drink's gone, Caroline." He turned his head and bawled, "Bert!" Back to Wolfe: "Well, she knows as much about it as anyone. She worked in my office three years. Somehow she got started playing golf, and she got good at it, and I figured it would be good publicity to have a golf champion for a niece, and she made it. That's better than anything she could do in the office. And better than anything her brother could do. My only nephew, and no good for anything at all. Are you, Jimmy?"

The young man grinned at him. "Not worth a damn."

"Yes, but you don't mean it, and I do. Just because your father and mother died when you were young . . . why I keep spending money on you is beyond me. It's about my only weakness. And when I think that my will leaves everything to you and your sister only because there's no one else in sight . . . it makes me hope I will never die. What do you call it? Immortality. When I think what you would do with a million dollars . . . let me ask you, Mr. Wolfe, what is your opinion of architecture?"

"Well . . . I like this house."

Jimmy cackled. "Ha! Wowie!"

His uncle disregarded him and cocked an eye at Wolfe. "You do actually? My nephew there designed it. It was only finished last year. I came originally from this part of the country . . . was born on this spot in an old shack. There is absolutely no money in architecture and never will be . . . I've looked into it. Where a nephew of mine ever got the idea . . ."

He went on and on, and Wolfe placidly opened another bottle of beer. I myself wasn't doing so bad, because it was by no means pratteria Scotch in my highball, and I had nearly finished my second one, and was so seated that I could take in the blonde on the canvas swing, with all her convolutions and what not. I quit listening to Pratt entirely, and got to wondering idly which was the more desirable quality in a girl, the ability to look as inviting as that stretched out on canvas, or the ability to save a man from a bull, and went on from that to something else, no matter what, when all of a sudden the pleasant sociable gathering was rudely interrupted. Four men came swinging around the corner of the house and tramped across the terrace. With a dim memory of our host's remark about being hounded around the fair grounds, and a dim idea that the look on their faces meant trouble, my hand was inside my coat touching my holster before I knew it, then I came to and pretended I needed to scratch my shoulder.

Pratt had jumped up and was using all his narrow forehead for a ferocious scowl, facing the intruders. The foremost, a wiry little item with a thin nose and sharp dark eyes, stopped right in front of him and told his face, "Well, Mr. Pratt, I think I've got it worked out to satisfy you."

"I'm already satisfied. I told you."

"But we're not." The keen eyes darted around. "If

you'd let me explain the arrangement I've been able—"

"It's a waste of time, Mr. Bennett. I've told you—"

"Permit me." The tone was brusque, and came from a solid-looking bird in a gray sport suit that was a dream, with the fitting accessories, including driving gloves on a warm day. "You're Pratt? Lew Bennett here has talked me into this, and I have to get back to Crowfield and out again for New York. I'm Cullen."

Bennett said nervously, "Daniel Cullen."

"Oh." Pratt looked interested and a little awed. "This is an honor, Mr. Cullen. My little place here. Sit down. Have a highball? Jimmy, push up some more chairs. No, you folks stay. Here, Mr. Cullen, meet my niece . . ." He did introductions all around, including titles and occupations. It appeared that Lew Bennett was the secretary of the National Guernsey League. The name of the big-boned guy with scraggly hair and a big tired face was Monte McMillan. Daniel Cullen, of course, was Daniel Cullen, just as J. P. Morgan is J. P. Morgan. The fourth one, who looked even tireder than Monte McMillan, was Sidney Darth, chairman of the North Atlantic Exposition Board. Bert was called and sent for drinks. Lily Rowan sat up to make room on the swing, and I noticed that Jimmy Pratt copped the place next to her. She looked around at the newcomers as if she was bored.

Lew Bennett was saying, "Mr. Cullen's in a hurry to get back, and I'm confident, Mr. Pratt, you'll appreciate what he's doing as well as we do. You won't lose a cent. It will be a happy outcome—"

"I want to say it's a damned outrage!" It was Cullen, glowering at Pratt. "It ought to be actionable! Where the devil!"

"Excuse me," Bennett put in hastily. "I've been all over that aspect of it, Mr. Cullen, and if Mr. Pratt doesn't see it our way . . . he just doesn't. It's quite useless . . . what I mean to say is, thank God you've come to the rescue." He turned to Pratt. "The arrangement is simply this, that Mr. Cullen has generously agreed to take Hickory Caesar Grindon."

Pratt grunted, then was silent. After a moment he asked sullenly, "What does he want with him?"

Bennett looked shocked. "He has one of the finest purebred Guernsey herds in the country."

Cullen growled, "You understand, Pratt, I don't need him. My senior herd sire is Mahwah Gallant Masterson who has 43 A R daughters. I have three junior sires who are lined out. I'm doing this as a favor to the breed and to the National Guernsey League."

Bennett said, "About the arrangement. Mr. Cullen is quite correct when he says he doesn't really need Caesar. He is acting very generously, but he isn't willing to pay you the sum you paid McMillan. I know, you've told me you offered it and you paid it and you're satisfied, but the fact remains that $45,000 is a terrific price for any bull. Why, Coldwater Grandee himself sold for $33,000 in 1932, and great as Caesar is, he isn't Grandee. In 1932 Grandee had 127 A R daughters and 15 A R sons. So the arrangement is this: Mr. Cullen will pay you $33,000, and Monte—Mr. McMillan will return $12,000 of the sum you paid him. You'll get all your money back. It can be paid now with Mr. Cullen's check, which I guess you know is good, and there'll be a truck here before dark to get

Caesar. Mr. Cullen wants to show him at Crowfield Thursday, if he can be got in shape. I hope he's not upset. I understand you've got him in a pasture."

Pratt turned on McMillan. "You told me this noon that you regarded the deal as closed for good and you wouldn't be a party to any effort to cancel it."

"I know I did." McMillan couldn't keep his hand from trembling a little as he put down his drink. "They've been riding me . . . they've been . . . I'm an old Guernsey man, Mr. Pratt."

"You should be ashamed to admit it!" Cullen exploded. "They should expel you from the league and freeze you out! Pratt doesn't know any better, he has that excuse at least. But you haven't! You knew what was going to happen to that bull before you sold him!"

"Sure." McMillan nodded wearily. "It's easy for you to talk, Mr. Cullen. What have you got, a couple of billion? What I had, after what the depression did to me, was my herd and nothing else. Just my herd. Then the anthrax came, only a month ago, and in one week what did I have? What did I have left out of my Hickory herd? Four calves, six cows, one junior sire, and Caesar. What could I do with Caesar under those conditions? Live on his fees? Where would that get me? I couldn't even buy grades to breed him to, let alone purebreds. I knew no stockman could pay high enough for him, so I sent telegrams offering him to a dozen of you gentlemen breeders, and what did I get? You all knew I was out on a limb, and the best offer was $9000! For Hickory Caesar Grindon. Then Mr. Pratt shows up and he tells me straight what he wants to do with Caesar, and of course I knew it was impossible, even in the fix I was in, but it was a temp-

tation, so to get rid of him I set a figure so high it was
ridiculous. $45,000!" McMillan picked up his glass,
looked into it, and put it down again. He said quietly,
"Mr. Pratt took out his checkbook and wrote out a
check and I took it. It wasn't you, Mr. Cullen, who
offered me $9000. As I remember it, your offer was
$7500."

Cullen shrugged. "I didn't need him. Anyway, as it
stands now, you'll be getting $33,000, or rather keep-
ing that out of what Pratt paid you. Under the circumstances, McMillan, you may consider yourself
damned lucky. What I'm doing is in effect philan-
thropy. I've had my superintendent on the phone, and
I'm not even sure I want Caesar's line in my herd.
There have been better bulls than Caesar before now,
and there will be—"

"No bull of yours, damn you!" McMillan's voice
shook with rage. "You damn lousy amateur!"
Abruptly he stopped himself, looked around at the
faces, and slowly drew the back of his hand across his
mouth. Then he leaned toward Cullen and said quietly
but pointedly, "How do you like that? Who are you to
make side remarks about any bull or any cow either?
Let alone Hickory Caesar Grindon! Caesar was the
finest bull, bar none, that ever got on the register!"

He passed his hand across his mouth again. "Yes, I
say 'was,' because he's not mine any more . . . and
he's not yours yet, Mr. Cullen. He was a double
grandson of Burleigh's Audacious. He had 51 A R
daughters and 9 A R sons. I was up all night the day
he was dropped—he sucked these fingers when he
was six hours old." The fingers trembled as he held
them out. "He took nine grands, the last one being at

Indianapolis, the National, last year. At five shows he has taken get of sire. Twelve of his daughters have topped 13,000 pounds of milk and 700 pounds of butterfat. And you say you're not even sure you want his line in your herd! Well, damn you, I hope you won't get it! At least I won't help you pay for it!"

He turned to the secretary of the National Guernsey League, Bennett, and said with his chin stiff, "I'll keep my $12,000, Lew. Count me out of your little deal."

What he got for that was an uproar. Bennett and Darth and Cullen all went for him. It was hard to get details out of all the confusion, but the gist of it seemed to be that McMillan was going back on his word and he couldn't do that, and the honor of the National Guernsey League and of all American stockmen was at stake, and it would put a crimp in the prestige of the North Atlantic Exposition if such a thing happened right next door to it, and McMillan would be keeping $33,000 which was enough anyhow, and so forth and so on. McMillan sat, looking sad and sore but stubborn, without trying to reply to them.

They were shocked into silence by an unexpected bomb tossed into the fray by Pratt.

"Let him alone!" Pratt yelled. "He's out of it anyhow. I don't want my money back from him or Mr. Cullen or anyone else. What I want is the bull, and I've got him, and a bill of sale. That's final."

They glared at him. Bennett sputtered, "You don't mean that. You can't mean it! Look here, I've told you—"

"I do mean it." Pratt's wide jaw was set. "I've paid a good price and I'm satisfied. I've made my arrangements and I'm going to stick to them. I've invited a hundred people—"

"But good God, after what I've . . ." Bennett jumped up, waving his arms, and it began to look as if I might have to reach into the holster after all. He raved. "I tell you, you can't do it! By God, you *won't* do it! You're crazy if you think you can get away with it, and I'll see that you don't! There's a dozen members of the league at Crowfield waiting for me to get back, and when they hear what I have to say, there'll be some action taken, don't think there won't!"

The others were on their feet too. Daniel Cullen rumbled, "You're a goddam maniac, Pratt."

Cullen grunted, and wheeled. "Come on, Bennett. Come on, Darth. I've got to catch a train." He strode off. The other two followed at his heels. They disappeared around the corner of the house.

After a silence Pratt's jaw relaxed a little and he looked across at the one who was left.

"You know, McMillan," he said, "I don't like the look of that fellow Bennett. Nor what he said either. He might even sneak around to that pasture right now, and I'm afraid the man I've got guarding it isn't much good. I know I wasn't supposed to get anything for my $45,000 except the bull, but I wonder if you'd mind . . ."

"Sure." McMillan was up, big-boned and lanky. "I'll go take a look. I . . . I wanted to look at him anyway."

"Could you stick around a while?"

"Sure."

The stockman lumbered off.

We sat, the nephew and niece looking worried,

Lily Rowan yawning, Pratt frowning. Wolfe heaved a sigh and emptied his glass.

Pratt muttered, "All the commotion."

Wolfe nodded. "Astonishing. About a bull. It might be thought you were going to cook him and eat him."

Pratt nodded back at him. "I am. That's what's causing all the trouble."

Chapter 3

Well, as the Emperor of India would say, that tore it. The children didn't appear to be shocked any, but I goggled at our host, and I could see by the sudden tilt to Wolfe's head that he was enjoying one of his real and rare surprises. He also betrayed it by repeating what he had already been told, which was equally rare.

"Eat that bull, Mr. Pratt?" he demanded.

Pratt nodded again. "I am. Perhaps you noticed a pit we have started to dig down by the lane. That's for a barbecue which will occur Thursday afternoon. Three days from now. I have invited a hundred guests, mostly from New York. My niece and nephew and their friend Miss Rowan have come for it. The bull will be butchered tomorrow. No local man will undertake it, and I'm getting one from Albany."

"Remarkable." Wolfe's head was still tilted. "I suppose an animal of that size would furnish 7 or 800 pounds of edible tissue. At $45,000 on the hoof, that would make it around $60 a pound. Of course you'll use only the more desirable cuts and a great deal will be wasted. Another way to calculate: if you serve a hundred guests the portions will be $450 each."

"It sounds terrible that way." Pratt reached for his glass, saw it was empty, and yelled for Bert. "But consider how little you can get for $45,000 in newspaper display or any other form of advertising. The radio would eat it up at a gulp, and what do you get for it? Nobody knows. But I know what I'll get out of this. Do you go in for psychology?"

"I . . ." Wolfe choked and said firmly, "No."

"You ought to. Look here. Do you realize what a stir it will make that the senior grand champion Guernsey bull of the United States is being barbecued and served in chunks and slices to a gathering of epicures? And by whom? By Tom Pratt of the famous pratterias! Let alone the publicity, do you know what the result will be? For weeks and months every customer that eats a roast beef sandwich in a pratteria will have a sneaking unconscious feeling that he's chewing a piece of Hickory Caesar Grindon! That's what I mean when I say psychology."

"You spoke of epicures."

"There'll be some. Mostly the barbecue guests will be friends and acquaintances and of course the press, but I'm going to run in a few epicures." Pratt jerked up. "By the way, I've heard you're one. Will you still be in Crowfield? Maybe you'd like to run out and join us. Thursday at one o'clock."

"Thank you, sir. I don't suppose Caesar's championship qualities include succulence, but it would be an experience."

"Certainly it would. I'll be phoning my agency in New York this evening. Can I say you'll be here? For the press."

"You may say so, of course. The judging of orchids will be Wednesday afternoon, and I shall probably have left for home. But you may say so. By the way, about this bull. I am only curious: you feel no compunction at slaughtering a beast of established nobility?"

"Why should I?" Pratt waved a hand. "They say this Caesar bull has so many A R daughters, that's the point they harp on. Do you know what A R means? Advanced Register. What a cow has to do to get on the Advanced Register is to produce a daily average of so much milk and so much butterfat over a period of one year. Well, there are over 40,000 A R Guernsey cows in this country, and only 51 of them are Caesar's daughters. Does that sound as if I was getting ready to barbecue the breed out of existence? To hear that bunch over at Crowfield talk you might think I was. I've had over forty telegrams today howling threats and bloody murder. That's that fellow Bennett; he's sicked his members on me."

"Their viewpoint, of course, is valid to them."

"Sure, and mine is to me. —Hey, you want a drink there, Mr. Goodwin. How about you, Miss Rowan? Oh, Bert! Bert!"

When Greasy-face appeared I let him proceed with his function, which I must admit he performed promptly and well. Three highballs were a notch above my ordinary indulgence, but after the blowout and smashup, and the pasture exercise, I felt a little extra would be not amiss. A little fed up with the champion bull, I moved to a chair closer to the champion niece and began to murmur at her. She graciously took it, and after a little I observed the blonde slanting one at me from the corner of her eye, so I tossed her a grin between murmurs. I could have expanded easily, but my prospect was not in fact at all rosy, since what I had to do before twilight was get Wolfe and the luggage and plants to Crowfield, outride him into a hotel and a room thereof, unpack, find forage he would swallow without gagging, discuss the matter of my inability to restrain the car from crashing into a tree and get it settled once and for all, and probably sit for a couple of hours and listen to him sigh. I was preparing to remark to the niece that it was after five o'clock and if she was going to drive us to Crowfield we had better get started, when I heard a climax being reached by my employer. Pratt was inviting him to stay for dinner and he was accepting. I scowled at him, hoping vindictively that the food would be terrible, for it would only complicate matters and make him almost too much for one man to handle if we got to our destination long after dark. He saw me scowling and let his lids cover half his eyes, and I pretended he wasn't there and concentrated on the niece again. I had decided she was all right, wholesome and quite intelligent, but she looked too darned strong. I mean a girl is a girl and an athlete is an athlete, though of course there are borderline cases.

In reply to an invitation from Caroline I was explaining that I would love to take her on at tennis if I hadn't twisted my wrist negotiating the fence, which was a lie, when the second attacking party arrived. Its personnel, as it suddenly made an appearance at the end of the terrace, left it uncertain at first whether it was another attack or not. In front was an extremely presentable number, I would say 22 or 3, wearing a belted linen thing and no hat, with yellowish brown eyes and warm trembly lips and such a chin. Behind her was a tall slender guy, not much younger than me, in brown slacks and pull-over, and backing him up was an individual who should not have been there, since the proper environment for that type is bounded by 42nd and 96th Streets on the south and north, and Lexington Avenue and Broadway on the east and west. In their habitat they don't look bad, in fact they help a lot in maintaining the tone, but out in the country like that, still wearing a Crawnley town suit including vest and a custom-made shirt and a Monteith tie, they jar.

The atmosphere they created was immediate and full of sparks. Our host's mouth fell open. Jimmy stood up with his face red. Caroline exclaimed something. Lily Rowan twisted her neck to see and showed a crease in her brow. The girl got as far as the table which was littered with empty glasses, let her yellowish brown eyes go around, and said:

"We should have telephoned. Shouldn't we?"

That met denial. Greetings crossed one another through the atmosphere. It appeared that the bird in the Crawnley suit was a stranger to the Pratts, since he had to be introduced as Mr. Bronson. Wolfe and I had our names called, and learned that the girl was Nancy Osgood and the tall slender guy was her brother Clyde. Once more the clarion was sounded for poor Bert, whereupon there seemed to be an increase in the general embarrassment. Miss Osgood protested that they didn't want to intrude, they really couldn't stay, they had been to the fair and had only stopped in on their way home, on an impulse. Clyde Osgood, who had a pair of binoculars dangling on a strap around his neck, gazed down at Pratt in a fairly provocative manner and addressed him:

"We just got chased away from your pasture by Monte McMillan. We were only taking a look at your bull."

Pratt nodded sort of unconcerned, but I could see his temples were tight. "That darned bull's causing a lot of trouble." He glanced at the sister, and back at the brother again. "It's nice of you children to drop in like this. Unexpected pleasure. I saw your father over at Crowfield today."

"Yeah. He saw you too." All at once Clyde stopped talking, and began to turn, slow but sure, as if something had gripped him and was wheeling him on a pivot. He took four steps and was confronting the canvas swing, looking down straight at Lily Rowan.

"How are you?" he demanded.

"I'm fine." She held her head tilted back to see him. "Just fine. You all right?"

"Yeah, I'm great."

"Good." Lily yawned.

That simple exchange seemed to have an effect on Jimmy Pratt, for he took on added color, though as near as I could tell his eyes were aimed at Nancy Osgood, who was passing a remark to Caroline. Caroline was insisting that they stay for a drink. Mr. Bronson, looking a little weary, as if the day at the fair had been too much for him, had sat down. Clyde abruptly turned away from the swing, crossed back over, and got onto the edge of the chair next to Pratt's.

"Look here," he said.

"Well, my boy?"

"We stopped in to see you, my sister and I."

"I think that was a good idea. Now that I've built

this place here . . . we're neighbors again, aren't we."

Clyde frowned. He looked to me like a spoiled kid, with a mouth that didn't quite go shut, and moving as if he expected things to get out of his way. He said, "Neighbors? I suppose so. Technically, anyhow. I wanted to speak to you about that bull. I know why you're doing it . . . I guess everyone around here does. You're doing it just to be offensive to my father —you keep out of this, Nancy, I'm handling this—"

His sister had a hand on his shoulder. "But Clyde, that's no way—"

"Let me alone." He shook her off and went after Pratt again. "You think you can get his goat by sneering at him, by butchering a bull that could top any of his in show competition. I'll hand it to you for one thing, you picked a good one. Hickory Caesar Grindon is a hard bull to put down. I say that not only on account of his record, but because I know cattle . . . or I used to. I wanted my father to buy Caesar in 1931, when he was only a promising junior. And you think you're going to butcher him?"

"That's my intention. But where you got the idea that I'm doing it deliberately to offend your father— nonsense. I'm doing it as an advertisement for my business."

"You are like hell. I know all about it . . . from the beginning. It's just another of your cheap efforts to make my father look cheap—you keep out of this, Sis!"

"You're wrong, my boy." Pratt sounded tolerant. "I don't do anything cheap . . . I can afford not to. Let me tell you something. I understand the best bull your father's got is getting pretty old. Well, if your

father came to me and asked for that bull I bought, I'd
be strongly inclined to let him have him as a gift. I
certainly would."

"No doubt! A gift!" Clyde was nearly overcome
with scorn. "Now I'll tell you. There was a lot of talk
over at Crowfield today. Of course, as a member of
the Guernsey League, my father was in on it. He was
sure that the plan Bennett arranged with Cullen and
McMillan wouldn't work . . . he said he knew you
since you were a boy and you wouldn't turn loose. My
sister Nancy got the idea of coming here to try to
persuade you, and I agreed to come along. On the way
we met Bennett and Darth and Cullen going back,
and they told us what had happened. I came on anyhow, though it didn't look like there was much chance
of talking you out of it. Now I'd like to make a bet
with you. Do you ever do any betting?"

"I'm not a gambler." Pratt chuckled. "I'm not exactly a confirmed gambler, but I don't mind an occasional friendly wager. I won a nice chunk on the 1936
election."

"Would you care to try a little bet with me? Say
$10,000?"

"On what?"

They got interrupted. A voice sounded, "Oh, there
you are," and Monte McMillan was coming across the
terrace. He sounded a little relieved. He approached
Pratt: "They were fooling around the fence on the
other side, and I told them they might as well go on,
and I wasn't sure where they got to. Not that I would
suspect the Osgood youngsters of stealing a bull . . ."

Pratt grunted. "Sit down and have a drink. Bert!
Bert!" He turned to Clyde: "What is it you want to
bet about, my boy?"

Clyde leaned forward at him. "I'll bet you $10,000 you don't barbecue Hickory Caesar Grindon."

His sister Nancy exclaimed, "Clyde!" Wolfe's eyes went half shut. The others made sounds, and even Lily Rowan showed some interest. McMillan, who had started to sit down, stopped himself at an angle and held it a second, and then slowly sank.

Pratt asked quietly, "What's going to stop me?"

Clyde turned the palms of his hands up. "It's either a bet or it isn't. That's all."

"$10,000 even that we don't barbecue Hickory Caesar Grindon."

"Right."

"Within what time?"

"Say this week."

"I ought to warn you I've consulted a lawyer. There's no legal way of stopping it, if I own him, no matter how much of a champion he is."

Clyde merely shrugged. The look on his face was one I've often seen in a poker game.

"Well." Pratt leaned back and got his thumbs in his armpits. "This is mighty interesting. What about it, McMillan? Can they get that bull out of that pasture in spite of us?"

The stockman muttered, "I don't know who would be doing it. If there's any funny business . . . if we had him in a barn . . ."

"I haven't got a barn." Pratt eyed Clyde. "One thing. What do we do, put up now? Checks?"

Clyde flushed. "My check would be rubber. You know that, damn it. If I lose I'll pay."

"You're proposing a gentleman's bet? With me?"

"All right, call it that. A gentleman's bet."

"By God. My boy, I'm flattered. I really am. But I

can't afford to do much flattering when $10,000 is involved. I'm afraid I couldn't bet unless I had some sort of inkling of where you would get hold of that amount."

Clyde got halfway out of his chair, and my feet came back automatically for a spring, but his sister pulled him back. She tried to pull him away, too, with urgent remarks about leaving, but he shook himself loose and even gave her a shove. He glared at Pratt with his jaw clamped:

"You damn trash, you say that to an Osgood! All right, I'll take some of your money, since that's all there is to you! If my father phones you to guarantee my side, does that make it a gentleman's bet?"

"Then you really do want to bet."

"I do."

"$10,000 even on the proposition as these people here have heard it."

"I do."

"All right. If your father guarantees it, it's a bet."

Clyde turned and started off without even a glance around for good-bye. His friend Bronson put down his drink and followed him. They had to wait at the edge of the terrace for Nancy, who, flustered as she was, managed a darn good exit under the circumstances. As she got away Monte McMillan stood up and remarked to Pratt:

"I've known that Osgood boy since he was a baby. I guess I'd better go and tell him not to do anything foolish."

He tramped off after them.

Lily Rowan said hopefully, "It sounds to me as if there's going to be dirty work at the crossroads." She patted the space beside her which Jimmy Pratt had vacated. "Come and sit here, Escamillo, and tell me what's going to happen."

I lifted the form, strolled gracefully over, deposited it, acquired her left hand, and studied the palm. "It's like this," I told her. "You will be very happy for a while, then you will take a long journey under water and will meet a bald-headed man sitting on some seaweed who you will think is William Beebe but who will begin talking to you in Russian. Not understanding Russian, you will take it for granted that you get the idea, but will discover to your horror that he was talking about something else. Give me the other hand to compare."

Jimmy Pratt, meanwhile, was haranguing his uncle. ". . . and you sit there and let him call you trash! I'd have liked to smack him! I *would* have smacked him—"

"Now, Jimmy." Pratt waved a hand. He chuckled. "You wouldn't smack an Osgood, would you? Take it easy, son. By the way, since you seem to be feeling belligerent, maybe you'd like to help out a little with that bull. I'm afraid we'll have to keep an eye on him all night. How about a little sentry duty?"

"Well, sir . . ." Jimmy looked uncomfortable. "The fact is . . . I've already told you . . . I don't approve of that. It seems to me a bull like that . . . a champion and so on . . ."

"You wouldn't like to help us guard him?"

"I'd appreciate it if you'd leave me out of that, Uncle Tom."

"All right. I guess we can manage somehow. — What's your feeling about it, Mr. Wolfe? Haven't I got a right to eat my own bull?"

Wolfe obliged with a philosophical lecture on written and unwritten law, degrees of moral turpitude, and the extravagant enthusiasms of bovine genetics. It sounded quite instructive and elevated the tone of the gathering to a plane high above such petty things as smacking an Osgood or eating beefsteak or winning a $10,000 bet. When he had finished, he turned to me with a suggestion: since he had accepted Mr. Pratt's kind invitation to dine there, a change of linen would be desirable, and the luggage was still in our car out by the roadside. Jimmy offered his services, but Caroline insisted it was her job, since it was she who had contracted to drive us to Crowfield, so I followed her from the terrace, across a wide lawn, around some shrubbery and flower beds, and down a path which took us to the graveled space in front of the garage, where a big sedan was parked near the yellow convertible. I stooped to peer under the trees to where I had caught a glimpse of a high long mound of freshly dug soil, with picks and shovels leaning against it. I had noticed it previously, as we drove by in the convertible after escaping from the pasture, but had not then realized its significance.

"Pit for the barbecue?" I inquired.

Caroline nodded. "I think it's pretty awful, but I couldn't very well refuse uncle's invitation to come up for it. Get in."

When she had swung the sedan around and had headed down the drive I said, "I ask this because it's none of my business. I'm interested in human nature. Which is it, advertising, or a Bronx cheer for Father Osgood?"

"I don't know. I'm thinking about something."

So I held myself aloof. The sedan emerged onto the highway and turned left, and in half a minute was swinging around the curve which I had seen from the other direction during my survey of the surroundings after the accident. In the other half of the minute she had arrived at the scene, spun the wheel with her strong wrists, done a U, and pulled up directly behind the relic. I got out. The angle of the low evening sun made long soft shadows with trees and telephone poles on the green of the pasture. Across its expanse, on the other side, I could see the top third of Monte McMillan above the fence, his face turned our way, and moving along this side of the boulder, with slow imperial tread, looking bigger than ever, was the bull. I had to admit he was a beaut, now that I could take an impersonal view.

There were two suitcases, two bags, the sprayer, and the crates of plants. After I got them all transferred I locked the car up again, took another glance at the bull who was soon to be served at 450 bucks a portion, and climbed in beside Miss Pratt. Still aloof, I didn't say anything, but sat quietly and waited for the spirit to move her. After a minute she moved, but only to turn her head to look at me.

"I want to tell you what I was thinking about."

I nodded politely.

"Lily Rowan."

I nodded again. "She calls me Escamillo. She told me that you and she are going to the fair tomorrow, and suggested that she and I might have lunch together."

"What did you tell her?"

"I told her I couldn't on account of my table manners. I don't like hitch-lunchers."

Caroline snorted. "She wasn't trying to hitch. She would pay the check. She's rich. Very. Maybe millions,

I don't know, anyway plenty. She's a vampire. She's dangerous."

"You mean she bites you in the neck?"

"I mean what I say. I used to think the talk about some woman being dangerous, you know, really dangerous, was romantic hooey, but it isn't. Lily Rowan is one. If she wasn't too lazy to make much of an effort there's no telling how many men she might ruin, but I know of at least three she has played the devil with. You saw Clyde Osgood today. Not that Clyde was ever one of nature's noblemen, but he was doing all right. He's just my age, 26. The Osgoods have owned this county for generations, they still have a couple of thousand acres, and after Clyde finished at college he buckled in and handled things for his father, who was away most of the time doing politics and things. People around here say he was really showing some sense. Then during a trip to New York two years ago he met Lily Rowan, and she took a fancy to him and got a spell of energy at the same time. She did worse than bite him in the neck. She swallowed him. Then last spring she spit him out again. That may not be very elegant, but can you describe the activities of a toad with elegance? Clyde hasn't returned to the country; he hangs around New York and tries to see her or tries not to see her. I don't know what he's doing up here now. Maybe he knew she was coming."

She stopped. I remarked, "And that's what you were thinking about."

"No, that only leads up to it." She frowned at me. "You're a detective. That's your business, isn't it?"

"Yep. 24 hour service."

"And you . . . you keep things confidential?"

"Sure, when they are confidential."

"Well, this is. Lily Rowan is after my brother
Jimmy."

I raised the brows. "And?"

"She mustn't get him. She hasn't got him . . .
yet. I would have supposed Jimmy had too much
sense, but apparently that has nothing to do with it.
Also I thought he was in love with Nan Osgood; I
thought that last winter. A month or so ago Lily
Rowan started after him. And even Jimmy . . . even
Jimmy will fall for it! How the devil does she do it?
Damn her!"

"I couldn't say. I could ask her."

"This isn't a joke. She'll ruin him."

"I don't regard it as a job. You asked a silly question. And her being up here . . . you invited her just
to help things along a little and have it over with?"

"I invited her because I thought that seeing her
like this . . . out here in the country . . . might
bring him to. But it hasn't."

"He still laps it up."

"Yes."

I hunched my shoulders. "Well, granted that I'm a
good detective, there doesn't seem to be anything to
detect. It seems to be what my employer calls a natural process, and there's no way of stopping it except
to send your brother to Australia for a pair of shoe-
strings or cut her throat."

"I could do that, cut her throat. I could murder
her. But maybe there is a way. That's what I was
thinking about. She said something about you today
while you were upstairs. Something that gave me an
idea."

"What did she say?"

"I can't tell you. I couldn't say it."

"Was it . . . well, personal?"

"Very personal."

"What was it?"

"I tell you I won't repeat it. But that, and other things, and her asking you to have lunch with her . . . I believe you could take her away from Jimmy. Provided you don't try. She likes to do the trying, when she gets energy enough. Something about you has attracted her; I knew that when she called you Escamillo."

"Go on."

"That's all. Except . . . of course . . . I don't mean to ask a favor of you. There's no reason why you should do me a favor, even as great a one as this. It's a matter of business. When you send me a bill I'll pay it, only if it's very big I might have to pay in installments."

"I see. First I act coy, then I let her ruin me, then I send you a bill—"

"I tell you this isn't a joke. It's anything but a joke. Will you do it?"

I screwed up my lips, regarding her. Then I got out a cigarette, offered her one which was refused, and lit up.

"Look," I said, "*I* think it's a joke. Let's say she goes ahead and ruins him. In my opinion, if he's worth the powder to blow him to hell, he'll soon get unruined. No man was ever taken to hell by a woman unless he already had a ticket in his pocket, or at least had been fooling around with timetables. God bless you, you say you want to hire me to pull her off. I couldn't take an outside job even if I wanted to, because I work for Nero Wolfe on salary. But since you want to make it strictly a matter of business, I'll do this for you: I'll eat lunch with her tomorrow, provided you'll pay the check. That will be $2, for which, inclusive, I'll make you a detailed report of progress."

She said briefly, "It isn't a joke. I'll give you the $2 when we get back to the house," and stepped on the starter.

It surely wouldn't have been too much to expect that I might have had a little peace and quiet during the hour that remained before dinnertime, but no such luck. I had unloaded the crates of plants and taken them upstairs to the bathroom, and had carted up the two suitcases, and my final journey was with the two bags. Entering the room with them and hearing a noise in the bathroom, I put the bags down and crossed to the open door and saw Wolfe there, with the lids of the crates lifted so he could inspect the orchids to see if they would require spraying. I said the plants looked to me to be in good shape, and he acknowledged the fact. Then I said that since our shirts and ties were in the suitcases, likewise toilet articles, I presumed it would be unnecessary to open the bags, though I had brought them up. Not looking at me, he murmured casually but distinctly:

"It would be well, I think, to unpack."

I started. "The whole works?"

"Yes."

"You mean take everything out?"

"Yes."

"And put it back in again after dinner?"

"No. We shall sleep here tonight."

I started to improvise a cutting remark, because I

am methodical by temperament and like to see plans
carried out when they have been made, but then I
reflected that after all this place unquestionably had it
all over any hotel room they were likely to be saving
for us in Crowfield, with the town overflowing with
exposition visitors. On the other hand it was always
bad policy to feed his conceit by displaying approval,
so without comment I returned to the bedroom and
began operations on the big suitcase. Pretty soon he
waddled in, removed his coat and vest and dropped
them on one of the beds, and started to unbutton his
shirt.

I inquired pleasantly, "How did you coerce Pratt
into having us as house guests? Just turn on the old
charm?"

"There was no coercion. Technically we are not
guests. Mr. Pratt was eager to adopt my suggestion."

"Oh." I whirled on him with my hands full of socks
and handkerchiefs. "You made a suggestion?"

"I did. I'm being perfectly frank about it, Archie; I
could let it appear that the suggestion originated with
Mr. Pratt, but it didn't; I offered it. Knowing of his
difficulty, it seemed a decent thing to do, after his
generous hospitality. He approved at once, and proposed a commission to me, and I accepted."

"I see." I was still holding the haberdashery.
"What kind of a commission, if you don't mind my
asking?"

"Not a very lucrative one. Nor very difficult. Surveillance."

"I thought so." I crossed and opened a drawer of
the bureau and arranged the socks and handkerchiefs
inside. Then I stood and watched him struggle out of

his shirt and heard the seams protesting. "I suspected it the minute you told me to unpack. Okay. That's a new one. Pasture patrol. Bodyguard for a bull. I sincerely trust you'll enjoy a good night's sleep, sir, having this lovely room all to yourself."

"Don't take a tone with me, Archie. It will be dull, that's all, for a man as fidgety—"

"Dull?" I waved a hand. "Don't you believe it. Dull, out there alone in the night, sharing my secrets with the stars? You don't know me. And glowing with satisfaction because just by being there I'll be making it possible for you to snooze in that excellent bed in this big airy room. And then the dawn! Mr. Wolfe, how I love the dawn!"

"You won't see the dawn."

"The hell I won't. Who'll bump me off, Clyde? Or will the bull get me?"

"Neither. I have made arrangements with Mr. Pratt and Mr. McMillan. The man called Dave will be on guard while we are dining. At 8:30 you will relieve him, and at 1 o'clock you will be relieved by Mr. McMillan. You often go to bed that late at home. You had better waken me by knocking when you come in. I am not accustomed to my room being entered at night."

"Okay." I resumed with the suitcase, and laid out a fresh shirt for him. "But darned if I'll lug that shotgun around. I'll take that up with McMillan. Incidentally, I've accepted a commission too. For the firm. Not a very lucrative one. The fee has already been paid, two bucks, but it'll be eaten up by expenses. The client is Miss Caroline Pratt."

Wolfe muttered, "Jabber."

"Not at all. She paid me two bucks to save her

brother from a fate worse than death. Boy, is it fun being a detective! Up half the night chaperoning a bull, only to be laid waste by a blonde the next day at lunch. Look, we'll have to send a telegram to Fritz; here's a button off."

Chapter 4

I didn't get to share any secrets with any stars. Clouds had started to gather at sundown, and by half past eight it was pitch-dark. Armed with a flashlight, and my belt surrounding a good dinner—not of course up to Fritz Brenner's standard, but far and away above anything I had ever speared at a pratteria—I left the others while they were still monkeying with coffee and went out to take over my shift. Cutting across through the orchard, I found Dave sitting on an upended keg over by the fence, clutching the shotgun.

"All right," I told him, cutting off the light to save juice. "You must be about ready for some chow."

"Naw," he said, "I couldn't eat late at night like this. I had some meat and potatoes and stuff at six o'clock. My main meal's breakfast. It's my stommick that wakes me up, I git so derned hungry I can't sleep."

"That's interesting. Where's the bull?"

"I ain't seen him for a half hour. Last I saw he was down yonder, yon side of the big walnut. Why the name of common sense they don't tie him up's beyond me."

"Pratt says he was tied the first night and bellowed all night and nobody could sleep."

Dave snorted. "Let him beller. Anybody that can't sleep for a bull's bellerin' had better keep woonies instead."

"What's woonies?"

He had started off in the dark, and I heard him stop. "Woonies is bulls with their tails at the front end." He cackled. "Got you that time, mister! Good night!"

I decided to take a look, and anyhow moving was better than standing still, so I went along the fence in the direction of the gate we had driven through in our rescue of Wolfe. It sure was a black night. After making some thirty yards I played the flashlight around the pasture again, but couldn't find him. I kept on to the other side of the gate, and that time I picked him up. He wasn't lying down as I supposed he would be, but standing there looking at the light. He loomed up like an elephant. I told him out loud, "All right, honey darling, it's only Archie, I don't want you to get upset," and turned back the way I had come.

It looked to me as if there was about as much chance of anyone kidnapping that bull as there was of the bull giving milk, but in any event I was elected to stay outdoors until one o'clock, and I might as well stay in the best place in case someone was fool enough to try. If he was taken out at all it would certainly have to be through a gate, and the one on the other side was a good deal more likely than this one. So I kept going, hugging the fence. It occurred to me that it would be a lot simpler to go through the middle of the pasture, and as dark as it was there was no danger of Caesar starting another game of tag, or very little danger at least ... probably not any, really ...

I went on around the fence. Through the orchard I could see the lighted windows of the house, a couple of hundred yards away. Soon I reached the corner of the fence and turned left and, before I knew it, was in a patch of briars. Ten minutes later I had rounded the bend in the road and was passing our sedan still nestled up against the tree. There was the gate. I climbed up and sat on the fence and played the light around, but it wasn't powerful enough to pick up the bull at that distance. I switched it off.

I suppose if you live in the country long enough you get familiar with all the little noises at night, but naturally you feel curious about them when you don't know what they are. The crickets and katydids are all right, but something scuttling through the grass makes you wonder what it could be. Then there was something in a tree across the road. I could hear it move around among the leaves, then for a long while it would be quiet, and then it would move again. Maybe an owl, or maybe some little harmless animal. I couldn't find it with the light.

I had been there I suppose half an hour, when a new noise came from the direction of the car. It sounded like something heavy bumping against it. I turned the light that way, and at first saw nothing because I was looking too close to the ground, and then saw quite plainly, edging out from the front fender, a fold of material that looked like part of a coat, maybe a sleeve. I opened my mouth to sing out, but abruptly shut it again and turned off the light and slid from the fence and sidestepped. It was just barely possible that the Guernsey League had one or two tough guys on the roll, or even that Clyde Osgood himself was tough or thought he was. I stepped along the grass to the back of the car, moved around it keeping close to the side, reached over the front fender for what was huddled there, grabbed, and got a shoulder.

There was a squeal and a wiggle, and a protest: "Say! That hurts!" I flashed the light and then turned loose and stepped back.

"For God's sake," I grumbled, "don't tell me you're sentimental about that bull too."

Lily Rowan stood up, a dark wrap covering the dress she had worn at dinner, and rubbed at her shoulder. "If I hadn't stumbled against the fender," she declared, "I'd have got right up against you before you knew I was there, and I'd have scared you half to death."

"Goody. What for?"

"Darn it, you hurt my shoulder."

"I'm a brute. How did you get here?"

"Walked. I came out for a walk. I didn't realize it was so dark; I thought my eyes would get used to it. I have eyes like a cat, but I don't think I ever saw it so dark. Is that your face? Hold still."

She put a hand out, her fingers on my cheek. For a second I thought she was going to claw, but the touch was soft, and when I realized it was going to linger I stepped back a pace and told her, "Don't do that, I'm ticklish."

She laughed. "I was just making sure it was your face. Are you going to have lunch with me tomorrow?"

"Yes."

"You are?" She sounded surprised.

"Sure. That is, you can have lunch with me. Why not? I think you're amusing. You'll do fine to pass away some time, just a pretty toy to be enjoyed for an idle moment and then tossed away. That's all any woman can ever mean to me, because all the serious side of me is concentrated on my career. I want to be a policeman."

"Goodness. I suppose we ought to be grateful that you're willing to bother with us at all. Let's get in your car and sit down and be comfortable."

"It's locked and I haven't got the key. Anyhow, if I sat down I might go to sleep and I mustn't because I'm guarding the bull. You'd better run along. I promised to be on the alert."

"Nonsense." She moved around the fender, brushing against me, and planted herself on the running board. "Come here and give me a cigarette. Clyde Osgood lost his head and made a fool of himself. How could anyone possibly do anything about that bull, with only the two gates, and one of them on the side towards the house and the other one right there? And you can't do any work on your career, here on a lonely road at night. Come and play with one of your toys."

I flashed the light on the gate, a hundred feet away, then switched it off and turned to join her on the running board. Stepping on an uneven spot, I got off balance and plumped down right against her. She jerked away.

"Don't sit so close," she said in an entirely new tone. "It gives me the shivers."

I reached for cigarettes, grinning in the dark. "That had the element of surprise," I said, getting out the matches, "but it's only fair to warn you that tactics bore me, and any you would be apt to know about would be too obvious. Besides, it was bad timing. The dangle-it-then-jerk-it-away is no good until after you're positive you've got the right lure, and you have by no means reached that point . . ."

I stopped because she was on her feet and moving off. I told the dark, where her form was dim, "The lunch is off. I doubt if you have anything new to contribute."

She came back, sat down again on the running board about a foot from me, and ran the tips of her fingers down my sleeve from shoulder to elbow. "Give me a cigarette, Escamillo." I lit for her and she inhaled. "Thanks. Let's get acquainted, shall we? Tell me something."

"For instance."

"Oh . . . tell me about your first woman."

"With pleasure." I took a draw and exhaled. "I was going up the Amazon in a canoe. I was alone because I had fed all our provisions to the alligators in a spirit of fun and my natives, whom I called boys, had fled into the jungle. For two months I had had nothing to eat but fish, then an enormous tarpon had gone off with my tackle and I was helpless. Doggedly I kept on up the river, and had resigned myself to the pangs of starvation when, on the fifth day, I came to a small but beautiful island with a woman standing on it about eight feet tall. She was an Amazon. I beached the canoe and she picked me up and carried me into a sort of bower she had, saying that what I needed was a woman's care. However, there did not appear to be anything on the island to eat, and she looked as if she wouldn't need to eat again for weeks. So I adopted the

only course that was left to me, laid my plans and set
a trap, and by sundown I had her stewing merrily in
an enormous iron pot which she had apparently been
using for making lemon butter. She was delicious. As
well as I can remember, that was my first woman. Of
course since then—"

She stopped me at that point and asked me to tell
her about something else. Her wrap had fallen open in
front, and she drew it to her again. We sat there for
two more cigarettes, and might have finished the rest
of my shift there on the running board, if it hadn't
been for a noise I heard from the pasture. It sounded
like a dull thud, very faint through the concert of the
crickets and katydids, and there was no reason to suppose it was anything alarming, but it served to remind me that the nearby gate wasn't the only possible
entry to the pasture, and I decided to take a look. I
stood up and said I was going to do a patrol around to
the other side. Lily protested that it was all foolish-
ness, but I started off and she came too. The bull
wasn't within range of my light.

She hung onto my arm to keep from stumbling,
she said, though it didn't appear she had done any to
speak of when she had been sneaking up on me. I
forgot about the briar patch along the stretch at the
far end, and she got entangled and I had to work her
loose. After we turned the next corner we were in the
orchard, fairly close to the house, and I told her she
might as well scoot, but she said she was enjoying it. I
hadn't found the bull, but he had seemed to have a
preference for the other end anyhow. We kept on
along the fence, left the orchard, and reached the
other gate, and still no bull. I stood still and listened,
and heard a noise, or thought I did, like someone

dragging something, and then went ahead, with Lily
trotting along behind, flashing the light into the pasture. The noise, I suppose it was, had made me un-
easy, and I was relieved when I saw the bull on ahead,
only ten yards or so from the fence. Then I saw he
was standing on his head, at least that was what it
looked like at that distance in the dim ray of light. I
broke into a jog. When I stopped again to direct the
light over the top of the fence, I could see he was
fussing with something on the ground, with his horns.
I went on until I was even with him, and aimed the
light at him again, and after one look I felt my wrist
going limp and had to stiffen it by clamping my fingers tight on the cylinder of the flash. I heard Lily's
gasp behind me and then her hoarse whisper:

"It's a . . . it's for God's sake make him stop!"

I supposed there was a chance he was still alive,
and if so there was no time to go hunt somebody who
knew how to handle a bull. I climbed the fence, slid off
inside the pasture, switched the light to my left hand
and with my right pulled my automatic from the holster, and slowly advanced. I figured that if he made a
sudden rush it would be for the light, so I held my left
arm extended full length to the side, keeping the light
spotted on his face. He didn't rush. When I was ten
feet off he lifted his head and blinked at the light, and
I jerked up the pistol to aim at the sky and let fly with
three shots. The bull tossed his head and pivoted like
lightning, and danced off sideways, shaking the
ground. He didn't stop. I took three strides and aimed
the light at the thing on the ground. One glance was
plenty. Alive hell, I thought. I felt something inside of
me start to turn, and tightened the muscles there. I
was sorry I had aimed at the sky, and lifted the light

to look for the bull, gripping the butt of the pistol, then I realized there was no sense in making a fool of myself, and walked over and leaned on the fence. Lily was making half hysterical requests for information, and I growled, "It's Clyde Osgood. Dead. Very dead. Beat it or shut up or something." Then I heard shouts from the direction of the house and headed the light that way and yelled:

"This way! Down beyond the pit!"

More shouts, and in a few seconds a couple of flashlights showed, one dancing on the lawn and one coming along the fence. Within three minutes after I had fired the pistol four of them were on the scene: Pratt, Jimmy, Caroline and McMillan. I didn't have much explaining to do, since they had lights and there it was on the ground. After one look Caroline turned her back and stood there. Pratt pushed his chest against the fence and pulled at his lower lip, looking. Jimmy climbed up on the fence and then climbed down again.

Pratt said, "Get him out. We have to get him out of there. Where's Bert? Where the hell is Bert?"

McMillan had walked over to the remains to inspect, and now came back and asked me, "What did you shoot at? Did you shoot at Caesar? Where is he?" I said I didn't know. Bert came trotting up with a big electric lantern. Dave appeared out of the darkness, with overalls on top of a nightshirt, carrying the shotgun. McMillan came back from somewhere and said the bull was up along the fence and should be tied up before the rest of us entered the pasture, and he couldn't find the tie-rope that had been left hanging on the fence and had I seen it or anyone else. We said no, and McMillan said any strong rope would do, and

Dave volunteered to bring one. I climbed up on the fence and sat there, and Caroline asked me something, I don't know what, and I shook my head at her.

It was after Dave had returned with some rope, and McMillan had gone off with it and come back in a few minutes and said the bull was tied up and we could go ahead, that I became aware that Nero Wolfe had joined us. I heard my name, and turned my head in surprise, and there he was, with his hat on and carrying his applewood stick, peering up at me where I was still sitting on the fence.

"You're not using that flashlight," he said. "May I borrow it?"

I demanded, "How did you get here without a light?"

"I walked. I heard shots and wondered about you. As I passed by, Mr. McMillan was tying the bull to the fence and he told me what had happened—or at least, what had been found. By the way, perhaps I should warn you once again to control the exuberance of your professional instincts. It would be inconvenient to get involved here."

"What would I be doing with professional instincts?"

"Oh. You've had a shock. When you regain your senses, be sure you regain your discretion also." He stuck out a hand. "May I have the light?"

I handed it to him, and he turned and went, along the fence. Then I heard McMillan calling to me to come and help, so I slid into the pasture on stiff knees and made myself walk back over there. Dave had brought a roll of canvas, and Jimmy and McMillan were spreading it on the ground while Pratt and Dave and Bert stood and looked on, Bert holding the electric lantern.

Pratt said in a shaky voice, "We shouldn't . . . if there's any chance . . . are you sure he's dead?"

McMillan, jerking at the canvas, answered him. "You got any eyes? Look at him." He sounded as if someone had hurt his feelings. "Give us some help, will you, Goodwin? Take his feet. We'll ease him onto the canvas and then we can all get hold. We'd better go through the gate."

I tightened my belly muscles again and moved.

We all helped with the carrying except Dave, who went on ahead to get the gate open. As we passed where the bull was tied he twisted his head around to look at us. Outside the pasture we put it down a minute to change holds and then picked it up again and went on. On the terrace there was hesitation and discussion of where to put it, when Caroline suddenly appeared and directed us to the room off of the living room that had a piano in it, and we saw that she had spread some sheets over the divan at one end. We got it deposited and stretched out, but left the flaps of the canvas covering it, and then stood back and stretched our fingers, nobody looking at anybody.

Dave said, "I never seen such a sight." He looked incomplete without the shotgun. "Godalmighty, I never seen anything like it."

"Shut up," Pratt told him. Pratt looked sick. He began pulling at his lower lip again. "Now we'll have to telephone . . . we'll have to notify the Osgoods. All right. A doctor too. We have to notify a doctor anyway. Don't we?"

Jimmy took hold of his uncle's elbow. "Brace up, Uncle Tom. It wasn't your fault. What the hell was he doing in that pasture? Go get yourself a drink. I'll do the phoning."

Bert bustled out as soon as he heard the word "drink." Caroline had disappeared again. The others shuffled their feet. I left them and went upstairs.

In our room Wolfe was in the comfortable upholstered chair, under a reading lamp, with one of the books we had brought along. Knowing my step, he didn't bother to glance up as I entered and crossed to the bathroom—we might have been at home in the office. I took off my shirt to scrub my hands and splash cold water over my face, then put it on again, and my necktie and coat, and went out and sat on the edge of a straight-backed chair.

Wolfe let his eyes leave the page long enough to ask, "Not going to bed? You should. Relax. I'll stop reading shortly. It's eleven o'clock."

"Yeah, I know it is. There'll be a doctor coming, and before he gives a certificate he'll probably want to see me. I was first on the scene."

He grunted and returned to his reading. I stayed on the edge of the chair and returned to my thoughts. I don't know when I began it, since it was unconscious, or how long I kept it up, but when Wolfe spoke again I became aware that I had been rubbing the back of my left hand with the finger tips of my right as I sat staring at various spots on the floor.

"You should realize, Archie, that that is very irritating. Rubbing your hand indefinitely like that."

I said offensively, "You'll get used to it in time."

He finished a paragraph before he dog-eared a page and closed the book, and sighed. "What is it, temperament? It was a shock, of course, but you have seen violence before, and the poor monstrosity life leaves behind when it departs—"

"I can stand the monstrosity. Go ahead and read your book. At present I'm low, but I'll snap out of it by morning. Down there you mentioned professional instinct. I may be short on that, but you'll allow me my share of professional pride. I was supposed to be keeping an eye on that bull, wasn't I? That was my job, wasn't it? And I sat over by the roadside smoking cigarettes while he killed a man."

"You were guarding the bull, not the man. The bull is intact."

"Much obliged for nothing. Phooey. You're accustomed to feeling pleased because you're Nero Wolfe, aren't you? All right, on my modest scale I permit myself a similar feeling about Archie Goodwin. When did you ever give me an errand that you seriously expected me to perform and I didn't perform it? I've got a right to expect that when Archie Goodwin is told to watch a pasture and see that nothing happens to a bull, nothing will happen. And you tell me that nothing happened to the bull, the bull's all right, he just killed a man . . . what do you call that kind of suds?"

"Sophistry. Casuistry. *Ignoratio elenchi.*"

"Okay, I'll take all three."

"It's the feeling that you should have prevented the bull from killing a man that has reduced you to savagery."

"Yes. It was my job to keep things from happening in that pasture."

"Well." He sighed. "To begin with, will you never learn to make exact statements? You said that I told you the bull killed a man. I didn't say that. If I did say that, it wouldn't be true. Mr. Osgood was almost certainly murdered, but not by a bull."

I goggled at him. "You're crazy. I saw it."

"Suppose you tell me what you did see. I've had no details from you, but I'll wager you didn't see the bull impale Mr. Osgood, alive, on his horns. Did you?"

"No. When I got there he was pushing at him on the ground. Not very hard. Playing with him. I didn't know whether he was dead or not, so I climbed the fence and walked over and when I was ten feet away—"

Wolfe frowned. "You were in danger. Unnecessarily. The man was dead."

"I couldn't tell. I fired in the air, and the bull beat it, and I took a look. I didn't have to apply any tests. And now you have the nerve to say the bull didn't kill him. What are you trying to do, work up a case because business has been bad?"

"No. I'm trying to make you stop rubbing the back of your hand so I can finish this chapter before going to bed. I'm explaining that Mr. Osgood's death was not due to your negligence and would have occurred no matter where you were, only I presume the circumstances would have been differently arranged. I was not guilty of sophistry. I might suggest a thousand dangers to your self-respect, but a failure on the job tonight would not be one. You didn't fail. You were told to prevent the removal of the bull from the pasture. You had no reason to suspect an attempt to harm the bull, since the enemy's purpose was to defend him from harm, and certainly no reason to suspect an effort to frame him on a charge of murder. I do hope you won't begin—"

He stopped on account of footsteps in the hall.

They stopped by our door. There was a knock and I said come in and Bert entered.

He looked at me. "Could you come downstairs? Mr. Osgood is down there and wants to see you."

I told him I'd be right down. After he had gone and his footsteps had faded away Wolfe said, "You might confine yourself to direct evidence. That you rubbed your hand and I endeavored to make you stop is our affair."

I told him that I regarded it as such and left him to his book.

Chapter 5

At the foot of the stairs I was met by Pratt, standing with his hands stuck deep in his pockets and his wide jaw clamped tight. He made a motion with his head without saying anything, and led me into the big living room and to where a long-legged gentleman sat on a chair biting his lip, and letting it go, and biting it again. This latter barked at me when I was still five paces short of him, without waiting for Pratt or me to arrange contact:

"Your name's Goodwin, is it?"

It stuck out all over him, one of those born-to-command guys. I never invite them to parties. But I turned on the control and told him quietly, "Yep. Archie Goodwin."

"It was you that drove the bull off and fired the shots?"

"Yes, doctor."

"I'm not a doctor! I'm Frederick Osgood. My son has been killed. My only son."

"Excuse me, I thought you looked like a doctor."

Pratt, who had backed off and stood facing us with his hands still in his pockets, spoke: "The doctor hasn't got here yet. Mr. Osgood lives only a mile away and came in a few minutes."

Osgood demanded, "Tell your story. I want to hear it."

"Yes, sir." I told him. I know how to make a brief but complete report and did so, up to the point where the others had arrived, and ended by saying that I presumed he had had the rest of it from Mr. Pratt.

"Never mind Pratt. Your story is that you weren't there when my son entered the pasture."

"My story is just as I've told it."

"You're a New York detective."

I nodded. "Private."

"You work for Nero Wolfe and came here with him."

"Right. Mr. Wolfe is upstairs."

"What are you and Wolfe doing here?"

I said conversationally, "If you want a good sock in the jaw, stand up."

He started to lift. "Why, damn you—"

I showed him a palm. "Now hold it. I know your son has just been killed and I'll make all allowances within reason, but you're just making a damn fool of yourself. What's the matter with you, anyway? Are you hysterical?"

He bit his lip. In a second he said, with his tone off a shade, "No, I'm not hysterical. I'm trying to avoid making a fool of myself. I'm trying to decide whether to get the sheriff and the police here. I can't understand what happened. I don't believe it happened the way you say it did."

"That's too bad." I looked him in the eye. "Because for my part of it I have a witness. Someone was with me all the time. A . . . a young lady."

"Where is she? What's her name?"

"Lily Rowan."

He stared at me, stared at Pratt, and came back to me. He was beyond biting his lip. "Is *she* here?"

"Yes. I'll give you this free: Mr. Wolfe and I had an accident to our car and walked to this house to telephone. Everyone here was a stranger to us, including Lily Rowan. After dinner she went for a walk and found me guarding the pasture and stayed to keep me company. She was with me when I found the bull and drove him off. If you get the police and they honor me with any attention they'll be wasting their time. I've told you what I saw and did, and everything I saw and did."

Osgood's fingers were fastened onto his knees like claws digging for a hold. He demanded, "Was my son with this Lily Rowan?"

"Not while she was with me. She joined me on the far side of the pasture around nine-thirty. I hadn't seen your son since he left here in the afternoon. I don't know whether she had or not. Ask her."

"I'd rather wring her neck, damn her. What do you know about a bet my son made today with Pratt?"

A rumble came from Pratt: "I've told you all about that, Osgood. For God's sake give yourself a chance to cool down a little."

"I'd like to hear what this man has to say. What about it, Goodwin? Did you hear them making the bet?"

"Sure, we all heard it, including your daughter and your son's friend—name of Bronson." I surveyed him with decent compassion. "Take some advice from an old hand, mister, from one who has had the advantage of watching Nero Wolfe at work. You're rotten at this, terrible. You remind me of a second-grade dick harassing a dip. I've seen lots of people knocked dizzy by sudden death, and if that's all that's wrong with you there's nothing anyone can give you except sympathy, but if you're really working on an idea the best thing you can do is turn it over to professionals. Have you got a suspicion you can communicate?"

"I have."

"Suspicion of what?"

"I don't know, but I don't understand what happened. I don't believe my son walked into that pasture alone, for any purpose whatever. Pratt says he was there to get the bull. That's an idiotic supposition. My son wasn't an idiot. He wasn't a greenhorn with cattle, either. Is it likely he would go up to a loose bull, and if the bull showed temper, just stand there in the dark and let it come?"

Another rumble from Pratt: "You heard what McMillan said. He might have slipped or stumbled, and the bull was too close—"

"I don't believe it! What was he there for?"

"To win ten thousand dollars."

Osgood got to his feet. He was broad-shouldered, and a little taller than Pratt, but a bit paunchy. He advanced on Pratt with fists hanging and spoke through his teeth. "You damn skunk. I warned you not to say that again . . ."

I slipped in between them, being more at home there than I was with bulls. I allotted the face to Osgood: "And when the doctor comes his duty would be to get you two bandaged up. That would be nice. If Pratt thinks your son was trying to win a bet that's what he thinks, and you asked for his opinion and you got it. Cut out the playing. Either wait till morning and get some daylight on it, or go ahead and send for the sheriff and see what he thinks of Pratt's opinion. Then the papers will print it, along with Dave's opinion and Lily Rowan's opinion and so forth, and we'll see what the public thinks. Then some intelligent reporters from New York will print an interview with the bull—"

"Well, Mr. Pratt! I'm sorry I couldn't make it sooner . . ."

We turned. It was a stocky little man with no neck, carrying a black bag.

"I was out when the call . . . oh. Mr. Osgood. This is terrible. A very terrible thing. Terrible."

I followed the trio into the next room, where the piano was, and the divan. There was no sense in Osgood going in there again, but he went. Jimmy Pratt, who had been sitting on the piano stool, got up and left. The doctor trotted over to the divan and put his bag down on a chair. Osgood crossed to a window and stood with his back to the room. When the sound came of the canvas being opened, and the doctor's voice saying "My God!" quite loud, involuntarily, Osgood turned his head half around and then turned it back again.

Thirty minutes later I went upstairs and reported to Wolfe, who, in yellow pajamas, was in the bathroom brushing his teeth:

"Doc Sackett certified accidental death from a wound inflicted by a bull. Frederick Osgood, bereaved father, who would be a duke if we had dukes or know the reason why, suspects a fly in the soup, whether for the same reason as yours or not I can't say, because you haven't told me your reason if any. I didn't

know your wishes in regard to goading him with innu-
endo . . ."

Wolfe rinsed his mouth and spat. "I requested you
merely to give direct evidence."

"There was no merely about it. I tell you Osgood is
in the peerage and he doesn't believe it happened the
way it did happen, his chief reason being that Clyde
was too smart to fall for a bull in the dark and that
there is no acceptable reason to account for Clyde being in the pasture at all. He offered those observa-
tions to Doc Sackett, along with others, but Sackett
thought he was just under stress and shock, which he
was, and refused to delay the certification, and arranged for an undertaker to come in the morning.
Whereupon Osgood, without even asking permission
to use the telephone, called up the sheriff and the
state police."

"Indeed." Wolfe hung the towel on the rack. "Remind me to wire Theodore tomorrow. I found a mealy
bug on one of the plants."

Chapter 6

At eleven o'clock Tuesday morning I stood working on a bottle of milk which I had brought in from a dairy booth, one of hundreds lining the enormous rotunda of the main exhibits building at the Crowfield exposition grounds, and watching Nero Wolfe being gracious to an enemy. I was good and weary. On account of the arrival of the officers of the law at Pratt's around midnight, and their subsequent antics, I hadn't got to bed until after two. Wolfe had growled me out again before seven. Pratt and Caroline had been with us at breakfast, but not Lily Rowan or Jimmy. Pratt, looking as if he hadn't slept at all, reported that McMillan had insisted on guarding the bull the remainder of the night and was now upstairs in bed. Jimmy had gone to Crowfield with a list of names which probably wasn't complete, to send telegrams cancelling the invitations to the barbecue. It seemed likely that Hickory Caesar Grindon's carcass would never inspire a rustic festivity, but his destiny was uncertain. All that had been decided about him was that he wouldn't be eaten on Thursday. He had been convicted by the sheriff and the state police, who had found lying in the pasture, near the spot where Clyde Osgood had died, a tie-rope with a snap at one end, which had been identified as the one which had been left hanging on the fence. Even that had not satisfied Frederick Osgood, but it had satisfied the police, and they had dismissed Osgood's suspicions as vague, unsupported, and imaginary. When, back upstairs packing, I had asked Wolfe if he was satisfied too, he had grunted and said, "I told you last night that Mr. Osgood was not killed by the bull. My infernal curiosity led me to discover that much, and the weapon that was used, but I refuse to let the minor details of the problem take possession of my mind, so we won't discuss it."

"You might just mention who did it—"

"Please, Archie."

I put it away with moth balls and went on with the luggage. We were decamping for a Crowfield hotel. The contract for bull-nursing was cancelled, and though Pratt mumbled something about our staying on to be polite, the atmosphere of the house said go. So the packing, and lugging to the car, and spraying the orchids and getting them on board too, and the drive to Crowfield with Caroline as chauffeur, and the fight for a hotel room which was a pippin—I mean the fight, not the room—and getting both Wolfe and the crates out to the exposition grounds and finding our space and getting the plants from the crates without injury . . . It was in fact quite a morning.

Now, at eleven o'clock, I was providing for replacement of my incinerated tissue by filling up with milk. The orchids had been sprayed and straightened and manicured and were on the display benches in the space which had been allotted to us. The above-mentioned enemy that Wolfe was being gracious to was a short fat person in a dirty unpressed mohair suit with keen little black eyes and two chins, by name Charles E. Shanks. I watched them and listened to them as I sipped the milk, because it was instructive. Shanks knew that the reason Wolfe had busted precedent and come to Crowfield to exhibit albinos which he had got by three new crosses with Paphiopedilum lawrenceanum hyeanum was to get an award over one Shanks had produced by crossing P. callosum sanderae with a new species from Burma; that Wolfe desired and intended to make a monkey of Shanks because Shanks had fought shy of the metropolitan show and had also twice refused Wolfe's offers to trade albinos; and that one good look at the entries in direct comparison made it practically certain that the judges' decision would render Shanks not only a monkey but even a baboon. Furthermore, Wolfe knew that Shanks knew that they both knew; but hearing them gabbing away you might have thought that when a floriculturist wipes his brow it is to remove not sweat but his excess of brotherly love; which is why, knowing the stage of vindictiveness Wolfe had had to arrive at before he decided on that trip, I say it was instructive to listen to them.

I had been subjected to a few minor vexations in connection with the pasture affair. During the battle for a room at the hotel I had been approached by a bright-eyed boy with big ears and a notebook who grabbed me by the lapel and said he wanted, not only for the local Journal but also for the Associated Press, as lurid an account as possible of the carnage and gore. I traded him a few swift details for his help on the room problem. A couple of other news retrievers, in town to cover the exposition I suppose, also came sniffing around; and while I had been helping Wolfe get the orchids primped up I had been accosted by a tall skinny guy in a pin-check suit, as young as me or younger, wearing a smile that I would recognize if I saw it in Siam—the smile of an elected person who expects to run again, or a novice in training to join the elected person class at the first opportunity. He looked around to make sure no spies were sneaking up on us at the moment, introduced himself as Mr. Whosis, Assistant District Attorney of Crowfield County, and told me at the bottom of his voice, shifting from the smile to Expression 9B, which is used when speaking of the death of a voter, that he would like to have my version of the unfortunate occurrence at the estate of Mr. Pratt the preceding evening.

Feeling pestered, I raised my voice instead of lowering it. "District Attorney, huh? Working up a charge of murder against the bull?"

That confused him, because he had to show that he appreciated my wit without sacrificing Expression 9B; also I attracted the attention of passers-by and a few of them stopped in the aisle to look at us. He did it pretty well. No, he said, not a charge of murder, nothing like that, not even against the bull; but certain inquiries had been made and it was felt desirable to supplement the reports of the sheriff and police by firsthand information so there could be no complaint of laxity. . . .

I drew the picture for him without any retouching or painting out, and he asked a few fairly intelligent questions. When he had gone I told Wolfe about him, but Wolfe had orchids and Charles E. Shanks on his mind and showed no sign of comprehension. A little later Shanks himself appeared on the scene and that was when I went for the bottle of milk.

There was an ethical question troubling me which couldn't be definitely settled until one o'clock. In view of what had happened at Pratt's place I had no idea that Lily Rowan would show up for the lunch date, and if she didn't what was the status of the two dollars Caroline had paid me? Anyhow, I had decided that if the fee wasn't earned it wouldn't be my fault, and luckily my intentions fitted in with Wolfe's plans which he presently arranged, namely to have lunch with Shanks. I wouldn't have eaten with them anyway, since I had heard enough about stored pollen and nutritive solutions and fungus inoculation for a while, so a little before one I left the main exhibits building and headed down the avenue to the right in the direction of the tent which covered the eatery operated by the ladies of the First Methodist Church. That struck me as an incongruous spot to pick for being undone by a predatory blonde, but she had said the food there was the best available at the exposition grounds, and Caroline's reply to an inquiry during the morning ride to Crowfield had verified it, so I smothered my conscience and went ahead.

It was another fine day and the crowd was kicking up quite a dust. Banners, balloons, booby booths and bingo games were all doing a rushing business, not to mention hot dogs, orange drinks, popcorn, snake charmers, lucky wheels, shooting galleries, take a slam and win a ham, two-bit fountain pens and Madam Shasta who reads the future and will let you in on it for one thin dime. I passed a platform whereon stood a girl wearing a grin and a pure gold brassière and a Fuller brush skirt eleven inches long, and beside her a hoarse guy in a black derby yelling that the mystic secret Dingaroola Dance would start inside the tent in eight minutes. Fifty people stood gazing up at her and listening to him, the men looking as if they might be willing to take one more crack at the mystic, and the women looking cool and contemptuous. I moseyed along. The crowd got thicker, that being the main avenue leading to the grandstand entrance. I got tripped up by a kid diving between my legs in an effort to resume contact with mamma, was glared at by a hefty milkmaid, not bad-looking, who got her toe caught under my shoe, wriggled away from the tip of a toy parasol which a sweet little girl kept digging into my ribs with, and finally left the worst of the happy throng behind and made it to the Methodist grub-tent, having passed by the Baptists with the snooty feeling of a man-about-town who is in the know.

Believe it or not, she was there, at a table against the canvas wall toward the rear. I pranced across the sawdust, concealing my amazement. Dressed in a light tan jersey thing, with a blue scarf and a little blue hat, among those hearty country folk she looked like an antelope in a herd of Guernseys. I sat down across the table from her and told her so. She yawned and said that what she had seen of antelopes' legs made it seem necessary to return the compliment for repairs, and before I could arrange a comeback we were interrupted by a Methodist lady in white apron who wanted to know what we would have.

Lily Rowan said, "Two chicken fricassee with dumplings."

"Wait a minute," I protested. "It says there they have beef pot roast and veal—"

"No." Lily was firm. "The fricassee with dumplings is made by a Mrs. Miller whose husband has left her four times on account of her disposition and returned four times on account of her cooking and is still there. So I was told yesterday by Jimmy Pratt."

The Methodist bustled off. Lily looked at me with a corner of her mouth curled up and remarked as if it didn't matter much, "The chief reason I came was to see how surprised you would look when you found me here, and you don't look surprised at all and you begin by telling me I have legs like an antelope."

I shrugged. "Go ahead and nag. I admit I'm glad you came, because if you hadn't I wouldn't have known about the fricassee. Your harping on legs is childish. Your legs are unusually good and you know it and so do I. Legs are made to be walked with or looked at, not talked about, especially not in a Methodist stronghold. Are you a Catholic? What's the difference between a Catholic and a river that runs uphill?"

She didn't know and I told her, and we babbled on. The fricassee came, and the first bite, together with dumpling and gravy, made me marvel at the hellishness of Mrs. Miller's disposition, to drive a man away from that. It gave me an idea, and a few minutes later, when I saw Wolfe and Charles E. Shanks enter the tent and get settled at a table on the other side, I excused myself and went over and told him about the fricassee, and he nodded gravely.

I was corralling the last of my rice when Lily asked me when I was going back to New York. I told her it depended on what time the orchids were judged on Wednesday; we would leave either Wednesday afternoon or Thursday morning.

"Of course," she said, "we'll see each other in New York."

"Yeah?" I swallowed the rice. "What for?"

"Nothing in particular. Only I'm sure we'll see each other, because if you weren't curious about me you wouldn't be so rude, and I was curious about you before I ever saw your face, when I saw you walking across that pasture. You have a distinctive way of walking. You move very . . . I don't know . . ."

"Distinctive will do. Maybe you noticed I have a distinctive way of getting over a fence too, in case of a bull. Speaking of bulls, I understand the barbecue is off."

"Yes." She shivered a little. "Naturally. I'm thinking of leaving this afternoon. When I came away at noon there was a string of people gawking along the fence, there where your car had been . . . where we were last night. They would have crossed the pasture and swarmed all over the place if there hadn't been a state trooper there." ·

"With the bull in it?"

"The bull was at the far end. That what's-his-name —McMillan—took him there and tied him up again." She shivered. "I never saw anything like last night . . . I had to sit on the ground to keep from fainting. What were they asking questions for? Why did they ask if I was with you all the time? What did that have to do with him getting killed by the bull?"

"Oh, they always do that in cases of accidental death. Eye-witnesses. By the way, you won't be leaving for New York today if they hold an inquest, only I don't suppose they will. Did they ask if you had seen Clyde Osgood around there after dinner, before you went for your walk and ran onto me?"

"Yes. Of course I hadn't. Why did they ask?"

"Search me." I put sugar in my coffee and stirred. "Maybe they thought you had deprived him of all hope or something and he climbed into the pasture to commit suicide. All kinds of romantic ideas, those birds get. Did they ask if Clyde had come to Pratt's place to see you?"

"Yes." Her eyes lifted up at me and then dropped back to her coffee cup. "I didn't understand that either. Why should they think he had come to see me?"

"Oh, possibly Clyde's father sicked them on. I know when I mentioned your name to him last night and said you were there, he nearly popped open. I got the impression he had seen you once in a nightmare. Not that I think you belong in a nightmare, with your complexion and so on, but that was the impression I got."

"He's just a pain." She shrugged indifferently. "He has no right to be talking about me. Anyway, not to you." Her eyes moved up me and over me, up from my chest over my face to the top of my head, and then slowly traveled down again. "Not to you, Escamillo," she said. I wanted to slap her, because her tone, and the look in her eyes going over me, made me feel like a potato she was peeling. She asked, "What did he say?"

"Not much." I controlled myself. "Only his expression was suggestive. He spoke of wringing your neck. I gathered that you and his son Clyde had once been friends. I suppose he told the police and sheriff that, or maybe they knew it already, and that's why they asked if Clyde came to see you last night."

"Well, he didn't. He would have been more apt to come to see Caroline than me."

That was turning a new page for me, but I covered
my surprise and inquired idly, "You mean Miss Pratt?
Why, did they have dealings?"

"They used to have." She opened the mirror of her
compact to study nature with an eye to improvement.
"I guess they were engaged, or about to be. Of course
you don't know about the Osgood-Pratt situation. The
Osgoods have been rich for generations, they go back
to a revolutionary general I think it was—their relatives in New York think the Social Register is vulgar.
To me that's all a bore . . . my mother was a wait-
ress and my father was an immigrant and made his
money building sewers."

"Yet look at you. I heard Pratt say yesterday that
he was born in an old shack on the spot where his new
house stands."

"Yes. His father worked as a stablehand for Osgood's father. Clyde told me about it. A farmer had a
beautiful daughter named Marcia and young Pratt got
himself engaged to her and Frederick Osgood came
back from college and saw her and married her. So
she became Clyde Osgood's mother, and Nancy's.
Pratt went to New York and soon began to make
money. He didn't marry, and as soon as he had time to
spare he started to find ways to annoy Osgood. When
he bought land up here and started to build, it looked
as if the annoyance might become really serious."

"And Clyde read up on family feuds and found that
the best way to cure it would be for him to marry
Pratt's niece. A daughter is better in such cases, but a
niece will do."

"No, it wasn't Clyde's idea, it was his sister's.
Nancy's." Lily closed her compact. "She was staying
in New York for the winter, studying rhythm at the

best night clubs, and met Jimmy and Caroline, and thought it might be helpful for the four of them to know each other, and when Clyde came down for a visit she arranged it. It made a sort of a situation, and she and Jimmy got really friendly, and so did Clyde and Caroline. Then Clyde happened to get interested in me, and I guess that reacted on Nancy and Jimmy."

"Did you and Clyde get engaged?"

"No." She looked at me, and the corner of her mouth turned up, and I saw her breasts gently putting the weave of the jersey to more strain as she breathed a deep one. "No, Escamillo." She peeled her potato again. "I don't suppose I'll marry. Because marriage is really nothing but an economic arrangement, and I'm lucky because I don't have to let the economic part enter into it. The man would be lucky too—I mean if a man attracted me and I attracted him."

"He sure would." I was wondering which would be more satisfactory, to slap her and then kiss her, or to kiss her and then slap her. "Did Clyde attract you much?"

"He did for a while." She shivered delicately. "You know how tiresome it is when someone you found exciting gets to be nothing but a nuisance? He wanted me to marry him, too. You mustn't think I'm heartless, because I'm not. Caroline would have been a swell wife for him, and I told him so. I rather thought they would make it up, and I hoped they would, and that's why I said he would have been more apt to come to see Caroline than me last night."

"Maybe he did. Have you asked her?"

"Good lord no. Me ask Caroline anything about

Clyde? I wouldn't dare mention his name to her. She hates me."

"She invited you up for the barbecue, didn't she?"

"Yes, but that was because she was being clever. Her brother Jimmy and I were beginning to be friendly, and she thought if he saw me out here in the country, a lot of me, he would realize how superficial and unhealthy I am."

"Oh. So you're unhealthy?"

"Terribly." The corner of her mouth went up another sixteenth of an inch. "Because I'm frank and simple. Because I never offer anything I don't give, and I never give anything and then expect to get paid for it. I'm frightfully unhealthy. But I guess I was wrong to say superficial. I doubt if Caroline thinks I'm superficial."

"Excuse me a minute," I said, and stood up.

Even in the midst of being ruined I had had Wolfe's table across the tent in the corner of my eye, partly to note his reaction to the fricassee, which had appeared to be satisfactory since he had ordered a second portion, and my interrupting my despoiler was on account of a sign from him. A man was standing by Wolfe's chair talking to him, and Wolfe had glanced in my direction with a lift to his brow which I considered significant. So I excused myself to Lily and got up and ambled over. As I arrived the man turned his head and I saw it was Lew Bennett, the secretary of the National Guernsey League.

"Archie, I must thank you." Wolfe put his napkin down. "For suggesting the fricassee. It is superb. Only female Americans can make good dumplings, and not many of them."

"Yes, sir."

"You have met Mr. Bennett."

"Yes, sir."

"Can you conveniently extricate yourself from that . . ." He turned a thumb in the direction I had come from.

"You mean right now?"

"As soon as may be. Now if you are not too involved. Mr. Bennett has been looking for me at the request of Mr. Osgood, who is waiting in the exposition office and wishes to see me. Mr. Shanks and I shall have finished our lunch in ten minutes."

"Okay. I'm badly involved but I'll manage it."

I went back to my table and told Lily we must part, and summoned the Methodist to give me a check. The damage proved to be $1.60, and, having relinquished a pair of dimes for the missionaries, I reflected with pride that the firm had cleaned up 20 cents net on the deal.

Lily said in a tone of real disappointment without any petulance that I could detect, "I had supposed we would spend the afternoon together, watching the races and riding on the merry-go-round and throwing balls at things . . ."

"Not ever," I said firmly. "Not the afternoon. Whatever the future may have in store for us, whatever may betide, I work afternoons. Understand once and for all that I am a workingman and I only play with toys at odd moments. I am working when you would least expect it. Throughout this delightful lunch with you, I have been working and earning money."

"I suppose while you were paying me all those charming compliments one part of your brain, the most important part, was busy on some difficult problem."

"That's the idea."

"Dear Escamillo. Darling Escamillo. But the afternoon comes to an end, doesn't it? What will you be doing this evening?"

"God knows. I work for Nero Wolfe."

Chapter 7

The room in the exposition offices, to which Bennett led us, on a kind of mezzanine in the Administration Building, was large and lofty, with two dusty windows in the board wall and plain board partitions for the other three sides. The only furniture were three big rough tables and a dozen wooden chairs. On one table were a pile of faded bunting and a bushel basket half-full of apples; the other two were bare. Three of the chairs were occupied. Sidney Darth, Chairman of the North Atlantic Exposition Board, was on the edge of one but jumped up as we entered; Frederick Osgood, the upstate duke, had sagging shoulders and a tired and bitter but determined expression; and Nancy Osgood sat with her spine curved and looked miserable all over.

Bennett did the introductions. Darth mumbled something about people waiting for him and loped off. Wolfe's eyes traveled over the furniture with a hopeless look, ending at me, meaning couldn't I for God's sake rustle a chair somewhere that would hold all of him, but I shook my head inflexibly, knowing how useless it was. He compressed his lips, heaved a sigh, and sat down.

Bennett said, "I can stay if you want . . . if I can be of any help . . ." Wolfe looked at Osgood and Osgood shook his head: "No thanks, Lew. You run along." Bennett hesitated a second, looking as if he wouldn't mind staying a bit, and then beat it. After the door had closed behind him I requisitioned a chair for myself and sat down.

Osgood surveyed Wolfe with an aristocratic scowl. "So you're Nero Wolfe. I understand you came to Crowfield to exhibit orchids."

Wolfe snapped at him, "Who told you so?"

The scowl got half startled away, but came right back again. "Does it matter who told me?"

"No. Nor does it matter why I came to Crowfield. Mr. Bennett said you wished to consult me, but surely not about orchids."

I restrained a grin, knowing that Wolfe was not only establishing control, which was practical and desirable, but was also relieving his resentment at having been sent for and having come, even if it was on his way anyhow.

"I don't give a damn about the orchids." Osgood preserved the scowl. "The purpose of your presence here is relevant because I need to know if you are a friend of Tom Pratt's, or are being employed by him, or have been. You were at his house last night."

"Relevant to what, sir?" Wolfe sounded patient with distress. "Either you want to consult me or you don't. If you do, and I find that I am in any way committed to a conflicting interest, I shall tell you so. You have started badly and offensively. Why the devil should I account to you for my presence here in

Crowfield or anywhere else? If you need me, here I am. What can I do for you?"

"Are you a friend of Tom Pratt's?"

Wolfe grunted with exasperation, got himself raised, and took a step. "Come, Archie."

Osgood raised his voice: "Where you going? Damn it, haven't I got a right to ask—"

"No, sir." Wolfe glared down at him. "You have no right to ask me anything whatever. I am a professional detective in good standing. If I accept a commission I perform it. If for any reason I can't undertake it in good faith, I refuse it. Come, Archie."

I arose with reluctance. Not only did I hate to walk out on what might develop into a nice piece of business, but also my curiosity had been aroused by the expression on Nancy Osgood's face. When Wolfe had got up and started to go she had looked relieved, and when after Osgood's protest he had started off again her relief had been even more evident. Little contrary things like that disturbed my peace of mind, so it suited me fine when Osgood surrendered.

"All right," he growled. "I apologize. Come back and sit down. Of course I've heard about you and your damned independence. I'll have to swallow it because I need you and I can't help it. These damn fools here . . . in the first place they have no brains and in the second place they're a pack of cowards. I want you to investigate the death of my son Clyde."

Sure enough, as Wolfe accepted the apology by returning to sit down, Nancy quit looking relieved and her hands on her lap, having relaxed a little, were clasped tight again.

Wolfe asked, "What aspect of your son's death do you want investigated?"

Osgood said savagely, "I want to know how he was killed."

"By a bull. Wasn't he? Isn't that the verdict of the legal and medical authorities?"

"Verdict hell. I don't believe it. My son knew cattle. What was he in the pasture at night for? Pratt's idea that he went there to get the bull is ridiculous. And he certainly wasn't ass enough to let himself be gored like that in the pitch-dark."

"Still he was gored." Wolfe shifted on the measly chair. "If not by the bull, then how and by what?"

"I don't know. I don't pretend to know. You're an expert and that's what I want you to find out. You're supposed to have intelligence above the average . . . what do you think? You were at Pratt's place. Knowing the circumstances as you do, do you think he was killed by the bull?"

Wolfe sighed. "Expert opinions cost money, Mr. Osgood. Especially mine. I charge high fees. I doubt if I can accept a commission to investigate your son's death. My intention is to leave for New York Thursday morning, and I shouldn't care to be delayed much beyond that. I like to stay at home, and when I am away I like to get back. Without committing myself to an investigation, my fee for an opinion, now, will be a thousand dollars."

Osgood stared. "A thousand dollars just to say what you think?"

"To say what I have deduced and decided, yes. I doubt if it's worth it to you."

"Then why the devil do you ask it?"

Nancy's voice came in, a husky protest, "Dad. I told you. It's foolish . . . it's all so foolish . . ."

Wolfe glanced at her, and back at her father, and shrugged. "That's the price, sir."

"For one man's guess."

"Oh, no. For the truth."

"Truth? You're prepared to prove it?"

"No. I sell it as an opinion. But I don't sell guesses."

"All right. I'll pay for it. What is it?"

"Well." Wolfe pursed his lips and half shut his eyes. "Clyde Osgood did not enter the pasture voluntarily. He was unconscious, though still alive, when he was placed in the pasture. He was not gored, and therefore not killed, by the bull. He was murdered, probably by a man, possibly by two men, barely possibly by a woman or a man and a woman."

Nancy had straightened up with a gasp and then sat stiff. Osgood was gazing at Wolfe with his clamped jaw working a little from side to side.

"That . . ." He stopped and clamped his jaw again. "You say that's the truth? That my son was murdered?"

"Yes. Without a guaranty. I sell it as an opinion."

"How good is it? Where did you get it? Damn you, if you're playing me—"

"Mr. Osgood! Really. I'm not playing, I'm working. I assure you my opinion is a good one. Whether it's worth what you're paying for it depends on what you do with it."

Osgood got up, took two steps, and was looking down at his daughter. "You hear that, Nancy?" he demanded, as if he was accusing her of something. "You hear what he says? I knew it, I tell you, I knew it." He jerked his head up. "Good God . . . my son dead . . . murdered . . ." He whirled to Wolfe, opened his mouth and closed it again, and went back to his chair and let himself down.

Nancy looked at Wolfe and asked indignantly, "Why do you say that? How can you know . . . Clyde was murdered? Why do you say it as if . . . as if you could know . . ."

"Because I had arrived at that opinion, Miss Osgood."

"But how? Why?"

"Be quiet, Nancy." Osgood turned to Wolfe. "All right, I've got your opinion. Now I want to know what you base it on."

"My deductions. I was there last night, with a flashlight."

"Deductions from what?"

"From the facts." Wolfe wiggled a finger at him. "You may have them if you want them, but see here. You spoke of 'these damn fools here' and called them a pack of cowards. Referring to the legal authorities?"

"Yes. The District Attorney and the sheriff."

"Do you call them cowards because they hesitate to institute an investigation of your son's death?"

"They don't merely hesitate, they refuse. They say my suspicions are arbitrary and unfounded. They don't use those words, but that's what they mean. They simply don't want to pick up something they're afraid they can't handle."

"But you have position, power, political influence—"

"No. Especially not with Waddell, the District Attorney. I opposed him in '36, and it was chiefly Tom Pratt's money that elected him. But this is murder! You say yourself it was murder!"

"They may be convinced it wasn't. That's quite

plausible under the circumstances. Do you suggest they would bottle up a murder to save Pratt annoyance?"

"No. Or yes. I don't care a damn which. I only know they won't listen to reason and I'm helpless, and I intend that whoever killed my son shall suffer for it. That's why I came to you."

"Precisely." Wolfe shifted in his chair again. "The fact is, you haven't given them much reason to listen to. You have told them your son wouldn't have entered the pasture, but he was there; and that he wasn't fool enough to let a bull kill him in the dark, which is conjectural and by no means a demonstrated fact. You have asked me to investigate your son's death, but I couldn't undertake it unless the police exert themselves simultaneously. There will be a lot of work to do, and I have no assistance here except Mr. Goodwin; and I can't commandeer evidence. If I move in the affair at all, the first stop must be to enlist the authorities. Is the District Attorney's office in Crowfield?"

"Yes."

"Is he there now?"

"Yes."

"Then I suggest that we see him. I engage to persuade him to start an investigation immediately. That of course will call for an additional fee, but I shall try not to make it extravagant. After that is done we can reconsider your request that I undertake an investigation myself. You may decide it isn't necessary, or I may regard it as impractical. Do you have a car here? May Mr. Goodwin drive it? He ran mine into a tree."

"I do my own driving. Or my daughter does. I don't like going back to that jackass Waddell."

"I'm afraid it's unavoidable." Wolfe elevated his bulk. "Certain things must be done without delay, and they will need authority behind them."

It turned out that the daughter drove. We found Osgood's big black sedan parked in a privileged and exclusive space at one side of the Administration Building, and piled in. I sat in front with Nancy. For the two miles into Crowfield the highway and streets were cluttered with the exposition traffic, and although she was impulsive with the wheel and jerky on the gas pedal, she did it pretty well. I glanced around once and saw Wolfe hanging onto the strap for dear life. We finally rolled up to the curb in front of a stretch of lawn and a big old stone building with its status carved above the entrance: CROWFIELD COUNTY COURT HOUSE.

Osgood, climbing out, spoke to his daughter: "You go on home, Nancy, to your mother. There was no sense in your coming anyway. I'll phone when there is anything to say."

Wolfe intervened, "It would be better for her to wait for us here. In case I take this job I shall need to talk with her without delay."

"With my daughter?" Osgood scowled. "What for? Nonsense!"

"As you please, sir." Wolfe shrugged. "It's fairly certain I won't want the job. For one thing, you're too infernally combative for a client."

"But why the devil should you need to talk to my daughter?"

"To get information. I offer you advice, Mr. Osgood: go home with your daughter and forget this quest for vengeance. There is no other form of human activity quite so impertinent as a competent murder

investigation, and I fear you're not equipped to tolerate it. Abandon the idea. You can mail me a check at
your convenience—"

"I'm going on with it."

"Then prepare yourself for annoyance, intrusion,
plague, the insolence of publicity—"

"I'm going on with it."

"Indeed." Wolfe inclined his head an inch toward
the lovely but miserable face of the daughter at the
steering wheel. "Then you will please wait here, Miss
Osgood."

Chapter 8

In all ordinary circumstances Wolfe's cocky and unlimited conceit prevents the development of any of the tender sentiments, such as compassion for instance, but that afternoon I felt sorry for him. He was being compelled to break some of his most ironclad rules. He was riding behind strange drivers, walking in crowds, obeying a summons from a prospective client, and calling upon a public official, urged on by his desperate desire to find a decent place to sit down. The hotel room we had managed to get—since we hadn't arrived Monday evening to claim the one we had reserved—was small, dark and noisy, and had one window which overlooked a building operation where a concrete mixer was raising cain. If you opened the window, cement dust entered in clouds. There was nowhere at all to sit near our space in the exhibits building. At the Methodist tent they had folding chairs. The ones at the room where we had gone to meet Osgood, where Wolfe had probably expected something fairly tolerable, had been little better; and obviously Wolfe regarded the District Attorney's office as a sort of forlorn last hope. I never saw him move faster than when we entered and a swift glance showed him there was just one upholstered, in dingy black leather, with arms. You might almost have called it a swoop. He stood in front of it for the introduction and then sank.

Carter Waddell, the District Attorney, was pudgy and middle-aged and inclined to bubble. I suppose he did special bubbling for Osgood, on account of sympathy for bereavement and to show that the 1936 election had left no hard feelings, not to mention his love for his country of which Osgood owned 2000 acres. He said he was perfectly willing to reopen the discussion they had had earlier in the day, though his own opinion was unaltered. Osgood said he didn't intend to discuss it himself, that would be a waste of time and effort, but that Mr. Nero Wolfe had something to say.

"By all means," Waddell bubbled. "Certainly. Mr. Wolfe's reputation is well known, of course. Doubtless we poor rustics could learn a great deal from him. Couldn't we, Mr. Wolfe?"

Wolfe murmured, "I don't know your capacity, Mr. Waddell. But I do think I have something pertinent to offer regarding the murder of Clyde Osgood."

"Murder?" Waddell stretched his eyes wide. "Now I don't know. *Petitio principii* isn't a good way to begin. Is it?"

"Of course not." Wolfe wriggled himself comfortable, and sighed. "I offer the word as something to be established, not as a postulate. Did you ever see a bull kill a man, or injure one with his horn?"

"No, I can't say I have."

"Did you ever see a bull who had just gored a man or a horse or any animal? Immediately after the goring?"

"No."

"Well, I have . . . long ago . . . a dozen times or more, at bullfights. Horses killed, and men injured . . . one man killed." Wolfe wiggled a finger. "Whether you've seen it or not, surely you can imagine what happens when a bull thrusts his horn deep into a living body, and tosses, and tears the wound. While the heart of the victim is still furiously pumping. Blood spurts all over the bull's face and head, and often clear to his shoulders and beyond. The bleeding of a man killed in that manner is frightful; the instant such a wound is made a torrent gushes forth. It was so in the case of Clyde Osgood. His clothing was saturated. I am told that the police report that where he was killed there is an enormous caked pool of it. Is that correct? You acknowledge it. Last night Mr. Goodwin, my assistant, found the bull turning Clyde Osgood's body over on the ground, with his horns, without much force or enthusiasm. The natural supposition was that the bull had killed him. Not more than fifteen minutes later, when the bull had been tied to the fence, I examined him at close range with a flashlight. He has a white face, and there was only one smudge of blood on it, and his horns were bloody only a few inches down from the tips. Was that fact included in the police report?"

Waddell said slowly, "I don't remember . . . no."

"Then I advise that the bull be inspected at once, provided he hasn't been already washed off. I assure you that my report is reliable." Wolfe wiggled a finger again. "I didn't come here to offer a conjecture, Mr. Waddell. I don't intend to argue it with you. Often in considering phenomena we encounter a suspicious circumstance which requires study and permits debate, but the appearance of the bull's face and head last night is not that, it is much more. It is conclusive proof that the bull didn't kill Clyde Osgood. You spoke of my reputation; I stake it on this."

"By God," Clyde Osgood's father muttered. "Well, by God. I looked at that bull myself, and I never thought . . ."

"I'm afraid you weren't doing much thinking last night," Wolfe told him. "It couldn't be expected of you. But it might have been expected of the police by the sanguine . . . particularly the rustic police."

The District Attorney, without any sign of bubbling, said, "You've made a point, I grant that. Of course you have. But I'd like to have a doctor's opinion about the bleeding—"

"It was all over his clothes and the grass. Great quantities. If you consult a doctor, let it be the one who saw the wound. In the meantime, it would be well to act, and act soon, on the assumption that the bull didn't do it, because that's the fact."

"You're very positive, Mr. Wolfe. Very."

"I am."

"Isn't it possible that the bull withdrew his horn so quickly that he escaped the spurt of blood?"

"No. The spurt is instantaneous, and bulls don't gore like that anyway. They stay in to tear. Has the wound been described to you?"

Waddell nodded. I noticed that he wasn't looking at Osgood. "That's another thing," he said. "That wound. If it wasn't made by the bull, what could possibly have done it? What kind of weapon?"

"The weapon is right there, not thirty yards from the pasture fence. Or was. I examined it."

I thought, uh-huh, see the bright little fat boy with

all the pretty skyrockets! But I stared at him, and so
did the others. Osgood ejaculated something, and
Waddell's voice had a crack in it as he demanded,
"You what?"

"I said, I examined it."

"The weapon that killed him?"

"Yes. I borrowed a flashlight from Mr. Goodwin,
because of a slight difficulty in believing that Clyde
Osgood would let himself be gored by a bull in the
dark. I had heard him remark, in the afternoon, that
he knew cattle. Later his father experienced the same
difficulty, but didn't know how to resolve it. I did so
by borrowing the light and inspecting the bull, and
perceived at once that the supposition which already
prevailed was false. The bull hadn't killed him. Then
what had?"

Wolfe squirmed in his chair, which was after all
eight inches too narrow, and continued, "It is an interesting question whether rapid and accurate brain
work results from superior equipment or from good
training. In my case, whatever my original equipment
may have been, it has certainly had the advantage of
prolonged and severe training. One result, not always
pleasant and rarely profitable, is that I am likely to
forget myself and concentrate on problems which are
none of my business. I did so last night. Within thirty
seconds after inspecting the bull's clean face, I had
guessed at a possible weapon. Knowing where it was,
I went and inspected it, and verified my guess. I then
returned to the house. By the time I arrived there I
had reached a conclusion as to how the crime had
been committed—and I have not altered it since."

"What was the weapon? Where was it?"

"It was rustic too. An ordinary pick for digging. In

the afternoon, in an emergency created by the bull—preceded by Mr. Goodwin's destruction of my car—I had been conveyed from the pasture by Miss Pratt in an automobile. We had passed by an excavation—the barbecue pit as I learned afterwards—with freshly dug earth and picks and shovels lying there. My guess was that a pick might have been used. I went with a flashlight to see, and found confirmation. There were two picks. One of them was perfectly dry, with bits of dried soil clinging to it, and the other was damp. Even the metal itself was still damp on the under side, and the wooden handle was positively wet. There was no particle of soil clinging to the metal. Obviously the thing had been thoroughly and recently washed, not more than an hour previously at the outside. Not far away I found the end of a piece of garden hose. It was connected somewhere, for when I turned the nozzle a little, water came. Around where the nozzle lay the grass was quite wet when I pressed my palm into it. It was more than a surmise, it was close to a certainty, that the pick had done the goring, got deluged with blood, been carefully washed with the garden hose and replaced on the pile of excavated soil where I found it."

"You mean—" Frederick Osgood stopped with his jaw clamped. His clenched fists, resting on his hams, showed white knuckles. He went on, harshly, "My son . . . was killed like that . . . dug at with a pick?"

Waddell was looking decomposed. He tried to bluster. "If all this is true—you knew it last night, didn't you? Why the hell didn't you spill it when the sheriff was there? When the cops were there on the spot?"

"I represented no interest last night, sir."

"What about the interest of justice? You're a citizen, aren't you? Did you ever hear of withholding evidence—"

"Nonsense. I didn't withhold the bull's face or the pick. You must know you're being silly. My cerebral processes, and the conclusions they lead me to, belong to me."

"You say the pick handle was wet and there was no dirt sticking to the metal. Couldn't it have been washed for some legitimate reason? Did you inquire about that?"

"I made no inquiries of anybody. At eleven o'clock at night the pick handle was wet. If you regard it as a rational project to find a legitimate nocturnal pick-washer, go ahead. The time might be better spent, if you need confirmation, in looking for blood residue in the grass around the hose nozzle and examining the pick handle with a microscope. It is hard to remove all vestige of blood from a piece of wood. Those steps are of course obvious, and others as well."

"You're telling me." The District Attorney sent a glance, half a glare, at Osgood, and away again, back at Wolfe. "Now look here, don't get me wrong . . . you neither, Fred Osgood. I'm the prosecutor for this county and I know my duty and I intend to do it and I try to do it. If there's been a crime I don't want to back off from it and neither does Sam Lake, but I'm not going to raise a stink just for the hell of it and you can't blame me for that. The people who elected me wouldn't want it and nobody ought to want it. And the way it looks to me—in spite of no blood on the bull and whether I find a legitimate nocturnal pick-washer or not—it still strikes me as cuckoo. Did he climb into the pasture carrying the pick—where the bull was—

and then Clyde Osgood climbed in after him and obligingly stood there while he swung the pick? Or was Clyde already in the pasture, and he climbed in with the pick and let him have it? Can you imagine aiming anything as clumsy and heavy as a pick at a man in the dark, and him still being there when it landed? And wouldn't the blood spurt all over you too? Who is he and where did he go to, covered with blood?"

Osgood snarled, "I told you, Wolfe. Listen to the damn fool.—Look here, Carter Waddell! Now I'll tell you something—"

"Please, gentlemen!" Wolfe had a palm up. "We're wasting a lot of time." He regarded the District Attorney and said patiently, "You're going about it wrong. You should stop squirming and struggling. Finding yourself confronted by an unpleasant fact . . . you're like a woman who conceals a stain on a table cover by putting an ash tray over it. Ineffectual, because someone is sure to move the ash tray. The fact is that Clyde Osgood was murdered by someone with that pick, and unhappily your function is to establish the fact and reveal its mechanism; you can't obliterate it merely by inventing unlikely corollaries."

"I didn't invent anything, I only—"

"Pardon me. You assumed the fictions that Clyde climbed the fence into the pasture and obligingly stood in the dark and permitted himself to be fatally pierced by a clumsy pick. I admit that the first is unlikely and the second next to incredible. Those considerations occurred to me last night on the spot. As I said, by the time I reached the house I had satisfied myself as to how the crime was committed, and I am still satisfied. I don't believe Clyde Osgood climbed the fence. He was first rendered unconscious, proba-

bly by a blow on the head. He was then dragged or
carried to the fence, and pushed under it or lifted over
it, and further dragged or carried ten or fifteen yards
into the pasture, and left lying on his side. The murderer then stood behind him with the pick and swung
it powerfully in the natural and ordinary manner, only
instead of piercing and tearing the ground it pierced
and tore his victim. The wound would perfectly resemble the goring of a bull. The blood-spurt would of
course soil the pick, but not the man who wielded it.
He got the tie-rope from where it was hanging on the
fence and tossed it on the ground near the body, to
make it appear that Clyde had entered the pasture
with it; then he took the pick to the convenient hose
nozzle, washed it off, returned it where he had got it,
and went—" Wolfe shrugged "—went somewhere."

"The bull," Waddell said. "Did the bull just stand
and look on and wait for the murderer to leave, and
then push the body around so as to have bloody
horns? Even a rustic sheriff might have noticed it if
he had had no blood on him at all."

"I couldn't say. It was dark. A bull may or may not
attack in the dark. But I suggest (1) the murderer,
knowing how to handle a bull in the dark, before performing with the pick, approached the bull, snapped
the tie-rope onto the nose ring, and led him to the
fence and tied him. Later, before releasing him, he
smeared blood on his horns. Or (2), after the pick had
been used the murderer enticed the bull to the spot
and left him there, knowing that the smell of blood
would lead him to investigate. Or (3), the murderer
acted when the bull was in another part of the pasture
and made no effort to manufacture the evidence of
bloody horns, thinking that in the excitement and

with the weight of other circumstances as arranged, it wouldn't matter. It was his good luck that Mr. Goodwin happened to arrive while the bull was satisfying his curiosity . . . and his bad luck that I happened to arrive at all."

Waddell sat frowning, his mouth screwed up. After a moment he blurted, "Fingerprints on the pick handle."

Wolfe shook his head. "A handkerchief or a tuft of grass, to carry it after washing it. I doubt if the murderer was an idiot."

Waddell frowned some more. "Your idea about tying the bull to the fence and smearing blood on his horns. That would be getting pretty familiar with a bull, even in the dark. I don't suppose anyone could have done it except Monte McMillan . . . he was Monte's bull, or he had been. Maybe you're ready to explain why Monte McMillan would want to kill Clyde Osgood?"

"Good heavens, no. There are at least two other alternatives. Mr. McMillan may be capable of murder, I don't know, and he was certainly resolved to protect the bull from molestation—but don't get things confused. Remember that the murder was no part of an effort to guard the bull; Clyde was knocked unconscious not in the pasture, but somewhere else."

"That's your guess."

"It's my opinion. I am careful with my opinions, sir; they are my bread and butter and the main source of my self-esteem."

Waddell sat with his mouth screwed up. Suddenly Osgood barked at him ferociously:

"Well, what about it?"

Waddell nodded at him, and then unscrewed his

mouth to mutter, "Of course." He got up and kicked
his chair back, stuck his hands in his pockets, stood
and gazed at Wolfe a minute, and then backed up and
sat down again. "Goddam it," he said in a pained voice.
"Of course. We've got to get on it as quick and hard as
we can. Jesus, what a mess. At Tom Pratt's place.
Clyde Osgood. Your son, Fred. And you know the
kind of material I have to work with—for instance
Sam Lake—on a thing like this . . . I'll have to pull
them away from the exposition . . . I'll go out and
see Pratt myself, now . . ."

He jerked himself forward and reached for the
telephone.

Osgood said to Wolfe, bitterly, "You see the prospect."

Wolfe nodded, and sighed. "It's an extraordinarily
difficult situation, Mr. Osgood."

"I know damn well it is. I may have missed the
significance of the bull's face, but I'm not a fool. The
devil had brains and nerve and luck. I have two things
to say to you. First, I apologize again for the way I
tackled you this afternoon. I didn't know you had
really earned your reputation, so many people
haven't, but I see now you have. Second, you can see
for yourself that you'll have to do this. You'll have to
go on with it."

Wolfe shook his head. "I expect to leave for New
York Thursday morning. Day after tomorrow."

"But my God, man! This is what you do, isn't it?
Isn't this your job? What's the difference whether you
work at it in New York or here?"

"Enormous; the difference, I mean. In New York I
have my home, my office in it, my cook, my accustomed surroundings—"

"Do you mean . . ." Osgood was up, spluttering. "Do you mean to say you have the gall to plead your personal comfort, your petty convenience, to a man in the position I'm in?"

"I do." Wolfe was serene. "I'm not responsible for the position you're in. Mr. Goodwin will tell you: I have a deep aversion to leaving my home or remaining long away from it. Another thing, you might not think me so petty if you could see and hear and smell the hotel room in which I shall have to sleep tonight and tomorrow night . . . and heaven knows how many more nights if I accepted your commission."

"What's wrong with it?"

"Everything imaginable."

"Then leave it. Come to my house. It's only sixteen miles out, and you can have a car until yours is repaired, and your man here can drive it . . ."

"I don't know." Wolfe looked doubtful. "Of course, if I undertake it I shall need immediately a good deal of information from you and your daughter, and your own home would be a good place for that . . ."

I stood up with my heels together and saluted him, and he glared at me. Naturally he knew I was on to him. Machiavelli was a simple little shepherd lad by comparison. Not that I disapproved by any means, for the chances were that I would get a fairly good bed myself, but it was one more proof that under no circumstances could you ever really trust him.

Chapter 9

With Nancy still chauffering, we drove to the hotel for our luggage, and then had to leave town by way of the exposition grounds in order to give the orchids a look and another spraying. Shanks wasn't around, and Wolfe made arrangements with a skinny woman who sat on an upturned box by a table full of dahlias, to keep an eye on our pots.

Driving into Crowfield that morning, Caroline Pratt had pointed out the Osgood demesne, the main entrance of which was only a mile from Pratt's place. It was rolling farm land, a lot of it looking like pasture, with three or four wooded knolls. The stock barns and other outbuildings were in plain view, but the dwelling, which was all of half a mile from the highway, was out of sight among the trees until the private drive straightened out at the beginning of a wide expanse of lawn. It was a big old rambling white house, with an old-fashioned portico, with pillars, extending along the middle portion of the front. It looked as if it had probably once been George Washington's headquarters, provided he ever got that far north.

There was an encounter before we got into the house. As we crossed the portico, a man approached from the other end, wiping his brow with his handkerchief and looking dusty and sweaty. Mr. Bronson had on a different shirt and tie from the day before, and another suit, but was no more appropriate to his surroundings than he had been when I first saw him on Pratt's terrace. Osgood tossed a nod at him, then, seeing that he intended to speak, stopped and said, "Hullo."

Bronson came up to us. I hadn't noticed him much the day before, with my attention elsewhere, but I remarked now that he was around thirty, of good height and well-built, with a wide full mouth and a blunt nose and clever gray eyes. I didn't like the eyes, as they took us in with a quick glance. He said deferentially, "I hope you won't mind, Mr. Osgood. I've been over there."

"Over where?" Osgood demanded.

"Pratt's place. I walked across the fields. I knew I had offended you by disagreeing this morning with your ideas about the . . . accident. I wanted to look it over. I met young Pratt, but not his father, and that man McMillan—"

"What did you expect to accomplish by that?"

"Nothing, I suppose. I'm sorry if I've offended again. But I didn't . . . I was discreet. I suppose I shouldn't be here, I should have left this morning, but with this terrible . . . with Clyde dead, and I'm the only one of his New York friends here . . . it seemed . . ."

"It doesn't matter," said Osgood roughly. "Stay. I said so."

"I know you did, but frankly . . . I feel very much de trop . . . I'll leave now if you prefer it . . ."

"Excuse me." It was Wolfe's quiet murmur. "You had better stay, Mr. Bronson. Much better. We may need you."

The clever eyes flickered at him. "Oh. If Nero Wolfe says stay . . ." He lifted his shoulders and let them down. "But I don't need to stay here. I can go to a Crowfield hotel—"

"Nonsense." Osgood scowled at him. "Stay here. You were Clyde's guest, weren't you? Stay here. But if you want to walk in the fields, there's plenty of directions besides the one leading to Pratt's."

Abruptly he started off, and we followed, as Bronson again lifted his handkerchief to his sweaty brow.

A few minutes later we were seated in a large room with French windows, lined with books and furnished for comfort, and were being waited on by a lassie with a pug nose who had manners far superior to Bert's but was way beneath him in speed and spirit as a drink-slinger. Nancy had disappeared but was understood to be on call. Osgood was scowling at a highball, Wolfe was gulping beer which, judging from his expression, was too warm, and I had plain water.

Wolfe was saying testily, "My own method is the only one available to me. I either use that or none at all. I may be only clearing away rubbish, but that's my affair. The plain fact is, sir, that last night, in Mr. Goodwin's presence, you behaved in an astonishing manner to him and Mr. Pratt. You were rude, arrogant and unreasonable. I need to know whether that was due to the emotional shock you had had, or to your belief that Mr. Pratt was somehow involved in the death of your son, or was merely your normal conduct."

"I was under a strain, of course," Osgood snapped. "I suppose I'm inclined to arrogance, if you want to call it that. I wouldn't like to think I'm habitually rude, but I would be rude to Pratt on sight if the circumstances were such that I couldn't ignore him. Last night I couldn't ignore him. Call it normal conduct and forget it."

"Why do you dislike and despise Mr. Pratt?"

"Damn it, I tell you that has nothing to do with it! It's an old story. It had no bearing—"

"It wouldn't account for a reciprocal hatred from Mr. Pratt that might have led him to murder?"

"No." Osgood stirred impatiently and put down his highball. "No."

"Can you suggest any other motive Mr. Pratt might have had for murdering your son? Make it plausible."

"I can't make it plausible or implausible. Pratt's vindictive and tricky, and in his youth he had fits of violence. His father worked for my father as a stablehand. In a fit of temper he might have murdered, yes."

Wolfe shook his head. "That won't do. The murder was carefully planned and executed. The plan may have been rapid and extempore, but it was cold and thorough. Besides, your son was not discovered in an effort to molest the bull, remember that. You insisted on that point yourself before you had my demonstration of it. What could have got Mr. Pratt into a murderous temper toward your son if he didn't find him trying to molest the bull?"

"I don't know. Nothing that I know of."

"I ask the same question regarding Jimmy Pratt."

"I don't know him. I've never seen him."

"Actually never seen him?"

"Well . . . seen him perhaps. I don't know him."

"Did Clyde know him?"

"I believe they were acquainted. They met in New York."

"Do you know of any motive Jimmy Pratt might have had for killing your son?"

"No."

"I ask the same question regarding Caroline Pratt."

"The same answer. They too met in New York, but the acquaintance was slight."

"Excuse me, boss," I put in. "Do I release cats in public?"

"Certainly." Wolfe shot me a glance. "We're talking of Mr. Osgood's son, who is dead."

"Okay. Clyde and Caroline Pratt were engaged to be married, but the clutch slipped."

"Indeed," Wolfe murmured. Osgood glared at me and said, "Ridiculous. Who the devil told you that?"

I disregarded him and told Wolfe, "Guaranteed. They were engaged for quite a while, only apparently Clyde didn't want his father to know that he had been hooked by a female Pratt who was also an athlete. Then Clyde saw something else and made a dive for it, and the Osgood-Pratt axis got multiple fracture. The something else was the young lady who was outdoors with me last night, named Lily Rowan. Later . . . we're up to last spring now . . . she skidded again and Clyde fell off. Since then he has been hanging around New York trying to get back on. One guess is that he came up here because he knew she would be here, but that's not in the guarantee. I haven't had a chance—"

Osgood was boiling. "This is insufferable! Preposterous gossip! If this is your idea—"

I growled at Wolfe, "Ask him why he wants to wring Lily Rowan's neck."

"Mr. Osgood, please." Wolfe keyed it up. "I warned you that a murder investigation is of necessity intrusive and impertinent. Either bear it or abandon it. If you resent the vulgarity of Mr. Goodwin's jargon I don't blame you, but nothing can be done about it. If you resent his disclosure of facts, nothing can be done about that either except to drop the inquiry. We have to know things. What about your son's engagement to marry Miss Pratt?"

"I never heard of it. He never mentioned it. Neither did my daughter, and she would have known of it; she and Clyde were very close to each other. I don't believe it."

"You may, I think, now. My assistant is careful about facts. What about the entanglement with Miss Rowan?"

"That . . . yes." As badly as Osgood's head needed a rest, it was a struggle for him to remove the ducal coronet. "You understand this is absolutely confidential."

"I doubt it. I suspect that at least a hundred people in New York know more about it than you do. But what do you know?"

"I know that about a year ago my son became infatuated with the woman. He wanted to marry her. She's wealthy, or her father is. She's a sex maniac. She wouldn't marry him. If she had she would have ruined him, but she did that anyway, or she was doing it. She got tired of him, but her claws were in him so deep he couldn't get them out, and there was no way of persuading him to act like a man. He wouldn't come home; he stayed in New York because she was there. He wasted a lot of my money and I cut off his income entirely, but that didn't help. I don't know what he has been living on the past four months, but I suspect my daughter has been helping him, though I decreased her allowance and forbade it. I went to New York in May and went to see the Rowan woman, and humiliated myself, but it did no good. She's a damned strumpet."

"Not by definition. A strumpet takes money. However . . . I see, at this point, no incentive for Miss Rowan to murder him. Miss Pratt . . . it might be. She was jilted, and she is muscular. Mortification could simmer in a woman's breast a long time, though she doesn't look it. When did your son arrive here from New York?"

"Sunday evening. My daughter and his friend Bronson rode up with him."

"Had you expected him?"

"Yes. He phoned from New York Saturday night."

"Was Miss Rowan already at Mr. Pratt's place?"

"I don't know. I didn't know she was there until your man told me last night, when I went over there."

"Was she, Archie?"

I shook my head. "No sale. I was working on another case at lunch."

"It doesn't matter. I'm only clearing away rubbish, and I doubt if it amounts to more than that." Back at Osgood: "Why did your son come after so long an absence? What did he say?"

"He came—" Osgood stopped. Then he went on, "They came to be here for the exposition."

"Why did he come, really?"

Osgood glared and said, "Damn it."

"I know, Mr. Osgood. We don't usually hang our linen on the line till it has been washed, but you've hired me to sort it out. Why did your son come to see you? To get money?"

"How did you know that?"

"I didn't. But men so often need money; and you had stopped your son's income. Was his need general or specific?"

"Specific as to the sum. He wanted $10,000."

"Oh." Wolfe's brows went up a trifle. "What for?"

"He wouldn't tell me. He said he would be in trouble if he didn't get it." Osgood looked as if it hurt where the coronet had been. "I may as well . . . he had used up a lot of money during his affair with that woman. I found out in May that he had taken to gambling, and that was one reason I cut him off. When he asked for $10,000 I suspected it was for a gambling debt, but he denied it and said it was something more urgent. He wouldn't tell me what."

"Did you let him have it?"

"No. I absolutely refused."

"He was insistent?"

"Very. We . . . there was a scene. Not violent, but damned unpleasant. Now . . ." Osgood set his jaw, and looked at space. He muttered with his teeth clamped, "Now he's dead. Good God, if I thought that $10,000 had anything to do—"

"Please, sir. Please. Let's work. I call your attention to a coincidence which you have probably already noticed: the bet your son made yesterday afternoon with Mr. Pratt was for $10,000. That raises a question. Mr. Pratt declined to make a so-called gentleman's wager with your son unless it was underwritten by you. I understand that he telephoned you to explain the difficulty, and you guaranteed payment by your son if he lost. Is that correct?"

"Yes."

"Well." Wolfe frowned at his two empty bottles. "It seems a little inconsistent . . . first you refuse to advance $10,000 needed urgently by your son to keep him out of trouble, and then you casually agree on the telephone to underwrite a bet he makes for that precise sum."

"There was nothing casual about it."

"Did you have any particular reason to assume that your son would win the bet?"

"How the hell could I? I didn't know what he was betting on."

"You didn't know that he had wagered that Mr. Pratt would not barbecue Hickory Caesar Grindon this week?"

"No. Not then. Not until my daughter told me afterwards . . . after Clyde was dead."

"Didn't Mr. Pratt tell you on the phone?"

"I didn't give him a chance. When I learned that Clyde had been to Tom Pratt's place and made a bet with him, and that Pratt had the insolence to ask me to stand good for my son—what do you think? Was I going to ask the dog for details? I told him that any debt my son might ever owe him, for a bet or anything else, or for $10,000 or ten times that, would be instantly paid, and I hung up."

"Didn't your son tell you what the bet was about when he got home a little later?"

"No. There was another scene. Since you have . . . you might as well have all of it. When Clyde appeared I was furious, and I demanded . . . I was in a temper, and that roused his, and he started to walk out. I accused him of betraying me. I accused him of arranging a fake bet with Pratt and getting Pratt to phone me, so that I would have to pay it, and then Pratt would hand him the money. Then he did walk out. As I said, I didn't find out until afterwards what the bet was about or how it was made. I left the house and got in a car and drove over the other side of Crowfield to the place of an old friend of mine. I didn't want to eat dinner at home. Clyde's friend, this Bronson, was here, and my daughter and my wife . . . and my presence wouldn't make it a pleasant meal. It was already unpleasant enough. When I got back, after ten o'clock, there was no one around but my wife, and she was in her room crying. About half an hour later the phone call came from Pratt's—his nephew. I went. That was where I had to go to find my son dead."

Wolfe sat looking at him, and after a moment sighed. "That's too bad," he said. "I mean it's too bad that you were away from home, and weren't on speaking terms with your son. I had hoped to learn from you what time he left the house, and under what circumstances, and what he may have said of his destination and purpose. You can't tell me that."

"Yes, I can. My daughter and Bronson have told me—"

"Pardon me. If you don't mind, I'd rather hear it from them. What time is it, Archie?"

I told him, ten after five.

"Thank you. —You realize, Mr. Osgood, that we're

fishing in a big stream. This is your son's home, hundreds of people in this county know him, one or more of them may have hated or feared him enough to want him dead, and almost anyone could have got to the far end of the pasture without detection, despite the fact that my assistant had the pasture under surveillance. It was a dark night. But we'll extend our field only if we're compelled to; let's finish with those known to be present. Regarding motive, what about Mr. McMillan?"

"None that I know of. I've known Monte McMillan all my life; his place is up at the north end of the county. Even if he had caught Clyde trying some fool trick with the bull—my God, Monte wouldn't murder him . . . and you say yourself—"

"I know. Clyde wasn't caught doing that." Wolfe sighed. "That seems to cover it. Pratt, McMillan, the nephew, the niece, Miss Rowan . . . and on motive you offer no indictment. I suppose, since this place is at a distance of only a mile or so from Mr. Pratt's, which might fairly be called propinquity, we should include those who were here. What about Mr. Bronson?"

"I don't know him. He came with Clyde and was introduced as a friend."

"An old friend?"

"I don't know."

"You never saw him or heard of him before?"

"No."

"What about the people employed here? There must be quite a few. Anyone with a grudge against your son?"

"No. Absolutely not. For three years he more or less supervised things here for me, and he was competent and had their respect, and they all liked him. Except—" Osgood stopped abruptly, and was silent, suspended, with his mouth open. Then he said, "Good God, I've just remembered . . . but no, that's ridiculous . . ."

"What is?"

"Oh . . . a man who used to work here. Two years ago one of our best cows lost her calf and Clyde blamed this man and fired him. The man has done a lot of talking ever since, denying it was his fault, and making some wild threats I've been told about. The reason I think of it now . . . he's over at Pratt's place. Pratt hired him last spring. His name is Dave Smalley."

"Was he there last night?"

"I presume so. You can find out."

I put in an oar: "Sure he was. You remember Dave, don't you? How he resented your using that rock as a waiting room?"

Wolfe surveyed me. "Do you mean the idiot who waved the gun and jumped down from the fence?"

"Yep. That was Dave."

"Pfui." Wolfe almost spat. "It won't do, Mr. Osgood. You remarked, correctly, that the murderer had brains and nerve and luck. Dave is innocent."

"He's done a lot of talking."

"Thank God I didn't have to listen to it." Wolfe stirred in the big comfortable chair. "We must get on. I offer an observation or two before seeing your daughter. First, I must warn you of the practical certainty that the official theory will be that your son did enter the pasture to molest the bull, in spite of my demonstration to Mr. Waddell. They will learn that Clyde bet Mr. Pratt that he would not barbecue Hick-

ory Caesar Grindon *this week*. They will argue that all
Clyde had to do to win the bet was to force a post-
ponement of the feast for five days, and he might have
tried that. They will be fascinated by the qualification
this week. It is true that there is something highly
significant in the way the terms of the bet were
stated, but they'll miss that."

"What's significant about it? It was a damned
silly—"

"No. Permit me. I doubt if it was silly. I'll point it
out to you when I'm ready to interpret it. Second,
whatever line Mr. Waddell takes should have our re-
spectful attention. If he offends, don't in your arrogance send him to limbo, for we can use his facts.
Many of them. We shall want, for instance, to know
what the various persons at Mr. Pratt's house were
doing last night between 9 o'clock and 10:30. I don't
know, because at 9 o'clock I felt like being alone and
went up to my room to read. We shall want to know
what the doctor says about the probable time of your
son's death. The presumption is that it was not more
than, say 15 minutes, before Mr. Goodwin arrived on
the spot, but the doctor may be helpful. We shall want
to know whether my conclusions have been supported
by such details as the discovery of blood residue in
the grass by the hose nozzle, and on the pick handle,
et cetera. Third, I'd like to repeat a question which
you evaded a while ago. Why do you hate Mr. Pratt?"

"I didn't evade it. I merely said it has no bearing
on this."

"Tell me anyway. Of course I'm impertinent, but
I'll have to decide if I'm also irrelevant."

Osgood shrugged. "It's no secret. This whole end
of the state knows it. I don't hate him, I only feel

contempt for him. As I told you, his father was one of my father's stablehands. As a boy Tom was wild, and aggressive, but he had ambition, if you want to call it that. He courted a young woman in the neighborhood and persuaded her to agree to marry him. I came home from college, and she and I were mutually attracted, and I married her. Tom went to New York and never made an appearance around here. Apparently he was nursing a grievance all the time, for about eight years ago he began to make a nuisance of himself. He had made a lot of money, and he used some of it and all his ingenuity concocting schemes to pester and injure me. Then two years ago he bought that land next to mine, and built on it, and that made it worse."

"Have you tried retaliation?"

"If I ever tried retaliation it would be with a horsewhip. I ignore him."

"Not a democratic weapon, the whip. Yesterday afternoon your son accused him of projecting the barbecue as an offense to you. The idea seemed to be that it would humiliate you and make you ridiculous if a bull better than your best bull was cooked and eaten. It struck me as farfetched. Mr. Pratt maintained that the barbecue was to advertise his business."

"I don't care a damn. What's the difference?"

"None, I suppose. But the fact remains that the bull is a central character in our problem, and it would be a mistake to lose sight of him. So is Mr. Pratt, of course. You reject the possibility that his festering grievance might have impelled him to murder."

"Yes. That's fantastic. He's not insane . . . at least I don't think he is."

"Well." Wolfe sighed. "Will you send for your daughter?"

Osgood scowled. "She's with her mother. Do you insist on speaking to her? I know you're supposed to be competent, but it seems to me the people to ask questions of are at Pratt's, not here."

"It's my competence you're hiring, sir. Your daughter comes next. Mr. Waddell is at Pratt's, where he belongs, since he has authority." Wolfe wiggled a finger. "If you please."

Osgood got up and went to a table to push a button, and then came back and downed his highball, which must have been as warm as Wolfe's beer by that time, in three gulps. The pug-nosed lassie appeared and was instructed to ask Miss Osgood to join us. Osgood sat down again and said:

"I don't see what you're accomplishing, Wolfe. If you think by questioning me you've eliminated everybody at Pratt's—"

"By no means. I've eliminated no one." Wolfe sounded faintly exasperated, and I perceived that it was up to me to arrange with Pug-nose for more and colder beer. "Elimination, as such, is tommyrot. Innocence is a negative and can never be established; you can only establish guilt. The only way I can apodictically eliminate any individual from consideration as the possible murderer is to find out who did it. You can't be expected to see what I am accomplishing; if you could do that, you could do the job yourself. Let me give you a conjecture for you to try your hand on: for example, is Miss Rowan an accomplice? Did she join Mr. Goodwin last night and sit with him for an hour on the running board of my car, which he had steered into a tree, to distract him while the crime was being committed? Or if you would prefer another sort of problem . . ."

He stopped with a grimace and began preparations to arise. I got up too, and Osgood started across the room toward the door which had opened to admit his daughter, and with her an older woman in a dark blue dress with her hair piled on top of her head. Osgood made an effort to head off the latter, and protested, but she advanced toward us anyhow. He submitted enough to introduce us:

"This is Mr. Nero Wolfe, Marcia. His assistant, Mr. Goodwin. My wife. Now dear, there's no sense in this, it won't help any . . ."

While he remonstrated with her I took a polite look. The farmer's beautiful daughter who, according to one school of thought, was responsible for Tom Pratt's unlucky idea of making beefsteak out of Hickory Caesar Grindon, was still beautiful I suppose; it's hard for me to tell when they're around fifty, on account of my tendency to concentrate on details which can't be expected to last that long. Anyway, with her eyes red and swollen from crying and her skin blotchy, it wasn't fair to judge.

She told her husband, "No, Fred, really, I'll be all right. Nancy has told me what you've decided. I suppose you're right . . . you always are right . . . now you don't need to look like that . . . you're perfectly right to want to find out about it, but I don't want just to shut myself away . . . you know Clyde always said it wasn't a pie if I didn't have my finger in it . . ." her lip quivered ". . . and if it is to be discussed with Nancy I want to be here . . ."

"It's foolish, Marcia, there's no sense in it." Osgood had hold of her arm. "If you'll just—"

"Permit me." Wolfe was frowning, and made his tone crisp. "Neither of you will stay. I wish to speak with Miss Osgood alone.—Confound it, sir, I am working, and for you! However I may want to sympathize with grief, I can't afford to let it interfere with my job. The job you want done. If you want it done."

Osgood glared at him, but said to his wife, "Come, Marcia."

I followed them three steps and halted him: "Excuse me. It would be to everyone's advantage if he had more beer, say three bottles, and make it colder."

Chapter 10

Nancy, sitting in the chair Osgood had vacated, looked more adamant than the situation seemed to call for, considering that Wolfe's client was her father. You might have thought she was confronted by hostile forces. Of course her brother had just been killed and she couldn't be expected to beam with cheerful eagerness, but her stiffness as she sat looked not only tense but antagonistic, and her lips, which only 24 hours before had struck me as being warm and trembly, now formed a thin rigid colorless line.

Wolfe leaned back and regarded her with half-closed eyes. "We'll be as brief as we can with this, Miss Osgood," he said, with honey in his mouth. "I thought we might reach our objective a little sooner with your father and mother absent."

She nodded, her head tilted forward once and back again, and said nothing. Wolfe resumed:

"We must manage to accompany your brother yesterday afternoon as continuously as possible from the time he left Mr. Pratt's terrace. Were you and Mr. Bronson and he riding in one car?"

Her voice was low and firm: "Yes."

"Tell me briefly your movements after leaving the terrace."

"We walked across the lawn and back to the car and got in and came—no, Clyde got out again because Mr. McMillan called to him and wanted to speak to him. Clyde went over to him and they talked a few minutes and then Clyde came back and we drove home."

"Did you hear his conversation with Mr. McMillan?"

"No."

"Was it apparently an altercation?"

"It didn't look like it."

Wolfe nodded. "Mr. McMillan left the terrace with the announced intention of advising your brother not to do anything foolish. He did it quietly then."

"They just talked a few minutes, that was all."

"So. You returned home, and Clyde had a talk with your father."

"Did he?"

"Please, Miss Osgood." Wolfe wiggled a finger. "Discretion will only delay us. Your father has described the . . . unpleasant scene, he called it . . . he had with his son. Was that immediately after you got home?"

"Yes. Dad was waiting for us at the veranda steps."

"Infuriated by the phone call from Mr. Pratt. Were you present during the scene?"

"No. They went into the library . . . this room. I went upstairs to clean up . . . we had been at Crowfield nearly all day."

"When did you see your brother again?"

"At dinnertime."

"Who was at table?"

"Mother and I, and Mr. Bronson and Clyde. Dad had gone somewhere."

"What time was dinner over?"

"A little after eight. We eat early in the country, and we sort of rushed through it because it wasn't very gay. Mother was angry . . . Dad had told her about the bet Clyde had made with Monte Cris—with Mr. Pratt, and Clyde was glum—"

"You called Mr. Pratt Monte Cristo?"

"That was a slip of the tongue."

"Obviously. Don't be perturbed, it wasn't traitorous, your father has told me of Mr. Pratt's rancor. You called him Monte Cristo?"

"Yes, Clyde and I did, and . . ." Her lip started to quiver, and she controlled it. "We thought it was funny when we started it."

"It may have been so. Now for your movements after dinner, please."

"I went to mother's room with her and we talked a while, and then I went to my room. Later I came downstairs and sat on the veranda and listened to the katydids. I was there when Dad came home."

"And Clyde?"

"I don't know. I didn't see him after I went upstairs with mother after dinner."

She wasn't much good as a liar; she didn't know how to relax for it. Wolfe has taught me that one of the most important requirements for successful lying is relaxed vocal cords and throat muscles; otherwise you are forced to put on extra pressure to push the lie through, and the result is that you talk faster and raise the pitch and the blood shows in your face.

Nancy Osgood betrayed all of those signs. I moved my eyes for a glance at Wolfe, but he merely murmured a question:

"So you don't know when your brother left the house? Left here to go to Pratt's?"

"No." She stirred a little, and was still again, and repeated, "No."

"That's a pity. Didn't he tell you or your mother that he was going to Pratt's?"

"So far as I know, he told no one."

There was an interruption, a knock at the door. I went to it and took from Pug-nose a tray with three bottles of beer, felt one and approved of the temperature, and taxied them across to Wolfe. He, opening and pouring, asked Nancy if she would have, and she declined with thanks. He drank, put down the empty glass, and wiped his lips with his handkerchief.

"Now Miss Osgood," he said in a new tone. "I have more questions to ask of you, but this next is probably the most material of all. When did your brother tell you how and why he expected to win his bet with Mr. Pratt?"

She stared a second and said, "He didn't tell me at all. What makes you think he did?" It sounded straight to me.

"I thought it likely. Your father says that you and your brother were very close to each other."

"We were."

"But he told you nothing of that wager?"

"He didn't have to tell me he made it, I heard him. He didn't tell me how or why he expected to win it."

"What was discussed as you rode home from Pratt's yesterday?"

"I don't know. Nothing in particular."

"Remarkable. The bizarre wager which had just been made wasn't mentioned?"

"No. Mr. Bronson was . . . well, it only takes a couple of minutes to drive here from Pratt's—"

"Mr. Bronson was what?"

"Nothing. He was there, that's all."

"Is he an old friend of your brother's?"

"He's not—no. Not an old friend."

"But a friend, I presume, since you and your brother brought him here?"

"Yes." She clipped it. She was terrible.

"Is he a friend of yours too?"

"No." She raised her voice a little. "Why should you ask me about Mr. Bronson?"

"My dear child." Wolfe compressed his lips. "For heaven's sake don't start that. I am a hired instrument of vengeance . . . hired by your father. Nowadays an Erinys wears a coat and trousers and drinks beer and works for pay, but the function is unaltered and should still be performed, if at all, mercilessly. I am going to find out who killed your brother. A part of the operation is to prick all available facts. I intend to look into Mr. Bronson as well as everyone else unlucky enough to be within range. For example, take Miss Pratt. Did you approve of your brother's engagement to marry Miss Caroline Pratt?"

She stared in consternation, opened her mouth, and closed it.

Wolfe shook his head at her. "I'm not being wily, to disconcert you and corner you. I don't think I need to; you have made yourself too vulnerable. To give you an idea, here are some questions I shall expect you to answer: Why, since you regard Mr. Bronson with loathing, do you permit him to remain as a guest

in this house? I know you loathe him, because when
he happened to brush against you yesterday on Mr.
Pratt's terrace you drew away as if slime had touched
your dress. Why would you prefer to have the mystery of your brother's death unsolved and to leave the
onus to the bull? I know you would, from the relief on
your face this afternoon when your father's incivility
started me for the door. Why did you tell me that you
didn't see your brother after dinner last evening? I
know it was a lie, because I was hearing and seeing
you when you said it. You see how you have exposed
yourself?"

Nancy was standing up, and the line of her mouth
was thinner than ever. She took a step and said, "My
father . . . I'll see if he wants—"

"Nonsense," Wolfe snapped. "Please sit down.
Why do you think I had your father leave? Shall I
send for him? He intends to learn who murdered his
son, and for the moment all other considerations surrender to that, even his daughter's dignity and peace
of mind. You won't get peace of mind by concealing
things, anyway. You must give satisfactory and complete answers to those questions, and the easiest way
is here, to me, at once."

"You can't do this." She fluttered a hand. Her chin
trembled, and she steadied it. "Really you can't. You
can't do this." She was beauty in distress if I ever saw
it, and if the guy harassing her had been anybody else
I would have smacked him cold and flung her behind
my saddle.

Wolfe told her impatiently, "You see how it is. Sit
down. Confound it, do you want to turn it into a
brawl, with your father here too and both of us shouting at you? You'll have to tell these things, for we

need to know them, whether they prove useful or not. You can't bury them. For example, your dislike for Mr. Bronson. I can pick up that telephone and call a man in New York named Saul Panzer, an able and industrious man, and tell him I want to know all he can discover about Bronson and you and your brother. You see how silly it would be to force us to spend that time and money. What about Mr. Bronson? Who is he?"

"If I told you about Bronson—" She stopped to control her voice. "I can't. I promised Clyde I wouldn't."

"Clyde is dead. Come, Miss Osgood. We'll learn it anyhow, I assure you we will. You know that."

"I suppose . . . you will." She sat down abruptly, buried her face in her hands, and was rigid. Her muffled voice came: "Clyde! Clyde!"

"Come." Wolfe was sharp. "Who is Bronson?"

She uncovered her face slowly, and lifted it. "He's a crook."

"A professional? What's his specialty?"

"I don't know. I don't know him. I only met him a few days ago. I only know what Clyde—"

She stopped, and gazed at Wolfe's face as if she was hoping that something would blot it out but knew that nothing would. "All right," she said. "I thought I had enough guts, but apparently I haven't. What good will it do? What good will it do you or dad or anyone to know that Bronson killed him?"

"Do you know it?"

"Yes."

"Bronson murdered your brother?"

"Yes."

"Indeed. Did you see it done?"

"No."

"What was his motive?"

"I don't know. It couldn't have been to get the money, because Clyde didn't have it."

Wolfe leaned back and heaved a sigh. "Well," he murmured. "I guess we must have it out. What money would Mr. Bronson have wanted to get, and why?"

"Money that Clyde owed him."

"The amount being, I presume, $10,000. Don't ask me how I know that, please. And Bronson was insisting on payment?"

"Yes. That was why he came up here. It was why Clyde came, too, to try to get the money from Father. He had to pay it this week or—" She stopped, and stretched out a hand, and let it fall again. "Please," she said, pleading. "*Please.* That's what I promised Clyde I wouldn't tell."

"The promise died with him," Wolfe told her. "Believe me, Miss Osgood, if you weren't bewildered by shock and grief you wouldn't get values confused like this. Was it money that Clyde had borrowed from Mr. Bronson?"

"No. It was money that Bronson had paid him."

"What had he paid it for?"

He pulled it out of her, patiently, in pieces. The gist of the story was short and not very sweet. Clyde had shot his wad on Lily Rowan, and had followed it with various other wads, pried loose from his father, requisitioned from his sister, borrowed from friends. Then he had invited luck to contribute to the good cause, by sundry methods from crackaloo to 10-cent bridge, and learned too late that luck's clock was slow. At a time when he was in up to his nose, a Mr. Howard Bronson permitted him to inspect a fistful of real money and expressed a desire to be introduced into certain circles, including the two most exclusive bridge clubs in New York; Clyde, with his family connections, having the entree to about everything from the aquarium up. But Clyde had needed the dough not some time tomorrow, but now, and Bronson had given it to him; whereupon Clyde had mollified a few debts and slid the rest down his favorite chute, before dawn. Following a lifelong habit, he had confided in his sister, and her horror added to his own belated reflections had shown him that in his desperation he had taken an order which no Osgood could possibly fill. He had so notified Bronson, with regret and the expressed intention of repaying the ten grand at the earliest opportunity, but Bronson had revealed a nasty streak. He wanted the order filled, or the cash returned, forthwith; and a complication was that Clyde had rashly signed a receipt for the money which included specifications of what Bronson was to get for it. Bronson threatened to show the receipt to the family connections. Bad all around. When Clyde decided, as a last resort, on a trip to Crowfield for an appeal to his father, Bronson's distrust of him had got so deplorable that he insisted on going along and he couldn't be ditched; and Nancy had accompanied them for the purpose of helping out with father. But father had been obdurate, and Monday it was beginning to look as if Clyde would have to confess all in order to get the money, which would be worse than bad, when on Pratt's terrace luck reared its pretty head again and Clyde made a bet.

Wolfe got all that out of her, patiently, with various details and dates, and then observed, having finished the second bottle of beer, that while it seemed

to establish Bronson as a man of disreputable motives
it didn't seem to include one for murder.

"I know it," Nancy said. "I told you he couldn't
have done it to get the money, because Clyde didn't
have it, and anyway if he had had it he would have
given it to him."

"Still you say he did it?"

"Yes."

"Why?"

"Because I saw Bronson follow Clyde over to
Pratt's place."

"Indeed. Last night?"

"Yes."

"Tell me about it."

The bag was open now, and most of the beans
gone. She dumped the rest: "It was around 9 o'clock,
maybe a little later. When I left mother's room I came
downstairs to look for Clyde, to ask him why he had
made the bet with Pratt. I was afraid he was going to
try something wild. I found him out by the tennis
court, talking with Bronson, and they shut up when
they heard me coming. I said I wanted to ask him
something and he came away with me, but he
wouldn't tell me anything. I told him I was pretty
sure I would be able to get the money through
mother, and reminded him that he had sworn to me he
would stop acting like a fool, and said if he did something else foolish it might be the finish of him. I told
him things like that. He said that for once I was
wrong and he was right, that what he was doing
wasn't foolish, that he had turned over a new leaf and
was being sensible and practical and I would agree
with him when I found out about it, but he wouldn't

tell me then. I insisted, but he was always stubborner than I was."

"You got no inkling of what he had in mind."

Nancy shook her head. "Not the slightest. He said something about not interfering with the barbecue."

"Give me his exact words, if you can."

"Well, he said, 'I'm not going to harm anyone, not even Monte Cristo, except to win his money. I'll even let him have his damn pot roast, and he won't know the difference until after it's over, if I can fix it that way.' That's about it."

"Anything else about the barbecue or the bull or anyone at Mr. Pratt's place?"

"No, nothing."

"You left him outdoors?"

"I did then. I came back to the house and ran up to my room and changed to a dark-colored sweater and skirt. Then I came down and left by the west wing because the veranda lights were on in front and I didn't want to be seen. I didn't know whether Clyde intended to go anywhere or do anything, but I was going to find out. I couldn't find him. Beyond the range of the veranda lights it was pitch-dark, but I made a tour and looked as well as I could, and listened, and there wasn't a sign of him. The cars were in the garage, and anyway if he had taken a car or one of the farm trucks I would have heard it. If he was up to anything it could only be at Pratt's, so I decided to try that. I went past the kennels and the grove and through a gate into the meadow, which was the shortest cut, and across another field to the end of the row of pines, the windbreak—"

"All this in the dark?" Wolfe demanded.

"Of course. I know every foot of it, this is where I

was born. I can find my way in the dark all right. I
was about halfway along the windbreak when I saw a
glimmer of a flashlight ahead, and I got careless and
started to trot, because I wanted to get closer to find
out if it was Clyde, and I stepped into a hole and
tumbled and made a lot of noise. The flashlight was
turned towards me, and Clyde's voice called, and I
saw it was no use and answered him. He came back to
me, and Bronson was with him, carrying a club, a
length of sapling. Clyde was furious. I demanded to
know what he was going to do, and that made him
more furious. He said . . . oh, it doesn't matter what
he said. He made me promise to go back home and go
to bed—"

"Again without divulging his campaign."

"Yes. He wouldn't tell me. I came back home as I
had promised I would. If only I hadn't! If only—"

"I doubt if it would have mattered. You have
enough distress, Miss Osgood, without trying to borrow. But you haven't told me yet why you think Mr.
Bronson murdered your brother."

"Why . . . he was there. He went to Pratt's with
him. He's the kind of man who would do anything
vile—"

"Nonsense. You had no sleep last night. Your mind
isn't working even on the lowest level. Do you know
when Bronson got back here?"

"No. I was on the veranda until Dad came—"

"Then there's a job for you. You'll be better doing
something. Find out from the servants if anyone saw
him return, and let me know. It may save some time."
Wolfe pushed his lips out, and in again. "I should think
Mr. Bronson would be a little apprehensive about

your disclosing his presence at Pratt's last night. Have you any idea why he isn't?"

"Yes I have. He . . . he spoke to me this morning. He said he had left Clyde at the end of the windbreak, where the fence is that bounds our property, and come back here and sat out by the tennis court and smoked. He said he thought my father was mistaken, that the bull had killed Clyde, and that everyone else would think so. He showed me the receipt Clyde had signed and given him, and said he supposed I wouldn't want Clyde's memory blackened by such a thing coming out, and that he was willing to give me a chance to repay him the money before going to my father about it, provided I would save him the annoyance of being questioned about last night by forgetting that I had seen him with Clyde."

"And even when further developments gave you the notion that he was the murderer, you decided to withhold all this to protect your brother's memory."

"Yes. And I wish I had stuck to it." She leaned forward at Wolfe, and a flush of determination showed faintly on her cheeks. "You got it out of me," she said. "But what Clyde wanted most was that Dad shouldn't know about it. Does Dad have to know? Why does he? What good will it do?"

Wolfe grimaced. "Can you pay Bronson the $10,000?"

"Not now. But I've been trying to think of a way ever since Bronson spoke to me this morning . . . didn't Clyde win his bet with Pratt? Surely he won't have that barbecue now, will he? Won't he owe the money?"

"My dear child." Wolfe opened his eyes at her. "What a remarkable calculation. Amazing. It deserves to bear fruit, and we must see what can be done. I underestimated you, for which I apologize. Also I think you deserve to be humored. If it is feasible, and it should be, your promise to your brother shall be kept. I have undertaken a specific commission from your father, to expose the murderer of his son, and I should think that can be managed without disclosing his contract with Bronson. That's a superb idea, to collect from Pratt to pay Bronson. I like it. By winning his last wager your brother vindicated, as far as he could, all his previous sacrifices in the shabby temple of luck. Magnificent and neat . . . and fine of you, very fine, to perceive the necessity of completing the gesture for him . . . I assure you I'll do all I can—"

He broke off and glanced at me because a knock sounded at the door. I lifted from my chair and started across, but it opened before I got there and two men entered. I halted, slightly popeyed, when I saw it was Tom Pratt himself and McMillan. Behind them, catching up with them, hustled a middle-aged woman in a black dress, looking indignant, calling to them something about Mr. Osgood not being in there, they should wait for him in the hall. . . .

Then affairs began to get simultaneous and confused. I caught a glimpse of Mr. Howard Bronson standing at one of the French windows, looking in, and saw that Wolfe had spotted him too. At the same time a purposeful tread sounded from the hall, and then Mr. Frederick Osgood was among us, wearing a scowl that beat all his previous records. He directed it at Pratt, ignoring inessentials. He stood solid and enraged three feet in front of him, glaring at him, and spoke like an irate duke:

"Out!"

McMillan started to say something, but Osgood exploded at him: "Damn you, Monte, did you bring this man here? Get him away at once! I don't want his foot on my place—"

"Now wait a second, Fred." McMillan sounded as if he wasn't brooking anything much either. "Just a second and give us a chance. I didn't bring him; no, but we came. There's hell to pay around here, and Pratt doesn't like it any better than you do, and neither do I. Waddell, and Sam Lake with a bunch of deputies, and a herd of state police, are tearing things apart over there, and if there's anything to be found we hope they find it. At least I do; Pratt can do his own talking. But in my opinion there's going to have to be some talking. Not only on account of Clyde, but on account of what happened an hour ago."

McMillan paused, returning Osgood's gaze, and then said heavily, "Caesar's dead. My bull Caesar."

Pratt growled, "My bull."

"Okay, Pratt, your bull." McMillan didn't look at him. "But he's dead. I bred him and he was mine. Now he's lying there on the ground dead."

Chapter 11

Osgood's scowl had got adulterated by a touch of bewilderment. But he exploded again: "What the devil do I care about your bull?" He transferred to Pratt: "You get out of here. Get!"

He was turned, and so were the others, by Wolfe's voice booming across the room. "Mr. Osgood! Please!"

Wolfe had left the comfortable chair and was approaching. I saw by the look on his face, knowing it as I did, that something had jolted and irritated him almost to the limit, and wondered what it could be. He joined the circle. "How do you do, gentlemen. Mr. Pratt, it is a poor return for your hospitality if I've offended you by renting my services to Mr. Osgood, and I hope you don't feel that way about it. Mr. Osgood, this is your house, but however you may resent Mr. Pratt's entering it, surely you can bottle your hostility for the present crisis. I assure you it's highly desirable. He seems to have brought vital news, with Mr. McMillan—"

Osgood, glaring at Pratt, rumbled, "You dirty abominable mud lark!"

Pratt, returning the glare, growled, "You goddam stuffed shirt!"

Fair enough, I thought, for a duke and a millionaire. Wolfe said, "Pfui. What if you are both right? —Mr. McMillan, please. What's this about the bull?"

"He's dead."

"What killed him?"

"Anthrax."

"Indeed. That's a disease, isn't it?"

"No. It's sudden and terrible death. Technically it's a disease, of course, but it's so swift and deadly that it's more like a snake or a stroke of lightning." The stockman snapped his fingers. "Like that."

Wolfe nodded. "I knew of it, vaguely, in my boyhood in Europe. But wasn't Caesar healthy this morning? When did you observe symptoms?"

"With anthrax you don't observe symptoms. Not often. You go to the pasture in the morning and find dead cattle. That's what happened at my place a month ago. It's what happened with Caesar at 5 o'clock this afternoon. One of Sam Lake's deputies went down to the far end of the pasture, where I had him tied behind a clump of birch, and found him keeled over dead. I had gone to Crowfield to see Lew Bennett. They phoned me and I came back out, and Pratt and I decided to come over here."

Osgood's scowl had got adulterated some more. I didn't know then that the sound of the word "anthrax," with the news that it had struck within a mile of his own herd, was enough to adulterate any man's scowl, no matter what had happened to him. Wolfe turned and said brusquely:

"Mr. Pratt. I'd like to buy the bull's carcass. What will you take for it?"

I stared at him, wondering if whatever had jolted him had thrown him off balance. Pratt stared too.

Osgood blurted, "You can't buy an anthrax carcass. The state takes it."

Pratt demanded, "What in the name of God do you want it for?"

McMillan said sourly, "They're already there. A member of the State Board was at Crowfield, and he got there as soon as I did, with a dozen men. Why, what did you expect to do with it?"

Wolfe sighed. "I suppose Mr. Waddell has told you of my demonstration of the fact that Clyde Osgood wasn't killed by the bull. The absence of blood on his face. I wanted the hide. Juries like visual evidence. What is the member of the State Board doing with his men? Carting it away?"

"No. You don't cart it away. You don't want the hide either. You don't touch it, because it's dangerous. You don't bury it, because the spores live in the soil for years. You don't even go close to it. What the state men are doing is collecting wood to pile it around the carcass for a fire." McMillan slowly shook his head. "He'll burn all night, Caesar will."

"How did he get it? I understand you delivered him to Mr. Pratt last Friday. Did he bring it with him from your place?"

"He couldn't have. It doesn't wait that long to kill. The question of how he got it . . . that's one thing we came over here to discuss." McMillan faced Osgood. He hesitated a second and said, "Look here, Fred, say we sit down. I'm about played out. We want to ask you something."

Osgood said curtly, "Come to the veranda."

I controlled a grin. By gum, he wasn't going to

have a mud lark sitting within his walls. They all moved, Wolfe followed, and I brought up the rear, after a glance to see that Nancy was just getting up from her chair and Bronson was no longer visible through the French window. I requested her not to forget to ask the servants what Wolfe had told her, and she nodded.

When I got to the veranda they were seated in a group in the wicker chairs and McMillan was telling Osgood, "We all want it cleared up and that's why Pratt and I came over here. Waddell will be along pretty soon. Someone had an idea, it doesn't matter who, after Caesar was found dead, and we thought it was only fair to tell you about it before it is followed up. If you want to know why I came to tell you . . . I came because everybody else was afraid to. It's Waddell's job, or Sam Lake's, not mine, and it will be up to them to investigate it if they decide to, but they asked me to come and discuss it with you first. Pratt offered to come, but we knew how far that would get and it might even lead to some more violence of which we've had plenty, so I came, and he came along with what I would call good intentions . . . he can tell you—"

Pratt began, "The fact is, Fred—"

"My name's Osgood, damn you!"

"All right. Take your name and stick it up your chimney and go to hell."

Osgood ignored him and demanded, "What do you want to discuss, Monte?"

"About Clyde," McMillan said. "You're going to be sore naturally, but it won't help any to fly off the handle. The fact is that Clyde was in that pasture. What for? Waddell and Sam Lake, and Captain Barrow of the state police, admit that Nero Wolfe's reconstruction of it is possible, but it's hard to believe, and one reason it's hard is that if somebody did all that, who was it? That's chiefly what has them stumped."

"Not unique," murmured Wolfe.

"Do you claim the bull killed him?" Osgood demanded.

"I don't claim anything." McMillan lifted his sagging shoulders. "Don't get me wrong, Fred. I told you I came to see you because the others, except Pratt, were afraid to. I don't claim anything. What they say is this, that the main difficulty with supposing that Clyde climbed into the pasture himself was to try to figure what for. I said myself this morning that it was dumb as hell for anybody to imagine that he went in there to get the bull, because that would have been plain crazy and Clyde wasn't a lunatic. What could he have intended to do with him? You can't hide a bull in a barrel. But when Caesar was found dead of anthrax . . . it was Captain Barrow who suggested it first as a possibility . . . that might account for Clyde entering the pasture. As you know, anthrax can be communicated subcutaneously, or by contact, or by ingestion. If Caesar was fed something last night, something that had been activated . . . well . . ."

Involuntarily I hunched forward and drew my feet under me, ready to move. Frederick Osgood was stiff, and his eyes glassy, with cold rage. His chronic scowl had been merely funny, but he didn't look funny now. He said in a composed and icy tone:

"Look out, Monte. By God, look out. If you're suggesting that my son deliberately poisoned that bull . . ."

McMillan said gruffly, "I'm not suggesting anything. I've told you I came here as a messenger. The fact is, I wanted to come, because I thought you ought to be warned by a friend. Waddell's attitude, and Captain Barrow's, is that it was you who insisted on an investigation, and if there is any part of it you don't like you've got yourself to thank for it. Anyhow, they'll be here any minute now, with the idea of finding out where Clyde had been the past few days and whether he had access, or could have had access, to any source of anthrax."

"Anybody who comes here—" Osgood had to stop to control his voice "—with that idea can go away again. So can you. It . . . it's infamous." He began to tremble. "By God—"

"Mr. Osgood!" It was Wolfe, using his sharpest tone. "Didn't I warn you? I said annoyance, intrusion, plague. Mr. McMillan is perfectly correct, you have yourself to thank for it."

"But I don't have to tolerate—"

"Oh yes you do. Anything from inanity to malevolence, though I doubt if we're dealing with the latter in this instance. I don't know Captain Barrow, but I can see Mr. Waddell, like a befuddled trout, leaping for such a fly as this in all innocence. It is amazing with what frivolity a mind like his can disregard a basic fact—in this case the fact that Clyde was not killed by the bull. I entreat you to remember what I said about our needing Mr. Waddell. It is really fortunate he's coming here, for now we can get information that we need without delay. If first you must submit to an inquiry which you regard as monstrous, you will do so because it is necessary. They represent authority . . . and here they are, I suppose . . ."

There was a sound of wheels crunching gravel, and a car swung into view on the drive and rolled to a stop at the foot of the veranda steps. First out was a state cossack in uniform, a captain, looking grim and unflinching, and following him appeared the district attorney, trying to look the same. They came up the steps and headed for the group.

I missed that battle. Wolfe got up from his chair and started off, and, seeing that he had his handkerchief in his hand, I arose and followed him. With a nod to Waddell as we passed he went on, entered the house, stopped in the main hall, turned to me and told me to wait there for him, and disappeared in the direction of the library. I stood and wondered what was causing all his violent commotion.

In a few minutes he came back looking disgruntled. He frowned at me and muttered, "Entirely too fast for us, Archie. We are being made to look silly. We may even have been outwitted. I got Mr. Bennett on the telephone, but drew a blank. Did you bring a camera along?"

"No."

"After this always have one. Take a car and get over there. Someone there must have a camera—the niece or nephew or Miss Rowan. Borrow it and take pictures of the carcass from all angles . . . a dozen or more, as many as you can get. Hurry, before they get that fire started."

I made myself scarce. It sounded fairly loco. As I trotted out to where Osgood's sedan was still parked, and got in and got it going, my mind was toying with theories that would account for Wolfe's sudden passion for photography, but I couldn't concoct one that wasn't full of holes. For instance, if all he wanted was to have it on record that the bull's face was comparatively clean, why pictures from all angles? I devised others, wilder and more elaborate, during the four minutes it took to drive to the highway and along it for a mile to Pratt's place, but none was any good. At the entrance to the drive a state cop stopped me and I told him I was sent by Waddell.

I parked in the space in front of the garage, alongside the yellow Wethersill standing there, and jumped out and headed for the house. But I was only halfway there when I heard a call:

"Hey! Escamillo!"

I turned and saw Lily Rowan horizontal, lifted onto an elbow, on a canvas couch under a maple tree. I trotted over to her, telling her on the way:

"Hullo, plaything. I want to borrow a camera."

"My lord," she demanded, "am I such a pretty sight that you just have to—"

"No. This is serious and urgent. Have you got a camera?"

"Oh, I see. You came from the Osgoods. Oh, I knew you were there. It's that yellow-eyed Nancy—"

"Cut it. I tell you I'm serious. I want to take a picture of the bull before they get their—"

"What bull?"

"*The* bull."

"Good heavens. What a funny job you have. No one will ever take another picture of *that* bull. They've started the fire."

"Goddam it! Where?"

"Down at the other end . . ."

I was off on the lope, which may have been dumb, but I was in the throes of emotion. I heard her clamoring, "Wait! Escamillo! I'm coming along!" but I kept going. Leaving the lawn, as I passed the partly dug pit for the barbecue, I could smell the smoke, and soon I could see it, above the clump of birches towards the far end of the pasture. I slowed to a trot and cussed out loud as I went.

There was quite a group there, 15 or 20 besides the ones tending the fire. I joined them unnoticed. A length of the fence had been torn down and we stood back of the gap. Apparently Hickory Caesar Grindon had had a ring built around him of good dry wood, in ample quantity, for there was so much blaze that you could only catch an occasional glimpse of what was left of him between the tongues of flame. It was hot as the devil, even at the distance we were standing. Four or five men in shirt sleeves, with sweat pouring from them, were throwing on more wood from nearby piles. The group of spectators stood, some silent, some talking. I heard a voice beside me:

"I thought maybe you might get around."

I turned for a look. "Oh, hello, Dave. What made you think I'd be here?"

"Nothin' particular, only you seem like a feller that likes to be around where things is goin' on." He pinched at his nose. "I'll be derned if it don't smell like a barbecue. Same smell exactly. You might close your eyes and think he was bein' et."

"Well, he's not. He won't be."

"He sure won't." Silence, while we watched the flames. In a little he resumed, "You know, it gets you thinkin', a sight like that, derned if it don't. A champion bull like that Caesar bein' burnt up with scorn. It's ignominious. Ain't it?"

"Absolutely."

"Yes it is." He pinched his nose again. "Do you read pohtry?"

"No. Neither do you."

"The hell I don't. A book my daughter give me one Christmas I've read twenty times, parts of it more. In one place it says 'I sometimes think that never grows so red the rose as where some buried Caesar bled.' Of course this Caesar's bein' burnt instead of buried, but there's a connection if you can see it."

I made a fitting reply and shoved off. There was no percentage in standing there getting my face roasted and I wasn't in a mood to listen to Dave recite poetry.

Up a ways, near the gate through which we had carried the canvas with its burden the night before, Lily Rowan sat on the grass holding her nose. I had a notion to stop and tell her with a sneer that it was only a pose to show how sensitive and feminine she was, since Dave's olfactory judgment had been correct, but I didn't even feel like sneering. I had been sent there on the hop with my first chance to get a lick in, and had arrived too late, and I knew that Nero Wolfe wouldn't be demanding a snapshot of a bull just to put it in his album.

Lily held her hands out. "Help me up."

I grabbed hold, gave a healthy jerk, and she popped up and landed flat against me; and I enclosed her with both arms and planted a thorough one, of medium duration, on her mouth, and let her go.

"Well," she said, with her eyes shining. "You cad."

"Don't count on that as a precedent," I warned her. "I'm overwrought. I may never feel like that again. I'm sore as the devil and had to relieve the tension somehow. May I use your telephone? Mr. Pratt's telephone."

"Go climb a tree," she said, and got her arm through mine, and we went to the house that way, though it is a form of intimacy I don't care for, since I have a tendency to fight shy of bonds. Nor did I respond to the melting quality that seemed to be creeping into her tone, but kept strictly to persiflage.

Caroline was on the terrace, reading, looking even more under the weather than she had that morning, and I paused for a greeting. I didn't see Jimmy anywhere. Lily went with me to the phone in an alcove of the living room, and sat and looked at me with a corner of her mouth turned up, as she had the day before. I got the number of Osgood's place, and was answered by a maid, and asked for Wolfe.

His familiar grunt came: "Hello, Archie."

"Hello. Hell all haywire. They already had the fire started and it's like an inferno. What can I do?"

"Confound it. Nothing. Return."

"Nothing at all I can do here?"

"No. Come and help me admire stupidity."

I hung up and turned to Lily: "Listen, bauble. What good would it do if you told anyone that I came here to take a picture of the bull?"

"None whatever." She smiled and ran the tips of her fingers down my arm. "Trust me, Escamillo."

Chapter 12

An hour later, after eight o'clock, Wolfe and I sat in the room that had been assigned to him upstairs, eating off of trays, which he hated to do except at breakfast. But he wasn't complaining. He never talked business at meals, and was glad to escape from his client. Osgood had explained that his wife wouldn't appear, and his daughter would remain with her, and that perhaps it would be as well to forego service in the dining room altogether, and Wolfe had politely assented. His room was commodious and comfortable. It was a little chintzy, but one of its chairs was adequate for his bulk, and the bed would have held two of him. It might have been supposed that the kitchen would be sharing in the general household derangement, but the covered dishes of broiled lamb chops with stuffed tomatoes were hot and tasty, the salad was way below Fritz's standard but edible, and the squash pie was towards the top.

Osgood's collision with Waddell and Captain Barrow had been brief, for it had ended by the time I got back. The captain was collecting fingerprints from everyone who had been at Pratt's place the night before,

without disclosing how dire his intent might be, and
since Wolfe had already obliged I figured I might as
well. After he had got my ten specimens collected and
marked and put away in his little case, he had announced that he was ready for a call on the foreman of
the stock barns, and at Wolfe's suggestion Osgood and
McMillan had accompanied him, and Pratt had departed for home, which left Wolfe and me alone with
District Attorney Waddell.

Waddell was glad to cooperate, he said, with Fred
Osgood's representative. More than willing. He had
pursued, and intended to pursue, the investigation
without fear or favor. No one had a supported alibi
except Lily Rowan and me. They had left the dinner
table before 9 o'clock. Wolfe had gone upstairs to
read. Pratt had gone to his desk in the room next to
the living room to look over some business papers.
McMillan had been shown to a room upstairs by Bert,
and had lain down with his shoes off for a nap until 1
o'clock, at which time he was to relieve me on guard
duty. He had slept lightly and the sound of the shots
had awakened him. Caroline had sat on the terrace for
a while and had then gone to the living room and
looked at magazines. Jimmy had been on the terrace
with his sister, and when she left he had remained
there, and sat and smoked. He had heard our voices,
Lily's and mine, as we had followed the pasture fence
on our tour, especially as we encountered the briar
patch, but remembered no other sounds above the
noise of the crickets and katydids. Bert had helped
with the dinner dishes until 10 o'clock and had then
sat in the kitchen and listened to the radio, with his
ear glued to it because it had to be kept pianissimo.
Dave Smalley—Waddell knew all about his having

been fired by Clyde Osgood—Dave, on parting from
me at a quarter to 9, had gone to his room in a wing of
the garage building, shaved himself, and retired.
Wolfe demanded, "Shaved?" in incredulity, and got
the explanation Dave had given, that he always
shaved at bedtime because he was too hungry to do it
before breakfast, and after breakfast there was no
time.

So far as that went, Waddell conceded, anyone
could have done it. When you went on and asked why
anyone would have done it, that was different. There
was no one there with anything like a decent known
motive to murder Clyde Osgood unless you wanted to
make an exception of Dave Smalley, but Dave was
harmless and always had been. Say someone had
caught Clyde sneaking in there after the bull. If it had
been Pratt, he would have simply ordered him off. If
it had been Jimmy, he would have socked him. If it
had been McMillan, he would have picked him up and
thrown him over the fence. If it had been Dave, he
would have yelled for help. If it had been Goodwin,
who was guarding the bull, of course he didn't
know. . . .

"I've explained," said Wolfe patiently, "that the
murder was planned. Did you examine the bull?"

"I looked at him, and so did Sam Lake and the
police. There was one splotch on his face and a little
caked on his horns, but not much, he had rubbed most
of that off. A bull likes to keep his horns clean."

"What about the grass around the hose and the
pick handle?"

"We sent the pick to Albany for laboratory inspection. There were a few, kind of clots, we found in the

grass, and we sent them too. We won't know until tomorrow."

"They'll report human blood, and then what? Will you still waste time blathering about Clyde approaching the bull with a meal of anthrax, and the bull, after consuming it, becoming resentful and goring him?"

"If they report human blood that will add weight to your theory, of course. I said I'd cooperate, Wolfe, I didn't agree to lap up your sarcasm."

"Pfui." Wolfe shrugged. "Don't think I don't understand your position, sir. You are fairly sure there has been a murder, but you want to leave a path open to a public pretense that there was none, in case you fail to solve it. You have made no progress whatever toward a solution and see no prospect of any, and you would abandon the attempt now and announce it as accidental death as a result of malicious trespass, but for me. You know I am employed by Mr. Osgood, who may be obstructed but not ignored, and you further know that I have the knack of arranging, when I do make a fool of myself, that no one shall know it but me."

"You make . . ." Waddell sputtered with anger. "You accuse me of obstructing justice? I'm the law officer of this county—"

"Bah! Swallow it, sir! You know perfectly well Clyde Osgood was murdered, and you descend to that gibberish about him poisoning that bull!" Wolfe halted abruptly, and sighed. "But there, I beg your pardon. I have forfeited the right to reproach even gibberish. I had this case like that, complete—" he showed a clenched fist "—and I let it go." The fist popped open.

"You don't mean you know the mur—"

"I mean I was lazy and conceited. You may quote

that. Forget my dispraise, it was beside the point; you do your best. So do I. That's the devil of it: my best wasn't good enough this afternoon. But it will be. Drop all notion of filing it as an accident, Mr. Waddell; you may as well close that path, for you won't be allowed to return by it . . ."

Soon after that McMillan and Captain Barrow had returned, and they had all left, after Wolfe had arranged for McMillan to pay us a visit at 9 o'clock that evening.

During dinner Wolfe wasn't talkative, and I made no special effort at conversation because he didn't deserve it. If he wanted to be charitable enough to concede Waddell a right to live, I wouldn't have objected to that, but he might have kept within bounds. Decorum is decorum. If he wanted to admit he had made a boob of himself and prattle about forfeiting rights, that was okay, but the person to admit it too wasn't a half-witted crime buzzard from the upstate sticks, but me. That's what a confidential assistant is for. The only thing that restrained me from letting my indignation burst into speech was the fact that I didn't know what the hell he was talking about.

McMillan was punctual. It was 9 on the dot, and we were sipping coffee, when a maid came to say he was below. I went down and told him that Wolfe calculated there might be more privacy if he didn't object to coming upstairs, and he said certainly not. On the upper landing we ran into Nancy and he stopped for a couple of words with her, having, as he had observed the day before, known the Osgood youngsters since they were babies.

Wolfe greeted him. He sat down and declined cof-

fee. Wolfe looked at him and sighed. I sipped coffee
and watched them over the rim of the cup.

Wolfe said, "You look tired."

The stockman nodded. "I'm about all in. I guess
I'm getting old. Scores of times I've stayed up all
night with a cow dropping a calf . . . but of course
this wasn't exactly the same as a cow dropping a calf."

"No. Its antithesis. Death instead of birth. It was
obliging of you to come over here; I dislike expedi-
tions at night. In my capacity as an investigator for
your friend Mr. Osgood, may I ask you some questions?"

"That's what I came for."

"Good. Then first, you left Mr. Pratt's terrace yesterday afternoon with the announced intention of telling Clyde not to do anything foolish. Miss Osgood has
told me that you called Clyde from the car and conversed with him a few minutes. What was said?"

"Just that. I knew Clyde had a streak of reckless-
ness in him—not bad, he wasn't a bad boy, just a little
reckless sometimes—and after what he had said to
Pratt I thought he might need a little quieting down. I
sort of made a joke of it and told him I hoped he
wasn't going to try to pull any Halloween stunt. He
said he was going to win his bet with Pratt. I told him
there was no way he could do it and the sensible thing
was to let me go and arrange with Pratt to call the bet
off. He refused, and I asked him how he expected to
win it, and of course he wouldn't tell me. That was all
there was to it. I couldn't get anything out of him, and
he went and got in his car."

"Without giving you the slightest hint of his intentions."

"Right."

Wolfe grimaced. "I hoped you would be able to tell me a little more than that."

"I can't tell you more than what happened."

"Of course not. But I had that much, which is nothing, from Mr. Waddell, as you told it to him. He is the district attorney. I represent your friend Mr. Osgood. I had rather counted on your willingness to disclose things to me which you might choose to withhold from him."

McMillan frowned. "Maybe you'd better say that again. It sounds to me as if you meant I'm lying about it."

"I do. —Now please!" Wolfe showed a palm. "Don't let's be childish about the depravity of lying. Victor Hugo wrote a whole book to prove that a lie can be sublime. I strongly suspect you're lying, and I'd like to explain why. Briefly, because Clyde Osgood wasn't an imbecile. I suppose you have heard from Mr. Waddell of my theory that Clyde didn't climb into the pasture, but was put there. I still incline to that, but whether he voluntarily entered the pasture or not, he certainly went voluntarily from his home to Pratt's place. What for?"

He paused to empty his coffee cup. McMillan, still frowning, sat and looked at him.

Wolfe resumed, "I risk the assumption that he wasn't merely out for a stroll. He had a purpose, to do something or see somebody. I counted Dave out. Miss Rowan was with Mr. Goodwin. Mr. Waddell tells me that the others, including you, profess complete ignorance of Clyde's presence on the premises. I find it next to impossible to believe that; the reason being, as I said, that Clyde was not an imbecile; for if he didn't go there to see someone I must assume that his object was some sort of design, singlehanded, against the bull, and that's preposterous. What design? Remove the bull from the pasture, lead him away and keep him hid somewhere until the week was up? Feed him anthrax to kill him and render him inedible? Glue wings on him and ride him, a bovine Pegasus, to the moon? The last surmise is no more unlikely than the first two."

"You're not arguing with me," McMillan said drily. "If I set out to try to prove anything I wouldn't know where to start. But about my lying—"

"I'm coming to it." Wolfe pushed at his tray, with a glance at me, and I got up and moved it out of his way. He went on, "Frankly, I am not now dealing with the murder. I haven't got that far. I must first find a reasonable hypothesis to account for Clyde's going there . . . or rather, let me go back still further and put it this way: I must find a reasonable hypothesis for his evident expectation of winning that bet. Didn't he tell you he expected to win the bet?"

"Yes."

"And he wouldn't tell you how?"

"No."

"Well." Wolfe compressed his lips. "That's what I can't believe. I can't believe that, because he could expect to win the bet only with your assistance."

McMillan stared, with his heavy brows down. "Now," he said finally, "I don't think you want to start talking like that. Not to me. I don't believe so."

"Oh yes I do," Wolfe assured him. "It's my one form of prowess. I do talk. But I mean no offense, I'm speaking only of Clyde's expectations. I must account for his expecting to win that bet before I can approach the murder at all. I have considered, thoroughly, all the possible schemes, as well as the impossible, he might have had in mind, and there is one which appears neat, not too atrocious, and practicable though perhaps difficult. I have said he couldn't have expected simply to remove the bull from the pasture, because he couldn't have hid him from the resulting search. But why couldn't he remove Caesar and put another bull in his place?"

The stockman snorted. "A good grade Holstein maybe."

"No. Humor me, sir. Take my question as serious and answer it. Why couldn't he?"

"Because he couldn't."

"But why not? There were, I don't know how many, Guernsey bulls at the exposition, only seventeen miles away, and cattle trucks there to haul them in. There were some much closer, here at his father's place, within leading distance. Might not one of them, though vastly inferior to the champion Caesar in the finer qualities which I don't know about, resemble him sufficiently in size and coloring to pass as a substitute? A substitute for only one day, since the butcher was to come on Wednesday? Who would have known the difference?"

McMillan snorted again. "I would."

"Granted. You could have mistaken no other bull for your Caesar. But everyone else might easily have been fooled. At the very least there was an excellent sporting chance of it. It is obvious at what point such a scheme might have entered Clyde's mind. Yesterday afternoon he was sitting on the pasture fence, looking at Hickory Caesar Grindon through his binoculars. It occurred to him that there was a bull of similar general appearance, size and markings, either in his father's herd or among the collection at the exposition, which he had just come from; and that accidental reflection blossomed into an idea. Chased away from the pasture, he went to the house and made the wager with Mr. Pratt. Followed from the terrace to his car by you, he called you aside and made a proposal."

Wolfe sighed. "At least he might have. Let's say his proposal was that he should, with your consent, remove Caesar and put another bull in his place. He would take Caesar to the Osgood barns. You would, during Tuesday, help to guard the substitute so that no one who would be at all likely to notice the deception would be permitted to approach too closely. With the substitute once butchered, on Wednesday, the danger would of course be over. On Thursday Mr. Pratt and his guests, with trumpets of publicity, would eat the barbecued bull. On Sunday, with the week expired, Clyde would present Mr. Pratt with irrefutable evidence that it was not Caesar who had been sacrificed and that he had therefore won the bet. Mr. Pratt would of course explode with rage, but in the end he would have to compose himself and admit his helplessness and pay the $10,000, for if the facts were made public the roar of laughter would obliterate him. Customers in a pratteria would say, 'Do you suppose this is really beef? It may be woodchuck.' Mr. Pratt would have to pay and keep his mouth shut. He couldn't even take Caesar back, for what would he do with him? Clyde Osgood would get the $10,000, and doubtless a part of his proposal would be that you would get Caesar. I don't know how that would work out, since officially Caesar would be dead, but there might be a way around that difficulty, and as a minimum benefit you could breed his exceptional qualities into your herd."

Wolfe intertwined his fingers at his abdominal peak. "That, of course, is merely the outline of the proposal. Clyde had probably developed it in detail, including the time and manner of shuffling the bulls. The most auspicious time for that would have been after 1 o'clock, when you would be the one on guard, but you might have refused to involve yourself to that extent; and therefore one possibility is that the shuffling was set for earlier and had actually taken place. Caesar may be alive at this moment. The bull who died of anthrax may have been only a substitute. I offer that only as a conjecture; obviously it is tenable only on the supposition that you agreed to Clyde's proposal and entered into his scheme . . . and you know more about that than I do. But leaving that entirely aside, what do you think of the scheme itself? Do you detect any flaws?"

McMillan was eying him with a grim smile. He said calmly, "You're slick, aren't you?"

"Moderately." Wolfe's eyes closed and came half open again. "But don't make the mistake of supposing that I'm trying to waylay you. I may be passably slick, but my favorite weapon is candor. Here is my position, sir. I can account satisfactorily for Clyde's expectation of winning that bet only by assuming that he concocted such plan as I have outlined. If he did so, you either acceded or refused. In either case, I would like to know what he said. Don't think I am insulting you by reckoning that you might have withheld facts from Mr. Waddell. I would myself be reluctant to trust him with a fact of any delicacy. I appeal to you, did Clyde make you a proposal, and did you accept or decline?"

McMillan still wore the grim smile. "You're slick all right. Maybe the next thing is, did I murder him? Maybe I murdered him because he insulted me?"

"I'm never facetious about murder. Besides, I haven't got to the murder yet. I need first to justify Clyde's optimism about his bet, and establish what he came here to do or whom to see. Did he make you a proposal?"

"No." McMillan abruptly stood up.

Wolfe lifted his brows. "Going?"

"I don't see much point in staying. I came as a favor to Fred Osgood."

"And as a favor to him, you have no information at all that might help? Nothing that might explain—"

"No. I can't explain a damn thing." The stockman took three heavy steps and turned. "Neither can you," he declared, "by trying to smear any of the mess on me."

He strode to the door and opened it, and it closed after him.

Wolfe sighed, shut his eyes, and sat. I stood and looked at him a minute, detecting none of the subtle signs of glee or triumph on his map, and then treated myself to a healthy sigh and got busy with the trays. Not being sure whether a maid was supposed to be available at 10 o'clock at night, and not liking to dump the trays in the hall, I got them perched on my arms and sought the back stairs. That was a blunder, because the stairs were a little narrow and I nearly got stuck on a turn. But I navigated to the kitchen without disaster, unloaded, and proceeded via the pantry and dining room to the main hall. There was a light in the library, and through the open door I saw Howard Bronson reading a newspaper. No one else was visible, and I completed the circuit back to Wolfe's room by way of the main stair.

He was still dormant. I sat down and yawned, and said: "It is in the bag. Lily killed him, thinking that by erasing evidence of her past she could purify herself and perhaps some day be worthy of me. Caroline killed him to practise her follow-through. Jimmy killed him to erase Lily's past, making twice for that one motive. Pratt killed him to annoy Mr. Osgood. McMillan killed him because the substitute he brought for Caesar proved to be a cow. Dave killed him—"

"Confound it, Archie, shut up."

"Yes, sir. I'll close it forever and seal the crack with rubber cement the minute you explain at what time and by what process you got this nice little case like that." I doubled my fist, but the gesture was wasted because he didn't open his eyes.

He was in bad shape, for he muttered mildly, "I did have it like that."

"What became of it?"

"It went up in fire and smoke."

"The bull motif again. Phooey. Try and persuade me . . . and incidentally, why don't you stop telling people that I steered your car into a tree and demolished it? What good do you expect to accomplish by puerile paroxysms like that? To go back to this case you've dragged us into through your absolute frenzy to find an adequate chair to sit on, I suppose now it's hopeless? I suppose these hicks are going to enjoy the refreshing sight of Nero Wolfe heading south Thursday morning with his tail between his legs? Or shall I go on with the list until I offer one that strikes your fancy? Dave killed him because he missed breakfast the day he was fired two years ago and has never caught up. Bronson killed him . . . by the way, I just saw Mr. Bronson—"

"Bronson?"

"Yep. In the library reading a newspaper as if he owned the place."

"Go and get him." Wolfe stirred and his eyes threatened to open. "Bring him here."

"Now?"

"Now."

I arose and sallied forth. But on my way downstairs it occurred to me that I might as well make arrangements in case of a prolonged session, so I went to the kitchen first and abducted a pitcher of Advanced Register Guernsey milk from the refrigerator. With that in my hand, I strutted on to the library and told Bronson I hated to interrupt him but that Mr. Wolfe had expressed a desire for his company.

He looked amused and put down his newspaper and said he had begun to fear he was going to be slighted.

"No sirree," I said. "He'll banish that fear easy."

Chapter 13

He sat in the chair McMillan had vacated and continued to look tolerably amused. Wolfe, immovable, with his eyes nearly shut, appeared to be more than half asleep, which may or may not have deceived Bronson but didn't deceive me. I yawned. With the angle of the light striking Bronson as it did, his nose looked blunter than it had on the veranda, as if it had at some time been permanently pushed, and his clever gray eyes looked smaller.

Finally he said in a cultivated tone, "I understood you wanted to ask me something."

Wolfe nodded. "Yes, sir. Were you able to overhear much of my conversation with Miss Osgood this afternoon?"

"Not a great deal. In fact, very little." Bronson smiled. "What was that for, to see if I would make an effort at indignation? Let me suggest . . . we won't really need finesse. I know a little something about you, I'm aware of your resources, but I have a few myself. Why don't we just agree that you're not a fool and neither am I?"

"Indeed." Wolfe's lids had lifted so that his eyes

were more than slits. "Are you really a coolheaded man? There are so few."

"I'm fairly intelligent."

"Then thank heaven we can discuss facts calmly, without a lot of useless pother . . . facts which I have got from Miss Osgood. For instance, that you are what Mr. Osgood—and many other people—would call an unscrupulous blackguard."

"I don't . . ." Bronson flipped a hand. "Oh, well. Calling names . . ."

"Just so. I can excoriate stupidity, and often do, because it riles me, but moral indignation is a dangerous indulgence. Ethology is a chaos. Financial banditry, for example . . . I either condemn it or I don't; and if I do, without prejudice, where will I find jailers? No. My only excuse for labeling you an unscrupulous blackguard is the dictionary, and I do it to clarify our positions. I'm in the detective business, and you're in the blackguard business . . . and I want to consult with you about both. I am counting on you to help me in my investigation of a murder, and I also have a suggestion to make regarding one of your projects—the one that brought you here. Regarding the murder—"

"Perhaps we'd better take the last one first and get it out of the way. I'm always open to a reasonable suggestion."

"As you please, sir." Wolfe's lips pushed out, and in again. "You have a paper signed by Clyde Osgood. You showed it to Miss Osgood this morning."

"A receipt for money I paid him."

"Specifying the services he was to perform in return."

"Yes."

"The performance of which would render him like-wise a blackguard . . . in the estimation of his father."

"That's right."

Wolfe stirred. "I want that paper. Now wait. I offer no challenge to your right to expect your money back. I concede that right. But I don't like your methods of collection. You may have a right to them too, but I do not like them. Miss Osgood aroused my admiration this afternoon, which is rare for a woman, and I want to relieve the pressure on her. I propose that you hand the paper to Mr. Goodwin; it will be safe in his custody. Within 10 days at the outside I shall either pay you the $10,000, or have it paid, or return the paper to you. I make that pledge without reservation." Wolfe aimed a thumb at me. "Give it to him."

The blackguard shook his head, slowly and positively. "I said a reasonable suggestion."

"You won't do it?"

"No."

"The security is superlative. I rarely offer pledges, because I would redeem one, tritely, with my life."

"I couldn't use your life. The security you offer may be good, but the paper signed by Osgood is better, and it belongs to me. Why the deuce should I give it up?"

I looked at Wolfe inquiringly. "I'd be glad to undertake—"

"No, thanks, Archie. We'll pass it, at least for the present. —I hope, Mr. Bronson, that your antagonism will find—"

"I'm not antagonistic," Bronson interrupted. "Don't get me wrong. I said I'm not a fool, and I would be a fool to antagonize you. I know very well

I'm vulnerable, and I know what you can do. If I make an enemy of you I might as well leave New York. I've only been there two months, but if you wanted to take the trouble to trace me back I don't deny you could do it. You wouldn't find that a cell is waiting for me anywhere, but you could collect enough to make it damned hard going . . . too hard. I've had a bad break on this Clyde Osgood thing, but I can try again and expect better luck, and God knows I don't want you hounding me, and you wouldn't go to the expense and trouble just for the fun of it. Believe me, I'm not antagonistic. You have no right to get sore about my not surrendering that paper, because it's mine, but otherwise I'm for you. If I can help any I will."

"No finesse, Mr. Bronson?"

"None."

"Good. Then tell me first, where were you born?"

Bronson shook his head. "I said help you, not satisfy your curiosity."

"You've admitted I can trace you back if I care to take the trouble."

"Then take the trouble."

"Very well, I'll be more direct. Have you ever handled cattle?"

Bronson stared, then let out a short laugh and said, "My God, must I take it back about your not being a fool? Do you mean to say you're trying to fit me in that thing?"

"Have you ever handled cattle?"

"I've never had the slightest association with cattle. I know where milk and beef come from only because I read it somewhere."

"Where is the club you were carrying last night

when you accompanied Clyde Osgood to Pratt's place?"

"Club?"

"Yes. A rough club, a length of sapling."

"Why . . . I don't think . . . Oh yes. Sure, I remember. It was leaning up against a shed as we went by, and I just—"

"Where is it?"

"You mean now? After all—"

"Where did you leave it?"

"Why . . . I don't . . . Oh! Sure. When we got to the fence, where the trees ended, Clyde went on and I came back. He took the club with him."

"What for?"

Bronson shrugged. He had himself collected again. "Just to have it, I suppose. I notice you carry a heavy walking stick. What for?"

"Not to knock myself unconscious with. Did Clyde ask for the club? Did you offer it to him?"

"I don't know. It was quite casual, one way or the other. Why, was he knocked on the head? I thought he was killed with a pick, according to your—"

"You're supposed to be helping, sir, not chattering. I need the truth about that club."

"You've had it."

"Nonsense. You were obviously disconcerted, and you stalled." Wolfe wiggled a finger at him. "If you don't want my antagonism, beware. This is the most favorable chance you'll have to tell the truth, here privately with me in comparative amity. Isn't it a fact that you yourself carried the club to Mr. Pratt's place?"

"No. I didn't go there."

"You stick to that?"

"It's the truth."

"I warn you again, beware. But say we take that, for the moment, for truth, tell me this: why was Clyde going to Pratt's? What was he going to do there?"

"I don't know."

"What did he say he was going to do?"

"He didn't say."

Wolfe shut his eyes and was silent. I saw the tip of his index finger making little circles on the arm of his chair, and knew he was speechless with fury. After a minute Bronson began:

"I may as well—"

"Shut up!" Wolfe's lids quivered as he opened his eyes. "You're making a mistake. A bad one. Listen to this. You were demanding immediate repayment of your money. Clyde, unable to raise the sum in New York, came here to appeal to his father, and you were in such a hurry, or mistrusted him so greatly, or both, that you came along. You wouldn't let him out of your sight. His father refused his appeal, since Clyde wouldn't tell him what the money was needed for—to save the Osgood honor would be correct phrasing— and you were ready to disclose the facts to the father and collect your debt direct from him. Then Clyde, in desperation, made a bet. He couldn't possibly win the bet and pay you for 6 days, until the week expired, and what acceptable assurance could he give you that he would win it at all? Only one assurance could have induced you to wait: a satisfactory explanation of the method by which he expected to win. So he gave it to you. Don't try to tell me he didn't; I'm not a gull. He told you how he expected to win, and the steps he proposed to take. Very well, you tell me."

Bronson shook his head. "All I can say is, you're wrong. He didn't tell—"

"Pfui. I'm right. I know when I'm right. Beware, sir."

Bronson shrugged. "It won't get you anywhere to keep telling me to beware. I can't tell you what I don't know."

"Did Clyde Osgood tell you how and why he expected to win the bet?"

"No."

"Or what he intended to do at Pratt's or whom he expected to see there?"

"No."

"You're making a bad blunder."

"No, I'm not. I may be getting in bad with you, but I can't help it. For God's sake—"

"Shut up. You're a fool after all." Wolfe turned and snapped at me: "Archie, get that paper."

He might have prepared me by one swift glance before putting it into words, but when I complained to him about such things he always said that my speed and wit required no preparation, and I retorted that I could put up with less sarcastic flattery and more regard for my convenience.

On this occasion it didn't matter much. Bronson was about my size but I doubted if he was tough. However, it was a murder case, and Wolfe had just been insinuating that this gentleman had been on the scene of hostilities with a club in his hand, so I got upright and across to his neighborhood quick enough to forestall any foolish motions he might make. I stuck my hand out and said:

"Gimme."

He shook his head and got up without haste, kicking his chair back without looking at it, looking instead at me with his eyes still steady and clever.

"This is silly," he said. "Damned silly. You can't bluff me like this."

I asked without turning my head, "Do you want it, Mr. Wolfe?"

"Get it."

"Okay. —Reach for the moon. I'll help myself."

"No you won't." His eyes didn't flicker. "If you try taking it away from me, I won't fight. I'm not much of a coward, but I'm not in condition and I'd be meat for you. Instead, I'll yell, and Osgood will come, and of course he'll want a look at the paper that's causing the trouble." He smiled.

"You will?"

"I will."

"Back at you. If you do, I'll show you how I make sausage. I warn you, one bleat and I'll quit only when the ambulance comes. After Osgood reads the paper he'll offer to pay me to do it again. Hold that pose."

I started to reach, and I'll be damned if he didn't try a dive with his knee up, and without flashing a flag. He was fairly quick, but I side-stepped in time. It wasn't absolutely essential to punch him, but a guy as tricky as he was needed a lesson anyway, so I let him have it, a good stiff hook that lifted him out of his dive and turned him over. I was beside him, bending over him, by the time he got his eyes open again.

"Stay there," I told him. "I don't know which pocket it's in. Do you think you can remember that? If so, gimme."

His hand started for his inside breast pocket, and I reached in ahead of him and pulled out something that proved to be a handsome brown leather wallet with a monogram on it in platinum or maybe tin. He grabbed for it and I jerked away and told him to get up and sit down, and backed off a little to examine the loot.

"My word." I whistled. "Here's an accumulation of currency out of all proportion. A couple of thousand or more. Pipe down, you. I don't steal from blackguards. But I don't see . . . ah, here we are. Secret compartments you might say." I unfolded it and ran my eye over it, and handed it to Wolfe. "Return the balance?"

He nodded, reading. I handed the wallet back to Bronson, who was back on his feet. He looked a little disarranged, but he met my eye as he took the wallet from me, and I had to admit there was something to him, although misplaced; it isn't usual to meet the eye of a bird who has just knocked you down and made you like it. Wolfe said, "Here, Archie," and handed me the paper, and from my own breast pocket I took the brown ostrich cardcase, gold-tooled, given to me by Wolfe on a birthday, in which I carried my police and fire cards and operator's license. I slipped the folded paper inside and returned it to my pocket.

Wolfe said, "Mr. Bronson. There are other questions I meant to ask, such as the purpose of your trip to Mr. Pratt's place this afternoon, but it would be futile. I am even beginning to suspect that you are now engaged in an enterprise which may prove to be a bigger blunder than your conduct here with me. As for the paper Mr. Goodwin took from you, I guarantee that within 10 days you will get it back, or your money. Don't try any stratagems. I'm mad enough already. Good night, sir."

"I repeat . . . I've told you . . ."

"I don't want to hear it. You're a fool. Good night." Bronson went.

Wolfe heaved a deep sigh. I poured out a glass of milk, and sipped, and saw that he had an eye cocked at me. In a minute he murmured:

"Archie. Where did you get that milk?"

"Refrigerator."

"In the kitchen?"

"Yes, sir."

"Well?"

"Yes, sir. There's 5 or 6 bottles in there. Shall I bring you one?"

"You might have saved yourself a trip." His hand dived into his side coat pocket and came out clutching a flock of beer bottle caps. He opened his fist and counted them, frowning, and told me, "Bring two."

Chapter 14

At 10 o'clock the next morning, Wednesday, a motley group piled into Osgood's sedan, bound for Crowfield. All except Nero Wolfe looked the worse for wear—I couldn't say about me. Osgood was seedy and silent, and during a brief talk with Wolfe had shown an inclination to bite. Bronson no longer looked disarranged, having again donned the Crawnley suit he had worn Monday, but the right side of his jaw was swollen and he was sullen and not amused. Nancy, who took the wheel again, was pale and had bloodshot eyes and moved in jerks. She had already made one trip to Crowfield and back, for a couple of relatives at the railroad station. The funeral was to be Thursday afternoon, and the major influx of kin would be 24 hours later. Apparently Wolfe had changed his mind about immediately relieving the pressure on the woman he admired, for I had been instructed that there was no hurry about telling Miss Osgood that the paper her brother had signed was in my possession. Which, considering how I had got it, was in my judgment just as well.

During the 30-minute drive to Crowfield no one

said a word, except for a brief discussion between Osgood and Nancy to arrange for meeting later in the day, after errands had been performed. First we dropped Osgood on Main Street in front of an establishment with palms and ferns in the window and a small sign painted down in a corner which said Somebody or other, MORTICIAN. Our next stop was two blocks down, at the hotel, where Bronson left us, in a dismal all-around silence and unfriendly atmosphere that is probably the chief occupational hazard of the blackguard business.

Nancy muttered at me, "Thompson's Garage, isn't it?" and I told her yes, and three minutes later she let me out there, around on a side street, the idea being that since there might be a delay about the car she would proceed to deliver Wolfe at the exposition grounds, for which I was grateful, not wanting him muttering around underfoot.

The bill was $66.20, which was plenty, even including the towing in. Of course there was no use beefing, so I contented myself with a thorough inspection to make sure everything was okay, filled up with gas and oil; paid in real money, and departed.

Then I was supposed to find Lew Bennett, secretary of the National Guernsey League. I tried the hotel and drew a blank, and wasted 20 minutes in a phone booth, being met with busy lines, wrong numbers, and general ignorance. There seemed to be an impression that he was somewhere at the exposition, so I drove out there and after a battle got the car parked in one of the spaces reserved for exhibitors. I plunged into the crowd, deciding to start at the exposition offices, where I learned that this was a big cattle day and Bennett was in up to his ears. He would be around the exhibition sheds, which were at the other end of the grounds. Back in the crowd again, I fought through men, women, children, balloons, horns, popcorn and bedlam, to my objective.

I hadn't seen this part before. There was a city of enormous sheds, in a row, each one 50 yards long or more and half as wide. There weren't many people around. I popped into the first shed. It smelled like cows, which wasn't surprising, because it was full of them. A partition 5 feet high ran down the middle of the shed its entire length, and facing it, tied to it, were cattle, on both sides. Bulls and cows and calves. Two more rows of them faced the walls. But none of them looked like the breed I was most familiar with after my association with Hickory Caesar Grindon. A few spectators straggled down the long aisle, and I moseyed along to where a little squirt in overalls was combing tangles out of a cow's tail, and told him I was looking for Lew Bennett of the Guernsey League.

"Guernsey?" He looked contemptuous. "I wouldn't know. I'm a Jersey man."

"Oh. Excuse me. Personally, I fancy Guernseys. Is there a shed where they allow Guernseys?"

"Sure. Down beyond the judging lot. He might be at the lot. They're judging Ayrshires and Belted Swiss this morning, but they begin on Guernseys at 1 o'clock."

I thanked him and proceeded. After I had passed three sheds there was a large vacant space, roped off into divisions, and that was where the crowd was, several hundred of them, up against the ropes. Inside were groups of cattle, black with belts of white around their middles, held by men and boys with tie-ropes. Other men walked or stood around, frowning at

the cattle, accompanied by still others armed with
fountain pens and sheets of cardboard. One guy was
kneeling down, inspecting an udder as if he expected
to find the Clue of the Month on it. I couldn't see
Bennett anywhere.

I found him in the second shed ahead, which was
devoted to Guernseys. It was full of activity and wor-
riment—brushing coats, washing hoofs and faces,
combing tails, discussing and arguing. Bennett was
rushing back and forth. He didn't recognize me, and I
nearly had to wrestle him to stop him. I reminded him
of our acquaintance and said that Nero Wolfe wanted
to see him at the main exhibits building, or some more
convenient spot, as soon as possible. Urgent.

"Out of the question," he declared, looking fierce.
"I haven't even got time to eat. They're judging us at
1 o'clock."

"Mr. Wolfe's solving a murder for Mr. Frederick
Osgood. He needs important information from you."

"I haven't got any."

"He wants to ask you."

"I can't see him now. I just can't do it. After 1
o'clock . . . when they start judging . . . you say
he's at the main exhibits building? I'll see him or let
him know . . ."

"He'll lunch at the Methodist tent. Make it soon.
Huh?"

He said just as soon as possible.

It was noon by the time I got to our space in the
main exhibits building. It was judgment day for more
than Guernseys, as 4 o'clock that afternoon was zero
hour for the orchids. Wolfe was there spraying and
manicuring. The sprayer was a pippin, made specially
to his order, holding two gallons, with a compression

chamber and a little electric motor, weighing only 11 pounds empty. His rival and enemy, Shanks, was with him admiring the sprayer when I joined them. I told him the car was okay and named the extent of the damage, and described the plight of Mr. Bennett.

He grimaced. "Then I must wait here."

"Standing is good for you."

"And the delay. It is Wednesday noon. We have nothing left but shreds. I telephoned Mr. Waddell. The club carried to Mr. Pratt's place has not been found, and the police took no photographs of the bull. Pfui. Inspector Cramer's indefatigable routine has its advantages. Miss Osgood reports that none of the servants saw Bronson return. Our next move depends on Mr. Bennett."

"He says he has no information."

"But he has. He is ignorant of its application. Perhaps if you went back and explained? . . ."

"Not without using force. He says he hasn't got time to eat."

That of course silenced him. He grunted and returned to Shanks.

I propped myself against the edge of the dahlia table across the aisle and yawned. Dissatisfaction filled my breast. I had failed to bring what I had been sent for, which was infrequent and irritating. I had been relieved of $66.20 of Wolfe's money. We were going to dine and sleep that night in a house where family and relatives were preparing for a funeral. Wolfe had just stated that in the murder case we were supposed to be solving we had nothing left but shreds. Altogether, the outlook was not rosy. Wolfe and Shanks went on chewing the rag, paying no attention to the visitors passing up and down the aisle, and I stood propped, with no enthusiasm for any effort to combat the gloom. I must have shut my eyes for the first I knew there was a tug at my sleeve and a voice:

"Wake up, Escamillo, and show me the flowers."

I let the lids up. "How do you do, Miss Rowan. Go away. I'm in seclusion."

"Kiss me."

I bent and deposited a peck on her brow. "There. Thank you for calling. Nice to see you."

"You're a lout."

"I have at no time asked you to submit bids."

The corner of her mouth went up. "This is a public exposition. I paid my way in. You're an exhibitor. Go ahead and exhibit. Show me."

"Not exhibitionist. Exhibitor. Anyway, I'm only an employee." I took her elbow and eased her across the aisle. "Mr. Wolfe, you know Miss Rowan. She wants to be shown the orchids."

He bowed. "That is one compliment I always surrender to."

She looked him in the eye. "I want you to like me, Mr. Wolfe. Or not dislike me. Mr. Goodwin and I are probably going to be friends. Will you give me an orchid?"

"I rarely dislike women, and never like them, Miss Rowan. I have only albinos here. I'll give you orchids at 5 o'clock, after the judging, if you'll tell me where to send them."

"I'll come and get them."

The upshot of that was that she went to lunch with us.

The Methodist tent was fuller than the day before, probably because we got there earlier. Apparently Mrs. Miller had no off days, for the fricassee with dumplings was as good as the memory of it, and, thinking it might be my last appearance among the devout, I permitted myself to run the meal in two sections, as did Wolfe. He, as always in the company of good food, was sociable and expansive. Discovering that Lily had been in Egypt, he told about his house in Cairo, and they chatted away like a pair of camels, going on to Arabia and making quite a trip of it. She let him do most of the talking but made him chuckle a couple of times, and I began to suspect she wasn't very obvious and might even be smooth.

As I put down my empty coffee cup Wolfe said, "Still no Bennett. It's 1:30. Is it far to the cattle sheds?"

I told him not very.

"Then if you will please find out about him. Confound it, I must see him. If he can't come at once, tell him I'll be here until 3 o'clock, and after that at the exhibit."

"Right."

I got up. Lily arose too, saying that she was supposed to be with Mr. Pratt and Caroline and they were probably looking for her. She left the tent with me, whereupon I informed her that it was now working hours and I would be moving through the throngs too energetically for pleasant companionship. She stated that up to date she had failed to detect any taint of pleasantness in my make-up and would see me at 5 o'clock, and departed in the direction of the grandstand. My errand was the other way.

They were going strong at the judging lot. I was pleased to note that Guernseys were evidently a more popular breed than Belted Swiss or Ayrshires, as the crowd was much larger than it had been 2 hours earlier. Bennett was within the enclosure, along with judges, scorekeepers and cattle with attendants. For a second my heart stopped, as I caught sight of a bull I would have sworn was Hickory Caesar Grindon; then I saw he was a lighter shade of tan and had a much smaller white spot on his face. I maneuvered around to the other side where the crowd wasn't so thick, and stood there, and when I felt a pull at my sleeve I thought for an instant that Lily Rowan had tailed me.

But it was Dave, dressed up in coat and pants and shirt and tie, and a shiny straw hat. He cackled: "Didn't I say you like to be around where things is goin' on? First I seen you. Was you here when them derned fools put down Bella Grassleigh for that Silverville cow? Her with a barrel more like a deer than any good milker I ever saw."

"Good God," I said, "that's the worst I ever heard. I just got here. I don't suppose . . . well, I'll be derned. There's our friend Monte McMillan."

"Yep, I drove him in this morning." Dave shook his head. "Poor old Monte, got to start practically all over again. He's got it in mind to do some buyin' if prices is right, to build up another foundation. You wouldn't have thought a year ago . . ."

I missed the rest because I was diving under the rope. Bennett was momentarily disengaged, standing mopping his forehead, and I made for him. He blinked at me in the sunlight and said he was sorry, he hadn't been able to make it. I told him okay, that was forgiven, but couldn't he come to the Methodist tent right now. Impossible, he said, they were judging Produce of Dam and Breeders' Young Herd simulta-

neously. There was nothing he could tell Nero Wolfe
anyway. And I didn't belong there in the enclosure—

I got a little peremptory: "Wolfe's working on a
murder, and he says he needs to see you and can't
make another move until he does. Are you primarily a
citizen and a friend of Fred Osgood's, or a sergeant at
arms in a cattle tribunal? If you think justice among
the cows is more important . . ."

He said he wasn't a particular friend of Osgood's,
who as far as he was concerned was merely a member
of the League, and that he would be at the Methodist
tent, no fooling, within half an hour.

I got outside the ropes again, but instead of beat-
ing it I decided to hang around and wait for him. I
watched the judging for a few minutes, but couldn't
see very well on account of the mob, and so wandered
along in front of the sheds. There was no one around
at all, the judging being the current attraction, so naturally I observed the moving object that caught my
eyes, especially since the first sight showed me that
the object was familiar. It was Nancy Osgood, and the
glance she cast behind her as she entered one of the
sheds was either furtive or I was getting fanciful.
Even if she was furtive it was none of my business,
but a detective who minds his own business would be
a contradiction in terms, so I slid over to the shed and
inserted myself through the door.

She wasn't within view. There were plenty of
cows, black and white this time, and a few visitors
further down the aisle, but no Nancy. I strolled along
between the rows of hind ends. Toward the middle of
the shed there was a partitioned compartment on the
left, containing no cow; but an instant's peep disclosed
that it contained three other things: a large pile of

straw with a pitchfork handle protruding from its center, Nancy Osgood, and Jimmy Pratt. I would have
passed on, but I had been seen. Jimmy's voice was
gruff and discourteous:

"Well?"

I shrugged. "Well enough. Hoping you are the
same." I started to move on, but his voice came even
gruffer:

"Wait and look and listen. The more you see and
hear the more you can tell."

"Don't, Jimmy." Nancy sounded very distressed.
She turned her eyes, more bloodshot than ever, in my
direction: "Were you following me, Mr. Goodwin?
What for?"

A couple of passers-by seemed disposed to linger,
so I stepped inside the stall to keep it in the family.
"Yes," I told her, "I was. For about 40 seconds. I happened to see you enter this shed looking behind you
for bloodhounds, and followed you out of curiosity." I
surveyed young Pratt. "It's a good thing you're training for architecture instead of the diplomatic service.
You lack suavity. If this is a clandestine rendezvous
and you suspected I might report it, it might be better to rub me with salve than sandpaper."

He reached for his pocket. "Oh, in that case—"

I let him go on. His hand emerged with a modest
roll, from which, with unsteady fingers, he peeled a
ten. He thrust it at me with an objectionable smile
and asked, "Will that do?"

"Swell." I took it. "Munificent." My first impulse
was to stick it in the pocket of Nancy's jacket and tell
her to buy stocking with it, but at that moment our
party was joined by a lanky guy in overalls carrying a
pitchfork. With only a glance at us he rammed the

fork into the pile of straw and started to lift the load. I stopped him by shoving the $10 bill under his nose.

"Here, brother. I represent the exposition management. We've decided you fellows are overworked. Take this as an expression of our esteem."

He stared. "What's that?"

"Don't try to understand it, just take it. Redistribution of wealth. A form of communism."

"From the exposition management?"

"Right."

"I'll be derned. They must be crazy." He took the bill and stuffed it in his pocket. "Much obliged to you."

"Don't mention it." I waved airily. He elevated the load of straw, a big one, about one-fourth of the entire pile, above his shoulder with an expert twist, and departed.

"You said salve, didn't you?" Jimmy Pratt sounded resentful. "How the hell could I know you're Robin Hood? After what you said about salve, wasn't it natural to take you for a chiseler?" He turned to Nancy. "He knows all about Bronson and the paper Clyde signed, anyway, since he was there when you told Wolfe. As far as your father hearing about our being together is concerned . . ."

I was extremely glad he had shifted to Nancy, because it gave me an opportunity I was badly in need of. I grant that I have aplomb, but I'm not constructed of wood, and it still surprises me that nothing on my face gave them alarm. What I had seen was something that had been uncovered by the removal of a portion of the straw. Making a movement, my toe had touched some object that wasn't straw, and a downward glance had shown me what it was. It was a brown custom-made oxford perched on its heel, an inch of brown sock, and the cuff of one leg of a pair of Crawnley trousers.

So, as I say, I was glad Jimmy had shifted to Nancy, for it gave me an opportunity to kick at the straw capriciously and thereby get the shoe and sock and trouser cuff out of sight again. Nothing was left visible but straw.

Nancy was talking to me: "Perhaps I shouldn't, after Mr. Wolfe said he would help me, but I met Jimmy this morning and we . . . we had a talk . . . and I told him about that paper and Bronson still having it . . . and he thought he could do something about it and I was sure he shouldn't try it without seeing Mr. Wolfe first . . . and we arranged to meet here at 2 o'clock and discuss it . . ."

I had unobtrusively got myself moved around to where I could reach the pitchfork handle which was protruding erect from the center of the pile of straw. With my eyes respectfully attending to Nancy, my hand idly played with the straw, which is nice to touch, and without much effort it found the spot where the handle of the fork joined the tines. Two of my fingers—feeling with the ends of their nails, which don't leave prints—explored downward along a tine, but not far, not more than a couple of inches, before they were stopped by something that was neither tine nor straw. I kept the fingers there half a minute, feeling, and then slowly withdrew my hand.

Jimmy demanded, "What's the use of deadpanning her? Either you and Wolfe are going to act as decent as he talked—"

"Deadpan?" I grinned. "Not on your life. I wouldn't know about decency, but Wolfe and I always do what he says. But you children are only going to

make it harder by being indiscreet all over the fair
grounds. Osgood is a difficult enough client already.
For God's sake postpone this reunion for a day or two.
Everybody in the county knows you, and here you
stand in plain view. If you'll do what I say I'll guarantee that Wolfe and I will be as decent as doves . . .
and Osgood will never see that paper."

Jimmy was frowning. "Well?"

"Separate. Disunite. Immediately. You go out at
the other end and I'll take her this way."

"He's right, Jimmy. It was awfully foolish, but you
insisted—"

"Come on, beat it. Ten people have stopped to look
in here at us in the last three minutes."

"But I've got to know—"

"Damn it, do what I say!"

"Please, Jimmy."

He took her hand and looked her in the eye and
said her name twice as if he was leaving her bound to
a railroad track, and tore himself away. I told her to
come on and left the stall and turned right with her,
toward the door by which I had entered. Outside I
took her elbow and talked as we walked:

"I've got work to do and I'm leaving you. You've
acted like a female nincompoop. It's true that emotions are emotions, but brains are also brains. To go
running to Jimmy Pratt for help when you already
had Nero Wolfe's! You get away from here. I suppose
you have a date to meet your father somewhere. If so,
go there and wait for him and practice thinking."

"But I haven't . . . you talk as if—"

"I don't talk as if anything. Don't worry about how
I talk. Here's where I turn off. See you in kindergar-
ten."

I left her in the middle of a crowd, thinking that was as good a place as any, and elbowed my way across the current to where I could make better time without displaying any indications of panic. It took less than five minutes to get from there to the Methodist tent. Wolfe was still there, at the table, looking massively forlorn on the folding chair. He had probably never before digested good food under such difficult circumstances.

He frowned up at me. "Well? Mr. Bennett?"

I sat down and nodded and restrained my voice. "I have to make a brief but tiresome report. Item 1, Mr. Bennett will be here in 10 minutes or so. He said. Item 2, I found Nancy Osgood and Jimmy Pratt in a cowshed, discussing means of getting the paper which I have in my pocket. Item 3, in the same shed I found Mr. Bronson lying under a pile of straw, dead, with a pitchfork stuck through his heart. No one knows of the last item but me . . . or didn't when I left."

Wolfe's eyes went shut, then came half-open again. He heaved a deep sigh. "The fool. I told that man he was a fool."

Chapter 15

I nodded. "Yeah. You also told him you were beginning to suspect that he was engaged in an enterprise which might prove to be a big blunder.
Madam Shasta, in a booth down the line, calls it reading the future and charges a dime for it." I fished for a
pair of nickels and shoved them across at him. "I'll
bite. How did you know it?"

He ignored my offer. "Confound it," he muttered.
"Too late again. I should have phoned Saul or Fred
last evening to take a night train. Bronson should
have been followed this morning. Once compelled to
talk, he would have been all the evidence we needed. I
am not myself, Archie. How the devil can I be, dash-
ing around in all this furor . . . I have that scoundrel
Shanks to thank for it. Well." He sighed again. "You
say no one knows it?"

"Correct. Except the guy that did it. I was waiting
around for Bennett and saw Nancy enter a cowshed
and followed her in. She joined Jimmy Pratt in a stall
which also contained a pile of straw. I made it three
and we conversed. A cow nurse came and removed
part of the straw, exposing a shoe and a trouser cuff.

No one saw it but me and I kicked straw over it. A pitchfork was thrust into the pile, upright, with straw covering it part way up the handle, and I took a sounding with my hand and discovered what its pincushion was. Right through his chest. His pump was gone. I accused Romeo and Juliet of indiscretion and hustled them out in separate directions, and came here."

"Then the discovery awaits removal of more straw."

"Yes. Which may have already happened, or may not occur until tomorrow."

"But probably sooner. You came away to escape clamor?"

"To notify you. And to tell you about Bennett. And to save Nancy from being annoyed, by her father for the company she keeps, and by the cops for practically sitting on a corpse."

"You were all seen by the man who removed the straw."

"Sure, and by various others. Shall I go back now and discover him?"

Wolfe shook his head. "That wouldn't help. Nor, probably, will there be a trail for the official pack, so there's no hurry. I wouldn't have guessed Bronson would be idiot enough to give him such a chance, but of course he had to meet him somewhere. But it is now all the more imperative—ah, thank goodness! Good afternoon, sir."

Lew Bennett, still in his shirt sleeves, out of breath, stood beside him and curtly acknowledged the greeting. "You want to see me? Worst time you could have picked. The very worst."

"So Mr. Goodwin has told me. I'm sorry, but I can't help it. Be seated, sir. Have some coffee?"

"I'll just stand. If I once sat down . . . what do you want?"

"Have you had lunch?"

"No."

"Preposterous." Wolfe shook his head at him. "In the midst of the most difficult and chaotic problems, I never missed a meal. A stomach too long empty thins the blood and disconcerts the brain.—Archie, order a portion of the fricassee.—For God's sake, sir, sit down."

I doubt if Wolfe influenced him much, it was the smell of food. I saw his nostrils quivering. He hesitated, and when I flagged a Methodist and told her to bring it with an extra dime's worth of dumplings, which was an idea Wolfe had invented, he succumbed and dropped into a chair.

Wolfe said, "That's better. Now. I've been hired by Mr. Osgood to solve a murder, and I need to know some things. You may think of my questions irrelevant or even asinine; if so you'll be wrong. My only serious fault is lethargy, and I tolerate Mr. Goodwin, and even pay him, to help me circumvent it. 48 hours ago, Monday afternoon on Mr. Pratt's terrace, you told him that there were a dozen members of your league waiting for you to get back, and that when they heard what you had to say there would be some action taken. You shouted that at him with conviction. What sort of action did you have in mind?"

Bennett was staring at him. "Not murder," he said shortly. "What has that got—"

"Please." Wolfe wiggled a finger at him. "I've told

you I'm not an ass. I asked you a simple straightfor-
ward question. Can't you simply answer it? I know
you were shouting at Mr. Pratt in a rage. But what
sort of action did you have in mind?"

"No sort."

"Nothing whatever?"

"Nothing specific. I was furious. We all were.
What he intended to do was the most damnable outrage and insult—"

"I know. Granting your viewpoint, I agree. But
hadn't ways and means of preventing it been discussed? For example, had anyone suggested the possibility of removing Hickory Caesar Grindon secretly
and putting another bull in his place?"

Bennett started to speak, and stopped. His eyes
looked wary. "No," he said curtly.

Wolfe sighed. "All right. I wish you would understand that I'm investigating a murder, not a conspir-
acy to defraud. You should eat those dumplings hot. It
might be better to let this wait until you're
through—"

"Go ahead. When I'm through I'm going."

"Very well. I didn't ask if some of you had substituted another bull or tried, I asked merely if it had
been suggested in the heat of indignation. What I
really want to know is, would such a plan have been
feasible?"

"Feasible?" Bennett swallowed chicken. "It would
have been a crime. Legally."

"Of course. But—please give this consideration as
a serious question—might it have worked?"

He considered, chewing bread and butter. "No.
Monte McMillan was there."

"If Mr. McMillan hadn't been there, or had been a party to the scheme, might it have worked?"

"It might have."

"It would have been possible to replace Caesar with another bull sufficiently resembling him so that the substitution would be undetected by anyone not thoroughly familiar with his appearance, without a close inspection?"

"It might have."

"Yet Caesar was a national grand champion." Wolfe shifted, grimacing, on the folding chair. "Didn't he approach the unique?"

"Hell no. There's plenty of good bulls, and quite a few great ones. The grand champion stuff is all right, and it's valid, but sometimes the margin is mighty slim. Last year at Indianapolis, Caesar scored 96 and Portchester Compton 95. Another thing of course is their get. The records of their daughters and sons. Caesar had 51 A R daughters—"

"And 9 A R sons. I know. And that of course would not be visible to the eye. But still I am not satisfied. If another bull was to be substituted for Caesar by . . . well, let us say Clyde Osgood . . . it couldn't be a near-champion, for the bull was destined to be butchered, and near-champions are valuable too. Would it be possible for an average bull, of comparatively low value, to have a fairly strong resemblance to a champion?"

"Might. At a distance of say a hundred yards. It would depend on who was looking."

"How does a bull score points?"

Bennett swallowed dumplings. "The scale of points we judge on has 22 headings, with a total of 100 points for perfection, which of course no bull ever got. Style and symmetry is 10 points. Head 6, horns 1, neck 3, withers 3, shoulders 2, chest 4, back 8, loin 3, hips 2, rump 6, thurls 2, barrel 10, and so on. The biggest number of points for any heading is 20 points for Secretions Indicating Color of Product. That's judged by the pigment secretions of the skin, which should be a deep yellow inclining toward orange in color, especially discernible in the ear, at the end of the tailbone, around the eyes and nose, on the scrotum, and at the base of horns. Hoofs and horns should be yellow. There is a very close relationship between the color of the skin, the color of the internal fat, and the milk and butter. Now that heading alone is 20 points out of the 100, and you can only judge it by a close-up inspection. As far as value is concerned, a bull's A R record is much more important than his show record. In the 1935 auctions, for instance, the price brought by A R bulls averaged over $2000. Bulls not yet A R but with A R dams averaged $533. Bulls not A R and without A R dams averaged $157. That same year Langwater Reveller sold for $10,000."

Wolfe nodded. "I see. The subtleties rule, as usual. That seems to cover the questions of value and superficial appearance. The next point . . . I was astonished by what you told me on the telephone yesterday when I called you from Mr. Osgood's house. I would have supposed that every purebred calf would receive an indelible mark at birth. But you said that the only ones that are marked—with a tattoo on the ear—are those of solid color, with no white."

"That's right."

"So that if Caesar had been replaced by another

bull it couldn't have been detected by the absence of any identifying mark."

"No. Only by comparing his color pattern with your knowledge of Caesar's color pattern or with the sketch on his Certificate of Registration."

"Just so. You spoke of sketches or photographs. How are they procured?"

"They are made by the breeder, at birth, or at least before the calf is six months old. On the reverse of the Application for Registration are printed outlines of a cow, both sides and face. On them the breeder sketches in ink the color pattern of the calf, showing white, light fawn, dark fawn, red fawn, brown and brindle. The sketches, filed in our office at Fernborough, are the permanent record for identification throughout life. Copies of them appear on the certificate of registration. If you buy a bull and want to be sure you are getting the right one, you compare his color and markings with the sketches."

"Then I did understand you on the telephone. It sounded a little haphazard."

"It's the universal method," declared Bennett stiffly. "There has never been any difficulty."

"No offense. If it works it works." Wolfe sighed. "One more thing while you have your pie and coffee. This may require some reflection. Putting it as a hypothesis that Clyde Osgood actually undertook to replace Caesar with a substitute, how many bulls are there within, say, 50 miles of here, which might have been likely candidates? With a fair resemblance to Caesar, the closer the better, in general appearance and color pattern? Remember it mustn't be another champion, worth thousands."

Bennett objected, "But I've told you, it couldn't have worked. No matter how close the resemblance was, Monte McMillan would have known. He would have known Hickory Caesar Grindon from any bull on earth."

"I said as a hypothesis. Humor me and we'll soon be through. How many such bulls within 50 miles?"

"That's quite an order." Bennett slowly munched a bite of pie, stirring his coffee, and considered. "Of course there's one right here, up at the shed. A Willowdale bull, 3-year-old. He'll never be in Caesar's class, but superficially he's a lot like him, color pattern and carriage and so on."

"Are you sure the one in the shed is the Willowdale bull?"

Bennett looked startled for an instant, then relieved. "Yes, it's Willowdale Zodiac all right. He was judged a while ago, and he's way down in pigment." He sipped some coffee. "There's a bull over at Hawley's, Orinoco, that might fill the bill, except his loin's narrow, but you might or might not notice that from any distance, depending on how he was standing. Mrs. Linville has one, over the other side of Crowfield, that would do even better than Orinoco, but I'm not sure if he's home. I understand she was sending him to Syracuse. Then of course another one would have been Hickory Buckingham Pell, Caesar's double brother, but he's dead."

"When did he die?"

"About a month ago. Anthrax. With most of the rest of McMillan's herd."

"Yes. That was a catastrophe. Was Buckingham also a champion?"

"Hell no. He and Caesar were both sired by old Hickory Gabriel, a grand and beautiful bull, but no matter how good a sire may be he can't be expected to hit the combination every time. Buckingham was good to look at, but his pigment secretion was bad and his daughters were inferior. He hadn't been shown since 1936, when he scored a 68 at Jamestown."

"In any case, he was dead. What about the Osgood herd? Any candidates there?"

Bennett slowly shook his head. "Hardly. There's a promising junior sire, Thistleleaf Lucifer, that might be figured in, but he's nearer brindle than red fawn. However, you might miss it if you had no reason to suspect it, and if you didn't have Caesar's pattern well in mind."

"What is Lucifer's value?"

"That's hard to say. At an auction, it all depends . . ."

"But a rough guess?"

"Oh, between $500 and $800."

"I see. A mere fraction of $45,000."

Bennett snorted. "No bull ever lived that was worth $45,000. McMillan didn't get that for Caesar as a proper and reasonable price for him. It was only a bribe Pratt offered to pull him in on a shameful and discreditable stunt. One or two of the fellows are inclined to excuse McMillan, saying that losing 80% of his herd with anthrax was a terrible blow and he was desperate and it was a lot of money, but I say nothing in God's world could excuse a thing like that and most of them agree with me. I'd rather commit suicide than let myself—hey, George, over here! I was just coming. What's up?"

One of the men I had noticed in the judging enclosure, a big broad-shouldered guy with a tooth gone in front, approached us, bumping the backs of chairs as he came.

"Can't they get along without me for 10 minutes?" Bennett demanded. "What's wrong now?"

"Nothin's wrong at the lot," the man said. "But we can't lead from the shed and back, on account of the crowd. There's a million people around there. Somebody found a dead man under a straw pile in the Holstein shed with a pitchfork through him. Murdered."

"Good God!" Bennett jumped up. "Who?"

"Don't know. You can't find out anything. You ought to see the mob . . ."

That was all I heard, because they were on their way out. A Methodist started after Bennett, but I intercepted her and told her I would pay for the meal. She said 90 cents, and I relinquished a dollar bill and sat down again across from Wolfe.

"The natural thing," I said, "would be for me to trot over there and poke around."

Wolfe shook his head. "It's after 3 o'clock, and we have business of our own. Let's attend to it."

He got himself erect and turned to give the folding chair a dirty look, and we departed. Outside it was simpler to navigate than formerly, because instead of moving crisscross and every other way the crowd was mostly moving fast in a straight line, toward the end of the grounds where the cattle sheds were, in the opposite direction from the one we took. They looked excited and purposeful, as if they had just had news of some prey that might be pounced on for dinner. By keeping on one edge we avoided jostling.

Charles E. Shanks wasn't anywhere in sight

around the orchid display, but Raymond Plehn, who was showing Laeliocattleyas and Odontoglossums, was there. It was the first we had seen of him, though of course we had looked over his entry, which wasn't in competition with ours. The building, with its enormous expanse of tables and benches exhibiting everything from angel food cake to stalks of corn 14 feet high, seemed to have about as many afternoon visitors as usual, who either hadn't heard the news from the Holstein shed or were contrary enough to be more interested in flowers and vegetables than in corpses.

Wolfe exchanged amenities with Plehn and then he and I got busy. One of our 18 plants had got temperamental and showed signs of wilt, so I stuck it under the bench and covered it with newspaper. We went over the others thoroughly, straightening leaves that needed it, re-staking a few, and removing half a dozen blossoms whose sepals had started to brown at the tips.

"On the whole, they look perky," I told Wolfe.

"Dry," he grunted, inspecting a leaf. "Thank heaven, no red spider yet.—Ah. Good afternoon, Mr. Shanks."

At 4 o'clock the judges came, with retinue and scale sheets. One of them was a moonfaced bird from the Eastern States Horticultural Society and the other was Cuyler Ditson, who had been a judge several times at the Metropolitan. The pair started to squint and inspect and discuss, and a modest crowd collected.

It was such a pushover, and was over and done with so soon as far as the albinos were concerned, that it seemed pretty silly after all the trouble we had gone to, even though Wolfe got the medal and all three ribbons, and all Shanks got was a consoling pat on the back. But they both knew how it would look in the next issue of the American Orchid Gazette, and they knew who would read it. Shanks was dumb enough to get mad and try to start an argument with Cuyler Ditson, and Raymond Plehn gave him the horselaugh.

When the judges left the crowd dispersed. Wolfe and Plehn started to exercise their chins, and when that began I knew it would continue indefinitely, so I saw myself confronted by boredom. Wolfe had said that when the judging was over he would want to spray with nicotine and soap, and I dug the ingredients from the bottom of one of the crates, went for a can of water, and got the mixture ready in the sprayer. He did a thorough job of it, with Plehn assisting, put the sprayer down on the bench, and started talking shop again. I sat on a box and yawned and permitted my mind to flit around searching for honey in an idea that had occurred to me on account of one of the questions Wolfe had asked Bennett. But I hoped to heaven that wasn't the answer, for if it was we were certainly out on a limb, and as far as any hope of earning a fee from Osgood was concerned we might as well pack up and go home.

I glanced at my wrist and saw it was 10 minutes to 5, which reminded me that Lily Rowan was coming for orchids at 5 o'clock and gave me something to do, namely, devise a remark that would shatter her into bits. She had the appearance of never having been shattered to speak of, and it seemed to me that she was asking for it. To call a guy Escamillo in a spirit of fun is okay, but if you do so immediately after he has half-killed himself hurdling a fence on account of a bull chasing him, you have a right to expect whatever he may be capable of in return.

I never got the remark devised. The first interruption was the departure of Raymond Plehn, who was as urbane with his farewells as with other activities. The second interruption was more removed, when first noted, and much more irritating: I saw a person pointing at me. Down the aisle maybe ten paces he stood pointing, and he was unquestionably the lanky straw-handler in overalls whom I had last seen in the Holstein shed three hours previously. At his right hand stood Captain Barrow of the state police, and at his left District Attorney Waddell. As I gazed at them with my brow wrinkled in displeasure, they moved forward.

I told Wolfe out of the corner of my mouth. "Looky. Company's coming."

Apparently they had figured that the cow nurse would no longer be needed, for he lumbered off in the other direction, while the other two headed straight for their victim, meaning me. They looked moderately sour and nodded curtly when Wolfe and I greeted them.

Wolfe said, "I understand you have another dead man on your hands, and this time no demonstration from me is required."

Waddell mumbled something, but Barrow disregarded both of them and looked at me and said, "You're the one I want a demonstration from. Get your hat and come on."

I grinned. "Where to, please?"

"Sheriff's office. I'll be glad to show you the way. Wait a minute."

He extended a paw at me. I folded my arms and stepped back a pace. "Let's all wait a minute. I have a gun *and* a license. The gun is legally in my possession. We don't want a lot of silly complications. Do we?"

Chapter 16

Wolfe said sweetly, "I give you my word, Captain, he won't shoot you in my presence. He knows I dislike violence. I own the gun, by the way. Give it to me, Archie."

I took it from the holster and handed it to him. He held it close to his face, peering at it, and in a moment said, "It's a Worthington .38, number 63092T. If you insist on having it, Captain—illegally, as Mr. Goodwin correctly says—write out a receipt and I'll let you take it from me."

Barrow grunted. "To hell with the comedy. Keep the damn gun. Come on, Goodwin."

I shook my head. "I'm here legally too. What are you after? If you want a favor, ask for it. If you want to give orders, show me something signed by somebody. You know the rules as well as I do. In the meantime, don't touch me unless you're absolutely sure you can pick up anything you drop."

Waddell said, "We know the law some, in a rustic sort of way. A murder has been committed, and Captain Barrow wants to ask you some questions."

"Then let him ask. Or if he wants a private conference let him request my company and not yap at me." I transferred to Barrow. "Hell, I know what you want. I saw that ape that came in with you pointing me out. I know he saw me this afternoon alongside a pile of straw in the Holstein shed, talking with two acquaintances. I also know, by public rumor, that a dead man has been found under a pile of straw in that shed with a pitchfork sticking in him. I suppose it was the same pile of straw, I'm lucky that way. And you want to know why I was there and what I and my acquaintances were talking about and what was my motive for sticking the pitchfork into the man, and the doctor said the man had been dead two hours and six minutes and will I therefore give a timetable of my movements from 10 o'clock this morning up to 2:37 p.m. Right?"

"Right," Barrow said agreeably. "Only we're more interested in the dead man's movements than we are in yours. When did you see him last?"

I grinned. "Try again. I abandoned that trick years ago. First tell me who he is or was."

Barrow's eyes weren't wandering from my face. "His name was Howard Bronson."

"I'll be damned." I screwed up my lips and raised my brows in polite surprise. "Clyde Osgood's friend? Identified?"

"Yes. By Osgood and his daughter. When did you see him last?"

"At ten-thirty this morning, as he got out of Osgood's car in front of the hotel. Miss Osgood and Mr. Wolfe and I went on in the car."

"Did you know him well?"

"Never saw him before Monday afternoon."

"Any intimate relations with him?"

"Nope."

"Any close personal contacts with him?"

"Well—no."

"Well what?"

"Nothing. No."

"Any financial transactions? Did you pay him any money or did he pay you any?"

"No."

"Then will you explain how it happens that an empty brown leather wallet found in his pocket was covered with your fingerprints, inside and outside?"

Of course the boob had telegraphed the punch. If he hadn't, if he had fired that at me to begin with, he might have been gratified at a couple of stammers and a little hemming and hawing, but as it was he allowed me plenty of time for preparation.

I grinned at him. "Sure I'll explain. Last evening at Osgood's house I found a wallet on the veranda. I looked in it for papers to identify the owner, and found it was Bronson's, and returned it to him. It never occurred to me to wipe off my prints."

"Oh. You had it ready."

"Had what ready?" I demanded innocently. "The wallet?"

"The explanation."

"Yeah, I carry a big stock for the country trade." I compressed my lips at him. "For God's sake use your bean. If I had croaked the guy and frisked the wallet, or if I had found him dead and frisked it, would I have left my signature all over it? Do I strike you as being in that category? Maybe I can offer you a detail though. You say the wallet was empty. Last night when I found it, and when I returned it to him, it was bulging with a wad which I estimated roughly at 2000 bucks."

At that point Nero Wolfe's genius went into action. I say genius not because he concocted the stratagem, for that was only quick wit, but because he anticipated the need for it far enough ahead of time to get prepared. I didn't recognize it at the moment for what it was; all I saw, without paying it any attention, was that, apparently bored by a conversation he had no part in, he slipped the pistol into his coat pocket and picked up the sprayer and began fussing with the nozzle and the pressure handle.

"You advise me to use my bean," Barrow was saying. "I'll try. Did you remove anything from the wallet?"

"Today? I haven't seen it. I only found it once."

"Today or any other time. Did you?"

"No."

"Did you take anything from Bronson at all? His person or his effects?"

"No."

"Are you willing to submit to a search?"

My brain didn't exactly reel, but the wires buzzed. For half a second five or six alternatives chased each other around in a battle royal. Meanwhile I was treating Barrow to a grin to show how serene I was, and also, out of the corner of an eye, I was perceiving that Nero Wolfe's right index finger, resting half concealed by his coat on the pressure lever, was being wiggled at me. It was a busy moment. Hoping to God I had interpreted the wiggle correctly, I told Barrow affably, "Excuse the hesitation, but I'm trying to decide which would annoy you more, to deny you the courtesy and compel you to take steps, or let you go ahead and find nothing. Now that my gun is gone and you can't disarm me—"

The spray of nicotine and soap, full force under high pressure, hit him smack in the face.

He spluttered and squeaked and jumped aside, blinded. That was another busy moment. My hand shot into my breast pocket and out again and without stopping for reflection slipped my ostrich card case into the side coat pocket of District Attorney Waddell, who had stepped toward the captain with an ejaculation. Except for that I didn't move. Barrow grabbed for his handkerchief and dabbed at his eyes. There were murmurings from onlookers. Wolfe, offering his own handkerchief, said gravely:

"A thousand apologies, Captain. My stupid carelessness. It won't hurt you, of course, but nevertheless—"

"Shut it or I'll shut it for you." There were still pearly drops on Barrow's chin and ears, but he had his eyes wiped. He faced me and demanded savagely, "A goddam slick trick, huh? Where did you ditch it?"

"Ditch what? You're crazy."

"You're damn right I'm crazy." He whirled to Waddell: "What did he do when that fat slob sprayed my eyes shut?"

"Nothing," said Waddell. "He didn't do anything. He stood right here by me. He didn't move."

"I can add my assurance," Wolfe put in. "If he had moved I would have seen him."

Barrow glared at him savagely. "You're so slick you slide, huh?"

"I have apologized, sir."

"To hell with you. How'd you like to go along to the courthouse with us?"

Wolfe shook his head. "You're in a huff, Captain. I don't blame you, but I doubt if it's actionable. To arrest me for accidentally spraying you with soap would seem . . . well, impulsive—"

Barrow turned his back on him to confront Waddell. "You say he didn't move?"

"Goodwin? No."

"He didn't hand Wolfe anything?"

"Positively not. He wasn't within 10 feet of him."

"He didn't throw anything?"

"No."

A dozen or so onlookers had collected, down the aisle in either direction. Barrow raised his voice at them: "Did any of you see this man take anything from his pocket and hand it to the fat man or put it somewhere or throw it? Don't be afraid to speak up. I'm Captain Barrow and it's important."

There were head shakings and a few muttered negatives. A woman with a double chin said in a loud voice, "I was watching you, that spray in your face, it was like a scene in the movies, but if he'd done any throwing or anything like that I'm sure I'd have seen him because my eye takes in everything."

There were a couple of nervous giggles and Barrow abandoned his amateurs. He looked around, and I felt sorry for him. I still hadn't moved. There was no place within perhaps 6 feet where I could possibly have hidden anything. In the direction I faced were pots of orchid plants on the benches; behind me was the table of dahlia blooms in vases; both were way beyond my reach. I stood with my arms folded.

Barrow had pretty well regained his handsome and unflinching dignity. He composedly wiped with his handkerchief behind his ears and under his chin and told me: "I'm taking you to the courthouse for questioning in connection with the murder of Howard Bronson. If you're still trying to decide how to annoy me, it'll take me maybe twenty minutes to get a legal commitment as a material witness—"

"Permit me," Wolfe put in, purring. "We surely owe you some complaisance, Captain, after this regrettable accident. I don't believe I'd insist on a warrant, Archie. We really should cooperate."

"Whatever you say, boss."

"Go. After all, it is a little public here for a privy interview. I may join you later. —In the meantime, Mr. Waddell, if you can spare a few minutes, I'd like to tell you of a discovery I made last evening, touching both Clyde Osgood and Mr. Bronson. I questioned Bronson for nearly an hour, and I think you'll find it interesting."

"Well . . . I was going with Captain Barrow . . ."

Wolfe shrugged. "Now that Bronson has also been murdered, it is doubly interesting."

"What about it, Captain?"

"Suit yourself," Barrow told him. "You're the district attorney, you're in charge. I can handle Goodwin." He sounded as if all he required was a red-hot poker and a couple of thumbscrews. "Shall I go on?"

Waddell nodded. "I'll be along pretty soon."

I told Wolfe, "When the young lady comes for the orchids, tell her I've gone to pick huckleberries."

Walking the length of the main exhibits building to the exit, and through the crowds beyond the end of the grandstand, Barrow kept behind, with his left elbow about 10 inches back of my right one, proving that he had been to police school. A patrol car, with the top down and a trooper behind the wheel, was waiting there. I was instructed to get in with the driver and Barrow climbed in behind. His eyes weren't leaving me for a second, and I reflected that his hunch that I had something I would like to discard had probably been reinforced by Wolfe's performance with the sprayer.

In 5 minutes, in spite of the exposition traffic, we were pulling up at the courthouse. Instead of entering at the front, as with Osgood when calling on Waddell the day before, we went around to a side entrance that was on the ground level. The hall was dark and smelled of disinfectant and stale tobacco juice. The trooper preceding us turned the knob of a door marked SHERI F, with one F gone, and I followed him in with Barrow at my rear. It was a big dingy room with decrepit desks and chairs, at one desk in a corner being the only occupant, a bald-headed gentleman with a red face and gold-rimmed specs who nodded at us and said nothing.

"We're going through you," Barrow announced.

I nodded indifferently and struck a pose. I know that the whole included all its parts and that that was one of the parts, and it had been necessary for Wolfe to toss me to the dogs so that he could have a private interview with the district attorney's coat pocket. So I tolerated it, and got additional proof that they had been to police school. They did everything but rip my seams. When they had finished I returned the various items to their proper places, and sat down. Barrow stood and gazed down at me. I was surprised he didn't go and wash his face, because that nicotine and soap must have stung. Tough as they come, those weather-beaten babies.

"The mistake you made," I told him, "was coming in there breathing fire. Nero Wolfe and I are respectable law-abiding detectives."

He grunted. "Forget it. I'd give a month's pay to know how you did it, and maybe I'll find out sometime, but not now. I'm not going to try any hammering. Not at present." He glanced to see that the trooper was ready at a desk with notebook and pencil. "I just want to know a few things. Do you maintain that you took nothing from Bronson at any time?"

"I do."

"Did you suspect him of being implicated in the murder of Clyde Osgood?"

"You've got the wrong party. Mr. Wolfe does all the suspecting for the firm, ask him. I'm the office boy."

"Do you refuse to answer?"

"No indeed. If you want to know whether I personally suspected Bronson of murder, the reply is no. No known motive."

"Wasn't there anything in his relations with Clyde that might have supplied a motive?"

"Search me. You're wasting time. Day before yesterday at 2 o'clock the Osgoods and Pratts and Bronson were all complete strangers to Mr. Wolfe and me. Our only interest in any of them is that Osgood hired us to investigate the murder of his son. You started investigating simultaneously. If you're discouraged with what you've collected and want our crop as a handout, you'll have to go to Mr. Wolfe. You said you wanted to question me in connection with the murder of Howard Bronson."

"That's what I'm doing."

"Go ahead."

He kicked a chair around and sat down. "Wolfe interviewed Bronson last night. What was said at that interview?"

"Ask Mr. Wolfe."

"Do you refuse to answer?"

"I do, you know. I'm a workingman and don't want to lose my job."

"Neither do I. I'm working on a murder, Goodwin."

"So am I."

"Were you working on it when you entered the shed this afternoon where Bronson was killed?"

"No, not at that moment. I was waiting for Lew Bennett to tear himself away from the judging lot. I happened to see Nancy Osgood going into the shed and followed her out of curiosity. I found her in there in the stall talking to Jimmy Pratt. I knew her old man would be sore if he heard of it, which would have been too bad under the circumstances, so I advised them to postpone it and scatter, and they did so, and I went back to the Methodist tent where my employer was."

"How did they and you happen to pick the spot where Bronson's body was?"

"I didn't pick it, I found them there. I don't know why they picked it, but it would seem likely that it wasn't cause and effect. I imagine they would have chosen some other spot if they had known what was under the pile of straw."

"Did you know what was under it?"

"I'll give you three guesses."

"Did you?"

"No."

"Why were you so eager to get them out of there in a hurry?"

"I wouldn't say I was eager. It struck me they were fairly dumb to feed gossip at this particular time."

"You wouldn't say that you were eager to keep it quiet that they had been there, and you had?"

"Eager? Nope. Put it that I was inclined to feel it was desirable."

"Then why did you bribe the shed attendant?"

Of course he had telegraphed it again. But even so it was an awkward and undesirable question.

"I was waiting for that," I told him. "Now you have got me where it hurts, because the only explanation I can offer, which is the true one, is loony. There are times when I feel kittenish, and that was one. I'll give it to you verbatim." I did so, words and music, repeating the conversation just as it had occurred, up to the departure of the beneficiary. "There," I said, "Robin Hood, his sign. And when a corpse was discovered there, the louse thought I had been bribing him with a measly tenspot, and so did you. I swear to God I'll lay for him tonight and take it away from him."

Barrow grunted. "You're good at explanations. The fingerprints on the wallet. I suppose a man like Bronson would leave a wallet containing two thousand dollars lying around on a veranda. Now this. Do you realize how good you are?"

"I told you it was loony. But lacking evidence to the contrary, you might assume that I'm sane. Do I look like a goof who would try to gag a stranger in a case of murder with a ten dollar note? Should I start serious bribing around here, the per capita income of this county would shoot up like a skyrocket. And by the way, does that clodhopper say that I made any suggestions about silence or even discretion?"

"We're all clodhoppers around here. You try telling a jury of clodhoppers that you're in the habit of tossing out ten dollar bills for the comic effect."

I snorted. "Unveil it, brother. What jury? My peers sitting on my life? Honest, are you as batty as that?"

"No." The Captain squinted at me and rubbed a spot on the side of his neck. "No, Goodwin, I'm not. I'm not looking forward to the pleasure of hearing a jury's opinion of you. Nor do I bear any grudge because you and your boss started the stink on the Osgood thing. I don't care how slick you are or where you come from or how much you soak Osgood for, but now that the bag has been opened it is going to be emptied. Right to the bottom. Do you understand that?"

"Go ahead and jiggle it."

"I'm going to. And nothing's going to roll out of my sight while I'm not looking. You say ask Wolfe, and I'm going to, but right now I'm asking you. Are you going to talk or not?"

"My God, my throat's sore now."

"Yeah. I've got the wallet with your prints all over it. I've got the bill you gave the shed attendant. Are you going to tell me what you got from Bronson and where it is?"

"You're just encouraging me to lie, Captain."

"All right, I'll encourage you some more. This morning a sheriff's deputy was in the hotel lobby when Bronson entered. When Bronson went to a phone booth and put in a New York call, the deputy got himself plugged in on another line. He heard

Bronson tell somebody in New York that a man named Goodwin had poked him in the jaw and taken the receipt from him, but that he expected to pull it off anyway. Well?"

"Gee," I said, "that's swell. All you have to do is have the New York cops grab the somebody and run him through the coffee grinder—"

"Much obliged. What was the receipt for and where is it?"

I shook my head. "The deputy must have heard wrong. Maybe the name was Doodwin or Goldstein or DiMaggio—"

"I *would* like to clip you. Jesus, I would enjoy stretching you out." Barrow breathed. "Are you going to spill it?"

"Sorry, nothing to spill."

"On the hotel register you wrote your first name as Archie. Is that correct?"

"Yep."

He turned to his colleague. "Bill, you'll find Judge Hutchins waiting upstairs. Run up and swear out a material witness commitment. Archie Goodwin. Hurry down with it, we've got to shake a leg."

I raised the brows. The cossack made it snappy. I asked, "How's the accommodations?"

"Fair. A little crowded on account of the exposition. Any time you're ready to talk turkey—"

"No speak English. This will get you a row of ciphers and the finger of scorn and a bellyache."

He merely looked unflinching. We sat. In a few minutes his pal returned with a document, and I asked to see it and was obliged. Barrow took it and asked me to come on, and I went between them down the dark hall, around a corner and along another hall,

and into another office smaller than the one we had
left but not so dingy, with WARDEN on the door. A
sleepy-looking plump guy sat at a desk which had a
vase of flowers on it besides miscellany. He let out a
low growl when he saw us, like a dog being disturbed
in the middle of comfort. Barrow handed him the paper and told him:

"Material witness in the Bronson case. We've gone
through him; I suppose you'll want to take his jack-
knife. I'll stop in later for my copy or get it in the
morning. Any time he asks for me, day or night, I
want to see him."

The warden pushed a button on his desk, ran his
eyes over the paper, looked at me, and cackled. "By
golly, bud, you should have put on some old clothes.
The valley service here is terrible."

Chapter 17

It was certainly an antique. Apparently it was a whole wing of the ground floor of the courthouse. The cells faced each other, two rows of them, one on either side of a long corridor. Mine was two doors from the far end. My cellmate was a chap in a dark blue suit with a pointed nose and sharp brown eyes and a thick mop of well-brushed hair. At the time I was locked in, which was around 6 o'clock, he was sitting on one of the cots brushing the hair. The dim light from the little barred window, too high to see out of, made things seem gloomy. We exchanged greetings and he went on brushing. Pretty soon he asked:

"Got any cards or dice with you?"

"Nope."

"They didn't strip you, did they?"

"They took my knife."

He put the brush down and nodded. "You can't kick on that. Were you working out at the grounds? I've never seen you around before."

"You wouldn't. My name is Archie Goodwin, and I'm from New York and am being squeezed." I waved a hand and sat down on the other cot, which was covered with a dirty gray blanket. "Forget it. Were you working out at the grounds?"

"I was until yesterday afternoon. Spoon-bean. Are you hungry?"

"I could eat. But I hesitate to send in an order—"

"Oh, not on the house. No. They feed at 5, and it's the usual. But if you're hungry and happen to have a little jack . . ."

"Go ahead."

He went over to the door and tapped three times with his fingernail on one of the iron bars, waited a second, and tapped twice. In a couple of minutes slow footsteps sounded in the corridor, and as they got to our apartment my mate said in a tone restrained but not particularly secretive, "Here, Slim."

I got up and ambled across. It wasn't the keeper who had escorted me in, but a tall skinny object with an Adam's apple as big as a goose egg. I got out the Nero Wolfe expense wallet, extracted a dollar bill, and told him that I required two ham sandwiches and a chocolate egg malted. He took it but shook his head and said it wasn't enough. I told him I knew that but hadn't wanted to spoil him, and parted from another one, and asked him to include 5 evening papers in the order.

By the time he returned, in a quarter of an hour, my mate and I were old friends. His name was Basil Graham, and his firsthand knowledge of geography and county jails was extensive. I spread my lunch out on the cot with a sheet of the newspaper for a tablecloth, and it wasn't until the last crumb had disappeared that he made a proposal which might have withered the friendship in the bud if I hadn't been firm. His preparations were simple but interesting. From under the blanket of his cot he produced three teaspoons of the five and dime variety, and a small white bean. Then he came over and picked up one of my newspapers and asked, "May I?" I nodded. He put the newspaper on the floor and sat on it, and in front of him, on the concrete, ranged the three teaspoons in a row, bottoms up. He had nifty fingers. Under one of the spoons he put the bean and then looked up at me like the friend he was.

"You understand," he said, "I'm just showing you how it's done. It will pass the time. Sometimes the hand is quicker, sometimes the eye is quicker. It's not a game of chance, but a game of skill. Your eye against my hand. Your eye may be quicker than my hand, and we can only tell by trying. It never hurts to try. Which spoon is the bean under?"

I told him, and it was. He tried again, his fingers darting, and again it was. The next time it wasn't. The next three times it was, and he began to act flustered and surprised and displeased with himself.

I shook my head. "Don't do it, Basil," I said regretfully. "I'm not a wise guy exactly, but I'm a tightwad. If you go on working up indignation at yourself because my eye is so much quicker than your hand, you might get so upset you would actually offer to make a bet on it, and I would have to refuse. As a matter of fact, you are extremely good, both at manipulating the bean and at getting upset, but the currency you saw in the wallet is not my own, and even if it was I'm a tightwad."

"It don't hurt to try, does it? I just want to see—"
"No, I don't lather."

He cheerfully put the spoons and the bean away, and the friendship was saved.

It began to get dark in the cell, and after a while the lights were turned on. Somehow that only made it gloomier, since there was no light in the cell itself. The only way I could have read the paper, except for the headlines, which were screaming murder, would have been to hold it up against the bars of the door to catch the light from the corridor, so I gave it up and devoted myself to Basil. He was certainly a good-natured soul, for he had been nabbed after only one day's work at the exposition and expected to be fined 50 samoleons on the morrow, but I suppose if you embrace spoonbean as a career you have to be a philosopher to begin with. The inside of my nose was beginning to smart from the atmosphere. In a cell across the corridor someone started to sing in a thin tenor, *I'm wearing my heart away for you, it cries out may your love be true,* and from further down the line groans sounded, interrupted by a voice like a file growling, "Let him sing, let him sing, what the hell, it's beautiful."

Basil shrugged. "Just bums," he said tolerantly.

My wrist watch said 10 minutes to 8 when footsteps stopped at our address again, a key was turned in the lock, and the door swung open. A keeper I hadn't seen before stood in the gap and said, "Goodwin? You're wanted." He stepped aside to let me out, relocked the door, and let me precede him down the corridor. "Warden's office," he grunted.

Three men were standing in the office: Nero Wolfe, under self-imposed restraint, Frederick Osgood, scowling, and the warden, looking disturbed. I told them good evening. Osgood said, "Come on, Ollie, we'll step outside." The warden muttered something about the rules, Osgood got impatient and brusque, and out they went.

Wolfe stood and looked at me with his lips compressed. "Well?" he demanded. "Where were your wits?"

"Sure," I said bitterly, "brazen it out. Wits my eye. Fingerprints on the wallet. I bribed the shed attendant with ten bucks of Jimmy Pratt's money, which I'll explain to you some day if I don't rot in this dungeon. But chiefly, a deputy sheriff says that this morning at the hotel he heard Bronson tell somebody in New York on the telephone that a man named Goodwin poked him in the jaw and took a receipt away from him. Ha ha ha. Did you ever hear anything so droll? Even so, they don't think I'm a murderer. They only think I'm reticent. They're going to break my will. Of course if I *had* taken a receipt from Bronson and if they should find it—"

Wolfe shook his head. "Since you didn't, they can't. Which reminds me . . ."

His hand went into his pocket and came out again with my card case in it. I took it and inspected it, saw that it contained its proper items and nothing else, and put it where it belonged.

"Thanks. No trouble finding it?"

"None. It was quite simple. I had a talk with Mr. Waddell after you left and told him of my interview with Mr. Bronson last evening whatever I thought might be helpful. Then he went, and I telephoned the courthouse and could learn nothing. I found myself marooned. Finally I succeeded in locating Mr. Osgood, and his daughter came for me. She had been questioned, but not, I imagine, with great severity—ex-

cept by her father. Mr. Osgood is difficult. He
suspects you of arranging the meeting between his
daughter and Mr. Pratt's nephew, God knows why.
Watch him when he comes back in here; he might
even leap at you. He agreed to control himself if I
would question you about it."

"Good. You came to question me. I was wondering
what you came for."

"For one thing . . ." He hesitated, which was
rare. He went on, "For one thing, I came to bring that
package for you. The Osgood housekeeper kindly prepared it."

I looked and saw a four-bushel bundle, wrapped in
brown paper, on a table. "Saws and rope ladders?" I
demanded.

He said nothing. I went and tore some of the paper
off and found that it contained a pillow, a pair of blan-
kets, and sheets. I returned to confront Wolfe.

"So," I said. "So that's the way it is. I believe you
mentioned wits a minute ago?"

He muttered ferociously, "Shut up. It has never
happened before. I have telephoned, I have roared
and rushed headlong, and Mr. Waddell cannot be
found. Since I learned you were detained—he's deliberately hiding from me, I'm convinced of it. The judge
won't set bail without the concurrence of the District
Attorney. We don't want bail anyway. Pfui! Bail for
my confidential assistant! Wait! Wait till I find him!"

"Uh-huh. You wait at Osgood's, and I wait in a
fetid cell with a dangerous felon for a mate. By
heaven, I will play spoon-bean with your money. As
for the package you kindly brought, take it back to
the housekeeper. God knows how long I'll be here,

and I don't want to start in by getting a reputation as a sissy. I can take it, and it looks like I'm going to."

"You spoke of money. That was my second reason for coming."

"I know, you never carry any. How much do you want?"

"Well . . . twenty dollars. I want to assure you, Archie—"

"Don't bother." I got out the expense wallet and handed him a bill. "I can assure you that I shall come out of here with bugs—"

"Once when I was working for the Austrian government I was thrown into jail in Bulgaria—"

I strode to the door and pulled it open and bellowed into the hall: "Oh, warden! I'm escaping!"

He appeared from somewhere in a lumbering trot, stumbling. Behind him came Osgood, looking startled. From the other direction came the sound of a gallop, and that proved to be the keeper, with a revolver in his hand. I grinned at them: "April fool. Show me to my room. I'm sleepy. It's the country air."

Osgood rumbled, "Clown." The warden looked relieved. I tossed a cheery good night to Wolfe over my shoulder, and started off down the hall with the keeper trailing me.

Basil was seated on his cot brushing his hair. He asked me what the yelling had been for and I told him I had had a fit. I asked him what time the lights went out and he told me 9 o'clock, so I proceeded to get my bed made. Having had the forethought to order 5 copies of the newspaper, there was more than enough to cover the cot entirely with a double thickness. Basil suspended the brushing momentarily to watch me arranging it with ample laps, and when I was nearly through he observed that it would rustle so much that I wouldn't be able to sleep and neither would he. I replied that when I once got set I was as dead as a log, and he remarked in a sinister tone that it might not turn out that way in my present quarters. I finished the job anyhow. Down the line somewhere two voices were raised in an argument as to whether February 22nd was a national holiday, and others joined in.

It was approaching 9 o'clock when the key was turned in our lock again and the keeper appeared in the door and told me I was wanted.

"Cripes," Basil said, "we'll have to install a telephone."

It couldn't be Wolfe, I thought. There was no one else it could be except Waddell or Barrow, and there wasn't a chance of getting put on the sidewalk by them, and if they wanted to harry me they could damn well wait until morning. I decided to be contrary.

"Whoever it is, tell him I've gone to bed."

Even in the dim light, I seemed to perceive that the keeper looked disappointed. He asked, "Don't you want to see her?"

"Her?"

"It's your sister."

"Oh. I'll be derned. My dear sister."

My tone must have been good, for there was no audible derision as for the second time I preceded the keeper along the corridor. I went for two reasons, the first being curiosity. It might conceivably be Nancy or Caroline, but my guess was Lily, and the only way of finding out was to go and see. Second, I felt I should cooperate. 9 o'clock at night was no visiting time at a jail, and if it was Lily she must have been liberal in her negotiations with the warden, and I hated to see money wasted. It was the first time I could remember that anyone had paid cash to have a look at me, and I thought it was touching. So I trotted along.

It was Lily. The warden was at his desk, and stayed there, and the keeper closed the door and stood in front of it. Lily was in a chair in a dark corner, and I crossed to her.

"Hello, sis." I sat down.

"You know," she said, "I was wondering last night what would be the best thing to do with you, but it never occurred to me to lock you up. When you get out of here I'll try it. When will that be, by the way?"

"No telling. In time to spend Christmas at home, I hope. How are dad and ma and Oscar and Violet and Arthur—"

"Fine. Is it cosy?"

"Marvelous."

"Have you had anything to eat?"

"Plenty. There's a caterer."

"Have you got money?"

"Sure, how much do you want?"

She shook her head. "No, really. I'm flush." She opened her bag.

I reached and shut it. "No, you don't. Jimmy Pratt gave me 10 dollars today and that's partly why I'm here. Money is the root of all evil. Is there anything I can do for you?"

"Why, Escamillo. I came to see you."

"I'm aware of that. Did you bring any bedding?"

"No, but I can get some. Do you want some?"

"No, thanks. I was just curious. I have plenty of newspaper. But would you like to do me a favor?"

"I won't sleep if I can't do you a favor."

"Will you be up at midnight?"

"I can stay up."

"Do so. At midnight get Osgood's on the phone and ask to speak to Mr. Nero Wolfe. Tell him you're Mrs. Titus Goodwin and that you are at the Crowfield Hotel, having just come in an airplane from Cleveland, Ohio. Tell him that you got a telegram from your son Archie saying that he is in jail, stranded and abandoned and in despair. Tell him you want to know what the hell he had me put in jail for and you'll have the law on him, and you'll expect to see him first thing in the morning and he must be prepared to rectify his ghastly mistake without delay. And atone for it. Tell him he'll have to atone for it." I considered. "I guess that will do."

She nodded. "I've got it. Is any of it straight?"

"No, it's firecrackers."

"Then why don't I rout him out tonight? Make him come to the hotel right away and look for me. I mean at midnight."

"My God, no. He'd kill me. That will be sufficient. You follow instructions."

"I will. Anything else?"

"Nope."

"Kiss me."

"I can't until I wash my face. Anyway, I told you that wasn't a precedent. I have to be careful. I kissed a girl once in the subway and when she came to she was on top of the Empire State Building. She had floated out through a grating and right on up."

"Goodness. Did you ever send one clear to heaven?"

"The place is full of them."

"When are you going to get out of here?"

"I don't know. You might ask Wolfe on the phone tonight."

"Well." She looked at me, and I was reminded how she had peeled me like a potato in the Methodist tent. "What I really came for. Any bail, any amount, I could have it arranged for by 11 o'clock in the morning. Shall I?"

"I might come high."

"I said any amount."

"I wouldn't bother. It would make Wolfe jealous. Thanks just the same."

The keeper's hoarse voice sounded:

"After 9 o'clock, chief. What about the lights?"

I got up and told him, "Okay, I'll help you. Good night, sis."

Chapter 18

At 9 o'clock Thursday morning Basil sat on the edge of his cot brushing his hair. I sat on the edge of mine, with the newspapers still on it but a good deal the worse for wear, scratching my shoulder and my thigh and my right side and my left arm, with my forehead wrinkled in concentration, trying to remember the title of a book on prison reform which I had observed on Wolfe's library shelves at home but had never bothered to look at. It was a shame I hadn't read it because if I had I would have been much better prepared for a project which I had already got a pretty good start on. The idea of the project had occurred to me during breakfast for which meal I had limited myself to the common fare of my fellows for the sake of the experience, and I had got the start during the fifteen minutes from 8:30 to 8:45, when we had all been in the corridor together for what was called morning exercise, with a keeper and an ostentatious gun stationed at the open end.

Basil asked, "How many have we got?"

I told him four signed up and three more practically certain. I gave up trying to remember the
name of the book and took my memo pad from my
pocket and looked over the sheets I had written
on:

For the Warden, the District Attorney,
the Attorney-General, the State Legislature,
and the Governor.

MINIMUM BASIC DEMANDS
OF THE CROWFIELD COUNTY
PRISONERS UNION

1. Recognition of the C.C.P.U.
2. The closed shop.
3. Collective bargaining on all controversial
matters except date of release and possession by
our members of objects which could be used for
attack or escape.
4. No lockouts.
5. Food. (Food may be defined as nutritive material absorbed or taken into the body of an or-
ganism which serves for purposes of growth,
work or repair, and for the maintenance of the
vital processes.) We don't get any.
6. Running water in all cells.
7. Abolition of all animals smaller than rabbits.
8. Cell buckets of first grade enamel with good
lids.
9. Daily inspection of bedding by a committee of
public-spirited citizens, with one member a
woman.
10. Adequate supply of checkers and dominoes.
11. Soap which is free of Essence of Nettles, or
whatever it is that it now contains.

12. Appointment by our President of a Committee on Bathing, with power to enforce decisions. Signed this 15th day of September, 1938.

Archie Goodwin, *President.*

Basil Graham, *Vice-President, Secretary and Treasurer.*

Four other signatures followed.

I looked up with a dissatisfied frown. It was all right for a start, but there were 21 people inhabiting that corridor by actual count. I said in a resolute tone, "It has to be 100 per cent before nightfall. The fact is, Basil, you may be all right as Vice-President and/or Secretary and/or Treasurer, but you're no damn good as an agitator. You didn't get anybody."

He put the brush down. "Well," he said, "you made 3 mistakes. Demand number 9 will have to be amended by striking out the last five words. They simply don't like the idea of a woman poking around the cells. Demand number 12 is bad in toto. Even when he's out of jail a man resents having his personal liberties interfered with, and when he's in jail the feeling is greatly intensified. But worst of all was your offering them a dime apiece to join. That made them suspicious and we're going to have a hard time overcoming it."

"I don't see you making any strenuous effort."

"Is that so. I could make a suggestion right now. Are you game to step it up to two bits per capita?"

"But you said—"

"Never mind what I said. Are you?"

"Well . . ." I figured it. "Three seventy-five. Yes."

"But you wouldn't play spoon-bean, a game of skill. It's a funny world." He arose and approached.

"Give me that ultimatum." I tore off the sheet and handed it to him and he went to the door and tapped on a bar with his fingernail, 3 and 2. In a minute the skinny one with the Adam's apple appeared and Basil began talking to him in a low tone. I got up and sauntered over to listen.

"Tell them," Basil said, "that the offer of a dime to join is withdrawn. Tell them that the privilege of being charter members expires at noon and after that we may let them in and we may not. Tell them that our platform is Brotherhood, Universal Suffrage, and Freedom. Tell—"

"Universal Suffering?"

"No. Suf—leave that one out. Brotherhood and Freedom. Tell them that if they don't like the idea of a public-spirited woman coming around and the provisions with regard to bathing, the only way these demands can be changed is by the membership of the C. C. P. U., which is organized and functioning, and if they don't become members they can't help change them. Incidentally, our President will pay you two bits for each and every one you get to sign."

"Two bits? That's on the level?"

"Absolutely. Wait a minute, come back here. Since you're a trusty and are therefore technically one of us, you're eligible to join yourself if you want to. But you don't get any two bits for signing yourself up. It wouldn't be ethical. Would it, President Goodwin? Wouldn't that be *e pluribus unum corpus delicti*?"

"Right."

"Okay. Go ahead, Slim. Noon is the deadline."

Basil went back and sat down and picked up the brush. "No damn good as an agitator?" he inquired sarcastically.

"As an agitator, above average," I admitted. "As a treasurer, only so-so. You're inclined to overdraw."

I don't know to this day what the C. C. P. U. membership amounted to at its peak. When Slim had got 4 new members signed up he came to our cell and requested a dollar before proceeding further, and I paid him, and by 10 o'clock he had 4 more and got another dollar, but at that point I was removed from the scene by a keeper coming to get me. I started out, but Basil interposed to say that I had better leave the other $1.75 with him, since I had assumed the obligation, just in case. I told him he shouldn't be so pessimistic about the President but agreed that his point was valid, and shelled out.

Captain Barrow, still with no sign of flinching, was waiting in the hall outside the warden's office. He told me curtly to come on, and from behind my elbow directed me out of that wing of the building, up two flights of stairs, and along an upper corridor to a door which I had entered on Tuesday afternoon in the company of Osgood and Wolfe. We passed through the anteroom to the inner chamber, and there sat District Attorney Waddell at his desk, with bleary eyes that made him look pudgier than ever.

I marched up to the desk and told him offensively, "Nero Wolfe wants to see you, mister."

Barrow snarled, "Sit down, you."

I sat, and scratched my thigh and shoulder and side and arm ostentatiously.

Waddell demanded, "What about it? Have you changed your mind?"

"Yes," I said, "I have. I used to think that the people who make speeches and write books about prison reform are all sentimental softies, but no more. They may or may not—"

"Turn it off," Barrow growled. "And quit scratching."

Waddell said sternly, "I advise you not to be flippant. We have evidence that you possess vital information in a murder case. We want it." He laid a fist on his desk and leaned forward. "We're going to get it."

I grinned at him. "I'm sorry, you'll have to excuse me. My head is fairly buzzing with this new idea I've got and I can't think of anything else, not even murder." I erased the grin and pointed a finger at him and made my tone ominous: "Your head will soon be buzzing too. Don't think it won't. The C. C. P. U. is going to clean up, and how would you like to be kicked out of office?"

"Bah. You damn fool. Do you think Osgood runs this county? What's the C. C. P. U.?"

I knew he'd ask, since elected persons are always morbid about organizations. I told him impressively, "The Crowfield County Prisoners Union. I'm President. We'll be 100 percent by noon. Our demands include—"

I stopped and got my feet under my chair ready for leverage, because Barrow had got up and taken two steps and from his expression I thought for a second he was going to haul off and aim one. He halted and said slowly, "Don't get scared, I couldn't do it here. But there's a room down in the basement or I could take you out to the barracks. Get this. You cut the comedy."

I shrugged. "If you fellows really want to talk seriously, I'll tell you something. Do you?"

"You'll find out how serious we are before we finish with you."

"Okay. First, if you think you can scare me by threats about basements you're too dumb for a mother's tears. Common sense is against it, the probabilities are against it, and I'm against it. Second, the comedy. You asked for it by starting it, yesterday afternoon. You have no judgment. It's perfectly true that there are people who can be opened up by making faces at them and talking loud, but if I was one of them how long do you think I'd last as Nero Wolfe's favorite employee, eating with him at his table? Look at me, anyhow! Can't you tell one kind of mug from another kind? Third, the situation we're in. It's so simple I understand it myself. You think I have knowledge which is your legal property because you're cops working on a murder, and I say I haven't. Under those circumstances, what can I do? I can keep my mouth shut. What can you do? You can arrest me and put me under bond to appear on demand. Finally, when you've gathered up everything you can find and put it in order, you can either pin something on me, like obstruction of justice or accessory or perjury if I've been under oath, or any of that crap, or you can't. I return for a moment to your objection to my comedy. You deserved it because you've acted like a pair of comics yourselves."

I turned my palms up. "Were any of the words too long for you?"

Barrow sat down and looked at Waddell. The District Attorney said, "We don't think you have knowledge of facts, we know you have. And that's no comedy. Will you give them to us?"

"Nothing to give."

"Do you know your jeopardy? Have you had legal advice?"

"I don't need it. Didn't you hear my lecture? Find a lawyer that can beat it."

"You mentioned a bond. If you apply for release on bail, I'll oppose it. If your application is granted, it will be as high as I can make it."

"That's jake. Don't start worrying your little head about that on top of all your other troubles. I don't believe a rustic judge can look me in the eye and hold me without bail. The amount is a matter of indifference. My sister's father is a rich sewer tycoon."

"Your father? Where?"

"I said my sister's father. My family connections are none of your business, and besides, they're too complicated for you to understand. He is also occasionally my mother's father, on account of the fact that on the telephone last night my sister was my mother. But he isn't my father because I've never met him."

Barrow's head was twisted with his eyes fixed on me searchingly. "By God, I don't know," he said in a tone of doubtful surprise. "Maybe we ought to have Doc Sackett examine you."

Waddell disagreed. "It would cost 5 dollars and it's not worth it. Put him back in the cooler. If he's starting any trouble down there with this C. C. P. U. stuff, tell Ollie to put him in solitary. Tell Ollie he'd better investigate—"

The door popped open and Nero Wolfe walked in.

He looked neat and rested, with a clean yellow shirt on and the brown tie with tan stripes which Constanza Berin had sent him from Paris, but his shoes hadn't been shined. My glance took in those details as he crossed the room to us with his customary unhurried waddle. I scratched my leg furiously.

He stopped in front of me and demanded, "What are you doing? What's the matter?"

"Nothing. I itch."

"Look at your coat. Look at your trousers. Did you sleep in them?"

"What do you think I slept in, silken raiment? I'm glad you stopped in, it's nice to see you. We've been chatting. They're just sending me back to the you know. Did you hear from my mother? She's stricken."

He muttered, "Pfui," turned from me and looked at the other two and said good morning, and cast his eyes around. Then he took a step toward Barrow and said in his best manner, "Excuse me, Captain, but you have the only chair that is endurable for me. I'm sure you wouldn't mind changing." Barrow opened his mouth, but shut it again and got up and moved.

Wolfe nodded thanks, sat down, and directed a composed gaze at the district attorney. "You're a hard man to catch, sir," he observed. "I spent hours last evening trying to find you. I even suspect I was being evaded."

"I was busy."

"Indeed. To any effect?"

Barrow growled. Waddell leaned forward again with his fist on his desk. "Look here, Wolfe," he said in a nasty tone. "I've concluded you're no better than a waste of time, and probably worse. Thinking over what you told me about your talk with Bronson, what does it add up to? Zero. You were stringing me. You talk about evading! For the present I've only got one thing for you: a piece of advice. Either instruct your man here to open up and spill it, or do so yourself."

Wolfe sighed. "You're in a huff. Yesterday Captain Barrow, now you. You gentlemen are extraordinarily touchy."

"I'm touchy enough to know when I'm being strung. I don't enjoy it. And you're making a mistake when you figure that with Fred Osgood behind you, you can get away with anything you want to. Osgood may have owned this county once, but not any more, and he may be headed for a disagreeable surprise himself."

"I know." Wolfe was mild, and look resigned. "It's incredible, but judging from rumors that have reached Mr. Osgood you are actually entertaining a theory that Bronson killed his son, and the killing of Bronson was an eye for an eye. Mr. Waddell, that is infantile. It is so obviously infantile that I refuse to expound it for you. And your suggestion that I rely on Mr. Osgood's position and influence to protect me from penalties I have incurred is equally infantile. If I palaver with you at all—"

"You don't need to," Waddell snapped. "Peddle it somewhere else." Abruptly he stood up. "For two cents I'd stick you in with Goodwin. Beat it. On out. The next time I listen to you it will be in a courtroom. Take Goodwin down, Captain."

"Oh, no." Wolfe was still mild. "No, indeed. I bothered to see you only on Mr. Goodwin's account. You'll listen to me now."

"And who'll tell me why?"

"I will. Because I know who murdered Clyde Osgood and Howard Bronson, and you don't."

Barrow straightened. Waddell stared. I grinned, and wished Basil was there to tell me which spoon the bean was under.

"Furthermore," Wolfe went on quietly, "there is a very slim chance that you could ever find out, and no chance at all that you would ever be able to prove it. I have already found out, and I shall soon have proof. Under the circumstances, I should say it is even your duty to listen to me."

Barrow snapped, "I'd suggest having a judge listen to you."

"Pfui. For shame, Captain! You mean threaten me with the same treatment you have given Mr. Goodwin? I merely tell the judge I blathered. If he proves to be also an imbecile and holds me, I procure bail and then what do you do? You are helpless. I assure you—"

Waddell exploded, "It's a goddam cheap bluff!"

Wolfe grimaced. "Please, sir. My reputation . . . but no, I have too much respect for my reputation—"

"You say you *know* who murdered Clyde Osgood? And Bronson?"

"I do."

"Then by God you're right. I'll say I'll listen to you." Waddell sat down and pulled his phone over, and after a moment barked into it, "Send Phillips in."

Wolfe raised his brows. "Phillips?"

"Stenographer."

Wolfe shook his head. "Oh, no. You misunderstand. I only came for Mr. Goodwin. I need him."

"You do? So do we. We're keeping him. I repeat to you what I've told him, if there's an application for bail I'll oppose it."

The door opened and a young man with pimples appeared. Waddell nodded at him and he took a chair, opened his notebook, poised his pen, and inquired, "Names?" Waddell muttered at him, "Later. Take it."

Wolfe, disregarding the performance, said in a satisfied tone, "Now we've arrived at the point. It's Mr. Goodwin I want. If you hadn't eluded me last night I'd have got him then. Here are the alternatives for you to choose from. It is simplified for me by the fact that the sheriff, Mr. Lake, happens to be a protégé of Mr. Osgood's, while you are not. I understand you and Mr. Lake are inclined to pull in opposite directions.

"First. Release Mr. Goodwin at once. With his help I shall shortly have my proof perfected, and I'll deliver it to you, with the murderer, alive or dead.

"Second. Refuse to release Mr. Goodwin. Keep him. Without his help and therefore with more difficulty, I'll get the proof anyway, and it and the murderer will go to Mr. Lake. I am told that the *Crowfield Daily Journal* will be glad to cooperate with him and see that a full and correct account of his achievement is published, which is fortunate, for the public deserves to know what it gets for the money it pays its servants. It's a stroke of luck for you that you have Mr. Goodwin. But for that, I wouldn't be bothering with you at all."

Wolfe regarded the district attorney inquiringly. "Your choice, sir?"

I grinned. "He means take your pick."

Barrow growled at me, "Close your trap."

Waddell declared, "I still think it's a bluff."

Wolfe lifted his shoulders a quarter of an inch and dropped them. "Then it's Mr. Lake."

"You said you know who murdered Clyde Osgood

and Howard Bronson. Do you mean one man committed both crimes?"

"That won't do. You get information after my assistant is released, not before,—and when I'm ready
to give it."

"In a year or two, huh?"

"Hardly that long. Say within 24 hours. Less than
that, I hope."

"And you actually know who the murderer is and
you've got evidence?"

"Yes, to the first. I'll have satisfactory evidence."

"What kind of evidence?"

Wolfe shook his head. "I tell you it won't do. I'm
not playing a guessing game, and I won't be pumped."

"Convincing evidence?"

"Conclusive."

Waddell sat back, pulled at his ear, and said nothing. Finally he turned to the stenographer and told
him, "Give me that notebook and beat it." That command having been obeyed, he sat again a minute and
then looked at Barrow and demanded sourly, "What
about it, Captain? What the hell are we going to do?"

"I don't know." Barrow compressed his lips. "I
know what I'd like to do."

"That's a big help. You've had 6 or 8 men on this
thing and they haven't dug up a single solitary frag-
ment, and this smart elephant knows who did it and
will have conclusive evidence within 24 hours. So he
says." Waddell suddenly jerked up his chin and
whirled to Wolfe: "Who knows it besides you? If Lake
or any of his deputies have been holding out on me—"

"No," Wolfe assured him. "That's all right. They're
in the boat with you and Captain Barrow, with no
hooks and no bait."

"Then when did you pick it up? Where have you been? Goodwin certainly didn't help any, since we collared him soon after Bronson's body was found. By God, if this is a stall . . ."

Wolfe shook his head. "Please. I've known who killed Clyde Osgood since Monday night; I knew it as soon as I saw the bull's face; and I knew the motive. Your incredulous stare only makes you look foolish. Likewise with Mr. Bronson; the thing was obvious."

"You knew all about it when you were sitting there in that chair Tuesday afternoon? Talking to me, the district attorney?"

"Yes. But there was no evidence—or rather, there was, but before I could reach it it had been destroyed. Now I must find a substitute for it, and shall."

"What was the evidence that was destroyed?"

"Not now. It's nearly 11 o'clock, and Mr. Goodwin and I must be going. We have work to do. By the way, I don't want to be annoyed by surveillance. It will be futile, and if we're followed I shall consider myself released from the bargain."

"Will you give me your word of honor that you'll do just what you've agreed to do, with no reservations and no quibbling?"

"Not a word of honor. I don't like the phrase. The word 'honor' has been employed too much by objectionable people and has been badly soiled. I give you my word. But I can't sit here talking about it all day. I understand that my assistant has been legally committed, so the release must be legal too."

Waddell sat and pulled at his ear. He frowned at Barrow, but apparently read no helpful hint on the captain's stony countenance. He reached for his telephone and requested a number, and after a little wait spoke into it: "Frank? Ask Judge Hutchins if I can run up and see him for a minute. I want to ask him to vacate a warrant."

Chapter 19

I asked, "Shall I go get him?"

Wolfe said, "No. We'll wait."

We were in a room at the exposition offices, not the one where we had met Osgood Tuesday afternoon. This was smaller and contained desks and files and chairs and was cluttered with papers. It was noon. On leaving the courthouse with Wolfe I had been surprised to find that our sedan was parked out front; he explained that an Osgood employee had brought it from where I had left it the day before. He had instructed me to head for the exposition grounds, and our first stop had been the main exhibits building, where we gave the orchids an inspection and a spraying, and Wolfe arranged with an official for their care until Saturday, and the crating and shipping when the exposition closed. Then we had walked to the offices and been shown to Room 9. I was allowed to know that we expected to meet Lew Bennett there, but he hadn't arrived, and at noon we were still waiting for him.

I said, "If you ask my opinion, I think the best thing we can do is disguise ourselves as well as possible and jump in the car and drive like hell for New York. Or maybe across the line to Vermont and hide out in an old marble quarry."

"Stop that scratching."

I stuck my hands in my pockets. "You realize that I have been studying your face for 10 years, its lights and its shadows, the way it is arranged, and the way you handle it. And I say in all disrespect that I do not believe that the evidence which you mentioned to those false alarms is in existence."

"It isn't."

"I refer to the evidence which you promised to deliver within 24 hours."

"So do I."

"But it doesn't exist."

"No."

"But you're going to deliver it?"

"Yes."

I stared. "Okay. I suppose it was bound to happen sooner or later, but it's so painful to see that I wish it had happened to me first. Once at my mother's knee, back in 1839 I think it was—"

"Shut up, I'm going to make it."

"What? The bughouse?"

"The evidence. There is none. The bull was cremated. Nothing else remained to demonstrate the motive for murdering Clyde, and even if there had been other incriminating details—and there were none—they would have been useless. As for Bronson, Mr. Lake reports a vacuum. No fingerprints, except yours on the wallet, no one who remembers seeing him enter the shed, no one who saw him in anybody's company, no one with any discoverable motive. From the New York end, tracing his phone call, so far nothing—

and of course there can be nothing. A complete vacuum. Under the circumstances there is only—ah! Good morning, sir."

The Secretary of the National Guernsey League, having entered and shut the door behind him, approached. He looked like a man who has been interrupted, but nothing like as exasperated as he had been the preceding day. His greeting was affable but not frothy, and he sat down as if he didn't expect to stay long.

Wolfe said, "Thank you for coming. You're busy of course. Remarkable, how many ways there are of being busy. I believe Mr. Osgood told you on the phone that I would ask a favor in his name. I'll be brief. First the relevant facts: the records of your league are on file in your office at Fernborough, which is 110 miles from here, and the airplane belonging to Mr. Sturtevant, who takes passengers for hire at the airport at the other end of these grounds, could go there and return in 2 hours. Those are facts."

Bennett looked slightly bewildered. "I guess they are. I don't know about the airplane."

"I do, I've inquired. I've even engaged Mr. Sturtevant's services, tentatively. What I would like to have, sir, before 3 o'clock, are the color pattern sketches of Hickory Caesar Grindon, Willowdale Zodiac, Hawley's Orinoco, Mrs. Linville's bull whose name I don't know, and Hickory Buckingham Pell. Mr. Sturtevant is ready to leave at a moment's notice. You can accompany him, or Mr. Goodwin can, or you can merely give him a letter."

Bennett was frowning. "You mean the original sketches?"

"I understand no others are available. Those on certificates are scattered among the owners."

Bennett shook his head. "They can't leave the files, it's a strict rule. They're irreplaceable and we can't take risks."

"I understand. I said you can go yourself. When they come you can sit me here at this table with them and they can be constantly under your eye. I need only half an hour with them, possibly less."

"But they mustn't leave the files. Anyhow, I can't get away."

"This is the favor requested by Mr. Osgood."

"I can't help it. It . . . it isn't reasonable."

Wolfe leaned back and surveyed him. "One test of intelligence," he said patiently, "is the ability to welcome a singularity when the need arises, without excessive strain. Strict rules are universal. We all have a rule not to go on the street before clothing ourselves, but if the house is on fire we violate it. There is a conflagration here in Crowfield—metaphorically. People are being murdered. It should be extinguished, and the incendiary should be caught. The connection between that and the sketches in your files may be hidden to you, but not to me; for that you will have to accept my word. It is vital, it is essential, that I see those sketches. If you won't produce them as a favor to Mr. Osgood, you will do so as obligation to the community. I must see them."

Bennett looked impressed. But he objected. "I didn't say you couldn't see them. You can, anybody can, at our office. Go there yourself."

"Preposterous. Look at me."

"I don't see anything wrong with you. The airplane will carry you all right."

"No." Wolfe shuddered. "It won't. That's another thing you must accept my word for, that to expect me to get into an airplane would be utterly fantastic. Confound it, you object to violating a minor routine rule and then have the effrontery to suggest—have you ever been up in an airplane?"

"No."

"Then for heaven's sake try it once. It will be an experience for you. You'll enjoy it. I'm told that Mr. Sturtevant is competent and trustworthy and has a good machine. Get those sketches for me."

That was really what decided the question, 5 minutes later—the chance of a free airplane ride. Bennett gave in. He made a notation of the sketches Wolfe wanted, made a couple of phone calls, and was ready. I went with him to the landing field; we walked because he wanted to stop at the Guernsey cattle shed on the way. At the field we found Sturtevant, a good-looking kid with a clean face and greasy clothes, warming up the engine of a neat little biplane painted yellow. He said he was set and Bennett climbed in. I backed out of harm's way and watched them taxi across the field, and turn, and come scooting across the grass and lift. I stood there until they were up some 400 feet and headed east, and then walked back to the exposition grounds proper, to meet Wolfe at the Methodist tent as arranged. One rift in a gray sky was that I was to get another crack at the fricassee, and after my C. C. P. U. breakfast I had a place for it.

But it wasn't a leisurely meal, for it appeared that we had a program—that is, Wolfe had it and I was to carry it out. After all his gab about violating rules, he kept his intact about the prohibition of business while eating, and since he was in a mood there wasn't much

conversation. When the pie had been disposed of and
the coffee arrived, he squirmed to a new position on
the folding chair and began to lay it out. I was to
take the car and proceed to Osgoods, and bathe and
change my clothes. Since the house would be full of
funeral guests, I was to make myself as unobtrusive
as possible, and if Osgood himself failed to catch sight
of me at all, so much the better, as I was still under
suspicion of having steered his daughter to a rendezvous with the loathsome Pratt brat. I was to pack our
luggage and load it in the car, have the car filled with
gas and oil and whatever else it had an appetite for,
and report at the room where we had met Bennett
not later than 3 o'clock.

"Luggage?" I sipped coffee. "Poised for flight,
huh?"

Wolfe sighed. "We'll be going home. Home."

"Any stops on the way?"

"We'll stop at Mr. Pratt's place." He sipped. "By
the way, I'm overlooking something. Two things.
Have you a memorandum book with you? Or a notebook?"

"I've got a pad. You know the kind I carry."

"May I have it? And your pencil. It would be well
to use the kind of pencil that is carried, though I think
it will never get to microscopes. Thank you." He
frowned at the pad. "Larger sheets would be better,
but this will serve, and it wouldn't do to buy one in
Crowfield." He put the pad and pencil in his pocket.
"The second thing, I must have a good and reliable
liar."

"Yes, sir." I tapped my chest.

"No, not you. Rather, in addition to you."

"Another liar besides me. Plain or fancy?"

"Plain. But we're limited. It must be one of the three persons who were there when I was standing on that rock in the pasture Monday afternoon."

"Well." I pursed my lips and considered. "Your friend Dave might do for a liar. He reads poetry."

"No. Out of the question. Not Dave." Wolfe opened his eyes at me. "What about Miss Rowan? She seems inclined to friendship. Emphatically, since she visited you in jail."

"How the devil did you know that?"

"Not knowledge. Surmise. Your mother's voice on the telephone was hers. We'll discuss that episode after we get home. You must have suggested that performance to her, therefore you must have been in communication with her. People in jail aren't called to the telephone, so she couldn't have phoned you. She must have gone to see you. Surely, if she is as friendly as that, she would be pliant."

"I don't like to use my spiritual appeal for business purposes."

"Proscriptions carried too far lead to nullity."

"After I analyze that I'll get in touch with you. My first impulse is to return it unopened."

"Will she lie?"

"Good lord, yes. Why not?"

"It's important. Can we count on it?"

"Yes."

"Then another detail is for you to telephone, find her, and make sure she will be at Mr. Pratt's place from 3 o'clock on. Tell her you will want to speak to her as soon as we arrive there." He caught the eye of a Methodist, and when she came to his beckoning requested more coffee. Then he told me, "It's after 1 o'clock. Mr. Bennett is over halfway to Fernborough. You haven't much time."

I emptied my cup and left him.

The program went without a hitch, but it kept me on the go. I phoned Pratt's first thing, for Lily Rowan, and she was there, so I checked that off. I warmed up the concrete out to Osgood's, and by going in the rear entrance and up the back stairs avoided contact with the enraged father. I probably wouldn't have been noticed anyway, for the place was nearly as crowded as the exposition. There must have been a hundred cars, which was why I had to park long before I got to the end of the drive, and of course I had to carry the luggage. Upstairs I caught a glimpse of Nancy, and exchanged words with the housekeeper in the back hall downstairs, but didn't see Osgood. The service began at 2 o'clock, and when I left the only sound in the big old house, coming from the part I stayed away from, was the rise and fall of the preacher's voice pronouncing the last farewell for Clyde Osgood, who had won a bet and lost one simultaneously.

At 5 minutes to 3, with clean clothes and a clean body, not to mention the mind, with the car, filled with luggage and the other requisites, parked conveniently near, and without any satisfactory notion of the kind of goods Wolfe's factory was turning out in the line of evidence, though I had a strong inkling of who the consignee was to be, I sought Room 9 in the exposition offices. Sturtevant had apparently made good on his schedule, for the factory was in operation. Wolfe was there alone, seated at a table, with half a dozen sketches of bulls, on small sheets of white paper about 6 by 9 inches, arranged neatly in a row. One of them, separate, was directly under his eye, and he kept glancing back and forth from it to the sheet of my memo pad on which he was working with my pencil. He looked as concentrated as an artist hell bent for a masterpiece. I stood and observed operations over his shoulder for a few minutes, noting that the separate sheet from which he seemed to be drawing his inspiration was marked "Hickory Buckingham Pell," and then gave it up and sat down.

"What about Bennett keeping his sketches under his eye?" I demanded. "Did you worm yourself into his confidence, or bribe him?"

"He went to eat. I'm not hurting his sketches. Keep quiet and don't disturb me and don't scratch."

"I don't itch any more."

"Thank heaven."

I sat and diverted myself by trying different combinations on the puzzle we were supposed to be solving. At that point, thanks to various hints Wolfe had dropped, I was able to provide fairly plausible answers to most of the questions on the list, but was still completely stumped by the significance of the drawing practice he was indulging in. It seemed fanciful and even batty to suppose that by copying one of Bennett's sketches he was manufacturing evidence that would solve a double murder and earn us a fee and fulfil his engagement with Waddell, but the expression on his face left no doubt about his expectations. He was, by his calculations, sewing it up. I tried to work it into my combinations somehow, but couldn't get it to fit. I quit, and let my brain relax.

Lew Bennett entered with a toothpick in his mouth. As he did so Wolfe put my memo pad, with the pages he had worked on still attached, into his breast pocket, and the pencil. Then he sighed, pushed back his chair and got to his feet, and inclined his head to Bennett.

"Thank you, sir. There are your sketches intact. Guard them; preserve them carefully; you already thought them precious; they are now doubly so. It is a wise precaution for you to insist that they be made in ink, since that renders any alteration impossible without discovery. Doubtless Mr. Osgood will find occasion to thank you also. Come, Archie."

When we left, Bennett was leaning over the table squinting at the sketches.

Down at the parking space Wolfe climbed into the front seat beside me, which meant that he had things to say. As I threaded my way slowly along the edge of the darting crowds, he opened up: "Now, Archie. It all depends on the execution. I'll go over it briefly for you. . . ."

Chapter 20

At Pratt's place I parked in the graveled space in front of the garage, and we got out. Wolfe left me and headed for the house. Over at a corner of the lawn Caroline was absorbed in putting practice, which might have been thought a questionable occupation for a young woman, even a Metropolitan champion, on the afternoon of her former fiancé's funeral, but under the circumstances it was open to differing interpretations. She greeted me from a distance as I passed by on my way to meet Lily Rowan as arranged on the phone.

Lily stayed put in the hammock, extending a hand and going over me with a swift and comprehensive eye.

I said, "You're not so hot. Wolfe recognized your voice on the telephone last night."

"He didn't."

"He did."

"He agreed to meet me at the hotel at six in the morning."

"Bah. You laid an egg, that's all. However, you got him out of bed at midnight, which was something.

Thank you for doing me the favor. Now I want to offer to do you one, and I'm in a hurry. How would you like to take a lesson in detective work?"

"Who would give it to me?"

"I would."

"I'd love it."

"Fine. This may be the beginning of a worthwhile career for you. The lesson is simple but requires control of the voice and the facial muscles. You may not be needed, but on the other hand you may. You are to stay here, or close by. Sometime in the next hour or two I may come for you, or send Bert—"

"Come yourself."

"Okay. And escort you to the presence of Mr. Wolfe and a man. Wolfe will ask you a question and you will tell a lie. It won't be a complicated lie and there is no possibility of your getting tripped up. But it will help to pin a murder on a man, and therefore I want to assure you that it is not a frame-up. The man is guilty. If there were a chance in a million that he's innocent—"

"Don't bother." The corner of her mouth went up. "Do I have any company in the lie?"

"Yes. Me; also Wolfe. What we need is corroboration."

"Then as far as I'm concerned it isn't a lie at all. Truth is relative. I see you've washed your face. Kiss me."

"Pay in advance, huh?"

"Not in full. On account."

After about 30 or 32 seconds I straightened up again and cleared my throat and said, "Whatever is worth doing at all is worth doing well."

She was smiling and didn't say anything.

"This is it," I said. "Now quit smiling and listen."

It didn't take long to explain it. Four minutes later I was on my way to the house.

Wolfe was on the terrace with Pratt and Jimmy and Monte McMillan. Jimmy looked sullen and preoccupied, and I judged from his eyes that he was having too many highballs. McMillan sat to one side, silent, with his eyes fixed on Wolfe. Pratt was raving. He appeared to be not only sore because the general ruction had spoiled his barbecue plans and ruined the tail end of his country sojourn, but specifically and pointedly sore at Wolfe for vague but active reasons which had probably come to him on the bounce from District Attorney Waddell. Even so his deeper instincts prevailed, for when I arrived he interrupted himself to toss me a nod and let out a yell for Bert.

But Wolfe, who, I noticed, had already disposed of a bottle of beer, shook his head at me and stood up. "No," he said. "Please, Mr. Pratt. I don't resent your belligerence, but I think before long you may acknowledge its misdirection. You may even thank me, but I don't ask for that either. I didn't want to disturb you. I needed to have a talk with Mr. McMillan in private. When I told him so on the phone this morning and we tried to settle on a meeting place that would ensure privacy, I took the liberty of suggesting your house. There was a special reason for it, that the presence of Miss Rowan might be desirable."

"Lily Rowan? What the hell has she got to do with it?"

"That will appear. Or maybe it won't. Anyhow, Mr. McMillan agreed to meet me here. If my presence is really offensive to you we'll go elsewhere. I thought perhaps that room upstairs—"

"I don't give a damn. But if there's anything on my mind I'm in the habit of getting it off—"

"Later. Indulge me. It will keep. If you'll permit us to use the room upstairs? . . ."

"Help yourself." Pratt waved a hand. "You'll need something to drink. Bert! Hey, *Bert!*"

Jimmy shut his eyes and groaned.

We got ourselves separated. McMillan, who still hadn't opened his mouth, followed Wolfe, and I brought up the rear. As we started up the stairs, with the stockman's broad back towering above me, I got my pistol from the holster, to which it had been previously restored, and slipped it into my side coat pocket, hoping it could stay there. There was one item on Wolfe's bill of fare that might prove to be ticklish.

The room was in apple-pie order, with the afternoon sun slanting in through the modern casement windows which Wolfe had admired. I moved the big upholstered chair around for him, and placed a couple more for McMillan and me. Bert appeared, as sloppy and efficient as ever, with beer and the makings of highballs. As soon as that had been arranged and Bert had disappeared, McMillan said:

"This is the second time I've gone out of my way to see you, as a favor to Fred Osgood. It's sort of getting monotonous. I've got 7 cows and a bull at Crowfield that I've just bought that I ought to be taking home."

He stopped. Wolfe said nothing. Wolfe sat leaning back in the big upholstered chair, motionless, his hands resting on the polished wooden arms, gazing at the stockman with half-shut eyes. There was no indication that he intended either to speak or to move.

McMillan finally demanded, "What the hell is this, a staring match?"

Wolfe shook his head. "I don't like it," he said. "Believe me, sir, I take no pleasure from it. I have no desire to drag it out, to prolong the taste of victory. There has already been too much delay, far too much." He put his hand in his breast pocket, withdrew the memo pad, and held it out. "Take that, please, and examine the first three sheets. Thoroughly.—I'll want it back intact, Archie."

With a shrug of his broad shoulders, McMillan took the pad and looked it over. His head was bent and I couldn't see his face. After inspecting the sheets twice over he looked up again.

"You've got me," he declared. "Is there a trick to it?"

"I wouldn't say a trick." Wolfe's tone took on an edge. "Do you identify those sketches?"

"I never saw them before."

"Of course not. It was a bad question. Do you identify the original they were drawn from?"

"No I don't. Should I? They're not very good."

"That's true. Still I would have expected you to identify them. He was your bull. Today I compared them with some sketches, the originals on the applications for registration, which Mr. Bennett let me look at, and it was obvious that the model for them was Hickory Buckingham Pell. Your bull that died of anthrax a month ago."

"Is that so?" McMillan looked the sheets over again, in no haste, and returned his eyes to Wolfe. "It's possible. That's interesting. Where did you get these drawings?"

"That's just the point." Wolfe laced his fingers

across his belly. "I made them myself. You've heard of that homely episode Monday afternoon, before your arrival. Mr. Goodwin and I started to cross the pasture and were interrupted by the bull. Mr. Goodwin escaped by agility, but I mounted that boulder in the center of the pasture. I was there some 15 minutes before I was rescued by Miss Pratt. I am vain of my dignity, and I felt undignified. The bull was parading not far off, back and forth, and I took my memorandum pad from my pocket and made those sketches of him. The gesture may have been childish, but I got satisfaction from it. It was . . . well, a justification of my point of vantage on the boulder. May I have the pad back, please?"

McMillan didn't move. I arose and took the pad from him without his seeming to notice it, and put it in my pocket.

McMillan said, "You must have a screw loose. The bull in the pasture was Caesar. Hickory Caesar Grindon."

"No, sir. I must contradict you, for again that's just the point. The bull in the pasture was Hickory Buckingham Pell. The sketches I made Monday afternoon prove it, but I was aware of it long before I saw Mr. Bennett's official records. I suspected it Monday afternoon. I knew it Monday night. I didn't know it was Buckingham, for I had never heard of him, but I know it wasn't Caesar."

"You're a goddam liar. Whoever told you—"

"No one told me." Wolfe grimaced. He unlaced his fingers to wiggle one. "Let me make a suggestion, sir. We're engaged in a serious business, deadly serious, and we'll gain nothing by cluttering it up with frivolous rhetoric. You know very well what I'm doing, I'm undertaking to demonstrate that Clyde Osgood and Howard Bronson died by your hand. You can't refute my points until I've made them, and you can't keep me from making them by calling me names. Let's show mutual respect. I can't expose your guilt by shouting 'murderer' at you, and you can't disprove it by shouting 'liar' at me. Nor by pretending surprise. You must have known why I asked you to meet me here."

McMillan's gaze was steady. So was his voice: "You're going to undertake to prove something."

"I am. I have already shown proof that Caesar, the champion, was never in that pasture."

"Bah. Those drawings? Anybody would see through that trick. Do you suppose anyone is going to believe that when the bull chased you on that rock you stood there and made pictures of him?"

"I think so." Wolfe's eyes moved. "Archie, get Miss Rowan."

I wouldn't have left him like that if he had had the sketches on him, but they were in my pocket. I hotfooted it downstairs and across the lawn and under the trees to the hammock, which she got out of as she saw me coming. She linked her arm through mine, and I had to tolerate it for business reasons, but I made her trot. She offered no objections, but by the time we got upstairs to our destination she was a little out of breath. I had to admit she was a pretty good pupil when I saw her matter-of-fact nods, first to Wolfe and then to McMillan. Neither of them got up.

Wolfe said, "Miss Rowan. I believe Mr. Goodwin has informed you that we would ask you for an exercise of memory. I suppose you do remember that on

Monday afternoon the activity of the bull marooned me on a rock in the pasture?"

She smiled at him. "I do."

"How long was I on the rock?"

"Oh . . . I would say 15 minutes. Between 10 and 20."

"During that time, what was Miss Pratt doing?"

"Running to get her car and driving to the pasture and arguing with Dave about opening the gate, and then driving to get you."

"What was Dave doing?"

"Waving the gun and arguing with Esca . . . Mr. Goodwin and arguing with Caroline and jumping around."

"What were you doing?"

"Taking it in. Mostly I was watching you, because you made quite a picture—you and the bull."

"What was I doing?"

"Well, you climbed to the top of the rock and stood there 2 or 3 minutes with your arms folded and your walking stick hanging from your wrist, and then you took a notebook or something from your pocket and it looked as if you were writing in it or drawing in it. You kept looking at the bull and back at the book or whatever it was. I decided you were making a sketch of the bull. That hardly seemed possible under the circumstances, but it certainly looked like it."

Wolfe nodded. "I doubt if there will ever be any reason for you to repeat all that to a judge and jury in a courtroom, but if such an occasion should arise would you do it?"

"Certainly. Why not?"

"Under oath?"

"Of course. Not that I would enjoy it much."

"But you would do it?"

"Yes."

Wolfe turned to the stockman. "Would you care to ask her about it?"

McMillan only looked at him, and gave no sign. I went to open the door and told Lily, "That will do, Miss Rowan, thank you." She crossed and stopped at my elbow and said, "Take me back to the hammock." I muttered at her, "Go sit on your thumb. School's out." She made a face at me and glided over the threshold, and I shut the door and returned to my chair.

McMillan said, "I still say it's a trick. And a damn dirty trick. What else?"

"That's all." Wolfe sighed. "That's all, sir. I ask you to consider whether it isn't enough. Let us suppose that you are on trial for the murder of Clyde Osgood. Mr. Goodwin testifies that while I was on the rock he saw me looking at the bull and sketching on my pad. Miss Rowan testified as you have just heard. I testify that at that time, of that bull, I made those sketches, and the jury is permitted to compare them with the official sketches of Caesar and Buckingham. Wouldn't that satisfactorily demonstrate that Buckingham was in the pasture, and Caesar wasn't and never had been?"

McMillan merely gazed at him.

Wolfe went on, "I'll answer your charge that it's a trick. What if it is? Are you in a position to condemn tricks? As a matter of fact, I do know, from the evidence of my own eyes, that the bull was Buckingham. I had the opportunity to observe him minutely. Remember that I have studied the official sketches. Buckingham had a white patch high on his left shoulder; Caesar had not. The bull in the pasture had it.

The white shield on Buckingham's face extended well below the level of the eyes; on Caesar it was smaller and came to a point higher up. Not only did I see the face of the bull in the pasture on Monday afternoon, but that night I examined it at close range with a flashlight. He was Buckingham. You know it; I know it; and if I can help a jury to know it by performing a trick with sketches I shall certainly do so. With Mr. Goodwin and Miss Rowan to swear that they saw me making them, I think we may regard that point as established."

"What else?"

"That's all. That's enough."

McMillan abruptly stood up. I was on my feet as soon as he was, with my gun in sight. He saw it and grinned at me without any humor, with his gums showing. "Go ahead and stop me, son," he said, and started, not fast but not slow, for the door. "Make it good though."

I dived past him and got to the door and stood with my back against it. He halted three paces off.

Wolfe's voice came, sharp, "Gentlemen! Please! If you start a commotion, Mr. McMillan, the thing is out of my hands. You must realize that. A wrestling match would bring people here. If you get shot you'll only be disabled; Mr. Goodwin doesn't like to kill people. Come back here and face it. I want to talk to you."

McMillan wheeled and demanded, "What the hell do you think I've been doing for the past month except face it?"

"I know. But you were still struggling. Now the struggle's over. You can't go out of that door; Mr. Goodwin won't let you. Come and sit down."

McMillan stood for a minute and looked at him.

Then slowly he moved, back across the room to his chair, sat, put his elbows on his knees, and covered his face with his hands.

Wolfe said, "I don't know how you feel about it. You asked me what else. If you mean what other proof confronts you, I repeat that no more is needed. If you mean can I offer salve to your vanity, I think I can. You did extremely well. If I had not been here you would almost certainly have escaped even the stigma of suspicion."

Wolfe got his fingers laced again. I returned the gun to my pocket and sat down. Wolfe resumed: "As I said, I suspected Monday afternoon that the bull in the pasture was not the champion Caesar. When Clyde offered to bet Pratt that he would not barbecue Hickory Caesar Grindon, he opened up an amusing field for conjecture. I diverted myself with it while listening to Pratt's jabber. How did Clyde propose to win his bet? By removing the bull and hiding him? Fantastic; the bull was guarded, and where could he be hid against a search? Replace the bull with one less valuable? Little less fantastic; again, the bull was guarded, and while a substitute might be found who would deceive others, surely none would deceive you, and you were there. I considered other alternatives. There was one which was simple and plausible and presented no obstacles at all: that the bull in the pasture was not Hickory Caesar Grindon and Clyde had detected it. He had just come from the pasture, and he had binoculars, and he knew cattle. I regarded the little puzzle as solved and dismissed it from my mind, since it was none of my business.

"When the shots fired by Mr. Goodwin took us all to the pasture Monday night, and we found that Clyde had been killed, it was still none of my business, but the puzzle gained in interest and deserved a little effort as an intellectual challenge. I examined the bull, looked for the weapon and found it, and came to this room and sat in this chair and satisfied myself as to the probabilities. Of course I was merely satisfying myself as a mental exercise, not the legal requirements for evidence. First, if the bull wasn't Caesar you certainly knew it, and therefore you had swindled Pratt. How and why? Why, to get $45,000. How, by selling him Caesar and then delivering another bull, much less valuable, who resembled him. Then where was Caesar? Wouldn't it be highly dangerous for you to have him in your possession, since he had been legally sold, and cooked and eaten? You couldn't call him Caesar, you wouldn't dare to let anyone see him. Then you didn't have him in your possession. No one did. Caesar was dead."

Wolfe paused, and demanded, "Wasn't Caesar dead when you took the $45,000 from Pratt?"

McMillan, his face still covered with his hands, was motionless and made no sound.

"Of course he was," Wolfe said. "He had died of anthrax. Pratt mentioned at dinner Monday evening that he had first tried to buy Caesar from you, for his whimsical barbecue, more than six weeks ago, and you had indignantly refused. Then the anthrax came. Your herd was almost entirely destroyed. One morning you found that Caesar was dead. In your desperation an ingenious notion occurred to you. Buckingham, who resembled Caesar superficially but was worth only a fraction of his value, was alive and well. You announced that Buckingham had died, and the carcass was destroyed; and you told Pratt that he could have

Caesar. You couldn't have swindled a stockman like that, for the deception would soon have been found out; but the swindle was in fact no injury to Pratt, since Buckingham would make just as good roast beef as Caesar would have made. Of course, amusing myself with the puzzle Monday evening, I knew nothing of Buckingham, but one of the probabilities which I accepted was that you had delivered another bull instead of Caesar, and that Caesar was dead.

"Clyde, then, had discovered the deception, and when you heard him propose the bet to Pratt, and the way he stated its terms, you suspected the fact. You followed him out to his car and had a brief talk with him and got your suspicions confirmed, and he agreed to return later that evening and discuss it with you. He did so. You were supposed to be asleep upstairs. You left the house secretly and met Clyde. I am giving you the probabilities as I accepted them Monday evening. Clyde informed you that he knew of the deception and was determined to expose it in order to win his bet with Pratt. You, of course, faced ruin. He may have offered a compromise: for instance, if you would give him $20,000 of the money Pratt had paid you he would use half of it to settle his bet, keep the other half for himself, and preserve your secret. I don't know, and it doesn't matter. What happened was that you knocked him unconscious, evolved a plan to make it appear that he had been killed by the bull, and proceeded to execute it. I was inclined to believe, looking at the bull's horns Monday night, that you had smeared blood on them with your hands. You should have been much more thorough, but I suppose you were in a hurry, for you had to wash off the pick and get back to the house and into the upstairs room unobserved. You didn't know, of course, whether the thing would be discovered in 5 minutes or 5 hours—since Mr. Goodwin was on the other side of the pasture talking to Miss Rowan."

Wolfe opened his eyes. "Do I bore you or annoy you? Shall I stop?"

No movement and no response.

"Well. That was the way I arranged the puzzle Monday evening, but, as I say, it was none of my business. It didn't become my business until the middle of Tuesday afternoon, when I accepted a commission from Mr. Osgood to solve the murder, having first demonstrated that there had been one. At that moment I expected to have the job completed within a few hours. Only two things needed to be done to verify the solution I had already arrived at: first, to question everyone who had been at Pratt's place Monday evening, for if it turned out that you could not have left the house secretly—for instance, if someone had been with you constantly—I would have to consider new complexities; and second, to establish the identity of the bull. The first was routine and I left it to Mr. Waddell, as his proper province, while I investigated Clyde's background by conversing with his father and sister. The second, the proof that the bull was not Caesar, I intended to procure, with Mr. Bennett's assistance, as soon as I heard from the district attorney, and that delay was idiotic. I should not have postponed it one instant. For less than 3 hours after I had accepted the case I learned from your own lips that the bull was dead and his carcass was to be immediately destroyed. I tried; I phoned Mr. Bennett and learned that there was no single distinguishing mark or brand on Guernsey bulls, and Mr. Goodwin rushed over to take photographs; but the bull was already half consumed by fire. You acted quickly there, and in time. Of course you gave him the anthrax yourself. It would be . . . perhaps you would tell me how and when you did it."

McMillan said nothing.

Wolfe shrugged. "Anyhow, you were prompt and energetic. As long as the bull was destined to be cooked and eaten—this was to be the day for that, by the way—you ran little risk of exposure. But when all thought of the barbecue was abandoned, and it was suspected that Clyde had been murdered, the bull's presence, alive or dead, was a deadly peril to you. You acted at once. You not only killed him, you did it by a method which insured that his carcass would be immediately destroyed. You must have been prepared for contingencies.

"As for me, I was stumped. You had licked me. With all trace of the bull gone but his bones, there seemed no possible way of establishing your motive for murdering Clyde. I had no evidence even for my own satisfaction that my surmise had been correct—that the bull was not Caesar. Tuesday evening I floundered in futilities. I had an interview with you and tried to draw you out by suggesting absurdities, but you were too wary for me. You upbraided me for trying to smear some of the mess on you, and left. Then I tried Bronson, hoping for something—anything. That kind of man is always impervious unless he can be confronted with facts, and I had no facts. It's true that he led me to assumptions: that Clyde had told him how and why he expected to win the bet, and that Bronson therefore knew you were guilty—

might even have been there himself, in the dark—and that he was blackmailing you. I assumed those things, but he admitted none of them, and of course I couldn't prove them.

"Yesterday morning I went for Bennett. I wanted to find out all I could about identifying bulls. He was busy. Mr. Goodwin couldn't get him. After lunch I was still waiting for him. Finally he came, and I got a great deal of information, but nothing that would constitute evidence. Then came the news that Bronson had been murdered. Naturally that was obvious. Suspecting that he was blackmailing you, I had told the man he was a fool and he had proved me correct. There too you acted promptly and energetically. Men like you, sir, when once calamity sufficiently disturbs their balance, become excessively dangerous. They will perform any desperate and violent deed, but they don't lose their heads. I wouldn't mind if Mr. Goodwin left me with you in this room alone, because it is known that we are here; but I wouldn't care to offer you the smallest opportunity if there were the slightest room for your ingenuity."

McMillan lifted his head and broke his long silence. "I'm through," he said dully.

Wolfe nodded. "Yes, I guess you are. A jury might be reluctant to convict you of first degree murder on the testimony of my sketches, but if Pratt sued you for $45,000 on the ground that you hadn't delivered the bull you sold, I think the sketches would clinch that sort of case. Convicted of that swindle, you would be through anyway. About the sketches. I had to do that. 3 hours ago there wasn't a shred of evidence in existence to connect you with the murders you committed. But as soon as I examined the official sketches of Buckingham and Caesar I no longer surmised or deduced the identity of the bull in the pasture; I knew it. I had seen the white patch on the shoulder with my own eyes, and I had seen the extension of the white shield on his face. I made the sketches to support that knowledge. They will be used in the manner I described, with the testimony of Miss Rowan and Mr. Goodwin to augment my own. As I say, they will certainly convict you of fraud, if not of murder."

Wolfe sighed. "You killed Clyde Osgood to prevent the exposure of your fraud. Even less, to avoid the compulsion of having to share its proceeds. Now it threatens you again. That's the minimum of the threat."

McMillan tossed his head, as if he were trying to shake something off. The gesture looked familiar, but I didn't remember having seen him do it before. Then he did it again, and I saw what it was: it was the way the bull had tossed his head in the pasture Monday afternoon.

He looked at Wolfe and said, "Do me a favor. I want to go out to my car a minute. Alone."

Wolfe muttered, "You wouldn't come back."

"Yes, I would. My word was good for over 50 years. Now it's good again. I'll be back within 5 minutes, on my feet."

"Do I owe you a favor?"

"No. I'll do you one in return. I'll write something and sign it. Anything you say. You've got it pretty straight. I'll do it when I come back, not before. And you asked me how I killed Buckingham. I'll show you what I did it with."

Wolfe spoke to me without moving his head or his eyes. "Open the door for him, Archie."

I didn't stir. I knew he was indulging himself in one of his romantic impulses, and I thought a moment's reflection might show him its drawbacks; but after only half a moment he snapped at me, "Well?"

I got up and opened the door and McMillan, with a heavy tread but no sign of the blind staggers, passed out. I stood and watched his back until the top of his head disappeared on his way downstairs. Then I turned to Wolfe and said sarcastically, "Fortune-telling *and* character-reading. It would be nice to have to explain—"

"Shut up."

I kicked the door further open and stood there, listening for the sound of a gunshot or a racing engine or whatever I might hear. But the first pertinent sound, within the 5 minutes he had mentioned, was his returning footsteps on the stairs. He came down the hall, as he had promised, on his feet, entered without glancing at me, walked to Wolfe and handed him something, and went to his chair and sat down.

"That's what I said I'd show you." He seemed more out of breath than the exertion of his trip warranted, but otherwise under control. "That's what I killed Buckingham with." He turned his eye to me. "I haven't got any pencil or paper. If you'll let me have that pad . . ."

Wolfe held the thing daintily with thumb and forefinger, regarding it—a large hypodermic syringe. He lifted his gaze. "You had anthrax in this?"

"Yes. Five cubic centimeters. A culture I made myself from the tissues of Caesar's heart the morning I found him dead. They gave me hell for cutting him open, but—" He shrugged. "I did that before I got the idea of saying the carcass was Buckingham instead of Caesar. I only about half knew what I was doing that morning, but it was in my mind to use it on myself— the poison from Caesar's heart. Watch out how you handle that. It's empty now, but there might be a drop left on the needle, though I just wiped it off."

"Will anthrax kill a man?"

"Yes. How sudden depends on how he gets it. In my case collapse will come in maybe twenty minutes, because I shot more than two cubic centimeters of that concentrate in this vein." He tapped his left forearm with a finger. "Right in the vein. I only used half of it on Buckingham."

"Before you left for Crowfield Tuesday afternoon."

"Yes." McMillan looked at me again. "You'd better give me that pad and let me get started."

I got out the pad and tore off the three top sheets which contained the sketches, and handed it to him, with my fountain pen. He took it and scratched with the pen to try it, and asked Wolfe, "Do you want to dictate it?"

"No. Better in your own words. Just—it can be brief. Are you perfectly certain about the anthrax?"

"Yes. A good stockman is a jack of all trades."

Wolfe sighed, and shut his eyes.

I sat and watched the pen in McMillan's hand moving along the top sheet of the pad. Apparently he was a slow writer. The faint scratch of its movement was the only sound for several minutes. Then he asked without looking up:

"How do you spell 'unconscious'? I've always been a bad speller."

Wolfe spelled it for him, slowly and distinctly.

I watched the pen starting to move again. My gun, in my pocket, was weighting my coat down, and I transferred it back to the holster, still looking at the pen. Wolfe, his eyes closed, was looking at nothing.

Chapter 21

That was two months ago.

Yesterday, while I was sitting here in the office typing from my notebook Wolfe's dictated report on the Crampton-Gore case, the phone rang. Wolfe, at his desk in his oversize chair, happening not to be pouring beer at the moment, answered at his instrument. After a second he grunted and muttered:

"She wants Escamillo."

I lifted my receiver. "Hello, trifle. I'm busy."

"You're always busy." She sounded energetic. "You listen to me a minute. You probably don't know or don't care that I seldom pay any attention to my mail except to run through it to see if there's a letter from you. I've just discovered that I did after all get an invitation to Nancy's and Jimmy's wedding, which will be tomorrow. I know you did. You and I will go together. You can come—"

"Stop! Stop and take a breath. Weddings are out. They're barbaric vestiges of . . . of barbarism. I doubt if I'd go to my own."

"You might. You may. For a string of cellophane pearls I'd marry you myself. But this wedding will be amusing. Old Pratt and old Osgood will be there and you can see them shake hands. Then you can have cocktails and dinner with me."

"My pulse remains steady."

"Kiss me."

"Still steady."

"I'll buy you some marbles and an airgun and roller skates . . ."

"No. Are you going to ring off now?"

"No. I haven't seen you for a century."

"Okay. I'll tell you what I'll do. I'm going to the Strand tomorrow evening at 9 o'clock to watch Greenleaf and Baldwin play pool. You can come along if you'll promise to sit quietly and not chew gum."

"I wouldn't know a pool from a pikestaff. But all right. You can come here for dinner—"

"Nope. I'll eat at home with my employer. I'll meet you in the lobby of the Churchill at 8:45."

"My God, these public assignations—"

"I am perfectly willing to be seen with you in public."

"8:45 tomorrow."

"Right."

I replaced the instrument and turned to my typewriter. Wolfe's voice came:

"Archie."

"Yes, sir."

"Get the dictionary and look up the meaning of the word 'spiritual.' "

I merely ignored it and started on paragraph 16 of the report.

The Golden
Spiders

Introduction

My library owes no debt to Mr. Dewey's decimals, none to alphabetical order. The Nero Wolfe novels are shelved among "books of comfort," which I loosely define as novels riveting enough to hold my attention in the dreaded dentist's chair, yet never filled with onstage gore. Reading a Nero Wolfe is akin to visiting the home of an old friend or returning to the same inn on Cape Cod each year, nodding in delight at the familiar star-patterned quilt on the same canopied bed in the usual room, finding the idyllic view from the patio unchanged, unspoiled.

During stressful times I've devoured the Wolfe novels, charging so briskly through the canon that many of the titles seem interchangeable. Caught without reading material in an airport, I have, more than once, purchased a title I already own, only to discover the error at ten thousand feet. I'll cheerfully reread a Wolfe novel for the fourth or fifth time rather than resort to an airline magazine.

What should the reader expect from a Nero Wolfe novel—besides superb plotting, well-developed main characters, and crisp prose?

Introduction

A quick summary of the house rules:

At 325 West Thirty-fifth Street, Wolfe devotes the hours of 9 to 11 A.M. and 4 to 6 P.M. to the cultivation and propagation of orchids.

Theodore Horstmann, gardener par excellence, supervises Wolfe's participation in the above.

Fritz prepares outstanding cuisine.

No interruptions are allowed during meals; conversation is encouraged.

All guests and clients are offered refreshment.

Archie Goodwin, Wolfe's stalwart assistant, answers the door. He is available for a wisecrack. He'll punch a bad guy in the jaw. He'll dance with a woman if she's on the "right" side of thirty, and he can samba and rumba with the best.

Other than a well-heeled widow or two (clients), murderesses (surely more than statistically justifiable), and the occasionally glimpsed Lily Rowan, (whose name combines both flower and tree; perhaps she should be kept in the potting shed), *no women are allowed* within the all-male clubhouse on West Thirty-fifth. They are not even to be included among the cleaning crew. The entire gender is suspect and illogical. Each and every one might burst into tears, which would be *intolerable*!

Since the maintenance of the brownstone requires a substantial monthly outlay of cash, Nero Wolfe uses his Holmesian powers of observation and deduction to solve crimes that have baffled, or will soon baffle, the New York police force.

The Golden Spiders is atypical Stout, atypical Wolfe, and as such I take particular delight in introducing it to both devoted fans and new readers. The novel begins with humor, involves a child, and contains a personal element of vengeance. All rarities.

Introduction

The opening of a Nero Wolfe novel is usually a set piece, a ritualistic "feather-duster" scene, containing the obligatory paragraphs defining Fritz's and Theodore's roles in the Thirty-fifth Street ménage as well as a description of the red leather chair and the immense globe in Wolfe's spacious book-lined office.

As practiced by Rex Stout, the consummate pro, the detective novel generally begins with the client's initial visit, scheduled well within Wolfe's carefully prescribed hours. The client sits in the red leather chair. The client may be telling the truth; the client may be lying. If the client has sufficient financial assets, Wolfe takes the case.

The Golden Spiders starts in the kitchen with a fit of Wolfian petulance brought on by a disagreement over the proper preparation of starlings. Archie, amused by Wolfe's childish behavior, invites a child, a neighborhood tough who'd never ordinarily be admitted to Wolfe's presence, much less considered as a client, to join Wolfe at the table, shattering precedent and rules alike.

Archie's playfulness has terrible consequences.

We accept that the writer of amateur-sleuth detective novels has a built-in credibility problem. Why does our hardworking chef, writer, or actor keep stumbling over those unpleasant corpses? Why doesn't the chef, writer, or actor behave in a normal fashion, i.e., call the police and leave the investigation to them? It's less obvious that the writer of the professional detective series has her or his motivational problems as well. How does the detective become personally involved in each case? A fictional detective is not a neurosurgeon, for whom emotional detachment might be considered a plus. If she or he is to grasp and hold the reader, even the most curmudgeonly detective must find a reason beyond the check at the rainbow's end to pursue a case to its conclusion. Generally, it's Archie, our Everyman on a good day, who provides this sympathy, this bond. Rarely does Wolfe become engaged, much less enraged, by the crime in question.

Wolfe hates interruptions during meals. He dislikes children. He abhors deviations from his schedule. All of these indignities are heaped upon him in *The Golden Spiders*. They grate. They affect his appetite. They cause him to accept a retainer of four dollars and thirty cents from—horrors!—a teary-eyed woman.

They do my heart good.

I have loved and read these books all my life, and yet I rub my hands in secret satisfaction.

Let the old misogynist suffer.

Linda Barnes
June 1994

Chapter 1

When the doorbell rings while Nero Wolfe and I are at dinner, in the old brownstone house on West Thirty-fifth Street, ordinarily it is left to Fritz to answer it. But that evening I went myself, knowing that Fritz was in no mood to handle a caller, no matter who it was.

Fritz's mood should be explained. Each year around the middle of May, by arrangement, a farmer who lives up near Brewster shoots eighteen or twenty starlings, puts them in a bag, and gets in his car and drives to New York. It is understood that they are to be delivered to our door within two hours after they were winged. Fritz dresses them and sprinkles them with salt, and, at the proper moment, brushes them with melted butter, wraps them in sage leaves, grills them, and arranges them on a platter of hot polenta, which is thick porridge of fine-ground yellow cornmeal with butter, grated cheese, and salt and pepper.

It is an expensive meal and a happy one, and Wolfe always looks forward to it, but that day he put on an exhibition. When the platter was brought in, steaming, and placed before him, he sniffed, ducked his head and sniffed again, and straightened to look up at Fritz.

"The sage?"

"No, sir."

"What do you mean, no, sir?"

"I thought you might like it once in a style I have suggested, with saffron and tarragon. Much fresh tarragon, with just a touch of saffron, which is the way—"

"Remove it!"

Fritz went rigid and his lips tightened.

"You did not consult me," Wolfe said coldly. "To find that without warning one of my favorite dishes has been radically altered is an unpleasant shock. It may possibly be edible, but I am in no humor to risk it. Please dispose of it and bring me four coddled eggs and a piece of toast."

Fritz, knowing Wolfe as well as I did, aware that this was a stroke of discipline that hurt Wolfe more than it did him and that it would be useless to try to parley, reached for the platter, but I put in, "I'll take some if you don't mind. If the smell won't keep you from enjoying your eggs?"

Wolfe glared at me.

That was how Fritz acquired the mood that made me think it advisable for me to answer the door. When the bell rang Wolfe had finished his eggs and was drinking coffee, really a pitiful sight, and I was toward the end of a second helping of the starlings and polenta, which was certainly edible. Going to the hall and the front, I didn't bother to snap the light switch because there was still enough twilight for me to see, through the one-way glass panel, that the customer on the stoop was not our ship coming in.

I pulled the door open and told him politely, "Wrong number."

I was polite by policy, my established policy of promoting the idea of peace on earth with the neighborhood kids. It made life smoother in that street, where there was a fair amount of ball throwing and other activities.

"Guess again," he told me in a low nervous alto, not too rude. "You're Archie Goodwin. I've gotta see Nero Wolfe."

"What's your name?"

"Pete."

"What's the rest of it?"

"Drossos. Pete Drossos."

"What do you want to see Mr. Wolfe about?"

"I gotta case. I'll tell him."

He was a wiry little specimen with black hair that needed a trim and sharp black eyes, the top of his head coming about level with the knot of my four-in-hand. I had seen him around the neighborhood but had nothing either for or against him. The thing was to ease him off without starting a feud, and ordinarily I would have gone at it, but after Wolfe's childish performance with Fritz I thought it would do him good to have another child to play with. Naturally he would snarl and snap, but if Pete got scratched I could salve him afterward. So I invited him in and escorted him to the dining room.

Wolfe was refilling his coffee cup. He shot a glance at Pete, who I admit was not dressed up, put the pot down, looked straight at me, and spoke.

"Archie. I will not have interruptions at meals."

I nodded sympathetically. "I know, but this wasn't a meal. Call eggs a meal? This is Mr. Peter Drossos. He wants to consult you about a case. I was going to tell him you're busy, but I remembered you got sore because Fritz didn't consult you, and I didn't want you to get sore at Pete too. He's a neighbor of ours, and you know, love thy neighbor as thyself."

Ragging Wolfe is always a gamble. A quick reflex explosion may split the air; but if it doesn't, if he takes a second for a look at it, you're apt to find yourself topped. That time he took several seconds, sipping coffee, and then addressed our caller courteously. "Sit down, Mr. Drossos."

"I'm not mister, I'm Pete."

"Very well, Pete, sit down. Turn more to face me, please. Thank you. You wish to consult me?"

"Yeah, I gotta case."

"I always welcome a case, but the timing is a little unfortunate because Mr. Goodwin was going out this evening to see a billiard match, and now of course he will have to stay here to take down all that you say and all that I say. Archie, get your notebook, please?"

As I said, it's always a gamble. He had his thumb in my eye. I went across the hall to the office for a notebook and pen, and when I returned Fritz was there with coffee for me and cookies and a bottle of Coke for Pete. I said nothing. My pen and notebook would do the recording almost automatically, needing about a fifth of my brain, and I would see the rest of it devising plans for getting from under.

Pete was talking. "I guess it's okay him taking it down, but I gotta watch my end. This is strictly under the lid."

"If you mean it's confidential, certainly."

"Then I'll spill it. I know there's some private eyes you can't open up to, but you're different. We know all about you around here. I know how you feel about the lousy cops, just like I do. So I'll lay it out."

"Please do."

"Okay. What time is it?"

I looked at my wrist watch. "Ten to eight."

"Then it happened an hour ago. I know sometimes everything hangs on the time element, and right after it happened I went and looked at the clock in the drugstore near the corner, and it was a quarter to seven. I was working the wipe racket there at the corner of Thirty-fifth and Ninth, and a Caddy stopped—"

"Please. What's the wipe racket?"

"Why, you know, a car stops for the light and you hop to it with a rag and start wiping the window, and if it's a man and he lets you go on to the windshield you've got him for at least a dime. If it's a woman and she lets you go on, maybe you've got her and maybe not. That's a chance you take. Well, this Caddy stopped—"

"What's a Caddy?"

From the look that appeared in the sharp black eyes, Pete was beginning to suspect that he had picked the wrong private eye. I cut in to show him that anyhow one of us wasn't a moron, telling Wolfe, "A Cadillac automobile."

"I see. It stopped?"

"Yeah, for the light. I went for the window by the driver. It was a woman. She turned her face around to me to look straight at me and she said something. I don't think she made any sound, or anyway if she did I didn't hear anything through the window because it was up nearly to the top, but she worked her lips with it and I could tell what it was. She said, 'Help. Get a cop.' Like this, look."

He made the words with his lips, overdoing it some, without producing any noise. Wolfe nodded appreciatively. He turned to me. "Archie. Make a sketch of Pete's mouth doing that pantomime."

"Later," I said obligingly. "After you've gone to bed."

"It was plain as it could be," Pete went on. " 'Help, get a cop.' It hit me, it sure did. I tried to keep my face deadpan, I knew that was the way to take it, but I guess I didn't, because the man was looking at me and he—"

"Where was the man?"

"There on the seat with her. There was just them two in the car. I guess he saw by my face something had hit me, because he jabbed the gun against her harder and she jerked her head around—"

"Did you see the gun?"

"No, but I'm not a dope, am I? What else would make her want a cop and then jerk her head like that? What do you think it was, a lead pencil?"

"I prefer the gun. And then?"

"I backed up a little. All I had was a piece of rag, and him with a six gun. Now this next part—don't get me wrong, I got no use for cops. I feel about cops just like you. But it happened so quick I didn't realize just what I was doing, and I admit I looked around for a cop. I didn't see one, so I hopped to the sidewalk to see around the corner, and by the time I looked again the light had changed, and there went the car. I tried to flag another car to trail it, but nobody would stop. I thought I might catch it at Eighth Avenue and ran as fast as I could down Thirty-fifth, but it hit a green light at Eighth and went on through when I was only halfway there. But I got the license number."

He reached in his pants pocket, pulled out a little scrap of paper, and read from it: "Connecticut, Y,Y, nine, four, three, two."

"Excellent." Wolfe returned his empty cup to the saucer. "Have you given that to the police?"

"Me?" Pete was scornful. "The cops? Look, am I screwy? I go to the precinct and tell a flattie, or even say I get to a sarge and tell him, and what? First he don't believe me and then he chases me and then I'm marked. It don't hurt *you* to be marked, because you're a private eye with a license and you've got something on a lot of inspectors."

"I have? What?"

"Don't ask me. But everybody knows you're loaded with dirt on some big boys or you'd have been rubbed out long ago. But a kid like me can't risk it to be marked even if I'm straight. I hate cops, but you don't have to be a crook to hate cops. I keep telling my mother I'm straight, and I am straight, but I'm telling you it takes a lot of guts. What do you think of this case I got?"

Wolfe considered. "It seems a little—uh—hazy."

"Yeah, that's why I came to you. I went to a place I go to when I want to think, and I went all over it. I saw it was a swell case if I handled it right. The car was a Caddy, a dark gray fifty-two Caddy. The man looked mean, but he looked like dough, he looked like he might have two or three more Caddies. The woman did too. She wasn't as old as my mother, but I guess I can't go by that because my mother has done a lot of hard work, and I bet she never did work. She had a scratch on her face, on her left cheek, and her face was all twisted saying that to me, 'Help, get a cop'; but, thinking it over, I decided she was a good-looker. She had big gold spiders for earrings, spiders with their legs stretched out. Pure gold."

Wolfe grunted.

"Okay," Pete conceded, "they looked like gold. They wasn't brass. Anyhow, the whole layout said dough, and what I was thinking went like this: I got a case with people with dough, and how do I handle it so I'll get some? There might be up to fifty dollars in it if I handle it right. If he kills her I can identify him and get the reward. I can tell what she said to me and how he jabbed the gun in her—"

"You didn't see a gun."

"That's a detail. If he didn't kill her, if he just made her do something or tell him something or give him something, I can go and put it up to him, either he comes across with fifty bucks, or maybe a hundred, or I hang it on him."

"That would be blackmail."

"Okay." Pete brushed cookie crumbs from his fingers onto the tray. "That's why I decided I had to see you after I thought it over. I saw I couldn't handle it alone and I'd have to cut you in, but you understand it's my case. Maybe you think I was a sap to tell you that license number before we made a deal, but I don't. If you get onto him and corner him and try to cross me and hog it, I'll still have to identify him, so it will be up to me. If blackmail's out, you can figure it so it's not blackmail. What do you say we split fifty-fifty?"

"I'll tell you, Pete." Wolfe pushed his chair back and got his bulk comfortably settled in a new position. "If we are to join hands on your case I think I should tell you a few things about the science and art of detection. Mr. Goodwin will of course take it down, and when he types it he will make a copy for you. But first he'll make a phone call. Archie, you have that license number. Call Mr. Cramer's office and give them that number. Say that you have information that that car, or its owner or operator, may have been involved in a violation of a law in this city in the past two hours, and suggest a routine check. Do not be more definite. Say that our information is unverified and inquiry should be discreet."

"Hey," Pete demanded, "who's Mr. Cramer? A cop?"

"A police inspector," Wolfe told him. "You yourself suggested the possibility of murder. If there was a murder there is a corpse. If there is a corpse it should be found. Unless and until it is found, where's your case? We have no idea where to look for it, so we'll trick the police into finding it for us. I often make use of them that way. Archie. Of course you will not mention Pete's name, since he doesn't want to be marked."

As I went across to the office, to my desk, and dialed the number of Manhattan Homicide West, I was reflecting that of all Wolfe's thousand techniques for making himself obnoxious the worst was when he thought he was being funny. When I finished talking to Sergeant Purley Stebbins and hung up, I was tempted to just walk out and go up to watch Mosconi and Watrous handle their cues, but of course that wouldn't do because it would have been admitting he had called me good, and he would merely have shooed Pete out and settled down with a book and a satisfied smirk.

So I marched back to the dining room, sat down and took up my pen, and said brightly, "All right, they're alerted. Shoot the lecture on detection, and don't leave anything out."

Wolfe leaned back, put his elbows on the chair arms, and matched his fingertips. "You understand, Pete, that I shall confine myself to the problems and methods of the private detective who works at his profession for a living."

"Yeah." Pete had a fresh bottle of Coke. "That's what I want, how to rake in the dough."

"I had remarked that tendency in you. But you must not permit it to smother other considerations. It is desirable that you should earn your fees, but it is essential that you feel you have earned them, and that depends partly on your ego. If your ego is healthy and hardy, as mine is, you will seldom have difficulty—"

"What's my ego?"

"There are various definitions, philosophical, metaphysical, psychological, and now psychoanalytical, but as I am using the term it means the ability to play up everything that raises your opinion of yourself and play down everything that lowers it. Is that clear?"

"I guess so." Pete was frowning in concentration. "You mean, do you like yourself or don't you."

"Not precisely, but that's close enough. With a robust ego, your feeling—"

"What's robust?"

Wolfe made a face. "I'll try to use words you have met before, but when I don't, when one of them is a stranger to you, kindly do not interrupt. If you are smart enough to be a good detective, you are smart enough to guess accurately the meaning of a new word by the context—which means the other words I use with it. Also there is usually a clue. A moment ago I spoke of a healthy and hardy ego, and then, after your interruption, I spoke of a robust ego in the same connection. So obviously 'robust' means 'healthy and hardy,' and if you have the stuff of a good detective in you, you should have spotted it. How old are you?"

"Twelve."

"Then I should make allowances, and do. To continue: with a robust ego, your feeling about earning your fees can safely be left to your intelligence and common sense. Never collect or accept a fee that you feel you haven't earned; if you do, your integrity crumbles and your ego will have worms. With that one reservation, get all you can. As you must not take what you feel you haven't earned, so must you get what you feel you have earned. Don't even discuss a case with a prospective client until you know about his ability to pay. So much—"

"Then why—" Pete blurted, and stopped.

"Why what?"

"Nothing. Only you're discussing with me, just a kid."

"This is a special case. Mr. Goodwin brought you in to me, and he is my trusted and highly valuable assistant, and he would be disappointed if I didn't explore your affair thoroughly and let him take it down and type it." Wolfe favored me with a hypocritical glance and returned to Pete. "So much for your ego and your fees. As for your methods, they must of course be suited to your field. I pass over such fields as industrial espionage and divorce evidence and similar repugnant snooperies, since the ego of any man who engages in them is already infested with worms, and so you are not concerned. But take robbery. Say, for instance, a woman's jewel box has been looted, and she doesn't want to go to the police because she suspects—"

"Let's take murder. I'd rather start with murder."

"As you will." Wolfe was gracious. "You're getting this, are you, Archie?"

"You bet. With my tongue out."

"Good. But robbery or murder, no matter what, speaking generally, you must thoroughly understand that primarily you are practicing an art, not a science. The role of science in crime detection is worthy, honorable, and effective, but it has little part in the activities of a private detective who aspires to eminence. Anyone of moderate capacity can become adept with a vernier caliper, a camera, a microscope, a spectrograph, or a centrifuge, but they are merely the servants of detection. Science in detection can be distinguished, even brilliant, but it can never replace either the inexorable march of a fine intellect through a jungle of lies and fears to the clearing of truth, or the flash of perception along a sensitive nerve touched off by a tone of a voice or a flicker of an eye."

"Excuse me," I interposed. "Was that 'a tone of voice' or 'a tone of *a* voice'?"

"Neither," Wolfe lied. "It was 'a tone of some voice.'" He resumed to Pete, "The art of detection has many levels and many faces. Take one. Shadowing a man around New York without losing him is an extremely difficult task. When the police undertake it seriously they use three men, and even so they are often hoodwinked. There is a man who often works for me, Saul Panzer, who is a genius at it, working alone. I have discussed it with him and have concluded that he himself does not know the secret of his superlative knack. It is not a conscious and controlled operation of his brain, though he has a good one; it is something hidden somewhere in his nervous system—possibly, of course, in his skull. He says that he seems somehow to know, barely in the nick of time, what the man he is following is about to do—not what he has done or is doing, but what he intends. That's why Mr. Panzer might teach you everything he knows, and still you would never be his equal. But that doesn't mean you shouldn't learn all you can. Learning will never hurt you. Only the man who knows too little knows too much. It is only when you undertake to use what you have learned that you discover whether you can transform knowledge into performance."

Wolfe aimed a thumb at me. "Take Mr. Goodwin. It would be difficult for me to function effectively without him. He is irreplaceable. Yet his actions are largely governed by impulse and caprice, and that would of course incapacitate him for any important task if it were not that he has somewhere concealed in him—possibly in his brain, though I doubt it—a powerful and subtle governor. For instance, the sight of a pretty girl provokes in him an overwhelming reaction of appreciation and approval, and correlatively his acquisitive instinct, but he has never married. Why not? Because he knows that if he had a wife his reaction to pretty girls, now pure and frank and free, would not only be intolerably adulterated but would also be under surveillance and subject to restriction by authority. So the governor always stops him short of disaster, doubtless occasionally on the very brink. It works similarly with the majority of his impulses and whims, but now and then it fails to intervene in time, and he suffers mishap, as this evening when he was impelled to badger me when a certain opportunity offered. It has already cost him—what time is it, Archie?"

I looked. "Eighteen minutes to nine."

"Hey!" Pete leaped from his chair. "I gotta run! My mother—I gotta be home by a quarter to! See you tomorrow!"

He was on his way. By the time I was up and in the hall he had reached the front door and pulled it open, and was gone. I stepped to the threshold of the dining room and told Wolfe, "Damn it, I was hoping he would stay till midnight so you could finish. After that a billiard match will be pretty dull, but I might as well go."

I went.

Chapter 2

Next day, Wednesday, I was fairly busy. A hardware manufacturer from Youngstown, Ohio, had come to New York to try to locate a son who had cut his lines of communication, and had wired Wolfe to help, and we had Saul Panzer, Fred Durkin, and Orrie Cather out scouting around. That kept me close to my desk and the phone, getting reports and relaying instructions.

A little after four in the afternoon Pete Drossos showed up and wanted to see Wolfe. His attitude indicated that while he was aware that I too had a license as a private detective and he had nothing serious against me, he preferred to deal with the boss. I explained that Nero Wolfe spent four hours every day—from nine to eleven in the morning and from four to six in the afternoon—up in the plant rooms on the roof, with his ten thousand orchids, bossing Theodore Horstmann instead of me, and that during those hours he was unavailable. Pete let me know that he thought that was a hell of a way for a private eye to spend his time, and I didn't argue the point. By the time I finally got him eased out to the stoop and the door closed, I was ready to concede that maybe my governor needed oiling. Pete was going to be a damn nuisance, no doubt of it. I should have choked my impulse to invite him in as a playmate for Wolfe. Whenever I catch myself talking me into chalking one up against me, it helps to take a drink, so I went to the kitchen for a glass of milk. As I returned to the office the phone was ringing—Orrie Cather making a report.

At the dinner table that evening neither Wolfe nor Fritz gave the slightest indication that starlings had ever come between them. As Wolfe took his second helping of the main dish, which was Danish pork pancake, he said distinctly, "Most satisfactory." Since for him that was positively lavish, Fritz took it as offered, nodded with dignity, and murmured, "Certainly, sir." So there were no sparks flying when we finished our coffee, and Wolfe was so agreeable that he said he would like to see me demonstrate Mosconi's spectacular break shot I had told him about, if I cared to descend to the basement with him.

But I didn't get to demonstrate. When the doorbell rang as we were leaving the dining room, I supposed of course it was Pete, but it wasn't. The figure visible through the glass panel was fully twice as big as Pete, and much more familiar—Sergeant Purley Stebbins of Manhattan Homicide West. Wolfe went into the office, and I went to the front and opened the door.

"They went thataway," I said, pointing.

"Nuts. I want to see Wolfe. And you."

"This is me. Shoot."

"And Wolfe."

"He's digesting pork. Hold it." I slipped the chain bolt to hold the door to a two-inch crack, stepped to the office, told Wolfe Stebbins wanted an audience, stood patiently while he made faces, was instructed to bring the caller in, and returned to the front and did so.

Over the years a routine had been established for seating Sergeant Stebbins in our office. When he came with Inspector Cramer, Cramer of course took the big red leather chair near the end of Wolfe's desk, and Purley one of the yellow ones, which were smaller. When he came alone, I tried to herd him into the red leather chair but never made it. He always sidestepped and pulled up a yellow one. It wasn't that he felt a sergeant shouldn't sit where he had seen an inspector sit, not Purley. It may be he doesn't like to face a window, or possibly he just doesn't like red chairs. Some day I'll ask him.

That day he got his meat and muscle, of which he has a full share, at rest on a yellow chair as usual, eyed Wolfe a moment, and then twisted his neck to confront me. "Yesterday you phoned me about a car —a dark gray fifty-two Cadillac, Connecticut license YY nine-four-three-two. Why?"

I raised my shoulders and let them drop. "I told you. We had information, not checked, that the car or its owner or driver might have been involved in something, or might be. I suggested a routine inquiry."

"I know you did. Exactly what was your information and where did you get it?"

I shook my head. "You asked me that yesterday and I passed it. I still pass. Our informant doesn't want to be annoyed."

"Well, he's going to be. Who was it and what did he tell you?"

"Nothing doing." I turned a hand over. "You

know damn well this is just a bad habit you've got. If something has happened that makes you think I've got to tell you who and what, tell me what happened and let's see if I agree with you. You know how reasonable I am."

"Yeah, I sure do." Purley set his jaw and then relaxed it. "At six-forty this afternoon, two hours ago, a car stopped for a red light at the corner of Thirty-fifth Street and Ninth Avenue. A boy with a rag went to it and started wiping a window. He finished that side and started for the other side, and as he was circling in front of the car it suddenly jumped forward and ran over him, and kept going fast, across the avenue and along Thirty-fifth Street. The boy died soon after the ambulance got him to the hospital. The driver was a man, alone in the car. With excitement like that people never see much, but two people, a woman and a boy, agree about the license number, Connecticut YY nine-four-three-two, and the boy says it was a dark gray Cadillac sedan. Well?"

"What was the boy's name? The one that was killed."

"What's that got to do with it?"

"I don't know. I'm asking."

"His name was Drossos. Peter Drossos."

I swallowed. "That's just fine. The sonofabitch."

"Who, the boy?"

"No." I turned to Wolfe. "Do you tell it or do I?"

Wolfe had closed his eyes. He opened them to say, "You," and closed them again.

I didn't think it was necessary to tell Stebbins about the domestic crisis that had given me the impulse to take Pete in to Wolfe, but I gave him everything that was relevant, including Pete's second visit that afternoon. Though for once in his life he was satisfied that he was getting something straight in that office, he asked a lot of questions, and at the end he saw fit to contribute an unfriendly comment to the effect that worthy citizens like Nero Wolfe and Archie Goodwin might have been expected to show a little more interest in a woman with a gun in her ribs wanting a cop.

I wasn't feeling jaunty, and that stung me. "Specimens like you," I told him, "are not what has made this country great. The kid might have made it all up. He admitted he didn't see the gun. Or the woman might have been pulling his leg. If I had told you yesterday who had told me what, you would have thought I was screwy to spend a dime on it for a phone call. And I did give you the license number. Did you check on it?"

"Yes. It was a floater. It was taken from a Plymouth that was stolen in Hartford two months ago."

"No trace?"

"None so far. Now we'll ask Connecticut to dig. I don't know how many floater plates there are in New York this minute, but there are plenty."

"How good a description have you got of the driver?"

"We've got four and no two alike. Three of them aren't worth a damn and the other one may be—a man that had just come out of the drugstore and happened to notice the kid going to the car with his rag. He says the driver was a man about forty, dark brown suit, light complexion, regular features, felt hat pulled down nearly to his ears. He says he thinks he could identify him." Purley got up. "I'll be going. I'll admit I'm disappointed. I fully expected either

I'd get a lead from you or I'd find you covering for a client."

Wolfe opened his eyes, "I wish you luck, Mr. Stebbins. That boy ate at my table yesterday."

"Yeah," Purley growled, "that makes it bad. People have no business running over boys that ate at your table."

On that sociable note he marched out, and I went to the hall with him. As I put my hand on the doorknob a figure rose to view outside, coming up the steps to the stoop, and when I pulled the door open there she was—a skinny little woman in a neat dark blue dress, no jacket and no hat, with puffed red eyes and her mouth pressed so tight there were no lips.

Stebbins was just back of me as I addressed her. "Can I help you, madam?"

She squeezed words out. "Does Mr. Nero Wolfe live here?"

I told her yes.

"Do you think I could see him? I won't be long. My name is Mrs. Anthea Drossos."

She had been crying and looked as if she might resume any second, and a crying woman is one of the things Wolfe won't even try to take. So I told her he was busy, and I was his confidential assistant, and wouldn't she please tell me.

She raised her head to meet my eyes straight. "My boy Pete told me to see Mr. Nero Wolfe," she said, "and I'll just wait here till I can see him." She propped herself against the railing of the stoop.

I backed up and shut the door. Stebbins was at my heels as I entered the office and spoke to Wolfe. "Mrs. Anthea Drossos wants to see you. She says her boy Pete told her to. I won't do. She'll camp on the stoop all night if she has to. She might start crying in your presence. What do I do, take a mattress out to her?"

That opened his eyes all right. "Confound it. What can I do for the woman?"

"Nothing. Me too. But she won't take it from me."

"Then why the devil—pfui! Bring her in. That performance of yours yesterday—bring her in."

I went and got her. When I ushered her in Purley was planted back in his chair. With my hand on her elbow because she didn't seem any too sure of her footing, I steered her to the red leather number, which would have held three of her. She perched on the edge, with her black eyes—blacker, I suppose, because of the contrast with the inflamed lids—aimed at Wolfe.

Her voice was low and a little quavery, but determined. "Are you Mr. Nero Wolfe?"

He admitted it. She shifted the eyes to me, then to Stebbins, and back to Wolfe. "These gentlemen?" she asked.

"Mr. Goodwin, my assistant, and Mr. Stebbins, a policeman who is investigating the death of your son."

She nodded. "I thought he looked like a cop. My boy Pete wouldn't want me to tell this to a cop."

From her tone and expression it seemed pretty plain that she didn't intend to do anything her boy Pete wouldn't have wanted her to do, and therefore we had a problem. With Purley's deep suspicion that Wolfe, not to mention me, would rather be caught dead than with nothing up his sleeve, he sure wasn't going to bow out. But without hesitation he arose, said, "I'll go to the kitchen," and headed for the door.

My surprise lasted half a second, until I realized where he was going. In the alcove at the rear end of the hall, across from the kitchen, there was a hole in the wall that partitioned the alcove from the office. On the office side the hole was covered with a trick picture, and from the alcove side, when you slid a panel, you could see and hear movements and sounds from the office. Purley knew all about it.

As Purley disappeared I thought it just as well to warn Wolfe. "The picture."

"Certainly," Wolfe said peevishly. He looked at Mrs. Drossos. "Well, madam?"

She was taking nothing for granted. She got up and went to the open door to look both ways in the hall, shut the door, and returned to her seat. "You know Pete got killed."

"Yes, I know."

"They told me, and I ran down to the street, and there he was. He was unconscious but he wasn't dead. They let me ride in the ambulance with him. That was when he told me. He opened—"

She stopped. I was afraid it was going to bust, and so was she, but after sitting for half a minute without a muscle moving she had it licked and could go on. "He opened his eyes and saw me, and I put my head down to him. He said—I think I can tell you just what he said—he said, 'Tell Nero Wolfe he got me. Don't tell anybody but Nero Wolfe. Give him my money in the can.'"

She stopped and was rigid again. After a full minute of it Wolfe nudged her. "Yes, madam?"

She opened her bag, of black leather that had seen some wear but was good for more, fingered in it, extracted a small package wrapped in paper, and arose to put the package on Wolfe's desk.

"There's four dollars and thirty cents." She stayed on her feet. "He made it himself, it's his money that he kept in a tobacco can. That was the last thing he said, telling me to give you his money in the can; after that he was unconscious again, and he died before they could do anything at the hospital. I came away and came home to get his money and come and tell you. Now I'll go back." She turned, took a couple of steps, and turned again. "Did you understand what I told you?"

"Yes, I understand."

"Do you want me to do anything?"

"No, I think not. Archie?"

I was already there beside her. She seemed a little steadier on her feet than she had coming in, but I kept her arm anyway, on out to the stoop and down the seven steps to the sidewalk. She didn't thank me, but since she may not even have known I was there I didn't hold it against her.

Purley was in the hall when I re-entered, with his hat on. I asked him, "Did you shut the panel?"

"Taking candy from a kid I might expect," he said offensively. "But taking candy from a dead kid, by God!"

He was leaving, and I sidestepped to block him. "Oaf. Meaning you. If we had insisted on her taking it back she would have—"

I chopped it off at his grin of triumph. "Got you that time!" he croaked, and brushed past me and went.

So as I stepped into the office I was biting a nail. It is not often that Purley Stebbins can string me, but that day he had caught me off balance because my sentiments had been involved. Naturally I reacted by trying to take it out on Wolfe. I went to his desk for the little packet, unfolded the paper, and arranged the contents neatly in front of him: two dollar bills, four quarters, nine dimes, and eight nickels.

"Right," I announced. "Four dollars and thirty cents. Hearty congratulations. After income tax and deducting ten cents for expenses—the phone call to Stebbins yesterday—there will be enough left to—"

"Shut up," he snapped. "Will you return it to her tomorrow?"

"I will not. Nor any other day. You know damn well that's impossible."

"Give it to the Red Cross."

"You give it." I was firm. "She may never come again, but if she does and asks me what we did with Pete's money I won't feel like saying Red Cross and I won't feel like lying."

He pushed the dough away from him, to the other edge of the desk, toward me. "You brought him into this house."

"It's your house, and you fed him cookies."

That left it hanging. Wolfe picked up his current book from the other end of his desk, opened to his place, swiveled and maneuvered his seventh of a ton to a comfortable position, and started reading. I went to my desk and sat, and pretended to go over yesterday's reports from Saul and Fred and Orrie while I considered the situation. Somewhat later I pulled the typewriter around, put in paper, and hit the keys. The first draft had some flaws, which I corrected, and then typed it again on a fresh sheet. That time I thought it would do. I turned to face Wolfe and announced, "I have a suggestion."

He finished his paragraph, which must have been a long one, before glancing at me. "Well?"

"We're stuck with this dough and have to do

something with it. You may remember that you told Pete that the point is not so much to earn a fee as it is to feel that you earned it. I should think you would feel you earned this one if you blow it all on an ad in the paper reading something like this:

"Woman with spider earrings and scratch on cheek who on Tuesday, driving a car, told boy at Thirty-fifth Street and Ninth Avenue to get a cop, please communicate with Nero Wolfe at address in phone book."

I slid the paper across his desk to him. "In the *Times* the fee might not quite cover it, but I'll be glad to toss in a buck or two. I regard it as brilliant. It will spend Pete's money on Pete. It will make Cramer and Stebbins sore, and Stebbins has it coming to him. And since there's not one chance in a million that it will get a nibble, it won't expose you to the risk of any work or involvement. Last but not least, it will get your name in the paper. What do you say?"

He picked up the sheet and glanced over it with his nose turned up. "Very well," he agreed grumpily. "I hope to heaven this has taught you a lesson."

Chapter 3

The hardware manufacturer's son was finally spotted and corralled the next day, Thursday afternoon. Since that was a hush operation for more reasons than one—to show you how hush, he wasn't a hardware manufacturer and he wasn't from Youngstown—I can supply no details. But I make one remark. If Wolfe felt that he earned the fee he soaked that bird for, no ego was ever put to a severer test.

So Thursday was a little hectic, with no spare time for consideration of the question whether, if we had taken a different slant on the case Pete had come to share with us, Pete might still be breathing. In the detective business there are plenty of occasions for that kind of consideration, and while there is no percentage in letting it get you down, it doesn't hurt to take time out now and then for some auditing.

It had been too late Wednesday night to get the ad in for Thursday. Friday morning I had to grin at myself a couple of times. When I went down the two flights from my bedroom and entered the kitchen, the first thing I did after greeting Fritz was to turn

to the ads in the *Times* for a look at ours. That rated
a grin. It meant nothing, either professionally or personally, since the chance of getting an answer was
even slimmer than my estimate of one in a million.
The second grin came later, when I was dealing with
corn muffins and sausage—Fritz having taken
Wolfe's breakfast tray up to him according to schedule—with the *Times* in front of me on the rack, and
the phone rang and I nearly knocked my chair over
getting up to go for it. It was not someone answering
the ad. Some guy on Long Island wanted to know if
we could let him have three plants in bloom of Vanda
caerulea. I told him we didn't sell plants, and anyway
that Vandas didn't bloom in May.

But Pete's case was brought to us again before
noon, though not by way of the ad. Wolfe had just
got down to the office from the plant rooms and settled himself at his desk for a look at the morning
mail when the doorbell rang. Going to the hall and
seeing the ringer through the one-way panel, I had
no need to proceed to the door to ask him what he
wanted. That customer always wanted to see Wolfe,
and his arriving on the dot of eleven made it certain.

I turned and told Wolfe, "Inspector Cramer."

He scowled at me. "What does he want?" Childish again.

"Shall I ask him?"

"Yes. No. Very well."

I went and let him in. From the way he grunted a
greeting, if it could be called a greeting, and from the
expression on his face, he had not come to give Wolfe
a medal. Cramer's big red face and burly figure
never inspire a feeling of good-fellowship, but he had
his ups and downs, and that morning he was not up.
He preceded me to the office, gave Wolfe the twin of

the greeting he had given me, lowered himself into the red leather chair, and aimed a cold stare at Wolfe. Wolfe returned it.

"Why did you put that ad in the paper?" Cramer demanded.

Wolfe turned away from him and fingered in the little stack of papers on his desk that had just been removed from envelopes. "Archie," he said, "this letter from Jordan is farcical. He knows quite well that I do not use Brassavolas in tri-generic crosses. He doesn't deserve an answer, but he'll get one. Your notebook. 'Dear Mr. Jordan. I am aware that you have had ill success with—'"

"Save it," Cramer rasped. "Okay. Putting an ad in the paper is not a felony, but I asked a civil question."

"No," Wolfe said with finality. "Civil?"

"Then put it your way. You know what I want to know. How do you want me to ask it?"

"I would first have to be told why you want to know."

"Because I think you're covering something or somebody that's connected with a homicide. Which has been known to happen. From what you told Stebbins yesterday, you have no interest in the killing of that boy, and you have no client. Then you wouldn't spend a bent nickel on it, not you, and you certainly wouldn't start an inquiry that might make you use up energy. I might have asked you flat, who's your client, but no, I stick to the simple fact why did you run that ad. If that's not civil, civilize it and then tell me."

Wolfe took in a long-drawn sigh and let it out. "Archie. Tell him, please."

I obliged. It didn't take long, since he already had

Purley's report, and I had merely to explain how we had decided to disburse Pete's money, to which I had added $1.85 of my own. Meanwhile Cramer's hard gray eyes were leveled at me. I had often had to meet those eyes and stall or cover or dodge, so they didn't bother me any when I was merely handing it over straight.

When he had asked a couple of questions and had been answered, he moved the eyes to Wolfe and inquired abruptly, "Have you ever seen or heard of a man named Matthew Birch?"

"Yes," Wolfe said shortly.

"Oh. You have." A gleam showed in the gray eyes for a fraction of a second. If I hadn't known them so well I wouldn't have caught it. "I intend to make this civil. Would you mind telling me when and where?"

"No. In the *Gazette* day before yesterday, Wednesday. As you know, I never leave this house on business, and leave it as seldom as may be for anything whatever, and I depend on newspapers and the radio to keep me informed of the concerns and activities of my fellow beings. As reported, the body of a man named Matthew Birch was found late Tuesday night—or Wednesday, rather, around three A.M.—in a cobbled alley alongside a South Street pier. It was thought that a car had run over him."

"Yeah. I'll try to frame this right. Except for newspaper or radio items connected with his death, had or have you ever seen or heard of him?"

"Not under that name."

"Damn it, under any name?"

"Not to my knowledge."

"Have you any reason to suppose or suspect that the man found dead in that alley was someone you had ever seen or heard of in any connection whatever?"

"That's more like it," Wolfe said approvingly. "That should settle it. The answer is no. May I ask one? Have you any reason to suppose or suspect that the answer should be yes?"

Cramer didn't reply. He tilted his head until his chin touched the knot of his tie, pursed his lips, regarded me for a long moment, and then went back to Wolfe. He spoke. "This is why I came. With the message the boy sent you by his mother, and the way the car jumped him from a standstill and then tore off, already it didn't look like any accident, and now there are complications, and when I find complicated trouble and you even remotely involved I want to know exactly where and how you got on—and where you get off."

"I asked about reasons, not about animus."

"There's no animus. Here's the complication. The car that killed the boy was found yesterday morning, with that floater Connecticut plate still on it, parked up on One hundred and eighty-sixth Street. Laboratory men worked on it all day. They cinched it that it killed the boy, but not only that, underneath it, caught tight where an axle joins a rod, they found a piece of cloth the size of a man's hand. That piece of cloth was the flap torn from the jacket which was on the body of Matthew Birch when it was found. The laboratory is looking for further evidence that it was that car that killed Birch, but I'm no hog and I don't need it. Do you?"

Wolfe was patient. "For a working hypothesis, if I were working on it, no."

"That's the point. You are working on it. You put that ad in."

Wolfe's head wagged slowly from side to side to punctuate his civilized forbearance. "I'll stipulate," he conceded, "that I am capable of flummery, that I have on occasion gulled and hoaxed you, but you know I eschew the crudeness of an explicit lie. I tell you that the facts we have given you in this matter are guileless and complete, that I have no client connected with it in any way, and that I am not engaged in it and do not intend to be. I certainly agree—"

The phone ringing stopped him. I got it at my desk. "Nero Wolfe's office, Archie Goodwin speaking."

"May I speak to Mr. Wolfe, please?" The voice was low, nervous, and feminine.

"I'll see if he's available. Your name?"

"He wouldn't know my name. I want to see him—it's about his advertisement in the *Times* this morning. I want to make an appointment with him."

I kept it casual. "I handle his appointments. May I have your name, please?"

"I'd rather—when I come. Could I come at twelve o'clock?"

"Hold the wire a minute." I consulted my desk calendar, turning to a page for next week. "Yes, that'll be all right if you're punctual. You have the address?"

She said she did. I hung up and turned to report to Wolfe. "A character who probably wants to look at the orchids. I'll handle it as usual."

He resumed to Cramer. "I certainly agree that the evidence that the boy and Matthew Birch were killed by the same car is a noteworthy complication, but actually that should make it simpler for you. Even though the license plate is useless, surely you can trace the car itself."

Cramer's expression had reverted to the cold stare he had started with. "I have never had any notion," he stated, "that you are a crude liar. I have never seen you crude." He arose. In Wolfe's presence he always made a point of getting upright from a chair with the leverage of his leg muscles only, because Wolfe used hands and arms. "No," he said, "not crude," and turned and marched out.

I went to the hall to see the door close behind him and then returned to the office and my desk.

"The letter to Mr. Jordan," Wolfe instructed me.

"Yes, sir." I got my notebook. "First, though, I still say it was one in a million, but the one turned up this time. That was a woman on the phone about the ad. No name, and I didn't want to press her with company present. She made an appointment for noon today."

"With whom?"

"You."

His lips tightened. He released them. "Archie. This is insufferable."

"I know damn well it is. But considering that Cramer wasn't being civilized, I thought it might be satisfactory to have a little chat with her before phoning him to come and get her." I glanced up at the wall clock. "She'll be here in twenty minutes—if she comes."

He grunted. " 'Dear Mr. Jordan . . .' "

Chapter 4

She came. She was much more ornamental in the red leather chair than Inspector Cramer, or, for that matter, most of the thousands of tenants I had seen in it, but she sure was nervous. At the door, after I opened it and invited her in, I thought she was going to turn and scoot, and so did she, but she finally made her legs take her over the sill and let me conduct her to the office.

The scratch on her left cheek, on a slant down toward the corner of her mouth, was faint but noticeable on her smooth fair skin, and it was no wonder that Pete, looking straight at her face, had taken in the spider earrings. I agreed with him that they were gold, and they were fully as noticeable as the scratch. In spite of the scratch and the earrings and the jerky nervousness, on her the red leather chair looked good. She was about my age, which was not ideal, but I have nothing against maturity if it isn't overdone.

When Wolfe asked her, not too grumpily, what he could do for her, she opened her bag and got out two pieces of paper. The bag was of soft green suede, the same as the jacket she wore over a dark green woolen dress, and also the cocky little pancake tilted to one side of her head. It was an ensemble if I ever saw one.

"This," she said, "is just a clipping of your advertisement." She returned it to the bag. "This is a check made out to you for five hundred dollars."

"May I see it, please?"

"I don't—not yet. It has my name on it."

"So I would guess."

"I want to ask you—some things before I give you my name."

"What things?"

"Well, I—about the boy. The boy I asked to get a cop." Her voice wouldn't have been bad at all, in fact I might have liked it, if it hadn't been so jumpy. She was getting more nervous instead of less. "I want to see him. Will you arrange for me to see him? Or it would be—just give me his name and address. I think perhaps that would be enough for the five hundred dollars—I know you charge high. Or I might want—but first tell me that."

Wolfe invariably kept his eyes, when they were open, directly at the person he was talking to, but it had struck me that he was giving this visitor a specially keen inspection. He turned to me. "Archie. Please look closely at the scratch on her cheek."

I got up to obey. She had alternatives: sit and let me look, cover her face with her hands, or get up and go; but before she had time to choose I was there, bending over, with my eyes only a foot from her face.

She started to say something, then checked it as I straightened up and told Wolfe, "Made with something with a fine sharp point. It could have been a needle, but more likely a small scissors point."

"When?"

"The best guess is today, but it could have been yesterday I suppose. Not possibly three days ago." I stayed beside her.

"This is impudent!" she blurted. She left the chair. "I'm glad I didn't tell you my name!" She couldn't sweep out without sweeping through me.

"Nonsense." Wolfe was curt. "You couldn't possibly have imposed on me, even without the evidence of the scratch, unless you had been superlatively coached. Describe the boy. Describe the other occupants of the car. What time did it happen? What did the boy say? Exactly what did he do? And so on. As for your name, that is no longer in your discretion. Mr. Goodwin takes your bag, by force if necessary, and examines its contents. If you complain, we are two to one. Sit down, madam."

"This is contemptible!"

"No. It's our justifiable reaction to your attempt to humbug us. You are not under duress, but if you go you leave your name behind. Sit down and we'll discuss it, but first the name."

She may have been over-optimistic to think she could breeze into Nero Wolfe's office and fool him, but she wasn't a fool. She stood surveying the situation, all signs of nervousness gone, came to a conclusion, opened her bag, and got out an object which she displayed to Wolfe. "My driving license."

He took it and gave it a look and handed it back to her, and she seated herself. "I'm Laura Fromm," she said, "Mrs. Damon Fromm. I am a widow. My New York residence is at Seven-forty-three East Sixty-eighth Street. Tuesday, driving a car on Thirty-fifth Street, I told a boy to get a cop. I gathered from your advertisement that you can direct me to the boy, and I will pay you for it."

"So you don't admit this is an imposture."

"Certainly not."

"What time of day was it?"

"That's not important."

"What was the boy doing when you spoke to him?"

"Neither is that."

"How far away was the boy when you spoke to him, and how loudly did you shout?"

She shook her head. "I'm not going to answer any questions about it. Why should I?"

"But you maintain that you were driving the car and told the boy to get a cop?"

"Yes."

"Then you're in a pickle. The police want to question you about a murder. On Wednesday a car ran over the boy and killed him. Intentionally."

She gawked. "What?"

"It was the same car. The one you were driving Tuesday when the boy spoke to you."

She opened her mouth and closed it. Then she got words out. "I don't believe it."

"You will. The police will explain to you how they know it was the same car. There's no question about it, Mrs. Fromm."

"I mean the whole thing—you're making it up. This is—worse than contemptible."

Wolfe's head moved. "Archie, get yesterday's *Times*."

I went for it to the shelf where the papers are kept until they're a week old. Opening it to page eight and folding it, I crossed and handed it to Laura Fromm. Her hand was shaking a little as she took it, and to steady it while she read she called on the other hand to help hold it.

She took plenty of time for the reading. When her eyes lifted, Wolfe said, "There is nothing there to indicate that Peter Drossos was the boy you had accosted on Tuesday, but you don't need to take my word for that. The police will tell you about it."

Her eyes darted back and forth, from Wolfe to me and back again, and then settled on me. "I want— could I have some gin?"

She had let the newspaper drop to the floor. I picked it up and asked, "Straight?"

"That will do. Or a Gibson?"

"Onion?"

"No. No, thank you. But double?"

I went to the kitchen for the ingredients and ice. As I stirred I was thinking that if she was hoping for any cooperation from Wolfe it was too bad she had asked for gin, since in his book all gin drinkers were barbarians. That was probably why, when I took the tray in and put it on the little table beside her chair, he was leaning back with his eyes closed. I poured and served. First she swigged it, then had a few sips, and then swigged again. Meanwhile she kept her eyes lowered, presumably to keep me from looking in through them to watch her mind work.

Finally she emptied the glass the second time, put it on the tray and spoke. "A man was driving the car when it struck the boy."

Wolfe opened his eyes. "The tray, Archie?"

The smell of gin, especially with lunch only half an hour away, was of course repulsive. I took the vile object to the kitchen and returned.

". . . but though that isn't conclusive," Wolfe was saying, "since in a man's clothes you could pass for a man if you avoided scrutiny, I admit it is relevant. Anyhow, I am not assuming that you killed the boy. I tell you merely that by being drawn to me by that advertisement, and coming rigged in those earrings and that bogus scratch, you have put your foot in it, and if you stick to it that you were driving that car on Tuesday you will have fully qualified as a feeble-minded donkey."

"I wasn't."

"That's better. Where were you Tuesday afternoon from six-thirty to seven?"

"At a meeting of the Executive Committee of the Association for the Aid of Displaced Persons. It lasted until after seven. It was one of the causes my husband was interested in, and I am going on with it."

"Where were you Wednesday afternoon from six-thirty to seven?"

"What has that—oh. The boy was—yes. That was day before yesterday." She paused, not for long. "I was having cocktails at the Churchill with a friend."

"The friend's name, please?"

"This is ridiculous."

"I know it is. Almost as ridiculous as that scratch on your cheek."

"The friend's name is Dennis Horan. A lawyer."

Wolfe nodded. "Even so you are in for some disagreeable hours. I doubt if you have been willfully implicated in murder. I have had some experience watching faces, and I don't think your shock on hearing of the boy's death was feigned; but you'd better get your mind arranged. You're going to get it. Not from me. I don't ask why you tried this masquerade, because I'm not concerned, but the police will be insistent about it. I won't attempt to hold you here for them; you may go. You will hear from them."

Her eyes were brighter and her chin was higher.

It doesn't take gin long to get in a kick. "I don't have to hear from them," she said with assurance. "Why do I?"

"Because they'll want to know why you came here."

"I mean why do you have to tell them?"

"Because I withhold information pertinent to a crime only under dictation by my interest."

"I haven't committed any crime."

"That's what they'll want you to establish, but that won't satisfy their curiosity."

She looked at me, and I returned it. I may not be a Nero Wolfe at reading faces, but I too have had some experience at it, and I swear she was sizing me up, trying to decide if there was any way of lining me up with her in case she told Wolfe to go sit on a tack. I made it easy for her by looking manly, staunch and virtuous, but not actually hostile. I saw it on her face when she gave me up. Leaving me as hopeless, she opened the green suede bag, took from it a leather fold and a pen, opened the fold on the little table, and bent over it to write. Having written, she tore a small blue rectangle of paper from the fold and left her chair to put it in front of Wolfe on his desk.

"That's a check for ten thousand dollars," she told him.

"I see it is."

"It's a retainer."

"For what?"

"Oh, I'm not trying to bribe you." She smiled. It was the first time she had shown any reaction resembling a smile, and I gave her a mark for it. "It looks as if I'm going to need some expert advice, and maybe some expert help, and you already know

about it, and I wouldn't want—I don't care to consult
my lawyer, at least not now."

"Bosh. You're offering to pay me not to tell the
police of your visit."

"No, I'm not." Her eyes were shining but not
soft. "All right, I am, but not objectionably. I am
Mrs. Damon Fromm. My husband left me a large for-
tune, including a great deal of New York real estate.
I have position and responsibilities. If you report
this to the police I would arrange to see the Commissioner, and I don't think I would be abused, but I
would much rather not. If you'll come to my home at
noon tomorrow, I'll know what—"

"I don't go to people's homes."

"Oh yes, you don't." She frowned, but only for an
instant. "Then I'll come here."

"At noon tomorrow?"

"No, if it's here, eleven-thirty would be better because I have a one-o'clock appointment. Until then
you will not report my coming today. I want to—I
must see someone. I must try to find out something.
Tomorrow I will tell you all about it—no, I won't say
that. I'll say this: if I don't tell you all about it tomorrow you will inform the police if you decide you have
to. If I do tell you I will need your advice and I will
probably need your help. That's what the retainer is
for."

Wolfe grunted. His head turned. "Archie. Is she
Mrs. Damon Fromm?"

"I would say yes, but I won't sign it."

He went to her. "Madam, you tried one imposture and abandoned it only under pressure; this
could be another. Mr. Goodwin will go to a newspaper office and look at pictures of Mrs. Damon

Fromm, and phone me from there. Half an hour should do it. You will stay here with me."

She smiled again. "This *is* ridiculous."

"No doubt. But under the circumstances, not unreasonable. Do you refuse?"

"Of course not. I suppose I deserve it."

"You don't object?"

"No."

"Then it isn't necessary. You are Mrs. Fromm. Before you leave, an understanding and a question. The understanding: my decision whether to accept your retainer and work for you will be made tomorrow; you are not now my client. The question: do you know who the woman was who drove that car Tuesday and spoke to the boy?"

She shook her head. "Make your decision tomorrow, that's all right, but you won't report this visit before then?"

"No. That's understood. The question?"

"I'm not going to answer it now because I can't. I don't really *know*. I expect to answer it tomorrow."

"But you think you know?" Wolfe insisted.

"I won't answer it."

He frowned at her. "Mrs. Fromm. I must warn you. Have you ever seen or heard of a man named Matthew Birch?"

She frowned back. "No. Birch? No. Why?"

"A man of that name was run over by a car and killed Tuesday evening, and it was the same car as the one that killed Peter Drossos Wednesday. Since the car itself cannot be supposed ruthless and malign, someone associated with it must be. I am warning you not to be foolhardy, or even imprudent. You have told me next to nothing, so I don't know how imminent or deadly a doom you may be inviting, but I admonish you: beware!"

"The same car? Killed a man Tuesday?"

"Yes. Since you didn't know him you are not concerned, but I urge you to be discreet."

She sat frowning, "I am discreet, Mr. Wolfe."

"Not today, with that silly sham."

"Oh, you're wrong! I *was* being discreet! Or trying to." She got the leather fold and pen from the table, returned them to her bag, and closed it. She stood up. "Thank you for the gin, but I wish I hadn't asked for it. I shouldn't have." She offered a hand.

Wolfe doesn't usually rise when a woman enters or leaves the office. That time he did, but it was no special tribute to Laura Fromm or even to the check she had put on his desk. It was lunchtime, and he would have had to manipulate his bulk in a minute anyway. So he was on his feet to take her hand. Of course I was up, ready to take her to the door, and I thought it was darned gracious of her to give me a hand too, after the way I had repulsed her with my incorruptible look. I nearly bumped into her when, preceding me to the door, she suddenly turned to say to Wolfe, "I forgot to ask. The boy, Peter Drossos, was he a displaced person?"

Wolfe said he didn't know.

"Could you find out? And tell me tomorrow?"

He said he could.

There was no car waiting for her in front. Apparently the parking situation had compelled even Mrs. Damon Fromm to resort to taxis. When I returned to the office Wolfe wasn't there, and I found him in the kitchen, lifting the lid from a steaming casserole of lamb cutlets with gammon and tomatoes. It smelled good enough to eat.

"One thing I admit," I said generously. "You have damn good eyes. But of course pretty women's faces are so irresistible to you that you resented the scratch and so you focused on it."

He ignored it. "Are you going to the bank after lunch to deposit Mr. Corliss's check?"

"You know I am."

"Go also to Mrs. Fromm's bank and have her check certified. That will verify her signature. Fritz, this is even better than last time. Satisfactory."

Chapter 5

Before noon the next day, Saturday, I had plenty of dope on our prospective client. To begin with, five minutes spent in the *Gazette* morgue, by courtesy of my friend Lon Cohen, settled it that she was Mrs. Damon Fromm. She was good for somewhere between five million and twenty million, and since it was unlikely that we would ever want to bill her for more than a million or two, I didn't go any further into that. Her husband, who had been about twice her age, had died two years ago of a heart attack, leaving her the works. No children. She was born Laura Atherton, of a Philadelphia family of solid citizens, and had been married to Fromm seven years when he died.

Fromm had inherited a small pile and had built it into a mountain, chiefly in the chemical industry. His contributions to various organizations had caused an assortment of chairmen and chairladies and executive secretaries, upon news of his death, to have a deep and decent interest in the terms of his will, but except for a few modest bequests everything had gone to his widow. However, she had carried on with the contributions, and had also been generous with her time and energy, with special attention to Assadip, which was the cable code for the Association for the Aid of Displaced Persons, and the way it was usually spoken of by people who were thrifty with their breath.

If I give the impression that I had spent many hours on a thorough job of research, I should correct it. A quarter of an hour with Lon Cohen, after consulting the *Gazette*'s morgue, gave me all of the above except one item, which I got at our bank. There was no danger of Lon blatting around that Nero Wolfe was getting briefed on Mrs. Damon Fromm, since we had given him at least as many breaks on stories as he had given us on scuttlebutt.

At a quarter to twelve Saturday morning Wolfe was at his desk and I was standing at his elbow, rechecking with him the expense account of the job for Corliss (not his name), the hardware manufacturer (not his line). Wolfe thought he had found a twenty-dollar error in it, and it was up to me to prove he was wrong. It turned out to be a draw. Twenty dollars that I had charged against Orrie Cather should have been charged against Saul Panzer, which put me one down, but that made no difference in the grand total, which made us even. As I gathered up the sheets and crossed to the filing cabinet I glanced at my wrist. One minute to twelve.

"Twenty-nine minutes after eleven-thirty," I remarked. "Shall I phone her?"

He muttered no, and I went to the safe for the checkbook, to take care of some household bills, while Wolfe flipped the radio switch at his desk for the twelve-o'clock news. As I sat filling in the stubs my ears heard and I half listened:

"The coming Bermuda conference of the leaders of the United States, Great Britain, and France, which has been rendered somewhat doubtful by the fall of Premier Mayer, will probably be proceeded with as arranged. It is thought that Mayer's successor will be established in office in time to take the third place at the table.

"There is speculation in Tokyo that the three-day interval in the Korean truce negotiations granted at the request of the United Nations Command was intended to permit further consultation among representatives of the United Nations powers in the United States and at the Tokyo headquarters of General Mark W. Clark, the United Nations commander.

"The body of Mrs. Damon Fromm, wealthy New York socialite and philanthropist, was found early today lying in a passage between pillars of the East Side elevated highway now under construction. According to the police, she had been run over by a car, and it is not believed to have been an accident.

"An estimated million and a quarter New Yorkers got an impressive capsule demonstration of the might of American armed forces . . ."

Wolfe didn't turn it off. As far as I could tell from his expression, he was actually listening. But by the time the five minutes were up he was developing a scowl, and after flipping the switch he let it have his face without restraint.

"So," I said.

There were a dozen comments that could have been made, but none would have helped any. Wolfe certainly didn't need to be reminded that he had warned her not to be foolhardy or even imprudent. Also his scowl did not encourage comment. After a little he placed his palms on the arms of his chair and slowly moved them back and forth, rubbing the rough tapestry with a swishing sound. That went on for a while, then he folded his arms and sat straight.

"Archie."

"Yes, sir."

"How long will it take you to type an account of our conversation with Mrs. Fromm? Not verbatim. With your superlative memory you could come close to it, but that isn't necessary. Just the substance, adequately, as you would report to me."

"You could dictate it."

"I'm in no humor for dictation."

"Leave out anything?"

"Include only what is significant. Do not include my telling her that the same car killed Peter Drossos and Matthew Birch, since that has not been published."

"Twenty minutes."

"Type it in the form of a statement to be signed by you and me. Two carbons. Date it twelve noon today. You will take the original to Mr. Cramer's office immediately."

"Half an hour. For a signed statement I'll want to take more care."

"Very well."

I exceeded my estimate by less than five minutes. It covered three pages, and Wolfe read each page as it was finished. He made no corrections, and even no remarks, which was even stronger evidence of his state of mind than his refusal to dictate. We both signed it, and I stuck it in an envelope.

"Cramer won't be there," I told him. "Neither will Stebbins. Not with this to work on."

He said anyone would do, and I went.

I'm not a stranger at the Tenth Precinct on West 20th Street, which includes the headquarters of Manhattan Homicide West, but that day I saw no familiar faces until I mounted to the second floor and approached one at a desk with whom I was on speaking terms. I had been right; no Cramer and no Stebbins. Lieutenant Rowcliff was in charge, and the desk man phoned that I was there to see him.

If there were twenty of us, including Rowcliff, starving on an island, and we were balloting to elect the one we would carve up for a barbecue, I wouldn't vote for Rowcliff because I know I couldn't keep him down; and compared to his opinion of me, mine of him is sympathetic. So I wasn't surprised when, instead of having me conducted within, he came striding out and up to me, and rasped, "What do you want?"

I took the envelope from my pocket. "This," I said, "is not my application for a job on the force so I can serve under you."

"By God, if it were." He talked like that.

"Nor is it a citation—"

He jerked the envelope from my hand, removed the contents, darted a glance at the heading, turned to the third page, and darted another at the signatures.

"A statement by you and Wolfe. A masterpiece, no doubt. Do you want a receipt?"

"Not necessarily. I'll read it to you if you want me to."

"All I want of you is the sight of your back on the way out."

But without waiting for what he wanted, he wheeled and strode off. I told the one at the desk, "Kindly note that I delivered that envelope to that baboon at one-six Daylight Saving," and departed.

Back at the house, Wolfe had just started lunch, and I joined him in the operation on an anchovy omelet. He permits no talk of business at meals, and interruptions are out of the question, so it was further evidence of his state of mind when, as he was working on a fig and cherry tart, the phone ringing took me to the office, and I returned and told him, "A man named Dennis Horan on the line. You may remem—"

"Yes. What does he want?"

"You."

"We'll call him back in ten minutes."

"He's going places and won't be available."

He didn't even confound it. He didn't hustle any, but he went. I did too, and was at the phone at my desk before he reached his. He sat and got it to his ear.

"Nero Wolfe speaking."

"I'm Dennis Horan, Mr. Wolfe, counselor-at-law. There has been a terrible tragedy. Mrs. Damon Fromm is dead. Run over by a car."

"Indeed. When?"

"The body was found at five o'clock this morning." His voice was a thin tenor that seemed to want to squeak, but that could have been from the shock of the tragedy. "I was a friend of hers and handled some matters for her, and I'm calling about the check she gave you yesterday for ten thousand dollars. Has it been deposited?"

"No."

"That's good. Since she is dead of course it won't go through. Do you wish to mail it to her home address, or would you prefer to send it to me?"

"Neither. I'll deposit it."

"But it won't go through! Outstanding checks signed by a deceased person are not—"

"I know. It is certified. It was certified at her bank yesterday afternoon."

"Oh." A fairly long pause. "But since she is dead and can't use your services, since you can do nothing for her, I don't see how you can claim—I mean, wouldn't it be proper and ethical for you to return the check?"

"You are not my mentor in propriety and ethics, Mr. Horan."

"I don't say I am. But without any animus or prejudice, I put it to you, under the circumstances how can you justify keeping that money?"

"By earning it."

"You intend to earn it?"

"I do."

"How?"

"That's my affair. If you are an accredited representative of Mrs. Fromm's estate I am willing to discuss it with you, but not now on the telephone. I'll be available here at my office from now until four o'clock, or from six to seven, or from nine in the evening until midnight."

"I don't know—I don't believe—I'll see."

He hung up. So did we. Back in the dining room Wolfe finished his tart and his coffee in silence. I waited until we had returned to the office and he was adjusted in his chair to remark, "Earning it would be fine, but the main thing is to feel you've earned it.

No animus, but I doubt if delivering that statement to Rowcliff is quite enough. My ego is itching."

"Deposit the check," he muttered.

"Yes, sir."

"We need information."

"Yes, sir."

"See Mr. Cohen and get it."

"About what?"

"Everything. Include Matthew Birch, with the understanding that his knowledge of that connection is not to be disclosed unless the police release it or he gets it from some other source. Tell him nothing. It may be published that I am engaged on the case, but not the source of my interest."

"Do I tell him that Pete came to see you?"

"No."

"He would appreciate it. It would be an exclusive human interest story for him. Also it would show that your reputation—"

His fist hit the desk, which for him was a convulsion. "No!" he roared. "Reputation? Am I to invite the comment that it is a mortal hazard to solicit my help? On Tuesday, that boy. On Friday, that woman. They are both dead. I will not have my office converted into an anteroom for the morgue!"

"Yeah. Something of the sort had occurred to me."

"You were well advised not to voice it. The person responsible would have been well advised not to induce it. We will need Saul and Fred and Orrie, but I'll attend to that. Go."

I did so. I took a taxi to the *Gazette* office. The receptionist on the third floor, who had not only received me before but also had been, for three or four years, on the list of those who receive a box of orchids from Wolfe's plant rooms twice a year, spoke to Lon on the intercom and waved me in.

I don't know what Lon Cohen is on the *Gazette* and I doubt if he does. City or wire, daily or Sunday, foreign or national or local, he seems to know his way in and around without ever having to work at it. His is the only desk in a room about nine by twelve, and that's just as well because otherwise there would be no place for his feet, which are also about nine by twelve. From the ankles up he is fairly regular.

There were two colleagues in with him when I entered, but they soon finished and went. As we shook he said, "Stay on your feet. You can have two minutes."

"Nuts. An hour may do it."

"Not today. We're spinning on the Fromm murder. The only reason you got in at all, I want your release on the item that Nero Wolfe was making inquiries yesterday about Mrs. Fromm."

"I don't think—" I let it hang while I moved a chair and sat. "No, better not. But okay on an item that he is working on the murder."

"He is?"

"Yep."

"Who hired him?"

I shook my head. "It came by carrier pigeon, and he won't tell me."

"Take off your shoes and socks while I light a cigarette. A few applications to your tender flesh should do it. I want the name of the client."

"J. Edgar Hoover."

He made an unseemly noise. "Just a whisper, to me?"

"No."

"But it's open that Wolfe is working on the Fromm murder?"

"Yes. Just that."

"And the boy, Peter Drossos? And Matthew Birch? Them too?"

I gave him a look. "How come?"

"Oh, for God's sake. Wolfe's ad in the *Times* wanting to date a woman wearing spider earrings who had asked a boy at Ninth Avenue and Thirty-fifth Street to get a cop. Mrs. Fromm was wearing spider earrings, and you were here yesterday asking about her. As for Birch, the pattern. His body was found in a secluded spot, flattened by a car, and so was Mrs. Fromm's. I repeat the question."

"I answer it. Nero Wolfe is investigating the murder of Mrs. Fromm with his accustomed vigor, skill, and laziness. He will not rest until he gets the bastard or until bedtime, whichever comes first. Any mention you make of other murders should come on another page."

"No connection implied?"

"Not by him or me. If I should ask for information on Birch, it will be because you dragged him in yourself."

"Okay, hold everything. I want to catch the early."

He left the room. I sat and tried to argue Wolfe into letting Lon have the juicy item about the flap from Matthew Birch's pocket being found on the car that had killed Pete, but since Wolfe wasn't there I made no progress. Before long Lon came back, and after he had crossed to his desk and got his big feet under it I told him, "I still need an hour."

"We'll see. There's not much nourishment in that crumb."

It didn't take a full hour, but a big hunk of one. He gave me nearly everything I wanted without consulting any documents and with only two phone calls to shopmates.

Mrs. Fromm had had lunch Friday at the Churchill with Miss Angela Wright, Executive Secretary of Assadip—the Association for the Aid of Displaced Persons. Presumably she had gone to the Churchill upon leaving Wolfe's office, but I didn't go into that with Lon. After lunch, around two-thirty, the two women had gone together to the office of Assadip, where Mrs. Fromm signed some papers and made some phone calls. The *Gazette* didn't have her taped from around 3:15 to around five, when she had returned to her home on Sixty-eighth Street and had spent an hour or so working with her personal secretary, Miss Jean Estey. According to Lon, Angela Wright was a credit to her sex, since she would talk to reporters, and Jean Estey wasn't, since she wouldn't.

A little before seven o'clock Mrs. Fromm had left home, alone, to go out to dinner, driving one of her cars, a Cadillac convertible. The dinner was at the apartment of Mr. and Mrs. Dennis Horan on Gramercy Park. It wasn't known where she had parked the car, but in that neighborhood in the evening there are always spaces. There had been six people at the dinner:

Dennis Horan, the host
Claire Horan, his wife
Laura Fromm
Angela Wright
Paul Kuffner, public-relations expert
Vincent Lipscomb, magazine publisher

The party had broken up a little after eleven, and the guests had gone their ways separately. Mrs. Fromm had been the last to leave. The *Gazette* had a tip that Horan had taken her down to her car, but the police weren't saying, and it couldn't be checked. That was all on Laura Fromm until five o'clock Saturday morning, when a man on his way to work in a fish market, passing through the construction lane between the pillars, had found the body.

Just a few minutes before I reached the *Gazette* office the District Attorney had announced that Mrs. Fromm had been run over by her own car. The convertible had been found parked on Sixteenth Street between Sixth and Seventh Avenues, only a five-minute walk from the Tenth Precinct, and had yielded not only evidence of that fact but also a heavy tire wrench, found on the floor, which had been used on the back of Mrs. Fromm's head. Whether the murderer had been concealed in the car, under a rug behind the front seat, when Mrs. Fromm had come down to it, or whether he had been allowed by her to get in with her, then or later, it seemed better than a guess that he had picked a moment and spot to hit her with the wrench, replace her at the wheel, drive to an appropriate site, unoccupied and unobserved at that hour, unload her, and run the car over her. It would have been interesting and instructive to go down to Centre Street and watch the scientists working on that car, but they wouldn't have let me get within a mile of it, and anyhow I was busy with Lon.

As far as the *Gazette* knew, as of that moment the field was wide open, with no candidate favored either by the police or by any outside talent. Of course those who had been present at the dinner were in a glare, but it could have been anyone who had known where Mrs. Fromm would be, or even possibly someone who hadn't. Lon had no suggestions to offer, though he tossed in the comment that one *Gazette* female was being curious about Mrs. Horan's attitude toward the progress of the friendship between her husband and Mrs. Fromm.

I made an objection. "But if you want to fit in Pete Drossos and Matthew Birch, that's no good. Unless you can make it good. Who was Matthew Birch?"

Lon snorted. "On your way out buy a Wednesday *Gazette*."

"I've got one at home and I've read it. But that was three days ago."

"He hasn't changed any. He was a special agent of the Immigration and Naturalization Service, had been for twenty years, with a wife and three children. He had only twenty-one teeth, looked like a careworn statesman, dressed beyond his station, wasn't any too popular in his circle, and bet on the races through Danny Pincus."

"You said you counted Birch in because of the pattern. Was there any other reason?"

"No."

"Just to your old and trusted friend Goodwin. Any at all?"

"No."

"Then I'll do you a favor, expecting it back with interest at your earliest convenience. It's triple classified. The cops have it sewed up that the car that killed Pete Drossos was the one that killed Birch."

His eyes widened. "No!"

"Yes."

"Sewed up how?"

"Sorry, I've forgotten. But it's absolutely tight."

"I'll be damned." Lon rubbed his palms together. "This is sweet, Archie. This is very sweet. Pete and Mrs. Fromm, the earrings. Pete and Birch, the car. That ties Birch and Mrs. Fromm. You understand that the *Gazette* will now have a strong hunch that the three murders are connected and will proceed accordingly."

"As long as it's just a hunch, okay."

"Right. As for the car itself—as you know, the license plate was a floater; the car was stolen in Baltimore four months ago. It's been repainted twice."

"That hasn't been published."

"They released it at noon." Lon leaned to me. "Listen, I've got an idea. How can you be absolutely sure I'm to be trusted unless you try me? Here's your chance. Tell me how they know the same car killed Birch and the boy. Then I'll forget it."

"I forgot it first." I stood up and shook my pants legs down. "My God, are you a glutton! Dogs should be fed once a day, and you've had yours."

Chapter 6

When I got back to Thirty-fifth Street it was after four o'clock and the office was empty. I went to the kitchen to ask Fritz if there had been any visitors, and he said yes, Inspector Cramer.

I raised my brows. "Any blood flow?"

He said no, but it had been pretty noisy. I treated myself to a tall glass of water, returned to the office, and buzzed the plant rooms on the house phone, and when Wolfe answered I told him, "Home again. Regards from Lon Cohen. Do I type the report?"

"No. Come up and tell me."

That was not exactly busting a rule, like the interruption at lunch, but it was exceptional. It suited me all right, since as long as he stayed sore because he thought someone had made a monkey of him he would probably make his brain work. I went up the three flights and through the aluminum door into the vestibule, and the door to the warm room, where the Miltonia roezli and Phalaenopsis Aphrodite were in full bloom. In the next room, the medium, only a few of the big show-offs, the Cattleyas and Laelias, had flowers, which was all right with me, and anyway the biggest show-off in the place, named Wolfe, was there, helping Theodore adjust the muslin shaders. When I appeared he led the way to the rear, through the cool room into the potting room, where he lowered himself into the only chair present and demanded, "Well?"

I got onto a stool and gave it to him. He sat with his eyes closed and his nose twitching now and then for punctuation. In making a report to him one of my objectives is to cover it so well as I go along that at the end he won't have one question to ask, and that time I made it. When I had finished he held his pose a long moment, then opened his eyes and informed me, "Mr. Cramer was here."

I nodded. "So Fritz said. He also said it was noisy."

"Yes. He was uncommonly offensive. Of course he is under harassment, but so am I. He intimated that if I had told him yesterday of Mrs. Fromm's visit she would not have been killed, which is poppycock. Also he threatened me. If I obstruct the police investigation in any way I will be summoned. Pfui! Is he still downstairs?"

"Not unless he's hiding in the bathroom. Fritz said he left."

"I left him and came up here. I have phoned Saul and Fred and Orrie. What time is it?"

He would have had to turn his head to see the clock, so I told him. "Ten to five."

"They will be here at six or soon after. There has been no word from Mr. Horan. How old is Jean Estey?"

"Lon didn't specify, but he said young, so I suppose not over thirty. Why?"

"Is she comely?"

"No data."

"You have a right to know. At any rate, she is young. Saul or Fred or Orrie may find a crack for us, but I don't want to prowl around this cage while they try. I want to know what Mrs. Fromm did from three-fifteen to five o'clock yesterday afternoon, and what and whom her mind was on during the hour she spent with Miss Estey. Miss Estey can tell me—certainly the second, and probably the first. Get her and bring her here."

Don't misunderstand him. He knew it was fantastic. He hadn't the slightest expectation that under the circumstances I could get to Mrs. Fromm's personal secretary for a private chat, let alone convoy her to his office so he could pump her. But it would only cost him some taxi fare, so what the hell, why not let me stub my toe on the slim chance that I might raise some dust?

So I merely remarked that I would tell Fritz to set an extra place for dinner in case she was hungry, left him, went down one flight to my bedroom, stood by the window, and surveyed the problem. In ten minutes I concocted, and rejected, four different plans. The fifth one seemed more likely, at least with a faint chance of working, and I voted for it. For dressing the part nothing in my personal wardrobe would do, so I went to the closet where I kept an assortment of items for professional emergencies such as the present and got out a black cutaway and vest, striped trousers, a white shirt with starched collar, a black Homburg, and a black four-in-hand. Suitable shoes and socks were in my personal stock. When I had shaved and got into the costume I took a look in the full-length mirror and was impressed. All I needed was either a bride or a hearse.

Downstairs in the office I got a little Marley .22 from the collection in a drawer of my desk, loaded it, and stuck it in my hip pocket. That was a compromise. A shoulder holster with a .32 would have spoiled my contours in that getup, but long ago, after a couple of unpleasant experiences, one of which had made it necessary to have a bullet dug out of my chest, I had promised both Wolfe and myself that I would never go forth unarmed to deal with anyone involved in a murder, however remotely. That attended to, I went to the kitchen to give Fritz a treat.

"I've been appointed," I told him, "ambassador to Texas. Adieu."

He asked me to unbutton the shirt to show him my girdle.

It was 5:38 when I paid the taxi driver in front of the address on East Sixty-eighth Street. Across the street there was a little assembly of gawkers, but on this side a uniformed cop was keeping the citizens moving. The house was granite, set back a couple of yards, with iron railings higher than my head protecting the areaway on both sides of the entrance. As I headed for it the cop moved to meet me, but not actually to block me. Cops prefer not to block personages dressed as I was.

I stopped, looked at him mournfully, and said, "Arrangements."

He might have made it more difficult by accompanying me to the door, but three female sightseers gave me an assist just then by converging on the iron railing, and by the time he had persuaded them on their way I had entered the vestibule, pushed the button, and was speaking to a specimen with an aristocratic nose who had opened the door. His color scheme was the same as mine, but I had it on him in style.

"There has developed," I said sadly but firmly, "some confusion in the directions about the flowers, and it must be settled. I will have to see Miss Estey."

Since it would have been out of character to slide a foot across the sill against the open door I had to keep that impulse down, but when he opened it enough to give me room I lost no time in slipping past him. As he closed the door I remarked, "The morbid curiosity of the public at such a time is distressing. Will you please tell Miss Estey that Mr. Goodwin would like to consult her about the flowers?"

"This way, please."

He led me five paces along the hall to a door that was standing open, motioned me in, and told me to wait. The room was nothing like what I would have expected in the town residence of Mrs. Damon Fromm. It was smaller than my bedroom, and, in addition to two desks, two typewriter stands, and an assortment of chairs, it was crammed with filing cabinets and miscellaneous objects. The walls were covered with posters and photographs, some framed and some not. There were scores of them. After a general survey I focused on one item and then another, and was inspecting one inscribed, AMERICAN HEALTH COUNCIL, 1947, when I heard footsteps and straightened and turned.

She came in, stopped, and leveled greenish-brown eyes at me. "What's this about flowers?" she demanded.

The eyes didn't look as if they had been irritated by any great flood of tears, but they certainly were not merry. I might possibly have classed her under thirty in happier circumstances, but not as she was then. Comely, yes. She was not wearing earrings. There was no sign of a scratch on her cheek, but four days had passed since Pete had seen it, and he had given no specifications as to depth or outline. So there wasn't much hope of spotting any vestige of that scratch on Jean Estey or anyone else.

"Are you Miss Jean Estey?" I asked.

"Yes. What about flowers?"

"That's what I came to tell you. You may have heard the name Nero Wolfe."

"The detective?"

"Yes."

"Certainly."

"Good. He sent me. My name is Archie Goodwin, and I work for him. He wants to send flowers to Mrs. Fromm's funeral, and would like to know if there would be any objection to orchids, provided they are sprays of Miltonia roezli alba, which are pure white and are very beautiful."

She stared at me a second and then suddenly burst out laughing. It wasn't musical. Her shoulders were shaking with it, and she half walked and half stumbled to a chair, sat, lowered her head, and pressed her palms against her temples. The butler came to the threshold of the open door for a look, and I went to him and told him sympathetically that I had had experience with such crises, which was no lie, and that it might be well to shut the door. He agreed and pulled it shut himself. Then for a little I thought I might have to shock her out of it, but before long she started to calm down, and I went to a chair and sat. Soon she came erect and dabbed at her eyes with a handkerchief.

"What started me," she said, "was the way you're dressed. It's grotesque—dressed like that to come and ask if there's any objection to orchids!" She had to stop a moment to get her breathing in order. "There are to be no flowers. Now you may go."

"The costume was merely to get me in."

"I understand. Under false pretenses. What for?"

"To see you. Look, Miss Estey. I'm sorry my disguise brought on that little attack, but now you should sit quietly for a few minutes while your nerves catch up, and meanwhile why not let me explain? I suppose you know that Mrs. Fromm came to see Mr. Wolfe yesterday and gave him a check for ten thousand dollars."

"Yes. I handle her personal checking account."

"Did she tell you what it was for?"

"No. All she put on the stub was the word 'retainer.'"

"Well, I can't tell you what it was for, but she was to see Mr. Wolfe again today. The check was certified yesterday and will be deposited Monday. Mr. Wolfe feels a responsibility to Mrs. Fromm and considers that he is obliged to investigate her death."

She was breathing better. "The police are investigating it. Two of them left here just half an hour ago."

"Sure. If they solve it, fine. But if they don't, Mr. Wolfe will. Don't you want him to?"

"It doesn't matter what I want, does it?"

"It matters to Mr. Wolfe. The police can say to anybody involved, 'Answer this one, or else,' but he can't. He wants to talk with you and sent me to bring you to his office, and I can persuade you to come only by one of three methods. I could threaten you if I had a good menace handy, but I haven't. I could bribe you if I knew what to use for bait, but I don't. All that's left is to say that Mrs. Fromm came to see him and gave him that check, and he has reason to think that her death was connected with the matter she hired him to work on and therefore he feels obliged to investigate it, and he wants to start by talking with you. The question is whether you want to help. Naturally I should think you would, without any threats or bribes, even if I had some in stock. Our office is on Thirty-fifth Street. The cop out front will flag a taxi for us, and we can be there in fifteen minutes."

"You mean go now?"

"Sure."

She shook her head. "I couldn't. I have to—I couldn't." She was back in control, with all signs of the attack gone. "You say the question is whether I want to help, but that's not it, it's how I can help." She hesitated, studying me. "I think I'll tell you something."

"I'd appreciate it."

"I told you two policemen, detectives, left here half an hour ago."

"Yes."

"Well, while they were here, not long before they left, there was a phone call for one of them, and after he hung up he said I might be contacted by Nero Wolfe, probably through his assistant, Archie Goodwin, and I might be asked to go to see Nero Wolfe, and if so he hoped I would cooperate by going and then tell the police exactly what Wolfe said."

"That's interesting. Did you agree to cooperate?"

"No. I didn't commit myself." She got up, went to a desk, got a pack of cigarettes from a drawer, lit one, and took two healthy drags. She stood looking down at me. "The reason I told you that is purely selfish. I happen to think that Nero Wolfe is smarter than any policeman, but whether he is or not, Mrs. Fromm went to consult him yesterday and gave him that check, and I don't know what for. Since I'm her secretary of course I'm involved in this, I can't help that, but I'm not going to do anything to get more involved, and I certainly would be if I went to see Nero Wolfe. If I didn't tell the police what Wolfe said they would never let up on me, and if I did tell them —what if he asked me about something that Mrs. Fromm had told him confidentially and wouldn't want the police to know?"

She took another drag at the cigarette, went to a desk and mashed it in a tray, and came back. "So I told you. I'm just a sweet innocent small-town girl from Nebraska, I don't think. If ten years on your own in New York don't teach you how to avoid collisions in heavy traffic, nothing will. Here I am in this mess, but I'm not going to say or do anything to make it worse than it is—for me. I'm going to have to get a job. I don't owe Mrs. Damon Fromm anything—I worked for her, and she paid me, and nothing extravagant, either."

My head was tilted back to look up at her, with my face, if it was obeying orders, earnest and sympathetic. The starched collar was engraving the back of my neck. "You won't get an argument from me, Miss Estey," I assured her. "I've been in New York ten years too, and then some. You say the police wanted you to tell them what Nero Wolfe said, but how about Archie Goodwin? Did they ask you to tell them what I say?"

"I don't think so. No."

"Good. Not that I have anything special to say,

but I would like to ask a few questions if you'll sit down."

"I've been sitting answering questions all afternoon."

"I'll bet you have. Such as, where were you last night from ten o'clock to two o'clock?"

She stared. "You're asking me that?"

"No, just giving a sample of the kind of questions you've been answering all afternoon."

"Well, here's a sample of the kind of answers I gave. Yesterday between five and six Mrs. Fromm dictated about a dozen letters. A little after six she went up to dress, and I started on some phone calls she had told me to make. A little after seven, after she had gone out, I had dinner alone, and after dinner I typed the letters she had dictated and went out to mail them at the box at the corner. That was around ten o'clock. I came right back and told Peckham, the butler, I was tired and was going to bed, and went up to my room and turned on WQXR for the music, and went to bed."

"Fine. Then you live here?"

"Yes."

"Another example. Where were you Tuesday afternoon from six o'clock to seven?"

She went and sat down and cocked her head at me. "You're right, they asked me that too. Why?"

I shrugged. "I'm just showing you that I know the kind of questions cops ask."

"You are not. What is it about Tuesday afternoon?"

"First how did you answer it?"

"I couldn't until I thought back. That was the day Mrs. Fromm went to a meeting of the Executive Committee of Assadip—the Association for the Aid of Displaced Persons. She let me take a car—the convertible—and I spent the afternoon and evening chasing all over town trying to find a couple of refugees that Assadip wanted to help. I never found them, and I got home after midnight. I'd have a hard time accounting for every minute of that afternoon and evening, and I don't intend to try. Why should I? What happened Tuesday between six and seven?"

I regarded her. "How about a trade? Tell me where Mrs. Fromm was yesterday afternoon from three-fifteen to five o'clock, and what letters she dictated from five to six, and what phone calls she made, and I'll tell you what happened Tuesday."

"Those are more samples of what the police asked."

"Naturally. But these I like."

"She made no phone calls at all, but told me to make some later, to ask people to buy tickets for a theater benefit for the Milestone School. There were twenty-three names on the list, and the police have it. The letters she dictated were miscellaneous, just routine matters. Mr. Kuffner and Mr. Horan both said to let the police take the copies, so I did. If you want me to try to remember, I think—"

"Never mind. What did she do between the time she left the Assadip office and the time she got home?"

"I know two things she did. She went to a shop on Madison Avenue and bought some gloves—she brought them home with her—and she called at the office of Paul Kuffner. I don't know whether she did anything else. What happened Tuesday?"

"A car stopped for a light at the corner of Ninth Avenue and Thirty-fifth Street, and the woman driving it told a boy to get a cop."

Her brow wrinkled. "What?"

"I told you."

"But what has that to do with it?"

I shook my head. "Not in the bargain. I said I'd tell you what happened. This is a very complicated business, Miss Estey, and you may decide to tell the police what Archie Goodwin said, and they wouldn't like it if I went around telling the suspects exactly how all the—"

"I'm not a suspect!"

"I beg your pardon. I thought you were. Anyhow, I'm not—"

"Why should I be?"

"If for no other reason, because you were close to Mrs. Fromm and knew where she was last evening and that her car would be parked nearby. But even if you weren't I wouldn't spread it out for you. Mr. Wolfe might feel different. If you change your mind and come down to see him this evening after dinner, or tomorrow morning—say, eleven o'clock, when he'll be free—he might take a notion to empty the bag for you. He's a genius, so you never know. If you—"

The door swinging open stopped me. It swung wide, and a man trotted in. As he appeared he started to say something to Miss Estey, but, becoming aware that she had company, cut it off, stopped short, and proceeded to take me in.

When it seemed that neither was she performing introductions nor was he asking strangers' names, I broke the ice. "My name's Archie Goodwin. I work for Nero Wolfe." Seeing how he was taking me in, I added, "I'm in disguise."

He approached with a hand out, and I arose and took it. "I'm Paul Kuffner."

In size he had been shortchanged, the top of his head being about level with the tip of my nose. With his thin brown mustache trimmed so it wasn't quite parallel with the thick lips of his wide mouth, I wouldn't have called him well designed to make the sort of impression desirable for a handler of public relations, but I admit I'm prejudiced about a mustache trying to pass as a plucked eyebrow.

He smiled at me to show that he liked me, that he approved of everything I had ever said or done, and that he understood all my problems perfectly. "I'm sorry," he said, "that I have to break in like this and take Miss Estey away, but there are some urgent matters. Come upstairs, Miss Estey?"

It was a fine job. Instead of that he could have said, "Get out of this house and give me a chance to ask Miss Estey what the hell you're trying to put over," which was what he meant. But no, sir, he liked me too much to say anything that could possibly hurt my feelings.

When Miss Estey had got up and crossed to the door and passed through, and he had followed her to the sill, he turned to tell me, "It was a pleasure to meet you, Mr. Goodwin. I've heard a great deal about you, and Mr. Wolfe, of course. Sorry our meeting had to be at so difficult a moment." He stepped out of sight, but his voice carried in to me. "Oh, Peckham! Mr. Goodwin's going. See if he wants you to stop a cab for him."

A nice clean fast job. Apparently with that mustache he was in disguise too.

Chapter 7

I got back to the house in time to hear the briefing. Saul and Orrie were already there, sitting waiting, but Fred hadn't arrived. After greeting them, I reported to Wolfe, who was at his desk.

"I saw her and had a chat with her, but."

"Why the deuce are you arrayed like that?"

"I'm a mortician."

He made a face. "That abominable word. Tell me about it."

I obeyed, giving it in full, but that time he had questions. None of them got him anything, since I had delivered all the facts, and the impression I had got of Jean Estey and Paul Kuffner wasn't any help, even to me, let alone him, and when Saul went to answer the doorbell and brought Fred in, Wolfe dropped me at once and had them move chairs up to a line fronting his desk.

That trio was no great treat to look at. Saul Panzer, with his big nose lording it over his narrow face, in his brown suit that should have been pressed after he got caught in the rain, could have been a hackie or a street sweeper, but he wasn't. He was the smartest operative in the metropolitan area, and his talent for tailing, which Wolfe had praised to Pete Drossos, was only one little part of him. Any agency in town would pay him three times the market.

In bulk Fred Durkin would have made nearly two Sauls, but not in ability. He could tail all right, and you could count on him for any ordinary chore, but if he ran into something fancy he was apt to get twisted. You could trust him to hell and back.

As for Orrie Cather, when he confronted you with his confident dark brown eyes and a satisfied smile on his wavy lips, you had no doubt that his main concern was whether you realized how handsome he was. Of course that irritated any customer he tackled, but it also gave the impression that it wasn't necessary to watch your step, which might be dangerous, since his real concern was his reputation as a working detective.

Wolfe leaned back, rested his forearms on the arms of the chair, drew in a bushel of air, and audibly let it out. "Gentlemen," he said, "I am up to my thighs in a quagmire. Customarily, when I enlist your services, it is enough to define your specific tasks, but this time that won't do. You must be informed of the total situation in all its intricacy, but first a word about money. Less than twelve hours after the client gave me a check for ten thousand dollars, she was murdered. Since no successor to the cliency is in view, that's all I'll get. If it is unavoidable I am prepared, for a personal reason, to spend the major portion, even the entire sum, on the expense of the investigation, but not more. I don't ask you to be niggardly in your expenditures, but I must forbid any prodigality. Now here it is."

Beginning with my ushering Pete Drossos into the dining room Tuesday evening, and ending with

my report of my talk with Jean Estey, which Fred
had not heard, he went right through it, omitting
nothing. They sat absorbing it, each in his manner—
Saul slumped and relaxed, Fred stiff and straight,
with his eyes fastened on Wolfe as if he had to listen
with them too, and Orrie with his temple propped
against his fingertips for a studio portrait. As for me,
I was trying to catch Wolfe skipping some detail so I
would have the pleasure of supplying it when he was
through, but nothing doing. I couldn't have done a
better job myself.

He glanced up at the clock. "It's twenty past
seven, and dinner's ready. We're having fried
chicken with cream gravy and mush. We won't discuss this at the table, but I wanted you to have it in
your minds."

It was going on nine by the time we were back in
the office, having discussed all of five chickens, with
accessories, so fully that they were settled for good.
Wolfe, after getting arranged in his chair, scowled at
me and then at them.

"You don't look very alert," he said peevishly.

They didn't jerk to attention. While none of them
had had as much of him as I had, they knew how he
hated to work during the hour or so after dinner, and
what was eating him wasn't that they weren't alert
but that he didn't want to be.

"We can go downstairs," I suggested, "and play
some pool while you digest."

He snorted. "My stomach," he asserted, "is quite
capable of handling its affairs without pampering.
Has any of you gentlemen a pressing question before
I go on?"

"Maybe later," Saul suggested.

"Very well. It is, as you see, hopeless. It is excessively complex, but no sources of information are available to us. Archie can try with others as he did with Miss Estey, but he has no lever. The police will tell me nothing. On occasion, in the past, I have had tools wherewith to pry things out of them, but not this time. Since they know everything I know, I have nothing to bargain with. Of course we know presumptively what they're doing. They're finding out, or trying to, whether any woman known to Mrs. Fromm had a scratch on her cheek Tuesday evening or Wednesday. If they find her that could settle it; but they may not find her, since what that boy called a scratch, staring at her as he did, might have been a slight mark that she could have rendered practically unnoticeable as soon as she got a chance. Also the police are trying to find a woman known to Mrs. Fromm who wore spider earrings, and again, if they succeed, that could settle it."

Wolfe upturned a palm. "And they're trying to trace the car that killed the boy and Matthew Birch. They're examining every inch of Mrs. Fromm's car. They're rechecking Birch's movements and connections and associates. They're piecing together, minute by minute, everything Mrs. Fromm did and said after she left this office yesterday. They're badgering not only those who were with Mrs. Fromm last evening, but everyone who can be remotely suspected of knowledge of a pertinent fact. They're checking on the whereabouts of all possible culprits—for Tuesday evening when a woman told Peter Drossos to get a cop, for later that evening when Birch was killed, for Wednesday evening when the boy was killed, and for yesterday evening when Mrs. Fromm was killed. They're asking who had reason to fear or hate Mrs. Fromm or will profit in any way by her death. In those activities they are using a hundred men, or a thousand—all of them trained, and some of them competent."

He compressed his lips and shook his head. "They can't afford to fail on this one, and they won't dally. As we sit here they may have marked their prey and are ready to seize him. But until they do, I propose to use Mrs. Fromm's money or part of it, for a purpose that she would surely have sanctioned. With all their advantages, the police will certainly forestall us, but I intend to persuade myself that I am justified in keeping that money; and besides, I resent the assumption that people who come to me for help can be murdered with impunity. That's the personal reason."

"We'll get the bastard!" Fred Durkin blurted.

"I doubt it, Fred. You understand now why I called you to this conference and told you all about it instead of simply assigning you to errands as usual. I wanted you to know how hopeless it is, and also I wanted to consult you. There are dozens of possible approaches to the problem, and there are only three of you. Saul, where do you think you might start?"

Saul hesitated. He scratched his nose. "I'd like to start two places at once. Assadip and earrings."

"Why Assadip?"

"Because they're interested in displaced persons, and Birch was with the Immigration and Naturalization Service. That's the one chance I see for any connection between Birch and Mrs. Fromm. Of course the cops are on it, but on that kind of prying around anyone might get a lucky break."

"Since Angela Wright, the Executive Secretary of Assadip, was present at the dinner last evening, she is probably unapproachable."

"Not by a displaced person."

"Oh." Wolfe considered. "Yes, you might try that."

"And anyhow, if she's too busy with cops and so on, they must have a couple of stenographers and someone to answer the phone. I'll need a lot of sympathy."

Wolfe nodded. "Very well. In the morning. Take two hundred dollars, but a displaced person would not be lavish. What about earrings?"

"I couldn't do both."

"No, but what about them?"

"Well, I get around some, and I keep my eyes open, but I have never seen spider earrings, either on a woman or in a window. You said that Pete said big gold spiders with their legs stretched out. People would notice that. If she wore them before Tuesday, or after, the cops have already got her spotted or soon will have, and you're probably right, for us it's hopeless. But there's a chance she didn't, and was it the same ones Mrs. Fromm was wearing yesterday? It might pay to try to find some shop that ever sold any spider earrings. The cops are so busy on it from the other angle maybe they haven't started on that. Am I wrong?"

"No. You're seldom wrong. If we find that woman first—"

"I'll take it," Orrie said. "I've never seen any spider earrings either. How big were they?"

"The ones Mrs. Fromm wore yesterday were about the size of your thumbnail—that is, the circumference described by the tips of the extended legs. Archie?"

I responded. "I'd say a little larger."

"Were they gold?"

"I don't know. Archie?"

"My guess is yes, but don't quote me."

"Well made?"

"Yes."

"Okay. I'll take it."

Wolfe was frowning at him. "A month might do it."

"Not the way I'll work it, Mr. Wolfe. I did a favor once for a guy that's a salesman at Boudet's, and I'll start with him. That way I can get going tomorrow even if it is Sunday—I know where he lives. One thing I may have missed—is there any line at all on whether the ones Mrs. Fromm had on yesterday were the same as those the woman in the car was wearing Tuesday?"

"No."

"Then there may be two different pairs?"

"Yes."

"Right. I've got it. Last one across is a rotten egg."

"Will you need to pay your friend, the salesman at Boudet's?"

"Hell, no. He owes me a favor."

"Then take a hundred dollars. If you find anything that offers promise, avoid any hint that the police might be grateful for news of it. We might ourselves find it desirable to bid for official gratitude. At the slightest sign of a trail, phone me." Wolfe transferred to Durkin. "Fred, where do you start?"

Fred's big broad face showed pink. He had done jobs for Wolfe, off and on, for nearly twenty years, and being consulted on high-level strategy was something new to him. He clamped his jaw, swallowed, and said in a much louder voice than was called for, "Them earrings."

"Orrie has the earrings."

"I know he has, but look. Hundreds of people must've seen 'em on her. Elevator men, maids, waiters—"

"No." Wolfe was curt. "In all that area the police are so far ahead that we could never catch up. I have explained that. With our meager forces we must try to find a trail not already explored. Has anyone a suggestion for Fred?"

They exchanged glances. No one volunteered.

Wolfe nodded. "It is certainly difficult. One way to avoid panting along at the heels of the police, with the air polluted by their dust, is to make an assumption that they may not have made, and explore it. Let's try one. I assume that Tuesday afternoon, when the car stopped at the corner and the woman driver told the boy to get a cop, the man in the car with her was Matthew Birch."

Saul frowned. "I don't get it, Mr. Wolfe."

"Good. Then it probably hasn't occurred to the police. I admit it is extremely tenuous. But later that day, that night, that same car ran over Birch and killed him, in a place and manner indicating that it had carried him to the spot. Therefore, since he was in the car late in the evening, why not assume that he was in it early in the evening? I choose so to assume."

Saul maintained his frown. "But the way it stands, wouldn't the assumption be that the man who ran the car over the boy Wednesday was the one who had been with the woman Tuesday? Because he knew the boy could identify him? And on Wednesday Birch was dead."

"That's probably the police assumption," Wolfe conceded. "Its worth is obvious, so I don't reject it; I merely ignore it and substitute one of my own. Even a false assumption may serve a purpose. Columbus assumed that there was nothing but water between him and the treasures of the Orient, and he bumped into a continent." His eyes moved. "I don't expect you to bump into a continent, Fred, but you will proceed on my assumption that Birch was in the car with the woman. Try either to validate it or to disprove it. Take a hundred dollars—no, take three hundred, you never waste money. Archie will supply you with a photograph of Birch." He turned to me. "They should all have photographs of everyone involved. Can you get them from Mr. Cohen?"

"Not tonight. In the morning."

"Do so."

He surveyed his meager forces, left to right and back again. "Gentlemen, I trust I have not dulled your ardor by dwelling on the hopelessness of this enterprise. I wanted you to understand that the situation is such that any tidbit will be a feast. I have on occasion expected much of you; this time I expect nothing. It is likely that—"

The doorbell rang.

As I got up and crossed the room I glanced at my wrist. It was 9:55. In the hall, switching on the stoop light and approaching the door, I saw it was two men, both strangers. I opened up and told them good evening.

The one in front spoke. "We want to see Mr. Nero Wolfe."

"Your names, please?"

"Mine is Horan, Dennis Horan. I phoned him this morning. This is Mr. Maddox."

"Mr. Wolfe is busy. I'll see. Step in?"

They entered. I took them into the front room,

glanced at the soundproofed door connecting with the office to check that it was closed, invited them to sit, and left them. Going by way of the hall, I shut that door, returned to the office, and told Wolfe, "Two tidbits in the front room. One named Horan, who wanted you to cough up the ten grand, with a sidekick named Maddox."

He ran true to form. He glowered at me. Having finished with the briefing, he was all set to relax with a book, and here I was bringing him work to do. If we had been alone he would have indulged in one or two remarks, but after what he had just been telling the squad about hopelessness he had to control it, and I admit he did it like a man.

"Very well. Let Saul and Fred and Orrie out first, after you have given them expense money as specified."

I went to the safe for the dough.

Chapter 8

From their manner, and glances that passed between them as I ushered the callers into the office and got them into chairs, I gathered that I had been too hasty in assuming they were sidekicks. The glances were not affectionate.

Dennis Horan was a little too much. His eyelashes were a little too long, and he was a little too tall for his width and a little too old for campus tailoring. He needed an expert job of toning down, but since he had apparently spent more than forty years toning up I doubted if he would consider an offer.

Maddox made it plain to Wolfe that his name was James Albert Maddox. He had been suffering with ulcers from the cradle on, close to half a century—or if not, it was up to him to explain how his face had got so sour that looking at him would have turned his own dog into a pessimist. I put them into a couple of the yellow chairs which the boys had vacated, not knowing which of them, if either, rated the red leather one.

Horan opened up. He said that he had not intended, on the phone that morning, to intimate that Wolfe was doing or contemplating anything improper or unethical. He had merely been trying to safeguard the interests of his former friend and client, Mrs. Damon Fromm, who had been—

"Not your client," interposed Maddox in a tone that matched his face perfectly.

"I advised her," Horan snapped.

"Badly," Maddox snapped back.

They regarded each other. Not sidekicks.

"Perhaps," Wolfe suggested dryly, "it would be well for each of you to tell me, without interruption, to what extent and with what authority you represent Mrs. Fromm. Then contradictions can be composed or ignored as may seem desirable. Mr. Horan?"

He was controlling himself. His thin tenor was still thin, but it wasn't as close to a squeak as it had been on the phone. "It is true that I was never Mrs. Fromm's attorney of record in any action. She consulted me in many matters and showed that she valued my advice by frequently acting upon it. As counsel for the Association for the Aid of Displaced Persons, which I still am, I was closely associated with her. If she were alive I don't think she would challenge my right to call myself her friend."

"Are you an executor of her estate?"

"No."

"Thank you. Mr. Maddox?"

It hurt him, but he delivered. "My law firm, Maddox and Welling, was counsel for Damon Fromm for twelve years. Since his death we have been counsel for Mrs. Fromm. I am the executor of her estate. I interrupted because Mr. Horan's statement that Mrs. Fromm was his client was not true. I have something to add."

"Go ahead."

"This morning—no, this afternoon—Mr. Horan phoned and told me of the check Mrs. Fromm gave you yesterday, and of his conversation with you. His call to you was gratuitous and impertinent. My call on you now is not. I ask you formally, as Mrs. Fromm's counsel and executor of her estate, under what arrangement and for what purpose did she give you her check for ten thousand dollars? If you prefer to tell me privately, let us withdraw. Mr. Horan insisted on coming with me, but this is your house, and that young man looks quite capable of dealing with him."

If he intended the glance he shot at me to be complimentary, I'd hate to have him give me one of disapproval.

Wolfe spoke. "I don't prefer to tell you privately, Mr. Maddox. I prefer not to tell you at all."

Maddox didn't look any sourer, because he couldn't. "Do you know law, Mr. Wolfe?"

"No."

"Then you should seek advice. Unless you can establish that Mrs. Fromm received value for that payment, I can compel you to disgorge it. I am giving you a chance to establish it."

"I can't. She received nothing. As I told Mr. Horan on the phone, I intend to earn that money."

"How?"

"By making sure that the murderer of Mrs. Fromm is exposed and punished."

"That's ridiculous. That's the function of officers of the law. The information I got about you today, on inquiry, indicated that you are not a shyster, but you sound like one."

Wolfe chuckled. "You're prejudiced, Mr. Maddox. The feeling of virtuous lawyers toward shysters is the same as that of virtuous women toward prostitutes. Condemnation, certainly; but somewhere in it one tiny grain of envy, not to be recognized, let alone acknowledged. But don't envy me. A shyster is either a fool or a fanatic, and I am neither. I would like to ask a question."

"Ask it."

"Did you know that Mrs. Fromm intended to call on me, before she came?"

"No."

"Did you know that she had called on me, after she came?"

"No."

Wolfe's eyes moved. "You, Mr. Horan? Both questions."

"I don't see—" Horan hesitated. "I question your right to ask them."

Maddox looked at him. "Meet him, Horan. You insisted on coming. You have claimed that Mrs. Fromm consulted you on important matters. He's trying to lay ground. If he can establish that she told either you or me that she was coming to him, or had come, without disclosing what for, he'll take the position that manifestly she didn't want us to know and therefore he can't betray the confidence. Head him off."

Horan wasn't buying it. "I will not," he insisted, "submit to a cross-examination."

Maddox started to argue, but Wolfe cut in. "Your elucidation may be acute as far as it goes, Mr. Maddox, but you don't appreciate Mr. Horan's difficulty. He is stumped. If to my second question he says yes, you're right, I have a weapon and I'll use it. But if he says no, then I ask him how he knew that Mrs.

Fromm had given me a check. I'll want to know, and
I should think you will too."

"I already know. At least I know what he told
me. This morning, when he heard of Mrs. Fromm's
death, he telephoned her home and spoke with Miss
Estey, Mrs. Fromm's secretary, and she told him
about the check. I was in the country for the weekend, and Horan got me there. I drove to town immediately."

"Where in the country?"

Maddox's chin went up. "That's sheer impudence."

Wolfe waved it away. "At any rate, it's futile. I
beg your pardon, not for impudence but for stupidity. Force of habit impelled it. In this intricate maze
I must leave the conventional procedures, such as
inquiry into alibis, to the police. Since you're not
stumped, Mr. Horan, will you answer my questions?"

"No. On principle. You have no warrant to ask
them."

"But you expect me to answer yours?"

"No, not mine, because I have no warrant either.
But Mr. Maddox has, as executor of the estate. You'll
answer him."

"We'll see." Wolfe was judicious. He addressed
Maddox. "As I understand it, sir, you are not demanding that I return the money Mrs. Fromm paid
me."

"That depends. Tell me under what arrangement
and for what purpose it was paid, and I'll consider
the matter. I will not have the death of a valued client exploited and sensationalized by a private detective for his personal or professional profit."

"A worthy and wholesome attitude," Wolfe conceded. "I could remark that I would be hard put to

make the affair more sensational than it already is, but even so your attitude is admirable. Only here's the rub: I'll tell you nothing whatever of the conversation I had yesterday with Mrs. Fromm."

"Then you're withholding evidence!"

"Pfui. I have reported it to the police. In writing, signed."

"Then why not to me?"

"Because I'm not a simpleton. I have reason to think that the conversation was one of the links in a chain that led to Mrs. Fromm's death, and if that is so, the person most eager to know what she said to me is probably her murderer."

"I'm not her murderer."

"That remains to be seen."

For a moment I thought Maddox was going to choke. His throat swelled visibly. But a veteran lawyer has had lots of practice controlling his reactions, and he managed it. "That's worse than stupidity, it's drivel."

"I disagree. Have the police talked with you?"

"Certainly."

"How many of them?"

"Two—no, three."

"Would you mind telling me who they were?"

"A Captain Bundy, and a sergeant, and Deputy Commissioner Youmans. Also Assistant District Attorney Mandelbaum."

"Did any of them tell you what Mrs. Fromm consulted me about yesterday?"

"No. We didn't get onto that."

"I suggest that you see someone at the District Attorney's office—preferably someone you know well—and ask him to tell you. If he does so, or if any other official does, without important reservations,

I'll disgorge—your word—the money Mrs. Fromm
paid me."

Maddox was looking as if someone were trying to
persuade him that his nose was on upside down.

"I assure you," Wolfe went on, "that I am not ass
enough to withhold evidence in a capital crime, especially not one as sensational as this. Indeed, I am
meticulous about it. Unless the police have information about you that is unknown to me I doubt if they
have hitherto regarded you as a likely suspect, but
you may now find them a nuisance, after I have reported that you were so zealous to learn what Mrs.
Fromm said to me that you went to all this trouble.
That, of course, is my duty. This time it will also be
my pleasure."

"You are—" He was about to choke again. "You
are threatening to report this interview."

"Not a threat. Merely informing you that I will
do so as soon as you leave."

"I'm leaving now." He was up. "I'll replevy that
ten thousand dollars."

He wheeled and marched out. I followed to go
and open the door for him, but he beat me to it,
though he had to dive into the front room for his hat.
When I returned to the office Horan was on his feet
looking down at Wolfe, but no words were passing.
Wolfe told me, "Get Mr. Cramer's office, Archie."

"Wait a minute." Horan's thin tenor was urgent.
"You're making a mistake, Wolfe. If you really intend
to investigate the murder. Investigate how? You had
two of the persons closest to Mrs. Fromm and her
affairs here in your office, and you have chased one
of them out. Is that sensible?"

"Bosh." Wolfe was disgusted. "You won't even

tell me whether Mrs. Fromm told you she came to me."

"The context of your question was offensive."

"Then I'll try being affable. Will you give me the substance of what was said at the gathering at your home last evening?"

Horan's long eyelashes fluttered. "I doubt if I should. Of course I have told the police all about it, and they have urged me to be discreet."

"Naturally. But will you?"

"No."

"Will you describe, fully and frankly, the nature and course of your relations with Mrs. Fromm?"

"Certainly not."

"If I send Mr. Goodwin to the office of the Association for the Aid of Displaced Persons, for which you are counsel, will you instruct the staff to answer his questions fully and freely?"

"No."

"So much for affability." Wolfe turned. "Get Mr. Cramer's office, Archie."

I swiveled and dialed WA 9-8241, and got a prompt response, but then it got complicated. None of our dear friends or enemies was available, and I finally had to settle for a Sergeant Griffin, and so informed Wolfe, who took his instrument and spoke.

"Mr. Griffin? Nero Wolfe speaking. This is for the information of Mr. Cramer, so please see that he gets it. Mr. James Albert Maddox and Mr. Dennis Horan, both attorneys-at-law, called on me this evening. You have the names correctly? Yes, I suppose they are familiar. They asked me to tell them about my conversation with Mrs. Damon Fromm when she came to my office yesterday. I refused, and they insisted. I won't go so far as to say that Mr. Maddox tried to bribe me, but I got the impression that if I told him about the conversation he wouldn't press me to return the money Mrs. Fromm paid me; otherwise, he would. Mr. Horan concurred, at least tacitly. When Mr. Maddox left in a huff, Mr. Horan told me I was making a mistake. Will you please see that this reaches Mr. Cramer? No, that's all now. If Mr. Cramer wants details or a signed statement I'll oblige him."

Wolfe hung up and muttered at the lawyer, "Are you still here?"

Horan was going, but in three steps he turned to say, "You may not know law, but you know how to skirt the edges of slander. After this performance I wonder how you got your reputation."

He went, and I got to the hall in time to see him emerge from the front room with his hat and depart. After chain-bolting the door, I went back to the office and observed enthusiastically, "Well, you certainly pumped them good! Milked 'em and stripped 'em. Congratulations!"

"Shut up," he told me, and picked up a book, not to throw.

Chapter 9

I had been scheduled to leave Saturday afternoon for a weekend jaunt to Lily Rowan's fourteen-room shack in Westchester, but of course that had been knocked in the head—or rather, run over by a car. And my Sunday was no Sunday at all. Items:

Sergeant Purley Stebbins came bright and early, when Wolfe was still up in his room with his breakfast tray, to get filled in on the invasion by the lawyers. I accommodated him. He was suspicious when he arrived, and more suspicious when he left. Though I explained that my employer was a genius and time would show that his stiff-arming them was a brilliant stroke, Purley refused to believe that Wolfe would have those two corralled in his office and not do his damnedest to get a needle in. He did accept five or six crescents and two cups of coffee, but that was only because no man who has ever tasted Fritz's Sunday-morning crescents could possibly turn them down.

Wolfe and I both read every word of the accounts in the morning papers. Not that we hoped to get any hot leads, but at least we knew what the DA and

Cramer had seen fit to release, and there were a few morsels to file for reference. Angela Wright, the Executive Secretary of Assadip, had formerly worked for Damon Fromm, and had been put in the Assadip job by him. Mrs. Fromm had supported more than forty charities and worthy causes, but Assadip had been her pet. Vincent Lipscomb, the publisher who had been at the dinner party at Horan's apartment, had run a series of articles on displaced persons in his magazine, *Modern Thought*, and was planning another. Mrs. Dennis Horan had formerly been a movie star—well, anyhow, she had acted in movies. Paul Kuffner handled public relations for Assadip as a public service without remuneration, but he had also been professionally engaged in the interest of Mrs. Fromm personally. Dennis Horan was an authority on international law, belonged to five clubs, and had a reputation as an amateur chef.

There still wasn't a word about the flap from Matthew Birch's pocket that had been retrieved from the chassis of the car that had killed Pete Drossos. The police were hanging onto that one. But because of the similarity of the manner of the killings, the Birch murder was getting a play too.

Wolfe phoned his lawyer, Henry Parker, to ask about the process of a replevin and to tell him to get set for one in case Maddox kept his promise to make a grab for the ten grand. I had to track Parker down at a country club on Long Island.

Not a peep out of Jean Estey.

During the day three reporters phoned, and two made personal appearances on the stoop, but that was as far as they got. They didn't like it that the *Gazette* had had an exclusive on Nero Wolfe's working on the murder, and I sympathized with them.

My morning phone call to Lon Cohen at the *Gazette* was too early, and I left word for him to call me back, which he did. When I went there in the afternoon to collect a supply of prints of their best shots of the people we were interested in, I told Lon we could use a few dozen crucial inside facts, and he said he could too. He claimed they had printed everything they knew, though of course they had pecks of hot hearsay, such as that Mrs. Dennis Horan had once thrown a cocktail shaker at Mrs. Fromm, and that a certain importer had induced Vincent Lipscomb to publish an article favoring low tariffs by financing a trip to Europe. None of it seemed to me to be worth toting back to Thirty-fifth Street.

Anyway I had errands. For distribution of the photographs I met Saul Panzer at the Times Building, where he was boning up on displaced persons and Assadip; Orrie Cather at a bar and grill on Lexington Avenue, where he told me that the man who owed him a favor was playing golf at Van Cortlandt Park and could be seen later; and Fred Durkin at a restaurant on Broadway with his family, where Sunday dinner was $1.85 for adults and $1.15 for children. New York on a Sunday late in May is no place to open up a trail.

I made one little try on my own before heading back to Thirty-fifth Street. I don't remember ever doing a favor for a jewelry salesman, but I did a big one once for a certain member of the NYPD. If I had done my duty as a citizen and a licensed detective, he would have got it good and would still be locked up, but there were circumstances. No one knows about it, not even Wolfe. The man I did the favor for has given me to understand that he would like to hold my coat and hat if I ever get in a brawl, but as far as possible I've steered clear of him. That Sunday I thought what the hell, give the guy a chance to work it off, and I rang him and met him somewhere.

I said I would give him five minutes to tell me who had killed Mrs. Fromm. He said the way it was going it would take him five years and no guarantee. I asked him if that was based on the latest dispatches, and he said yes. I said that was all I wanted to know and therefore withdrew my offer of five minutes, but if and when he could make it five hours instead of five years I would appreciate it if he would communicate.

He asked, "Communicate what?"

I said, "That it's nearly ripe. That's all. So I can tell Mr. Wolfe to dive for cover."

"He's too damn fat to dive."

"I'm not."

"Okay, it's a deal. You sure that's all?"

"Absolutely."

"I thought maybe you were going to ask for Row-cliff's head with an apple in his mouth."

I went home and told Wolfe, "Relax. The cops are playing eeny, meeny, miney, mo. They know more than we do, but they're no closer to the answer."

"How do you know?"

"Gypsies. It's authentic, fresh, and strictly private. I saw the boys and gave them the photos. Do you want the unimportant details?"

"No."

"Any instructions?"

"No."

"No program for me for tomorrow?"

"No."

That was Sunday night.

Monday morning I got a treat. Wolfe never shows

downstairs until eleven o'clock. After breakfast in
his room he takes the elevator to the roof for the two
hours with the plants before descending to the office.
For morning communication with me he uses the
house phone unless there is something special. Apparently that morning was special, for when Fritz
came to the kitchen after taking breakfast up he announced solemnly, "Audience for you. *Levée!*" I spell
it French because he pronounced it so.

I had finished with the morning paper, in which
there was nothing to contradict my gypsies, and
when my coffee cup was empty I ascended the one
flight, knocked, and entered. On rainy mornings, or
even gray ones, Wolfe breakfasts in bed, after tossing the black silk coverlet toward the foot because
stains are bad for it, but when it's bright he has
Fritz put the tray on a table near a window. That
morning it was bright, and I had my treat. Bare-
footed, his hair tousled, with his couple of acres of
yellow pajamas dazzling in the sun, he was sensational.

We exchanged good mornings, and he told me to
sit. There was nothing left on his plate, but he wasn't
through with the coffee.

"I have instructions," he informed me.

"Okay. I was intending to be at the bank at ten
o'clock to deposit Mrs. Fromm's check."

"You may. You will proceed from there. You will
probably be out all day. Tell Fritz to answer the
phone and take the usual precautions with visitors.
Report by phone at intervals."

"The funeral is at two o'clock."

"I know, and therefore you may come home for
lunch. We'll see. Now the instructions."

He gave them to me. Four minutes did it. At the end he asked if I had any questions.

I was frowning. "One," I said. "It's clear enough as far as it goes, but what am I after?"

"Nothing."

"Then that's probably what I'll get."

He sipped coffee. "It's what I'll expect. You're stirring them up, that's all. You're turning a tiger loose in a crowd—or, if that's too bombastic, a mouse. How will they take it? Will any of them tell the police, and if so, which one or ones?"

I nodded. "Sure, I see the possibilities, but I wanted to know if there is any specific item I'm supposed to get."

"No. None." He reached for the coffee pot.

I went down to the office. In a drawer of my desk there is an assortment of calling cards, nine or ten different kinds, worded differently for different needs and occasions. I took some engraved ones with my name in the center and "Representing Nero Wolfe" in the corner, and on six of them I wrote in ink beneath my name, "To discuss what Mrs. Fromm told Mr. Wolfe on Friday." With them in my wallet, and the check and bankbook in my pocket, and a gun under my armpit, I was fully loaded, and I got my hat and beat it.

I walked to the bank, a pleasant fifteen-minute stretch on a fine May morning, and from there took a taxi to Sixty-eighth Street. I didn't know what the home of a deceased millionairess would be like on the day of her funeral, which was to be held in a chapel on Madison Avenue, but outside it was quieter than it had been Saturday. The only evidences of anything uncommon were a cop in uniform on the sidewalk, with nothing to do, and black crepe hanging on the door. It wasn't the same cop as on Saturday, and this one recognized me. As I made for the door he stopped me.

"You want something?"

"Yes, officer, I do."

"You're Archie Goodwin. What do you want?"

"I want to ring that bell, and hand Peckham my card to take to Miss Estey, and enter, and be conducted within, and engage in conversation—"

"Yeah, you're Goodwin all right."

That called for no reply, and he merely stood, so I walked past him into the vestibule and pushed the bell. In a moment the door was opened by Peckham. He may have been well trained, but the sight of me was too much for him. Instead of keeping his eyes on my face, as any butler worthy of the name should do, he let his bewilderment show as he took in my brown tropical worsted, light tan striped shirt, brown tie, and tan shoes. In fairness to him, remember it was the day of the funeral.

I handed him a card. "Miss Estey, please?"

He admitted me, but he had an expression on his face. He probably thought I was batty, since from the facts as he knew them that was the simplest explanation. Instead of ushering me down the hall, he told me to wait there, and went to the door to the office and disappeared inside. Voices issued, too low for me to catch the words, and then he came out.

"This way, Mr. Goodwin."

He moved aside as I approached, and I passed through the door. Jean Estey was there at a desk with my card in her hand. Without bothering with any greeting, she asked me abruptly, "Will you please close the door?"

I did so and turned to her. She spoke. "You know what I told you Saturday, Mr. Goodwin."

The greenish-brown eyes were straight at me. Below them the skin was puffy, either from too little sleep or too much, and while I still would have called her comely, she looked as if the two days since I had seen her had been two years.

I went to a chair near the end of her desk and sat. "You mean about the police asking you to see Nero Wolfe and pass it on?"

"Yes."

"What about it?"

"Nothing, only—well—if Mr. Wolfe still wants to see me, I think I might go. I'm not sure—but I certainly wouldn't tell the police what he said. I think they're simply awful. It's been more than two days since Mrs. Fromm was killed, fifty-nine hours, and I don't think they're getting anywhere at all."

I had to make a decision in about one second. With the line she was taking, it was a cinch I could get her down to the office, but would Wolfe want her? Which would he want me to do, get her to the office or follow my instructions? I don't know what I would have decided if I could have gone into a huddle with myself to think it over, but it had to be a flash vote and it went for instructions.

I spoke. "I'll tell Mr. Wolfe how you feel, Miss Estey, and I'm sure he'll be glad to hear it, but I ought to explain that what it says on that card— 'Representing Nero Wolfe'—is not exactly true. I'm here on my own."

She cocked her head. "On your own? Don't you work for Nero Wolfe?"

"Sure I do, but I work for me too when I get a good chance. I have an offer to make you."

She glanced at the card. "It says 'To discuss what Mrs. Fromm told Mr. Wolfe on Friday.' "

"That's right, that's what I want to discuss, but just between you and me."

"I don't understand."

"You soon will." I leaned toward her and lowered my voice. "You see, I was present during the talk Mrs. Fromm had with Mr. Wolfe. All of it. I have an extremely good memory. I could recite it to you word for word, or mighty close to it."

"Well?"

"Well, I think you would appreciate hearing it. I have reason to believe you would find it very interesting. You may think I'm sticking my neck out, but I have been Mr. Wolfe's confidential assistant for a good many years, and I've done some good work for him, and I've seen to it that he has learned to trust me, and if you call him up when I leave here, or go to see him, and tell him what I said to you, he'll think you're trying to pull a fast one. And when he asks me and I tell him you're a dirty liar, he'll believe me. So don't worry about my neck. I'll tell you about that talk, all of it, for five thousand dollars cash."

She said, "Oh," or maybe it was "Uh," but it was just a noise. Then she just stared.

"Naturally," I said, "I don't expect you to have that amount in your purse, so this afternoon will do, but I'll have to be paid in advance."

"This is incredible," she said. "Why on earth should I pay you five cents to tell me about that talk? Let alone five thousand dollars. Why?"

I shook my head. "That would be telling. After you pay and I deliver, you may or may not feel that you got your money's worth. I'm giving no guarantee of satisfaction, but I'd be a fool to come here with such an offer if all I had was a bag of popcorn."

Her gaze left me. She opened a drawer to get a pack of cigarettes, removed one, tapped its end several times on a memo pad, and reached for a desk lighter. But the cigarette didn't get lit. She dropped it and put the lighter down. "I suppose," she said, her eyes back to me, "I should be insulted and indignant, and I suppose I will, but now I'm too shocked. I didn't know you were a common skunk. If I had that much money to toss around I'd like to pay you and hear it. I'd like to hear what kind of a lie you're trying to sell me. You'd better go." She rose. "Get out of here!"

"Miss Estey, I think—"

"Get out!"

I have seen skunks in motion, both skunks unperturbed and skunks in a hurry, and they are not dignified. I was. Taking my hat from a corner of the desk, I walked out. In the hall Peckham showed his relief at getting rid of a lunatic undertaker without regrettable incident by bowing to me as he held the door open. On the sidewalk the cop thought he would say something and then decided no.

Around the corner I found a phone booth in a drugstore, called Wolfe and gave him a full report as instructed, and flagged a taxi headed downtown.

The address of my second customer, on Gramercy Park, proved to be an old yellow brick apartment house with a uniformed doorman, a spacious lobby with fine old rugs, and an elevator with a bad attack of asthma. It finally got the chauffeur and me to the eighth floor, after the doorman had phoned up and passed me. When I pushed the button at the door of 8B it was opened by a female master sergeant dressed like a maid, who admitted me, took my hat, and directed me to an archway at the end of the hall.

It was a large high-ceilinged living room, more than fully furnished, the dominant colors of its drapes and upholstery and rugs being yellow, violet, light green, and maroon—at least that was the impression gained from a glance around. A touch of black was supplied by the dress of the woman who moved to meet me as I approached. The black was becoming to her, with her ash-blond hair gathered into a bun at the back, her clear blue eyes, and her pale carefully tended skin. She didn't offer a hand, but her expression was not hostile.

"Mrs. Horan?" I inquired.

She nodded. "My husband will be furious at me for seeing you, but I was simply too curious. Of course I should be sure—you are the Archie Goodwin that works for Nero Wolfe?"

I got a card from my wallet and handed it to her, and she held it at an angle for better light. Then she widened her eyes at me. "But I don't—'To discuss what Mrs. Fromm told Mr. Wolfe'? With me? Why with me?"

"Because you're Mrs. Dennis Horan."

"Yes, I am, of course." Her tone implied that that angle hadn't occurred to her. "My husband will be furious!"

I glanced over my shoulder. "Perhaps we might sit over by a window? This is rather private."

"Certainly." She turned and found a way among pieces of furniture, and I followed. She took a chair at the far end near a window, and I moved one over close enough to make it cozy.

"You know," she said, "this is the most dreadful thing. The *most* dreadful. Laura Fromm was such a fine person." She might have used the same tone and expression to tell me she liked the way I had my hair cut. She added, "Did you know her well?"

"No, I saw her only once, last Friday when she came to consult Mr. Wolfe."

"He's a detective, isn't he?"

"That's right."

"Are you a detective too?"

"Yes, I work for Mr. Wolfe."

"It's simply fascinating. Of course there have been two men here asking questions—no, three— and Saturday more of them at the District Attorney's office, but they're really only policemen. You're truly a detective. I would never have thought a detective would be so—would dress so well." She made a pretty little gesture. "But here I am babbling along as usual, and you want to discuss something with me, don't you?"

"That was the idea. What Mrs. Fromm said to Mr. Wolfe."

"Then you'll have to tell me what she said. I can't discuss it until I know what it was. Can I?"

"No," I conceded, "but I can't tell you until I know how much you want to hear it."

"Oh, I *do* want to hear it!"

"Good. I thought you would. You see, Mrs. Horan, I was in the room all the time Mrs. Fromm and Mr. Wolfe were talking, and I remember every word they said. That's why I thought you would be extremely curious about it, so I'm not surprised that you are. The trouble is, I can't afford to satisfy your curiosity as a gift. I should have explained, I'm not here representing Nero Wolfe, that's why I said it's rather private. I'm representing just myself. I'll satisfy your curiosity if you'll lend me five thousand dollars to be repaid the day it rains up instead of down."

The only visible reaction was that the blue eyes widened a little. "That's an amusing idea," she said, "raining up instead of down. Would it be raining from the clouds up, or up from the ground to the clouds?"

"Either way would do."

"I like it better up from the ground." A pause. "What did you say about lending you some money? I beg your pardon, but my mind got onto the raining up."

I was ready to admit she was too much for me, but I struggled on. I abandoned the rain. "If you'll pay me five thousand dollars I'll tell you what Mrs. Fromm told Mr. Wolfe. Cash in advance."

Her eyes widened. "Was that what you said? I guess I didn't understand."

"I made it fancy by dragging in the rain. Sorry. It's better that way, plain."

She shook her pretty head. "It's not better for me, Mr. Goodwin. It sounds absolutely crazy, unless—oh, I see! You mean she told him something awful about me! That doesn't surprise me any, but what was it?"

"I didn't say she said anything about you. I merely—"

"But of course she did! She would! What was it?"

"No." I was emphatic. "Maybe I didn't make it plain enough." I stuck up a finger. "First you give me money." Another finger. "Second, I give you facts. I'm offering to sell you something, that's all."

She nodded regretfully. "That's the real trouble."

"What is?"

"Why, you don't really mean it. If you offered to

tell me for twenty dollars that might be different, and of course I'd love to know what she said—but five thousand! Do you know what I think, Mr. Goodwin?"

"I do not."

"I think you're much too fine a person to use this kind of tactics to stir up my curiosity just to get me talking. When you walked in I wouldn't have dreamed you were like that, especially your eyes. I go by eyes."

I also go by eyes up to a point, and hers didn't fit her performance. Though not the keenest and smartest I had ever seen, they were not the eyes of a scatterbrain. I would have liked to stay an hour or so to make a stab at tagging her, but my instructions were to put it bluntly, note the reaction, and move on; and besides, I wanted to get in as many as possible before funeral time. So I arose to leave. She was sorry to see me go; she even hinted that she might add ten to her counteroffer of twenty bucks; but I let her know that her remark about my tactics had hurt my feelings and I wanted to be alone.

Down on the street I found a phone booth to report to Wolfe and then took a taxi to Forty-second Street.

I had been informed by Lon Cohen that I shouldn't mark it against the Association for the Aid of Displaced Persons that they sported an elegant sunny office on the twenty-sixth floor of one of the newer midtown commercial palaces, because Mrs. Fromm owned the building and they paid no rent. Even so, it was a lot of dog for an outfit devoted to the relief of the unfortunate and oppressed. There in the glistening reception room I had an example before my eyes. At one end of a brown leather settee, slumped in weariness and despair, wearing an old gray suit two sizes too large for him, was a typical specimen. As I shot him a glance I wondered how it impressed him, but then I glanced again and quit wondering. It was Saul Panzer. Our eyes met, then his fell, and I went to the woman at the desk, who had a long thin nose and a chin to match.

She said Miss Wright was engaged and was available only for appointments. After producing a card and persuading her to relay not only my name but the message under it, I was told I would be received, but she didn't like it. She made it clear, with her tight lips and the set of her jaw, that she wanted no part of me.

I was shown into a large corner room with windows on two sides, giving views of Manhattan south and east. There were two desks, but only one of them was occupied, by a brown-haired female executive who looked almost as weary as Saul Panzer but wasn't giving in to it and didn't intend to.

She greeted me with a demand. "May I see your card, please?"

It had been read to her on the phone. I crossed and handed it over. She looked at it and then up at me. "I'm very busy. Is this urgent?"

"It won't take long, Miss Wright."

"What good will it do to discuss it with me?"

"I don't know. You'll have to leave that open, whether it does any good or not. I'm speaking strictly for myself, not for Nero Wolfe, and there's no—"

"Didn't Nero Wolfe send you here?"

"No."

"Did the police?"

"No. This is my idea. I've had some bad luck and

I need some cash, and I've got something to sell. I know this is a bad day for you, with Mrs. Fromm's funeral this afternoon, but this won't keep—at least I can't count on it—and I need five thousand dollars as soon as I can get it."

She smiled with one side of her mouth. "I'm afraid I haven't that much with me, if this is a stickup. Aren't you a reputable licensed detective?"

"I try to be. As I said, I've had some bad luck. All I'm doing, I'm offering to sell you something, and you can take it or leave it. It depends on how much you would like to know exactly what Mrs. Fromm told Mr. Wolfe. At five thousand dollars it might be a swell bargain for you, or it might not. You would be a better judge of that than I am, but of course you can't know until after you hear it."

She regarded me. "So that's it," she said.

"That's it," I concurred.

Her brown eyes were harder to meet than Jean Estey's had been, or Claire Horan's. My problem was to have the look of a man with a broad streak of rat in him, but also one who could be depended on to deliver as specified. Her straight hard gaze gave me a feeling that I wasn't dressed right for the part, and I was trying to give orders to my face not to show it. The face felt as if it might help to be doing something, so I used my mouth. "You understand, Miss Wright, this is a bona fide offer. I can and will tell you everything they said."

"But you would want the money first." Her voice was as hard as her eyes.

I turned a hand over. "I'm afraid that's the only way we could do it. You could tell me to go soak my head."

"So I could." Her mind was working. "Perhaps

we can arrange a compromise." She got a pad of paper from a drawer and pushed her desk pen across. "Pull up a chair, or use the other desk, and put your offer in writing, briefly. Put it like this: 'Upon payment to me by Angela Wright of five thousand dollars in cash, I will relate to her, in full and promptly, the conversation that took place between Laura Fromm and Nero Wolfe last Friday afternoon.' And date it and sign it, that's all."

"And give it to you?"

"Yes. I'll return it as soon as you have kept your side of the bargain. Isn't that fair?"

I smiled down at her. "Now really, Miss Wright. If I were as big a sap as that how long do you think I would have lasted with Nero Wolfe?"

She smiled back. "Would you like to know what I think?"

"Sure."

"I think that if you were capable of selling secrets you learned in Wolfe's office he would have known it long ago and would have thrown you out."

"I said I had some bad luck."

"Not that bad. I'm not a sap either. Of course you're right about one thing—that is, Mr. Wolfe is—I would like very much to know what Mrs. Fromm consulted him about. Naturally. I wonder what would actually happen if I scraped up the money and handed it over?"

"There's an easy way of finding out."

"Perhaps there's an easier one. I could go to Mr. Wolfe and ask him."

"I'd call you a liar."

She nodded. "Yes, I suppose you would. He couldn't very well admit he had sent you with such an offer."

"Especially if he didn't."

The brown eyes flashed for an instant and then were hard again. "Do you know what I resent most, Mr. Goodwin? I resent being taken for a complete fool. That's my vanity. Tell Mr. Wolfe that. Tell him that I don't mind his trying this little trick on me, but I do mind his underrating me."

I grinned at her. "You like that idea, don't you?"

"Yes, it appeals to me strongly."

"Okay, hang onto it. For that there's no charge."

I turned and went. As I passed through the reception room and saw Saul there on the settee I would have liked to warn him that he was up against a mind-reader, but of course had to skip it.

Down in the lobby I found a phone booth and reported to Wolfe and then went to a fountain for a Coke, partly because I was thirsty and partly because I wanted time out for a post-mortem. Had I bungled it, or was she too damn smart for me, or what? As I finished the Coke I decided that the only way to keep feminine intuition from sneaking through an occasional lucky stab was to stay away from women altogether, which wasn't practical. Anyhow, Wolfe hadn't seemed to think it mattered, since I had made her the offer and that was the chief point.

It was a short walk to my next stop, an older and dingier office building on Forty-third Street west of Fifth Avenue. After taking the elevator to the fourth floor and entering a door that was labeled *Modern Thoughts*, I got a pleasant surprise. Having on Sunday bought a copy of the magazine that Vincent Lipscomb edited, and looked through it before passing it to Wolfe, I had supposed that any female employed by it would have all her points of interest, if

any, inside her skull; but a curvy little number with
dancing eyes, seated at a switchboard, gave me one
bright glance and then welcomed me with a smile
which indicated that the only reason she had taken
the job was that she thought I would show up someday.

I would have enjoyed cooperating by asking her
what kind of orchids she liked, but it would soon be
noon, so I merely returned the smile, told her I
wanted to see Mr. Lipscomb, and handed her a card.

"A card?" she said appreciatively. "Real style,
huh?" Seeing what was on it, she gave me a second
look, still friendly but more reserved, inserted a plug
with lively fingers, pressed a button, and in a moment spoke into the transmitter.

She pulled out the plug, handed me the card, and
said, "Through there and third door on the left."

I didn't have to count to three because as I
started down the dark narrow hall a door opened and
a man appeared and bellowed at me as if I had been
across a river, "In here!" Then he went back in.
When I entered he was standing with his back to a
window with his hands thrust into his pants pockets.
The room was small, and the one desk and two chairs
could have been picked up on Second Avenue for the
price of a pair of Warburton shoes.

"Mr. Lipscomb?"

"Yes."

"You know who I am."

"Yes."

His voice, though below a bellow, was up to five
times as many decibels as were needed. It could
have been to match his stature, for he was two
inches above me, with massive shoulders that much
wider; or it could have been in compensation for his

nose, which was wide and flat and would have spoiled any map no matter what the rest of it was.

"This is a confidential matter," I told him. "Personal and private."

"Yes."

"And between you and me only. My proposition is just from me and it's just for you."

"What is it?"

"An offer to exchange information for cash. Since you're a magazine editor, that's an old story to you. For five thousand dollars I'll tell you about the talk Mrs. Fromm had with Mr. Wolfe last Friday. Authentic and complete."

He removed a hand from a pocket to scratch a cheek, then put it back. When he spoke his voice was down to a reasonable level. "My dear fellow, I'm not Harry Luce. Anyway, magazines don't buy like that. The procedure is this: you tell me in confidence what you have, and then, if I can use it, we agree on the amount. If we can't agree, no one is out anything." He raised the broad shoulders and let them drop. "I don't know. I shall certainly run a piece on Laura Fromm, a thoughtful and provocative piece; she was a great woman and a great lady; but at the moment I don't see how your information would fit in. What's it like?"

"I don't mean for your magazine, Mr. Lipscomb, I mean for you personally."

He frowned. If he wasn't straight he was good. "I'm afraid I don't get you."

"It's perfectly simple. I heard that talk, all of it. That evening Mrs. Fromm was murdered, and you're involved, and I have—"

"That's absurd. I am not involved. Words are my specialty, Mr. Goodwin, and one difficulty with them is that everybody uses them, too often in ignorance of their proper meaning. I'm willing to assume that you used that word in ignorance—otherwise it was slanderous. I am not involved."

"Okay. Are you concerned?"

"Of course I am. I wasn't intimate with Mrs. Fromm, but I esteemed her highly and was proud to know her."

"You were at the party at Horan's Friday evening. You were one of the last to see her alive. The police, who specialize in words too in a way, have asked you a lot of questions and will ask you more. But say you're concerned. Everything considered, including what I heard Mrs. Fromm tell Mr. Wolfe, I thought you might be concerned five thousand dollars' worth."

"This begins to sound like blackmail. Is it?"

"Search me. You're the word specialist. I'm ignorant."

His hands abruptly left his pockets, and for a second I thought he was going to make contact, but he only rubbed his palms together. "If it's blackmail," he said, "there must be a threat. If I pay, what then?"

"No threat. You get the information, that's all."

"And if I don't pay?"

"You don't get it."

"Who does?"

I shook my head. "I said no threat. I'm just trying to sell you something."

"Of course. A threat doesn't have to be explicit. It has been published that Wolfe is investigating the death of Mrs. Fromm."

"Right."

"But she didn't engage him to do that, since

surely she wasn't anticipating her death. This is how it looks. She paid Wolfe to investigate something or somebody, and that evening she was killed. He considered himself under obligation to investigate her death. You can't be offering to sell me information that Wolfe regards as being connected with her death, because you couldn't possibly suppress such evidence without Wolfe's connivance, and you're not claiming that, are you?"

"No."

"Then what you're offering is information, something Mrs. Fromm told Wolfe, that need not be disclosed as related to her death. Isn't that correct?"

"No comment."

He shook his head. "That won't do. Unless you tell me that, I couldn't possibly deal with you. I don't say I *will* deal if you do tell me, but without that I can't decide."

He about-faced and was looking out the window, if his eyes were open. All I had was his broad back. He stayed that way long enough to take his temperature, and then some. Finally he turned.

"I don't see that it would help any, Goodwin, for me to characterize your conduct as it deserves. Good God, what a way to make a living! Here I am, giving all my time and talent and energy in an effort to improve the tone of human conduct—and there you are. But that doesn't interest you—all you care about is money. Good God! Money! I'll think it over. I may phone you and I may not. You're in the book?"

I told him yes, Nero Wolfe's number, and, not caring to hear any more ugly facts about myself as compared to him, I slunk out. My cheerful little friend at the switchboard might have been willing to buck me up some, but I felt it would be bad for her to have any contact with my kind of character and went right on by.

Down the street I found a phone booth, dialed the number I knew best, and had Wolfe's voice in my ear.

"Ready with Number Four," I told him. "Lipscomb. Are you comfortable?"

"Go ahead. No questions."

His saying "No questions" meant that he was not alone. So I took extra care to give it all to him, including my spot opinion of the improver of the tone of human conduct. That done, I told him it was twenty minutes past twelve, to save him the trouble of looking up at the clock, and asked if I should proceed to Number Five, Paul Kuffner, the public-relations adviser who had operated on me so smoothly when he found me with Jean Estey.

"No," he said curtly. "Come home at once. Mr. Paul Kuffner is here, and I want to see you."

Chapter 10

The tone and wording of Wolfe's command had of course warned me what to expect, so I wasn't surprised at the dirty look he gave me as I entered the office. Paul Kuffner, in the red leather chair, didn't turn on the smile of enthusiastic approval he had favored me with Saturday, but I wouldn't have called his expression hostile. I suppose sound public relations rule out open hostility to a fellow being unless he actually chews on your ear. One little bite wouldn't be enough.

As I sat at my desk Wolfe spoke. "Don't sit there, Archie. Your right to sit at that desk is suspended." He pointed to one of the yellow chairs. "Move, please."

I was astounded. "What! What's the idea?"

"Move, please." He was grim.

I told my face that in addition to being astounded I was hurt and bewildered, as I arose, went to the yellow chair, lowered myself, and met his withering gaze. His tone matched. "Mr. Kuffner has made a shocking accusation. I want you to hear it from him. Mr. Kuffner?"

It pained Kuffner to have to say it. His thick

wide mouth puckered, making an arc of his plucked-
eyebrow mustache. He addressed me, not Wolfe. "I
am informed that you made an offer this morning to
a woman whose veracity I rely upon. She says that
you offered to tell her all about the talk Mrs. Fromm
had with Mr. Wolfe last Friday, if she would first pay
you five thousand dollars in cash."

I did not leap from my chair in indignation. Being
a veteran detective of wide experience under the
guidance of Nero Wolfe, I should be able to meet a
contemptible frame-up with some poise. I raised my
chin a quarter of an inch and asked him, "What's the
woman's name?"

He shook his head. "I haven't told Mr. Wolfe because she requested me not to. Of course you know
it."

"I've forgotten. Tell me."

"No."

"For God's sake." I was mildly disgusted. "If you
were a United States Senator, naturally I wouldn't
expect you to name my accuser, but since you're not,
go climb a tree."

Kuffner was distressed but stubborn. "It seems
to me quite simple. All I ask you to do is answer the
question, did you make such an offer to any woman
this morning?"

"Okay, say I answer it. Then you say that some
man told you that I stole the cheese out of his
mousetrap last night, and did I, and I answer that.
Then you say that some horse told you that I cut off
his tail—"

"That will do," Wolfe put in. "He does have a
point, Mr. Kuffner. Anonymous accusations are in
questionable taste."

"It's not anonymous to me. I know her."

"Then name her."

"I was asked not to."

"If you promised not to I'm afraid we're at an impasse. I'm not surprised that Mr. Goodwin makes this demand; he would be a ninny if he didn't. So that ends it. I shall not pursue it. If you are not justified in expecting an answer to an anonymous accusation, neither am I."

Kuffner puckered his mouth, and the mustache was a parenthesis lying on its back. His hand went automatically to his side pocket and came out with a cigarette case. He opened it and removed one, looked at it and became aware of it, and asked, "May I smoke?"

"No," Wolfe said flatly.

That was by no means a hard and fast rule. It had been relaxed not only for some men, but even for a few women, not necessarily prospective clients. Kuffner was frustrated and confused. A performance of a basic habit had been arbitrarily stopped, and also he had a problem. Taking a cigarette from a metal case with a clamp needs only a flick of a finger and thumb, but putting one back in is more complicated. He solved it by returning the case to his left side pocket and putting the cigarette in his right one. He was trying not to be flustered, but his voice showed it. "It was Miss Angela Wright."

I met it like a man. "Miss Wright told you that?"

"Yes."

"That I made her that offer?"

"Yes."

I got up and made for my desk. Wolfe asked, "What are you doing?"

"Phoning Miss Wright to ask her. If she says yes,

I'll call her a purebred liar and offer her a pedigree certificate for five thousand bucks."

"She's not there," Kuffner said.

"Where is she?"

"She was going to get a bite of lunch and then go to the chapel where the funeral will be held."

"Did you," Wolfe asked, "make Miss Wright an offer as described by Mr. Kuffner?"

"No, sir."

"Did you say anything to her that could have been reasonably construed as such an offer?"

"No, sir."

"Did anyone else hear your conversation with her?"

"Not unless that room is wired for sound."

"Then sit at your desk, please." Wolfe turned to the visitor. "If you have correctly reported what Miss Wright told you, it is an issue of veracity between her and Mr. Goodwin. I believe Mr. Goodwin. Other than what you have said, have you any evidence to impeach him?"

"No evidence, no."

"Do you still believe Miss Wright?"

"I—yes. I do."

"Then there we are. You realize, I suppose, that for me it is not exclusively a choice between Miss Wright and Mr. Goodwin as the liar, since I have no knowledge of what she told you except your own statement."

Kuffner smiled. He had caught up now and was bland again. "We might as well make it unanimous, Mr. Wolfe. I didn't mention this because it was only an inference by Miss Wright. It is her opinion that you sent Goodwin to her to make that offer. So for me too they are not the only alternatives."

Wolfe nodded, unconcerned. "Once the fabric is woven it may be embellished at will." He glanced at the clock. "It's twenty minutes to my lunchtime. We're at a dead end and might as well quit unless you want to proceed on a hypothesis. We can assume that either Miss Wright or you is lying, or we can assume that Mr. Goodwin is, or he and I both are. I'm quite willing, as a basis for discussion, to assume the last. That's the best position you could possibly have expected to occupy. What then?"

Kuffner was ready for it. "Then I ask you how you can justify making an improper and coercive proposal to Miss Wright."

"I reply that you have no mandate to regulate my conduct. Then?"

"I would decide—this would be with reluctance—I would probably decide that it was my duty to inform the police that you were interfering with official investigation of a murder."

"Nonsense. My talk with Mrs. Fromm has been reported to them, but not with a copyright. I'm not an attorney, and what a client says to me is not privileged. There was no interference or impropriety, and certainly no coercion. I had something that was legally and rightfully in my possession, a record of a talk, and I offered to sell it, with no attempt at compulsion or any hint of a disagreeable alternative. Your decision to report it to the police doesn't interest me."

Kuffner was smiling. "You certainly were prepared for that."

"I should have been. I framed the hypothesis. What next?"

The smile disappeared. "I would like to drop the hypothesis. Even if I could prove the offer was

made—and I can't, except for Miss Wright's word—
since you think you can justify it—and I'll grant
you're right for the sake of argument—where would
that get me? We haven't much time left—I must get
to the funeral—and I want to get down to business."

"Your business or mine?"

"Both." Kuffner leaned forward. "My professional
function, Mr. Wolfe, is to give advice to my clients,
and to some extent handle their affairs, so that they
and their activities will be regarded in a favorable
light. Mrs. Fromm was one of my clients. Another
was, and is, the Association for the Aid of Displaced
Persons. I have a strong feeling of obligation to Mrs.
Fromm which was not diminished by her death—on
the contrary, I will do anything in my power to see
that her memory and reputation are not damaged.
Also I am concerned about the Association. As far as
I know, there was no connection between her death
and the Association's affairs, but it is possible that
there was one. Do you know of any?"

"Go on, Mr. Kuffner."

"I am. I think it is more than possible, it is very
probable, that there was a connection between Mrs.
Fromm's death and her talk with you on Friday.
What she consulted you about must have been secret, because to my knowledge she told no one of
coming to see you. It would have been the natural
thing for her to tell me, that's obvious, but she
didn't. It must have been important, because she
certainly wouldn't have called on a private detective,
especially you, about anything trivial. And if it was
connected with whatever and whoever killed her, it
must have been more than important, it must have
been vital. I want to know about it—I *need* to know
about it. I have tried to get the police to tell me—

and they won't. You have just said that the record of
that talk is legally and rightfully in your possession
and it wouldn't be improper for you to sell it. I'll pay
you five thousand dollars for it. Cash in advance. If
you want it in currency I can have it this afternoon."

Wolfe was frowning at him. "Which is it, Mr.
Kuffner, black or white? You can't have it both ways.
You were going to report an iniquitous proposal to
the police, and now you are ready to be a party to it.
An extraordinary ethical somersault."

"No more extraordinary than yours," Kuffner
contended. "You were condemning Goodwin for it—
you even ordered him away from his desk—and then
you justified it."

"Certainly. Mr. Goodwin would have been offering to sell something that doesn't belong to him; it
belongs to me." Wolfe flipped a hand. "But your dex-
terity as a casuistic acrobat, though impressive, is
collateral. The question is, do I accept your offer?
The answer is no. I must decline it."

Kuffner's fist hit the chair arm. "You can't decline! You can't!"

"No?"

"No! I have a right to demand this as the representative of Mrs. Fromm's interests! You have no
right to decline! It's improper interference with my
legitimate function!"

Wolfe shook his head. "If there were no other
reason for my refusal it would be enough that I'm
afraid to deal with you. You're much too agile for me.
Only minutes ago it was improper interference for
me to offer to sell the information; now it's improper
interference for me to refuse to sell it. You have me
befuddled, and I must at least have time to get my

bearings. I know how to reach you." He glanced at
the clock. "You'll be late for the funeral."

That was true. Kuffner glanced at his wrist and
arose. He was obviously, from his face, deciding that
he must depart in a favorable light. He smiled at me
and then at Wolfe.

"I apologize," he said, "for being too free with my
accusations. I hope you'll make allowances. This is by
far the worst situation I've ever had to deal with. By
far. I'll be expecting and hoping to hear from you."

By the time I got back from showing him out
Wolfe had crossed the hall to the dining room.

Chapter 11

At six-thirty that afternoon I sat on a hard wooden chair in the office of Assistant District Attorney Mandelbaum, a smallish room, making a speech.

The audience of three was big enough for the room. At his desk was Mandelbaum, middle-aged, plump, to be classified as bald in two years. At his elbow was a Homicide dick named Randall, tall and narrow, with nothing covering his bones but his skin at the high spots. Jean Estey, in a chair near the end of the desk, around the corner from me, was in a dark gray dress which didn't go too well with her greenish-brown eyes, but presumably it was the best she had had in stock for the funeral.

The conference, consisting mostly of questions by Mandelbaum and answers by Miss Estey and me, had gone on for ten minutes or so when I felt that the background had been laid for my speech, and I proceeded to make it.

"I don't blame you," I told Mandelbaum, "for wasting your time, or even mine, because I know that nine-tenths of a murder investigation is barking up empty trees, but hasn't this gone on long enough?

Where are we? No matter what the facts are, I bow
out. If Miss Estey made it all up, you don't need me
to help you try to find out why. If she's telling the
truth and I made her that offer on my own, you told
Mr. Wolfe about it on the phone, and he's the one to
put me through the wringer, not you. If Wolfe sent
me to make her the offer, as you prefer to believe,
what's all the racket about? He could put an ad in
the paper offering to sell a transcript of his talk with
Mrs. Fromm to anyone who would pay the price,
which might not be very noble and you wouldn't like
it, but what would the charge read like? I came down
here at your request, and now I'd like to go home
and try to convince my employer that I'm not a viper
in his bosom."

It wasn't quite that easy, but after another five
minutes I was allowed to depart without shooting
my way out. Jean Estey didn't offer to kiss me good-
bye.

I really did want to get home, because I would
have to eat dinner early in order to keep a date with
Orrie Cather. Around five o'clock he had showed up
at the office with a report that seemed to justify an-
noying Wolfe in the plant rooms, and I had taken him
up. Wolfe was grumpy but he listened. The salesman
at Boudet's had never seen spider earrings, gold or
otherwise, but he had given Orrie a list of names of
people connected with manufacturers, importers,
wholesalers, and retailers, and Orrie had gone after
them, mostly by phone. By four o'clock he had been
about ready to report that there had never been a
spider earring in New York, when a buyer for a
wholesaler suggested that he speak to Miss Grummon, the firm's shopper.

Miss Grummon said yes, she had seen one pair of

spider earrings, and she didn't care to see more. One day a few weeks ago—she couldn't give the exact date—walking along Forty-sixth Street, she had stopped to inspect a window display and there they were, two big golden spiders in a green-lined case. She had thought them horrid, certainly not a design to suggest to her employers, and had been surprised to see them displayed by Julius Gerster, since most of the items offered in his small shop showed excellent taste.

So far fine. But Orrie had made straight for Gerster's shop and had stubbed his toe. He claimed he had made a good approach, telling Gerster he had seen the earrings in the window and wanted to buy them, but Gerster had clammed up from the beginning. He didn't deny that there had once been a pair of spider earrings in his shop, but neither did he admit it. His position, stated in the fewest possible words, was that he had no recollection of such an item, and if he had displayed it he didn't remember how or to whom they had been disposed of. Orrie's position, stated to Wolfe and me in enough words, was that Gerster was a goddam liar and that he wanted permission to pour gasoline on him and light him.

So Orrie and I were to call on Mr. Gerster at his home that evening, not by appointment.

During the day there had been various other occurrences not worth detailing—calls from Saul Panzer and Fred Durkin, who had found nothing to bring in, and nudges from Lon Cohen. One non-occurrence should be mentioned: there had been no word of a replevin by James Albert Maddox. Our lawyer, Parker, was feeling slighted.

I met Orrie at eight o'clock at the corner of Sev-

enty-fourth and Columbus, and we walked east to
the number, nearly to Central Park West, through a
monotonous drizzle that had started in late afternoon. If New York apartment houses can be divided
into two classes, those with canopies and those without, this one was in between. The stanchions were
there, from the entrance to the curb, but there was
no covering canvas. In the lobby we told the doorman "Gerster," and kept going to the elevator. The
elevator man said it was 11F.

The door was opened by an eighth-grader about
the age and build of Pete Drossos, but very neat and
clean. The instant I saw him I ditched the strategy
we had decided on and elected another. I said to Orrie, "Thanks for bringing me up. See you later." It
took him about a second to get it, which wasn't bad.
He said, "Don't mention it," and headed for the elevator. The boy had told me good evening, and I returned it, gave him my name, and said I wanted to
see Mr. Julius Gerster. He said, "I'll tell him, sir.
Please wait," and disappeared. I didn't cross the sill.
Soon a man came, clear up to me before speaking. He
was some shorter than me, and older, with a small
tidy face and black hair brushed back smooth, fully
as neat and clean as his son—at least I hoped it was
his son.

He asked politely but coolly, "You wanted to see
me?"

"I would like to if it's convenient. My name's
Goodwin, and I work for Nero Wolfe, the detective. I
want to ask you something about the murder of a
boy—a twelve-year-old boy named Peter Drossos."

His expression didn't change. As I was to see, it
never changed. "I know nothing about the murder of
any boy," he declared.

I contradicted him. "Yes, you do, but you don't know you do. What you know may be essential to the discovery of the boy's murderer. Mr. Wolfe thinks it is. May I come in for five minutes and explain?"

"Are you a policeman?"

"No, sir. Private detective. The boy was willfully run over by a car. It was a brutal murder."

He stepped aside. "Come in."

He took me not to the front, from where he had come, but along the hall in the other direction, into a small room with all its walls covered with books and pictures. There were a little desk in a corner, a chess table by a window, and two upholstered chairs. He motioned me to one, and, when I was seated, took the other.

I told him about Pete, not at great length, but enough for him to get the picture complete—his session with Wolfe and me, his second visit the next day only a few hours before Stebbins came with the news of his death, and Mrs. Drossos's call to bring the message and the four dollars and thirty cents. I didn't ham it, I just told it. Then I went after him.

"There are complications," I said, "that I won't go into unless you want them. For instance, Mrs. Damon Fromm was wearing gold spiders for earrings when she was killed Friday night. But what I'm asking your help on is who killed the boy. The police have got nowhere. Neither has Mr. Wolfe. In his opinion the best chance to start a trail is the earrings that Pete said the woman in the car was wearing. We can't find anyone who has ever seen any woman with such earrings—except Mrs. Fromm, of course—and Mr. Wolfe decided to try starting at the other end. He put a man on it, a man named Cather, to dig up someone who had ever sold spider earrings.

By this afternoon Cather was about ready to decide
there was no such person or firm in New York, and
then he hit it. A reliable person, who can be produced if necessary, told him that she saw a pair in
the window of your shop a few weeks ago. He went
to see you, and you said you had no memory of it."

I paused to give him a chance to comment, but he
offered none. His small tidy face displayed no reaction whatever.

I went on. "Of course I could raise my voice and
get tough. I could say that it's unbelievable that you
recently had an item as unusual as that in your shop
but don't remember anything about it. You could say
it may be unbelievable but it's true. Then I could say
that your memory will have to be warmed up, and
since I have no way of applying heat I'll have to turn
it over to someone who has, Inspector Cramer of the
Homicide Squad, though I would hate to do that."

I leaned back, at ease. "So I don't say it. I would
rather put it to you on the merits. That boy was deliberately murdered by someone he had done no
harm to. That was five days ago, and no trail has
been found. Possibly one never will be found unless
we can find the woman who was driving that car.
She was wearing spider earrings, and apparently
only one pair like that has ever been seen in New
York, and it was seen in your window less than a
month ago. I ask you, Mr. Gerster, does that have no
effect on your memory?"

He passed the tip of his tongue over his lips. "You
make it very difficult, Mr. Goodwin."

"Not me. The man who killed Pete made it difficult."

"Yes, of course. I knew nothing about that. I
don't usually read about murders in newspapers. I

did read a little about the death of Mrs. Fromm, including the detail that she was wearing spider earrings. You're quite right; they were unique. A man in Paris who picks up oddities for me included that one pair in a shipment which I received late in April. They were made by Lercari."

"You put them in your window?"

"That's right. This afternoon, when that man asked—what did you say his name is?"

"Cather."

"Yes. When he asked about them I preferred not to remember. I suspected that he was a policeman engaged in the investigation of Mrs. Fromm's death, though I didn't know why the earrings were important, and I have a deep aversion to any kind of notoriety. It would be very unpleasant to see my name in a headline. I shall be most grateful if you can keep it from appearing, but I ask for no promise. If any public testimony is required it will have to be given. I sold the earrings in the afternoon of Monday, May eleventh. A woman passing by saw them in the window and came in and bought them. She paid one hundred and forty dollars, with a check. It was Mrs. Damon Fromm."

It would have been an experience to play poker with that bird. I asked, "No doubt about it?"

"None. The check was signed 'Laura Fromm,' and I recognized her from pictures I had seen. I felt compelled to tell you this, Mr. Goodwin, after what you told me about the murder of that boy, though I realize that it won't help any, since Mrs. Fromm was the woman in the car and she is dead."

I could have told him that Mrs. Fromm was not the woman in the car, but I had promised my grandmother that I would never spout just to show people how much I knew, so I skipped it. I thanked him and told him I didn't think it would be necessary for his name to appear in headlines, and got up to go. When, at the door, I extended a hand and he took it courteously, his face had precisely the same expression as when he had first confronted me.

Orrie rejoined me down in the lobby. He waited till we were out on the sidewalk, in the drizzle again, to ask, "Did you crack him?"

"Sure, nothing to it. He said he would have been glad to tell you this afternoon but he caught you stashing a bracelet in your pocket. Mrs. Fromm bought them May eleventh."

"I'll be damned. Where does that leave us?"

"Not my department. Wolfe does the thinking. I just run errands that you have flubbed."

We flagged a taxi on Central Park West, and he went downtown with me.

Wolfe was in the office looking at television, which gives him a lot of pleasure. I have seen him turn it on as many as eight times in one evening, glare at it from one to three minutes, turn it off, and go back to his book. Once he made me a long speech about it which I may record some day. As Orrie and I entered he flipped the switch.

I told him. At the end I added, "I admit I took a risk. If the boy had been not his son but a nephew he would like to choke, I would have been sunk. I wish to recommend that if we peddle this to the cops we leave his name out. And Orrie wants to know where this leaves us."

He grunted. "So do I. Saul phoned. He has started something, but he doesn't know what."

"I told you I saw him at the Assadip office."

"Yes. His name is Leopold Heim and he is living

at a cheap hotel on First Avenue—it's here on my pad. He had a brief talk with Miss Wright, and one with her assistant, a Mr. Chaney. He appealed to them for help. He entered the country illegally and is in terror of being caught and deported. They told him that they cannot be accessory to a violation of law and advised him to consult a lawyer. When he said he knew no lawyer they gave him the name of Dennis Horan. That finnan haddie was too salty, and I'm thirsty. Will you have some beer, Orrie?"

"Yes, thanks, I will."

"Archie?"

"No, thank you. Beer likes me, but I don't like it."

He pressed a button on the rim of his desk and resumed. "Saul went to Mr. Horan's office and told him of his plight. Horan questioned him at length, taking many notes, and said that he would look into it as soon as possible and that Saul would hear from him. Saul went to his hotel room and stayed all afternoon. At six o'clock he went out for something to eat, and returned. Shortly before eight he had a caller, a man. The man gave no name. He said he had been aware for some time of Saul's predicament, and he sympathized with him and wanted to help. Since both the police and the FBI had to be dealt with, it would be costly. He estimated that the total amount required to prevent either exposure or harassment might go as high as ten thousand dollars."

He opened a drawer to get the gold opener, which bore an inscription from an ex-client, opened one of the bottles Fritz had brought, and poured.

When Fritz had opened Orrie's bottle, Wolfe continued, "Of course Saul protested in despair that it was impossible for him to procure such a sum. The man was prepared to make concessions. He said that it need not be paid in a lump; that weekly or monthly installments would be acceptable; that Saul could have twenty-four hours to explore expedients; and that an attempt to clear out would be disastrous. He said he would return at the same hour tomorrow, and left. Saul followed him. To attempt such a feat, following such a man in those circumstances, would of course be foolhardy for the most highly skilled operative, and even for Saul I would think it hazardous, but he managed it. He followed him to a restaurant on Third Avenue near Fourteenth Street. The man is now in the restaurant, eating. Saul phoned from across the street twenty minutes ago."

Wolfe drank beer. I had intended, when he was finished, to mix myself a healthy tall one to counteract the memory of the cold drizzle, but now I vetoed it. I could see Saul, and feel with him, in some little hole out of the drizzle, on Third Avenue, keeping his eyes peeled across the street past the El pillars, hoping to God his man wasn't phoning some pal to come for him in a car. Since it was Saul, the chances were that he already had a taxi parked down the block, but even so . . .

"I can take the sedan," I suggested, "and run Orrie over to Saul, and I'll lay back with the car. We three could hang onto Houdini."

Orrie gulped his beer down, stood up, and rumbled, "Let's go."

"I suppose so." Wolfe was frowning. Men willing, even eager, to go outdoors and brave the hubbub of the streets always discomposed him. At night, so much the worse; and at night in the rain it was outlandish. He sighed. "Go ahead."

The phone rang. He didn't reach for it, so I took

it at my desk. "Nero Wolfe's residence, Archie Goodwin speak—"

"This is Fred, Archie. The boss ought to hear it too."

"Can you make it snappy?"

"No, it'll take a while, and I'm going to need you. I'm up—"

"Hold it a second." I turned. "It's Fred, and he sounds hot. You go on. The best bet on a taxi is Tenth Avenue. If Fred doesn't need me worse than Saul I'll join you soon. If he does I won't."

Wolfe gave Orrie the address, and he beat it, and Wolfe picked up his phone.

I told the receiver, "Okay, Fred, Mr. Wolfe is on."

Wolfe demanded, "Where are you?"

"In a booth in a drugstore on Ninth Avenue. Fifty-fifth Street. I think I'm onto something. This morning I saw that guy at the *Gazette* that Archie sent me to, and he gave me a lot of stuff on Matthew Birch. Birch had several personal habits to choose from, but his main hangout was a dump on Ninth Avenue, Danny's Bar and Grill, between Fifty-fourth and Fifty-fifth. Danny's name is Pincus, and he runs a book. The place didn't open until eleven, and it was dead the first hour, and Danny didn't show until after one. I didn't camp, but I was in and out, asking everybody I saw about Birch. Of course the cops have been there often the past few days, and they probably thought I was just one more, until finally I decided what the hell. I told a little group that my name was O'Connor, and what was eating me about Birch was that I had been told that my wife had been seen in a car with him last Tuesday afternoon, not many hours before he was killed. A dark gray

Cadillac with a Connecticut plate. I said the car had been parked in front of Danny's Bar and Grill."

Wolfe grunted. "That was too specific."

"I guess it was, but I was playing for a rise, and you said I was to go on your assumption. And I got the rise. Most of them wasn't interested, except to tell me to forget it and get a new wife, but afterward one of them took me to a corner and wanted to know things. He was sharp, and I did the best I could. Finally he said it looked like I had a bum steer, but there was a guy that could give me the lowdown on Birch if anybody could, and if I wanted to see this guy a good time would be between nine-thirty and ten tonight, there at Danny's. A guy named Lips Egan."

"It is now nine-twenty-eight."

"I know it is. I was going to blow in right after nine-thirty, but I got to thinking. You ever hear of Lips Egan, Archie?"

"Not that I remember."

"I think I have. I think he used to beat carpets for Joe Slocum on the waterfront. If this is him maybe I showed too many cards and I'm going to be called, and I thought you might want to be around, but if you don't I can go ahead and play it."

"Go ahead and play it."

"Right." He didn't sound enthusiastic.

"But wait till I get there. Which side of the avenue is Danny's on?"

"West."

"Okay. I'm leaving now. I'll take the sedan. When you see me park across the street, go on into Danny's and keep your date. I'll stay in the car until I hear you scream or they roll your corpse out. If you leave with company I'll tail. If you leave alone head downtown and keep going, and as soon as I make sure you're loose I'll pick you up. Got it?"

"Yeah. How do I play him?"

"As Mr. Wolfe says, you got specific. You've bought it, Mr. O'Connor, so hang onto it. I'll find you a new wife."

"Any new instructions, Mr. Wolfe?"

"No. Proceed."

We hung up. From the drawer where I had put them on returning, I got a gun and holster and put them on. Wolfe sat scowling at me. Physical commotion and preparations for it irritate him, but as a practicing detective he defers to the necessity of putting people—me, for instance—in situations where they may get plugged or knifed or shoved off a cliff. In view of his distaste for such doings it's damn generous of him. I got an old hat and raincoat from the hall closet and left.

After getting the sedan from the garage around the corner, I crossed to Tenth Avenue and headed uptown. The drizzle was worse, if anything, and the mist thicker, but the staggered lights on Tenth Avenue keep you crawling anyhow. Turning right on Fifty-sixth, and again on Ninth Avenue, I made for the left side and slowed. There was a drugstore at the corner of Fifty-fifth. Ahead, across the street, a neon in a window said: DANNY'S BAR & GRILL. I rolled to the curb and stopped before I was even with Danny's, killed the engine, and cranked the right window down so I could see through the weather. In half a minute Fred appeared on the opposite side, proceeded to Danny's, and entered. It was 9:49.

Leaning back comfortably, through the open window I had a good view of Danny's except when passing cars intervened, and there weren't many. I decided to wait half an hour, until 10:19, before crossing the street and entering to see if Fred was still intact, but I didn't have to sweat it out that long. The dash clock said only two minutes past ten when Fred emerged with a man about half his size. The man had his right hand in his pocket and was at Fred's left elbow, so for a second I thought it was the old convoy game, but then Fred moseyed across the sidewalk, and the man headed uptown.

Fred stood at the curb, giving no sign, and I sat tight. The man turned left on Fifty-fifth. Three minutes passed, Fred standing and me sitting, and then a car came out of Fifty-fifth, turned into the avenue, and stopped where Fred was. The driver was Fred's companion, and he was alone. Fred got in beside him, and the car rolled.

With my engine still warm, there was nothing to it. I have good night eyes, and even in the drizzle I could give him a full block, and with Ninth Avenue wide and one-way I could keep over to my side, out of the range of his mirror. But I had barely catalogued those points in my favor when he left the avenue, swinging right into Forty-seventh Street. I made a diagonal across the bow of a thousand-ton truck, and the turn. He was on ahead. At Tenth Avenue a red light stopped him, and I braked to a crawl. When the light changed he turned uptown on Tenth, and I just did make the corner in time to see him swing, in the middle of the block, into the entrance of a garage. By the time I floated past he had disappeared inside. I went on by, turned into Forty-eighth, parked a foot beyond the building line, got out, and walked across the avenue to the west side.

The sign said NUNN'S GARAGE. It was an old brick building of three stories—nothing remarkable one way or another. I moved along to an entranceway across from it, stepped in out of the rain, and took a survey. The light inside was dim, and I couldn't see far into the entrance. On the two upper floors there was no light at all. The only adequate light was in a small room to the right of the entrance with two windows. In it were two desks and some chairs, but no people. When I had stood there ten minutes and still no sign of anyone, I decided that I didn't like it and it would be a good idea to try to find out why.

After going to the corner and crossing the avenue and coming back on the other side, I stopped smack in the middle of the entrance for a look. No one was in sight, but of course there could have been several platoons deployed among the congregation of cars and buses. I slipped in and to the left, behind a delivery truck, and stood and listened. There were faint sounds of movements, and then somewhere in the rear someone started to whistle "Oh, What a Beautiful Mornin'." As the whistler came nearer, off to the right, I edged around to the end of the truck. He finished his tune, but his footsteps were just as good on the concrete floor. He kept to the right—his left—almost to the entrance, and then a door opened and closed. He had gone into the office.

I moved fast but quietly, over nearly to the wall and then toward the rear through the maze of vehicles. When bumpers touched I detoured rather than risk a loose bolt under my weight. Halfway back I saw an objective, wooden stairs going up near the corner, and I made for it, but as I approached I became aware of a better objective. There were also steps going down, and up through the opening came the sound of voices. One of them was Fred's. I went

and stood at the top of the steps but couldn't catch
any words.

There's only one way to reconnoiter in such a situation without exposing your feet and legs before
your eyes have a chance. I lay down on my left side
with my shoulder above the first step, gripped the
upright with my right hand, and gently inched down
until my eye was level with the basement ceiling. At
first I saw nothing but another maze of cars and
parts of cars, fading into darkness, but as I twisted
my head around, nearly breaking my neck, I saw and
heard that the voices were coming through a doorway in a partition that was apparently one wall of a
built-in room. The door was open, but people in the
room couldn't see the stairs unless they came to the
door for a look.

I got to my feet and went downstairs, though not
that fast. All you can do on a wooden stair is keep to
the side, put your weight on each step a little at a
time, and hope to God it was a good carpenter. I
made it. The basement floor was concrete. I navigated it, now as silently as silence, across to the first
car at the right, and behind it, and then slipped along
to the next car, and the next. There, crouched in
shadow, I could look straight into the room and hear
their words. They were seated at a bare wooden table in the middle of the room, the little guy on the far
side, facing me, and Fred at the left, in profile.
Fred's hands were on the table. So were the little
guy's, but he had a gun in one of his. I wondered how
he got it staged that way, since Fred was not para-
lyzed, but that could wait. I got my gun from the
holster, and it felt good in my hand. With the car to
rest on, I could have picked any square inch on him.

He was talking. "Naw, I'm not like that. A guy

that plugs a man just because he likes to feel the trigger work, he's goin' to get into trouble someday. Hell, I'd just as soon not shoot anybody. But, like I told you, Lips Egan don't like to talk to a man with a gun on him, and that's his privilege. He ought to be here any minute. Why I'm makin' all this speech— keep your hands still—I'm goin' to lift yours now, and you're big enough to break me up, so don't get any idea that I never would pull a trigger. Here in this basement we could have a shooting gallery. Maybe we will."

From the way he held the gun, firm and steady but not tight, he was a damn liar. He did like to feel the trigger work. He kept it firm and steady while he pushed his chair back, got erect, and stepped around back of Fred. From behind a man it's a little awkward to take a gun from under his left armpit with your left hand, but he did it very neatly and quickly. I saw Fred's jaw clamp, but except for that he took it like a gentleman. The man backed up a step, took a look at Fred's gun, nodded approvingly, dropped it into his side pocket, went back to his chair, and sat.

"Was you ever in Pittsburgh, Pennsylvania?" he asked.

"No," Fred said.

"I met a guy there once that made his own cartridges. I've never saw nothin' like it. He claimed his own powder mixture had more zip, but that was all hooey; he was a goddam maniac, that's all it was. If I ever found myself falling for a nutty idea like that I'd quit and hoe beans. Sure enough, a coupla years later I heard that this guy got it out in St. Louis, Missouri. I guess he musta forgot to put in the zip."

He laughed. Until then I had had no special per-

sonal feeling toward him, but that laugh was objectionable.

"Was you ever in St. Louis, Missouri?" he asked.

"No," Fred said.

"Neither was I. I understand it's on the Missis-
sippi River. I'd like to see that goddam river. A guy
told me once there's alligators in it, but I'd have to
see 'em to believe 'em. About eight years ago I—"

A buzzer sounded—inside the room, I thought. A
long buzz, then two short, close together, then another long. The man sidled to the wall, keeping his
eyes and the gun on Fred, got his thumb on a button,
and pressed it. It looked like one short, two long, and
one short. Then he circled to the door and stood
straddling the sill, facing the stairs, but with Fred
well in range. In a moment there were footsteps
overhead, and then the feet appeared on the stairs,
descending. I ducked low, behind the car. It would
be natural for a new arrival to glance around, and I
wasn't ready to join the party.

"Hello, Mort."

"Hello, Lips. We been waiting."

"Is he clean?"

"Yeah, he had a S and W under his arm takin' his
tempachure."

I stayed down until the newcomer's steps had
crossed to the door and entered, then slowly came up
until one eye reached the glass of the car's door.
Mort had circled back to his former position and was
standing beside the chair. Lips Egan stood across
the table from Fred. He was fairly husky, with saggy
shoulders, and was gray all over except for his blue
shirt—gray suit, gray tie, gray face, and some gray
in his dark hair. The tip of his nose tilted up a little.

"Your name's O'Connor?" he asked.

"Yes," Fred said.

"What's this about Matt Birch and your wife?"

"Someone told me they saw her in a car with him last Tuesday afternoon. I think maybe she was cheating on me. Then he got killed that night."

"Did you kill him?"

Fred shook his head. "I never heard about her being with him until yesterday."

"Where were they seen?"

"The car was parked in front of Danny's. That's why I went there."

"What kind of a car?"

"Dark gray Caddy sedan, Connecticut plate. Look, all I want is about my wife. I just want to check her. This man, Mort, whoever he is, he told me you might be able to help me."

"Yeah, I might be. Where's his stuff, Mort?"

"I didn't go through him, Lips. I was waitin' for you. I just took his gun."

"Let's see his stuff."

Mort told Fred, "Go hug the wall."

Fred sat. "First," he said, "about that name O'Connor. I told you that because I didn't want to use mine, my wife being in it. My name's Durkin, Fred Durkin."

"I said go hug the wall. There back of you."

Fred moved. After he had gone three paces I would have had to edge to the right to keep him in view, and look over the hood, and there was no point in risking it. Mort disappeared too. Faint sounds came, and after a little Mort's voice, "Stay where you are," and then he backed into view and took an assortment of objects from his pockets, putting them on the table. They were the usual items of a man's cargo, but among them I recognized the yellow envelope which held the photos I had delivered to Fred the day before.

Lips Egan, going through the pile, concentrated on that and the wallet and notebook. He took his time with the photos. When he spoke his voice was quite different. Not that it had been sociable, but now it was nasty. "His name's Fred Durkin, and he's a private dick."

"He is? The dirty bastard."

You might have thought Egan had said he was a dope peddler. He did say, "Get him back in the chair."

Mort issued a command, and Fred returned into view. He lowered himself into the chair and spoke. "Look, Egan, a private dick has his private life. I heard that my wife—"

"Can it. Who you working for?"

"I'm telling you. I wanted to check—"

"I said can it. Where did you get these pictures?"

"That's another matter. That's just business."

"There's one of Birch. Where'd you get 'em?"

"I thought I might get a line on the murder of that Mrs. Fromm and pull something."

"Who you working for?"

"No one. I'm telling you. For myself."

"Nuts. Give me the gun, Mort, and get some cord and the pliers."

Mort handed the gun over, went to a chest of drawers in the rear and opened one, and returned with a brown ball of heavy cord and a pair of pliers. The pliers were medium-sized and had something wrapped around the jaws, but I couldn't tell what. He came up behind Fred. "Put your hands back here."

Fred didn't move.

"Do you want to get slammed with your own gun? Put your paws back."

Fred obeyed. Mort unrolled a length of cord, cut it off with a knife, went down on his knees, did a thorough job of tying Fred's wrists, and wrapped the ends of the cord around the rung of the chair and tied them. Then he picked up the pliers. I couldn't see what he did with them, but I didn't need to.

"Does that hurt?" he asked.

"No," Fred said.

Mort laughed. "You be careful. You're goin' to answer some questions. If you get excited and start jerkin' you're apt to lose a finger, so watch it. All set, Lips."

Egan was seated across from Fred, with the hand that held the gun resting on the tabletop. "Who you working for, Durkin?"

"I told you, Egan, myself. If you'll just tell me if you saw my wife with Birch, yes or no, that's all there is to it."

Fred finished his sentence, but he gave a little gasp and went stiff in the middle of it. I suppose I could have stood it a little while, maybe up to two minutes, and it would have been educational to see how much Fred could take; but if he got a finger broken, Wolfe would have to pay the doctor bill, and I like to protect the interests of my employer. So I slipped to the right, rested the gun on the hood, drew a bead on Egan's hand holding the gun, and fired. Then I was around the front of the car on the jump, with all the muscle I had, and springing for the door.

I had seen Mort drop Fred's gun into his left pocket, and unless he was a switch-hitter I figured that should give me about three seconds, especially since he was down on his knees. But he didn't wait to get up. By the time I made the door he had flung himself around behind Fred. I dropped flat and from there, looking underneath the seat of Fred's chair I saw his left hand leaving his pocket with the gun in it. I had dropped with my gun hand extended in front of me along the floor, and I pulled the trigger. Then I was on my feet again, or rather in the air, coming down behind Fred's chair. Mort, still on his knees, was reaching for the gun on the floor two feet away, with his right hand. I kicked him in the belly, saw him start to crumple, and jerked around for Egan. He was ten feet toward the rear, stooping over to pick up his gun. If I had known what his condition was I would have stood and watched. As I learned later, the bullet hadn't touched him. It had hit the cylinder of the gun, tearing it from his grip, and he had been holding it so tight that his hand had been numbed, and now he was trying to pick up the gun and couldn't. Not knowing that, I went for him, slammed him against the wall, picked up the gun, heard commotion behind me, and wheeled.

Fred had somehow got himself, chair and all, across to where his gun was, and was sitting there with both his feet on it. Mort was on the floor, writhing.

I stood and panted, shaking all over.

"Jesus H. Moses," Fred said.

I couldn't speak. Egan was standing against the wall, rubbing his right hand with his left one. Mort's left hand was bleeding. I stood and panted some more. When the shaking had about stopped I put Mort's gun in my pocket, got out my knife, and went to Fred and cut the cord.

He took his feet off of his gun, picked it up, stood,

and tried to grin at me. "You go lie down and take a nap."

"Yeah." I had about caught up on breathing. "That bird upstairs must be curious, and I'll go up and see. Keep these two quiet."

"Let me go. You've done your share."

"No, I'll take a look. Watch these babies."

"Don't worry."

I left the room, went to the foot of the stairs, and stood and listened. Nothing. With the gun in my hand and my head tilted back, I started up, slow and easy. I doubted if the garage man was much of a menace, but he could have phoned for help, and also Lips Egan might not have come alone. Having just proved I was a double-breasted hero before a witness, I intended to stay alive to enjoy the acclaim. So when my eyes were up to the level of the floor above I stopped again to look and listen. Still nothing. I went on up and was on the concrete. The route I had come by was as good as any, and I moved into the throng of cars and trucks. Halting every few feet to cock my ears, I was about halfway to the entrance where I became aware that someone was there, not far off to the right. That often happens. It's barely possible it comes by smell sometimes, but I think you get it either through your ears or your eyes, keyed up as they are, so faint you only feel it. Anyhow someone was there. I stopped and crouched.

I stuck there, huddled against a truck, straining my eyes and ears, for ten hours. Okay, make it ten minutes. It was enough. I began moving, one foot per minute, toward the rear of the truck. I wanted to see around the back end. It took forever, but I finally made it. I stood and listened and then stretched my neck and got my eye just beyond the edge of the truck's corner. A man was standing there an arm's length away, looking straight at me. Before he could move I stuck my head clear out.

"Hello, Saul," I whispered.

"Hello, Archie," he whispered back.

Chapter 12

I moved around the corner of the truck.

"Where's the floor man?" I whispered.

"Orrie's got him over back of the office, tied up. Orrie's sticking near the entrance."

I quit whispering. "Hooray. I'll recommend you for a raise. You tailed Lips Egan here?"

"I don't know his name, but we tailed him here. Then we thought we'd come in out of the rain, and the floor man spotted us, and we had to wrap him up. Then we heard two shots, and I started back to inquire, and I smelled you and stopped to think. You certainly are a noisy walker."

"So are you. I never heard such a din. Talk as loud as you want to. Egan is down in the basement with a friend, and Fred's there keeping them out of mischief."

Saul is hard to surprise, but that did it. "You mean it?"

"Come and see."

"How did you do it? Radar?"

"Oh, you'll usually find me where I'm needed. Guts Goodwin. I'll tell you later; we've got some work to do. Let's have a word with Orrie."

I led the way, and he followed. Orrie was standing not far in from the entrance. At sight of me his
eyes popped. "What the hell! How come?"

"Later. Fred's downstairs holding two guys. Saul
and I are going down for a game of pinochle. Any
kind of specimens are apt to turn up here, so watch
it. Is the floor man okay?"

"Saul and I okayed him."

"Right. Our lives are in your hands, so go to
sleep. Come on, Saul."

In the room in the basement Fred had the situation in hand. He was on the chair formerly occupied
by Mort, facing the door. Mort was stretched out on
his back over by the left wall, with his ankles tied,
and Egan was nearby, sitting on the floor, propped
against the wall, with his ankles likewise. Saul's appearance with me caused a little stir.

"So that's what kept you so long," Fred com-
mented, not pleased. "Do we need an army?"

Lips Egan muttered something.

"No," I told Fred, "I didn't send for him. He was
upstairs, came on Egan's tail. Orrie's up there too,
and we own the place."

"I'll be damned. Let me see Mort's gun."

I took it from my pocket and handed it to him,
and he inspected it. "Yeah, I thought so, here on the
cylinder. You didn't touch Egan. Mort's hand is a little messy, but I put a handkerchief around it, and
it'll keep a while. You kicked his stomach up to his
throat, and I tell him he ought to sit up so it can slide
down again, but he wants to rest."

I crossed to Mort, squatted, and took a look. His
color wasn't very good, but his eyes were open and
not glassy. I gave his abdomen a few gentle pokes
and asked if it hurt. Without wincing, he told me to

go do something vulgar, so I got erect, moved on to Egan, and stood looking down at him. Saul joined me.

"My name's Archie Goodwin," I told him. "I work for Nero Wolfe. So do my friends here. That's what you wanted Fred Durkin to spill, so now that's out of the way and it's our turn. Who are you working for?"

He didn't reply. He didn't even have the courtesy to look at me, but stared at his ankles. I said to Saul, "I'll empty him, and you do the other one," and we proceeded. I took my collection to the table, and Saul brought his. There was nothing worth framing in Mort's contribution except a driver's license in the name of Mortimer Ervin, but in Egan's pile was an item that showed real promise—a thick looseleaf notebook about four by seven, with a hundred pages, and each page had a dozen or so names and addresses. I flipped through it. The names seemed to be all flavors, and the addresses all in the metropolitan area. I handed it to Saul, and while he was taking a look I crossed to the chest of drawers, the only piece of furniture in the room that could have held anything, and went through it. I found nothing of any interest.

Saul called to me, "The last entry here is Leopold Heim and the address."

I went and glanced at it. "That's interesting. I didn't notice it." I slipped the book in my side pocket, the one that didn't have Mort's gun in it, and walked over to Egan. He glanced up at me, a really mean glance, and then returned to his ankles.

I addressed him. "If there's a thousand names in that book, and if each one donated ten grand, that would be ten million bucks. I suppose that's exaggerated, but discount it ninety per cent and you've still got a nice little sum. Do you care to comment?"

No reply.

"We haven't got all night," I said, "but I ought to explain that while we disapprove of blackmail rackets, especially this kind, that's not what we're working on. We're on a murder, or maybe I should say three murders. If I ask about your racket it's only to get at a murder. For instance, was Matthew Birch in with you?"

His chin jerked up, and he blurted at Saul, "You dirty little squirt!"

I nodded. "Now that's out, and you'll feel better. Was Birch in with you?"

"No."

"Who gave you the tip on Leopold Heim?"

"Nobody."

"How much is your cut of the dough, and who gets the rest?"

"What dough?"

I shrugged. "So you ask for it, huh? Take his arms, Saul."

I got his ankles, and we lugged him across to the opposite wall and put him down alongside a little stand that held a telephone. He started to wriggle around to prop himself against the wall, but I told Saul, "Keep him flat while I see if this phone's connected," and lifted the receiver and dialed a number. After only two whirrs a voice said, "Nero Wolfe speaking."

"Archie. I'm just testing a phone."

"It's midnight. Where the devil are you?"

"We're here together, all four of us, operating a garage on Tenth Avenue. We have customers waiting, and I'm too busy to talk. You'll hear from us later."

"I'm going to bed."

"Sure. Sleep tight."

I cradled the receiver, lifted the instrument, slid the stand along the wall out of the way, put the instrument on the floor a foot from Egan's shoulder as he lay, and called to Fred, "Bring that ball of cord."

He came with it, asking, "The crisscross?"

"Right. A piece about eight feet long."

While he was cutting it off I explained to Egan. "I don't know whether you've been introduced to this or not. It's a scientific method of stimulating the vocal cords. If and when you find you don't like it, the phone's right there by you. You can dial either police headquarters, Canal six-two-thousand, or the Sixteenth Precinct, Circle six-oh-four-one-six, which is right near here, but don't try dialing any other number. If you ring the cops we'll turn off the science and you can tell them anything you want to without interference. That's guaranteed. All right, Saul, pin his shoulders. Here, Fred."

We squatted by Egan's ankles, one on each side. It isn't complicated, but it's a little delicate if the patient has brittle bones. First you double the cord and noose it around the left ankle. Then you cross the legs, the right one over the left one, and work the toe of the right shoe under the left heel and around to the right side of it. For that the knees have to be bent. Pull the right ankle down as nearly even with the left ankle as possible, wind the doubled cord around them both, three tight turns, take a half-hitch and you've got it. If you grab the free ends of the cord and give a healthy yank straight down, away from the feet, the patient will probably pass out, so you don't do that. Even a gentle yank is not good technique. You merely hold the cord taut to maintain the tension. Meanwhile your colleague keeps the patient's shoulders in place, though even without him you have complete control. If you doubt it, try it.

With Saul at the shoulders and Fred at the end of the cord, I brought a chair over, sat, and watched Egan's face. He was trying to keep it from registering. "This hurts you more than it does me," I told him, "so any time you want to call the cops say so. If your legs are too uncomfortable to turn over to dial I'll cut the cord. A little tighter, Fred, just a little. Was Birch in on your racket?"

I waited ten seconds. His face was twisting, and he was breathing fast. "Did you see Birch in that car Tuesday afternoon?"

His eyes were shut, and he was trying to move his shoulders. Another ten seconds. "Who gave you the tip on Leopold Heim?"

"I want the cops," he said hoarsely.

"Right. Cut it, Fred."

Instead of cutting it, he undid the half-hitch, unwrapped the wind, and eased the left toe back under the heel. Egan started to pump his knees, slowly and carefully.

"No calisthenics," I told him. "Dial."

He turned on his side, lifted the receiver, and started to dial. Saul and I both watched. He hit the right holes, CA 6-2000. I heard him get an answer, and he said, "Police headquarters?" Then he dropped the receiver back in place and said to me, "You sonofabitch, you would?"

"Certainly," I told him, "I guaranteed it. Before we stimulate you again, a couple of points. You get one more chance to call the cops, that's all. You could keep this up all night. Second, it might be slick to come across now. If you're taking it for granted that your address book will get to the cops anyway, you're wrong. I'll give it to Mr. Wolfe, and he's working on a murder, and I don't think he'll feel like turning all those people over to the law. That's not his lookout. I make no promise, but I'm telling you. All right, Fred. Pin him, Saul."

That time we reversed it, crossing his left leg over his right, and we made the turns slightly tighter. Fred took the cord ends, and I returned to the chair. The reaction came quicker and stronger. In ten seconds his face began to twist. In ten more his forehead and neck went wet with sweat. His gray face got grayer, and his eyes opened and started to bulge. I was about to tell Fred to ease it a little when he gasped, "Let up!"

"Off a little, Fred. Just hold it. Was Birch in on the racket?"

"Yes!"

"Who's the boss?"

"Birch was. Take that cord off!"

"In a minute. It's better than pliers. Who's the boss now?"

"I don't know."

"Nuts. The cord had better stay a while. Did you see Birch in a car with a woman last Tuesday afternoon?"

"Yes, but it wasn't parked in front of Danny's."

"Slightly tighter, Fred. Where was it?"

"Going down Eleventh Avenue in the Fifties."

"A dark gray Caddy sedan with a Connecticut plate?"

"Yes."

"Was it Birch's car?"

"I never saw it before. But Birch worked with a hot-car gang too, and of course that Caddy was hot. Everything Birch had a hand in was hot."

"Yeah, he's dead now, so why not? Who was the woman with him?"

"I don't know. I was across the street and didn't see. Take the cord off! No more until it's off!"

He was breathing fast again, and his face was grayer, so I told Fred to give him a recess. When his legs had been unwound Egan thought he would bend them, then thought he would straighten them, then decided to postpone trying to move them.

I continued. "Didn't you recognize the woman?"

"No."

"Could you identify her?"

"I don't think so. They just went by."

"What time Tuesday afternoon?"

"Around half-past six, maybe a little later."

I would take that, anyhow on consignment. Pete Drossos had said it was a quarter to seven when the woman in the car had told him to get a cop. I almost hated to ask the next question for fear of Egan disqualifying himself by answering it wrong.

"Who was driving, Birch?"

"No, the woman. That surprised me. Birch wasn't a guy to have a woman driving him."

I could have kissed the louse. He had made it twenty to one on Wolfe's hit-or-miss assumption. I had a notion to get the photos of Jean Estey, Angela Wright, and Claire Horan from Fred's envelope and ask Egan if the woman in the car had resembled one of them, but skipped it. He had said he couldn't identify her, and he certainly wasn't going to take on more load than he already had.

I asked him, "Who do you deliver the dough to?"

"Birch."

"He's dead. Who to now?"

"I don't know."

"I guess we took the cord off too soon. If Leopold Heim had paid you the ten grand or any part of it, what would you have done with it?"

"Held onto it until I got word."

"Word from whom?"

"I don't know."

I got up. "The cord, Fred."

"Wait a minute," Egan pleaded. "You asked me where I got the tip on Leopold Heim. I got leads two ways, straight from Birch, and on the phone. A woman would call and give it to me."

"What woman?"

"I don't know. I've never seen her."

"How would you know it wasn't a trap? Just by her voice?"

"I knew her voice, but there's a password."

"What is it?"

Egan tightened his lips.

"You won't be using it anymore," I assured him, "so let's have it."

" 'Said a spider to a fly.' "

"What?"

"That's the password. That's how I got the lead on Leopold Heim. You asked who I would deliver dough to with Birch dead. I thought she would phone and tell me."

"Why didn't she tell you when she phoned you the lead on Heim?"

"I asked her, and she said she'd tell me later."

"What's her name?"

"I don't know."

"What number do you call her at?"

"I never call her. Birch was my contact. Now I wouldn't know how to get her."

"Phooey. We'll come back to that if we have to stimulate you. Why did you kill Birch?"

"I didn't kill him. I'm not a killer."

"Who did?"

"I don't know."

I sat down. "As I told you, what I'm interested in is murder. With that cord we could squeeze your guts out, but that wouldn't help us any; we just want facts, and facts we can check. If you didn't kill Birch and don't know who did, now tell me exactly how you've got it doped, and don't—"

A buzzer sounded. I left the chair. It went two short, one long, and one short. I said sharply, "Muzzle 'em." Saul pressed a palm over Egan's mouth, and Fred went to Mort. I stepped to the wall, to the button I had seen Mort use, and pushed it. Probably the one short, two long, and one short, wasn't the right answer this time, but it was as good as any ad lib. Then I left the room and, with my gun ready, stood three paces off from the foot of the stairs. I heard a voice up above, faintly, then silence, then footsteps, at first barely audible but getting louder. Then Orrie's voice came down. "Archie?"

"Yeah. Present."

"I'm bringing company."

"Fine. The more the merrier."

The steps reached the head of the stairs and started down. I saw well-shined black shoes, then well-pressed dark blue trouser legs, then a jacket to match, and to top it all the face of Dennis Horan. The face was very expensive. Behind him was Orrie with his gun visible.

"Hello there," I said.

He wasn't speaking, so I switched to Orrie. "How did he come?"

"In a car alone. He drove in, and I took it easy, not interested. He glanced at me but didn't say anything and went to a button on a pillar and pushed it. When a buzzer sounded I thought it was time to take a hand, so I showed my gun and told him to walk. Whoever pushed that buzzer may be—"

"That's all right, I did. Have you felt him?"

"No."

I went to Horan and patted him in the likely spots and some unlikely ones. "Okay. Go back up and tend to customers." Orrie went, and I sang out, "Saul! Take the muzzle off and tie his ankles and come here."

Horan started for the door of the room. I grabbed his arm and whirled him. He tried to pull away, and I gave him a good twist. "Don't think I'm not serious," I told him. "I know what number to call for an ambulance."

"Yes, it *is* serious," he agreed. His thin tenor needed oil. "Serious enough to finish you, Goodwin."

"Maybe, but right now I'm it, and it has gone to my head, so watch out." Saul came out. "This is Mr. Saul Panzer. Saul, this is Dennis Horan. We'll invite him to the conference later, but first I want to make a phone call. Take him over by the far wall. Don't disfigure him unless he insists on it. He's not armed."

I crossed to the room, entered, and shut the door. Fred was seated at the table massaging a finger, and the other two were as before. I pulled the little stand back to its place, picked up the phone and put it on the stand, seated myself, and dialed. This time it took more whirrs to get results, and then only a peevish mutter.

"Archie. I need advice."

"I'm asleep."

"Go splash your face with cold water."

"Good heavens. What is it?"

"As I told you, all four of us are here in a garage. We have two subjects in a room in the basement. One of them is a biped named Mortimer Ervin, who has probably got nothing for us. The other one is called Lips Egan. On his driver's license his first name is Lawrence. He's the article that called on Saul at his hotel, and Saul and Orrie tailed him here. He's a jewel. He had on him a notebook, now in my pocket, with about a thousand names and addresses of customers, and the last entry in it is Leopold Heim, so draw your own conclusions. We stimulated him some, and he claims that Matthew Birch was bossing the racket, but I haven't bought that. I have bought that he saw Birch in that Cadillac, Tuesday afternoon, with a woman driving. I have not bought that he didn't recognize her and couldn't identify her. Nor that—"

"Proceed with him. Why disturb me in the middle of it?"

"Because we've been disturbed. Dennis Horan drove in upstairs and gave a code signal to the basement on a buzzer, and Orrie took him and brought him down. He's out of earshot, but the other two are right here. I want your opinion on the kind and amount of stimulation to apply to a member of the bar. Of course he came to see Egan and he's in on the racket, but I haven't got it in writing."

"Is Mr. Horan bruised?"

"We've hardly touched him."

"Have you questioned him any?"

"No, I thought I'd call you."

"This is very satisfactory. Hold the wire while I wake up."

I did so. It was a full minute, maybe more, before his voice came again. "How are you arranged?"

"Fred and I are in the room in the basement with Ervin and Egan. Saul has Horan outside. Orrie's upstairs to receive visitors."

"Get Mr. Horan in and apologize to him."

"Oh, have a heart."

"I know, but he's a lawyer, and we won't give him cards to play. Has either Ervin or Egan shown a weapon?"

"Both. To Fred. They took his gun away, tied him in a chair, and were twisting his fingers around with pliers when I interrupted them."

"Good. Then you have them on two counts, attempted extortion from Saul and assault with a firearm on Fred. Here are your instructions."

He gave them to me. Some of it was too sketchy, and I asked him to elaborate. Finally I said I thought I had it. At the end he told me to hang on to Egan's notebook, mention it to no one, and put it in the safe as soon as I got home. I hung up, went and opened the door, and called to Saul to bring Horan in.

Horan's face was not so expressive. Apparently he had decided on a line, and it called for a deadpan. He took a chair like a lamb, showing no interest whatever in either Ervin or Egan beyond glances at the prostrate figures as he entered.

I addressed him. "If you'll excuse me, Mr. Horan, I have to say something to these two men. You listening, Ervin?"

"No."

"Suit yourself. You committed felonious assault on Fred Durkin with a loaded gun, and you committed battery on him with a pair of pliers. Are you listening, Egan?"

"I hear you."

"You also committed assault—with the gun I shot out of your hand. In addition, you attempted extortion from Saul Panzer, another felony. My own inclination would be to phone the cops to come and get you two birds, but I work for Nero Wolfe, and it's just possible he'll feel differently about it. He wants to ask you some questions, and I'm taking you both down to his place. If you prefer going to the station, say so, but that's your only alternative. If you try making a break you'll be surprised, or maybe you won't."

I turned to the lawyer. "As for you, Mr. Horan, I tender our sincere apologies. We were under quite a strain, having this run-in with these two characters, and Orrie Cather was a little too eager, and so was I. I just talked to Mr. Wolfe on the phone, and he said to give you his regrets for the way his employees treated you. I guess I should apologize for another little thing too—when I introduced Saul Panzer to you out there I forgot he had called at your office today under the name of Leopold Heim. That must have been confusing. That's all, unless you want to say something. Go on about your business, and I hope you won't hold this against us—no, wait a minute, I just got an idea."

I turned to Egan. "We want to be absolutely fair, Egan, and it just occurred to me that you might want a lawyer around while you're down at Mr. Wolfe's, and by coincidence this man is a lawyer. His name's Dennis Horan. I don't know whether he'd

care to represent you, but you can ask him if you
want to."

I thought and still think, that that was one of
Wolfe's neatest little notions, and I wouldn't have
missed the look on their faces for a week's pay. Egan
twisted his head around to see Horan, obviously to
get a steer. But Horan himself needed a steer. The
suggestion had caught him by surprise, and it had
too many aspects. To say yes would be risky, since it
would tie him to Egan, and he didn't know how much
Egan had spilled. To say no would be just as risky,
doubly risky, because Egan might think he was being ditched, and also because Egan was being taken
for a session with Nero Wolfe and there was no telling how he would stand up. It was too damned complicated and important to answer right off the bat,
and it was a treat to watch Horan blinking his long
eyelashes and trying to preserve his deadpan while
he worked on it.

Egan broke the silence. "I've got some cash on
me for a retainer, Mr. Horan. I understand it's kind
of a lawyer's duty to defend people in trouble."

"So it is, Mr. Egan." The tenor was squeezing
through. "I'm very busy right now."

"Yeah, I'm pretty busy too."

"No doubt. Yes. Of course." Horan straightened
his shoulders. "Very well. I'll see what I can do for
you. We'll have to have a talk."

I grinned at him. "Any talking you do," I stated,
"will have listeners. Let's go, boys. Untie 'em. Fred,
bring the pliers along for a souvenir."

Chapter 13

I need eight and a half hours' sleep and I prefer nine. Every morning when my bedside clock turns on the radio at seven-thirty I roll over to have it at the back of my ears. In a minute I roll over again, reach to turn it off, get comfortable, and try to figure that it's Sunday. But I know damn well Fritz will have my breakfast ready at 8:10. For two or three minutes I wrestle with the idea of getting him on the house phone to say I'll be a little late, then give up, kick the cover back, swing my legs around, get upright, and start to face realities.

That Tuesday morning was different. I had set the clock an hour earlier, for six-thirty, and when it clicked and the radio started one of those goddam cheerful morning jamborees I flipped the switch and got my feet to the floor in one desperate convulsion. I had been horizontal just two hours. I showered, shaved, combed and brushed, dressed, went downstairs, and entered the front room.

It was not a gay scene. Mortimer Ervin was stretched out on the carpet with his head resting on one of the cushions from the couch. Lips Egan was lying on the couch. Dennis Horan was in the uphol-

stered armchair, rumpled but not relaxed. Saul Panzer was on a chair with its back to the window, his
wards all in range without his having to overwork
his eyes.

"Good morning," I said gloomily. "Breakfast will
soon be served."

"This is insufferable," Horan squeaked.

"Then don't suffer it. I've told you at least five
times you're free to go. As for them, it's de luxe. A
couch and a soft carpet to rest on. Doc Vollmer, who
left his bed at two in the morning to dress Mort's
hand, is as good as they come. We're leaning over
backwards. Mr. Wolfe thought you might feel he was
taking an unfair advantage if he worked on them privately before notifying the law, so he didn't even get
up to have a look at them. He stayed isolated in his
room, either in bed or pacing the floor, I can't say
which. In your presence and hearing I phoned Manhattan Homicide at one-forty-seven A.M. and said
that Mr. Wolfe had something important to tell Inspector Cramer personally and would appreciate a
call from Cramer at his earliest convenience. As for
your desire to be alone with your client, we couldn't
possibly let a ruffian like Egan out of our sight.
Cramer would give us hell. How are you, Saul?"

"Fine. I had three hours' sleep before I relieved
Fred at five-thirty."

"You don't look it. I'll go see about breakfast."

While I was in the kitchen with Fritz, Fred came
in, fully dressed, with a staggering piece of news. He
and Orrie had been pounding their ears in the twin
beds in the south room, which is on the same floor as
mine, and had been aroused by the sound of tapping
on the ceiling of the room below, which was Wolfe's.
Fred had gone down to see, and had been told by

Wolfe to send Orrie to him at once. I would have had to dig deep in my memory for a precedent of Wolfe doing any business whatever before he had his breakfast.

Fritz had his hands full with eight breakfasts to prepare and serve, not counting his own, but Fred and I cooperated by putting a table in the front room and conveying food and equipment. We ate in the kitchen, and were disposing of our share of corn muffins and broiled ham and honey when Orrie marched in and commanded Fritz, "Forget these bums and attend to me. I have to go on a mission, and I'm hungry. Archie, go get me five hundred bucks. While you're gone I'll swipe your chair. Also give me the name of that outfit with a bunch of guys that make phone calls for so much per thousand."

I kept my chair until my breakfast was down, including a second cup of coffee, so he had to perch on the stool. Then I filled his orders. It was useless to try to guess what he was going to do with the five hundred, but if any substantial part of it was for buying phone calls wholesale I might try doping that for practice. Since I had reported to Wolfe in full up in his room after depositing our guests downstairs, he knew everything I did, but no more. Who could be the likely candidates for a thousand phone calls? It couldn't be the people listed in Egan's customer book, for it was locked in the safe—I saw it there when I got the currency from the expense drawer—and Orrie hadn't asked for it. I filed the question in my mind for further consideration during spare moments, if I had any. It wasn't the first time Wolfe had sent one of the help on an errand without consulting me.

By eight o'clock Fritz had brought Wolfe's tray

back down, and Orrie had left, and Fred and I had brought the breakfast things from the front room and were in the kitchen helping with the dishes, when the doorbell rang. I tossed the dishtowel to a table and went to the hall, and when I saw Inspector Cramer and Sergeant Purley Stebbins on the stoop I didn't have to keep them waiting while I sought instructions. I already had instructions, so, with a glance en route to make sure the door to the front room was closed, I went and opened up and welcomed them.

They stayed put. "We're on our way somewhere," Cramer rasped. "What do you want to tell me?"

"Nothing. Mr. Wolfe is the teller. Step in."

"I can't wait around for him."

"You won't have to. He's been anxiously expecting you for six hours."

They entered and headed for the office. As I entered behind them Cramer growled, "He's not here."

I ignored it, told them to be seated, went to my desk and buzzed Wolfe's room on the house phone, and told him who had arrived. Cramer got a cigar from a pocket, rolled it between his palms, inspected the end of it as if to see whether someone had dosed it with some rare and obscure poison, stuck it between his lips, and clamped his teeth on it. I had never seen him light one. Stebbins sat taking me in at a slant. He hated having his commanding officer coming there when a big murder case was sizzling, and I wouldn't bet that he wouldn't still have hated it even if he knew that we had the murderer, with ample evidence, wrapped up and waiting.

The sound of the descending elevator came, and in a moment Wolfe entered. He greeted the company with no enthusiasm, crossed to his desk, and before sitting down demanded, "What kept you so long? Mr. Goodwin phoned more than six hours ago. My house is full of questionable characters, and I want to get rid of them."

"Skip it," Cramer snapped. "We're in a hurry. What characters?"

Wolfe sat, taking his time to get arranged. "First," he said, "have you any comment about Miss Estey's charge that Mr. Goodwin offered to sell her a report of the conversation I had with Mrs. Fromm?"

"No. That's up to the District Attorney. You're stalling."

Wolfe shrugged. "Second, about the spider earrings. Mrs. Fromm bought them at a midtown shop on Monday afternoon, May eleventh. As you have doubtless discovered, there is probably no other pair like them in New York and never has been."

Stebbins got out his notebook. Cramer demanded, "Where did you get that?"

"By inquiry. I give you the fact; the way I got it is my affair. She saw them in a window, bought them, paid by check, and took them with her. Since you have access to her check stubs you can probably find the shop and verify this, but I can't imagine a sillier waste of time. I vouch for the fact, and reflection will show you that it is extremely significant."

"In what way?"

"No. Do your own interpreting. I supply only facts. Here's another. You know Saul Panzer."

"Yes."

"Yesterday he went to the office of the Association for the Aid of Displaced Persons, gave the name of Leopold Heim and as his address a cheap hotel on First Avenue, and talked both with Miss Angela Wright and a man named Chaney. He told them that he was in this country illegally and in fear of being exposed and deported, and asked for help. They said his plight was outside their field of activity, advised him to go to a lawyer, and gave him the name of Dennis Horan. He went and talked with Mr. Horan, and then went to his hotel. Shortly before eight o'clock in the evening a man arrived at his room and offered to protect him against exposure or harassment upon payment of ten thousand dollars. Mr. Panzer will give you all details. He was given twenty-four hours to scrape up all the money he could, and when the man left, Mr. Panzer followed him. He is pre-eminent at that."

"I know he is. Then what?"

"We'll shift to Mr. Goodwin. Before he proceeds I should explain that I had made an assumption about the man in the car with the woman last Tuesday when the woman told the boy to get a cop. I had assumed that the man was Matthew Birch."

Cramer's eyes widened. "Why Birch?"

"I don't have to expound it because it has been validated. It was Birch. Another fact."

"Show me. This one will have to be filled in good."

"By Mr. Goodwin. He'll get to it. Archie, start with Fred's phone call last evening and go on through."

I complied. Having known that this would be somewhere on the program, I had spent most of an hour carefully going over it, while I had been on guard duty in the front room from three-thirty to four-thirty, and had decided that only two major items should be omitted: the kind of stimulation used on Lips Egan, and Egan's notebook. The latter wouldn't be mentioned, and wasn't. Wolfe had said,

during our session up in his room, that if it proved
later to be essential evidence we would have to produce it, but not otherwise.

Except for those two items I delivered the crop.
Stebbins started taking notes but quit halfway
through. It was too much for him. I handed him
Mort's gun and exhibited the pliers, which had black
tape wrapped thick around the jaws to keep them
from breaking skin and bruising flesh. When I finished, Cramer and Stebbins sat looking at each
other.

Cramer turned to Wolfe. "This needs some sorting out."

"Yes," Wolfe agreed. "It does indeed."

Cramer turned to Stebbins. "Do we know this
Egan?"

"I don't, but I've been on Homicide all my life."

"Get Rowcliff and tell him to get on him fast."

I left my chair, and Purley got in it and dialed.
While he was phoning, Cramer sat holding his cigar
in his fingers, frowning at it, and rubbing his lips
with a knuckle of his other hand. It looked exactly as
if he were trying to make up his mind whether to
quit cigar-chewing. When Purley was through and
back in his chair, Cramer looked at Wolfe. "Horan's
in it up to his neck, but we can't hold him now."

"I'm not holding him. He is voluntarily cleaving
to his client."

"Yeah, I know. I hand you that one. It tagged
Horan all right. If we can make Egan sing we've got
it."

Wolfe shook his head. "Not necessarily the murderer. Possibly Egan knows as little about the
murders as you do."

It was a dirty crack, but Cramer ignored it.

"We'll give him a chance," he declared. "Plenty. I've got to sort this out. It's not absolutely tight that it was Birch in the car with the woman. Suppose it wasn't? Suppose the man in the car was one of the poor devils they had their hooks into. The woman was the one in the racket, the one that phones Egan the leads. She thought the man was going to kill her, so she told the boy to get a cop. Somehow she got out of it, but that night she got hold of Birch, who was running the racket, and killed him. Then he knew the boy could identify him—he might even have killed the woman, and her body hasn't been found—so the next day he killed the boy. Then he knew Mrs. Fromm was the head of that Association, so he killed her. My God, this makes it wide open, this racket and Horan in it. People like that are desperate, and there are thousands of them in New York—people here illegally and afraid of getting kicked out. They're soup for blackmailers. There must be a list somewhere of the ones these bastards were nicking, and I wish I had it. I would make it even money that the name of the murderer is on it. Would you?"

"No."

"Anything to be contrary. Why not?"

"You haven't done enough sorting, Mr. Cramer. But your snatching at a blackmail victim as the culprit shows that you're hard up. There have been three murders. Assuming, to keep it tidy, that there is only one murderer, have all the handy ones been eliminated?"

"No."

"Who has been?"

"Crossed off, nobody. Of course there are complications. For instance, Mrs. Horan says that Friday night her husband returned to the apartment ten minutes after he left with Mrs. Fromm to take her down to her car, and he went to bed and stayed there, but that's a wife corroborating a husband. If you're ready to nominate a candidate don't let me stop you. Have you got one?"

"Yes."

"The hell you have. Name him."

"The question was, have I a candidate, not am I ready to nominate. I may be ready in an hour, or in a week, but not now."

Cramer grunted. "Either you're grandstanding, which would be nothing new, or you're holding out. I admit you've made a haul—this racket, and Egan, and, by luck, Horan too—and much obliged. Okay. None of that names the murderer. What else? If you're after a deal, here I am. I'll give you anything and everything we've got, ask me anything you want to—of course that's what you're after—if you'll reciprocate and give me all you've got."

Stebbins made a noise and then tried to look as if he hadn't.

"That," Wolfe said, "is theoretically a fair and forthright proposal, but practically it's pointless. Because first, I've given you all I've got; and second, you have nothing I want or need."

Cramer and Stebbins gawked at him, both surprised and suspicious.

"You've already told me," Wolfe went on, "that no one has been eliminated, more than three days since Mrs. Fromm was killed. That will do for me. By now you have tens of thousands of words of reports and statements, and I admit it's possible that buried somewhere in them is a fact or a phrase I might think cogent, but even if you cart it all up here I don't intend to wade through it. For example, how many pages have you on the background and associates and recent comings and goings of Miss Angela Wright?"

"Enough," Cramer growled.

"Of course. I don't decry it. Such lines of inquiry often get you an answer, but manifestly in this case they haven't even hinted at one or you wouldn't be here. Would I find in your dossier the answer to this question: Why did the man who killed the boy in broad daylight, with people around on the street, dare to run the risk of later identification by one or more onlookers? Or to this one: How to account for the log of the earrings—bought by Mrs. Fromm on May eleventh, worn by another woman on May nineteenth, and worn by Mrs. Fromm on May twenty-second? Have you found any trace of the earrings beyond that? Worn by anyone at any time?"

"No."

"So I have provided my own answers, but since I can't expound them without naming my candidate, that will have to wait. Meanwhile—"

He halted because the door to the hall was opening. It swung halfway, enough for Fred Durkin to slip past the edge and signal to me to come.

I arose, but Wolfe asked him, "What is it, Fred?"

"A message for Archie from Saul."

"Deliver it. We're sharing everything with Mr. Cramer."

"Yes, sir. Horan wants to speak with you. Now. Urgent."

"Does he know Mr. Cramer and Mr. Stebbins are here?"

"No, sir."

Wolfe went to Cramer. "This man Horan is a hyena, and he irritates me. I should think you would prefer to deal with him on your own premises—and also the other two. Why don't you take them?"

Cramer regarded him. He took the cigar from his mouth, held it half a minute, and put it back between his teeth. "I would have thought," he said, not positively, "that I have seen you work all the dodges there are, but this is new. I'm damned if I get it. You had Horan and that lawyer Maddox here, and you chased them. The same with Paul Kuffner. Now Horan and the other two, there in your front room, and you don't even want to see them, and still you claim you're after the murderer. I know you too well to ask you why, but by God I'd like to find out." He swiveled his head around to Fred. "Bring Horan in here."

Fred, not moving, looked at Wolfe. Wolfe heaved a sigh. "All right, Fred."

Chapter 14

For a second I thought Dennis Horan was actually going to turn and scoot. He came wheeling in like a man with a purpose, stopped short when he saw we had company, forward marched four steps, recognized Cramer, and stopped short again. That was when I thought he was going to skedaddle.

"Oh," he said. "I don't want to butt in."

"Not at all," Cramer assured him. "Sit down. We were just talking about you. If you've got something to say, go right ahead. I've been told how you happen to be here."

Considering the atmosphere and circumstances, including the hard night he had been through, Horan did pretty well. He had to make a snap decision whether to make any change in his program because of the unexpected presence of the law, and apparently he managed it while he was placing a chair between Stebbins and Cramer and putting himself on it. Seated, he glanced from Cramer to Wolfe and back to Cramer.

"I'm glad you're here," he said.

"So am I," Cramer rumbled.

"Because," Horan went on, "you may feel that I owe you an apology, though I may not agree." The tenor was down a couple of notches. "You may think I should have told you about a talk I had Friday evening with Mrs. Fromm."

Cramer was giving him a hard eye. "You have told us about it."

"Yes, but not all of it. I had to make an extremely difficult decision, and I thought I made it right, but now I'm not so sure. Mrs. Fromm had told me something that might prove damaging to the Association for the Aid of Displaced Persons if it were made public. She was the president of the Association, and I was its counsel, and therefore what she told me was a privileged communication. Ordinarily, of course, it is improper for an attorney to divulge such a communication, but I had to decide whether this was a case where the public interest prevails. I decided that the Association had a right to rely on my discretion."

"I think the record will show that you gave no indication that you were withholding anything."

"I suppose it will," Horan conceded. "Possibly I even stated I had told you all that was said that evening, but you know how that is." He thought he would smile and then thought he wouldn't. "I had made a decision, that's all, and now I think it was wrong. At least I now want to reverse it. After dinner that evening Mrs. Fromm took me aside and told me something that shocked me greatly. She said she had received information that someone connected with the Association was furnishing names of people illegally in this country to a blackmailer, or a blackmail ring, and that the people were being persecuted; that the blackmailer, or the head of the ring, had been a man named Matthew Birch, who had been murdered Tuesday night; that a man named Egan was involved in it; and that—"

"Aren't you Egan's attorney?" Cramer demanded.

"No. That was a mistake. I acted on impulse. I've thought it over, and I've told him I can't act for him. Mrs. Fromm also told me that the meeting place of the blackmailers was a garage on Tenth Avenue— she gave me its name and address. She wanted me to go there at midnight that night, Friday. She said there was a pushbutton on the second pillar to the left in the garage, and I should give a signal with it, two short, one long, and one short, and then go to the rear and down a stair to the basement. She left it to me how to proceed with whomever I might find there, but she impressed on me that the main thing was to prevent any scandal that would injure the Association. That was like her! Thinking always of others, never of herself."

He paused, evidently momentarily overcome. Cramer asked, "Did you go?"

"You know I didn't, Inspector. As my wife and I have told you, after I took Mrs. Fromm down to her car I returned to my apartment and went to bed. I had told Mrs. Fromm that I would think it over. I would probably have decided to go the next night, Saturday, but in the morning the news came of Mrs. Fromm's death, and that terrible shock—" Horan had to pause again.

He resumed. "Frankly, I was hoping that you would find the murderer, and that there would be no connection between the crime and the affairs of the Association. So I didn't tell you of that talk. But Sunday came and went, and Monday, and I began to fear that I had made a mistake. Last evening I decided to try something. Around midnight I drove to that garage, drove right in, and there on the second pillar found the pushbutton. I pressed it, giving the signal as Mrs. Fromm had told me, and an answering signal came, a buzzer. As I was starting for the rear a man who had been lurking nearby drew a gun and ordered me to go as he directed. I did so. He took me back to a stair and commanded me to descend. At the foot of the stairs was another man with a gun, whom I recognized—Archie Goodwin."

He nodded sidewise at me. I didn't return it. He went on. "I had seen him Saturday evening in this office. While I no longer feared for my own safety, naturally I resented having guns pointed at me, and I protested. Goodwin summoned another man from within a room, also armed, and I was taken across to a wall and held there. I had seen this other man previously. He had called at my office yesterday morning, giving the name of Leopold Heim, and I had—"

"I know," Cramer said curtly. "Finish the garage."

"As you wish, Inspector, of course. Before long Goodwin called to this man, calling him Saul, to bring me to the room. There were three other men in there, one obviously with Goodwin, and the other two lying on the floor with their ankles bound. Goodwin said he had telephoned Nero Wolfe, and apologized to me. Then, after he had spoken briefly to the two on the floor, saying they had committed felonies and he was going to take them to Wolfe for questioning, he told one of them, the one he called Egan, that I was a lawyer and I might be willing to represent him. When the man asked me I said I would, and I must confess that that was ill-considered. I explain it, though I don't ask you to excuse it, by the fact that I was not in proper command of my faculties. I had been ordered around by men with guns, and besides I resented Goodwin's arbitrary transport of those men to the house of his employer when the proper procedure would have been to notify the authorities. So I agreed, and came here with them, and have been held here all night. I—"

"No," I objected. "Correction. Not held. I told you several times you could go whenever you wanted to."

"*They* were held, and I was held by the foolish commitment I had made. I admit it was foolish, and I regret it. Considering these latest developments, I have reluctantly concluded that Mrs. Fromm's death may after all have had some connection with the affairs of the Association, or with one of its personnel, and in that case my duty is plain. I am now performing it, fully and frankly, and, I hope, helpfully."

He got out a handkerchief and wiped his brow, his face, and his neck all around. "I have had no chance for a morning toilet," he said apologetically. That was a damn lie. There was a well-equipped bathroom with doors both from the front room and the office, and he had been in it. If, not having then decided to be full and frank and helpful, he hadn't wanted to have Egan out of his sight long enough to wash his face, that was his affair.

Cramer's hard eye hadn't softened any. "We're always grateful for help, Mr. Horan," he said, not gratefully. "Even when it's a little late. Who heard your talk with Mrs. Fromm?"

"No one. As I said, she took me aside."

"Did you tell anyone about it?"

"No. She told me not to."

"Who did she suspect of being implicated?"

"I told you. Matthew Birch, and a man named Egan."

"No. I mean who connected with the Association."

"She didn't say. My impression was that she suspected no one in particular."

"From whom had she got her information?"

"I don't know. She didn't tell me."

"That's hard to believe." Cramer was holding himself in. "She had a lot of details—Birch's name, and Egan's, and the name and address of the garage, and even the button on the pillar and the signal. She didn't tell you where she got all that?"

"No."

"Did you ask her?"

"Certainly. She said she couldn't tell me because she had been told in confidence."

Our four pairs of eyes were on him. He kept his, with their swollen red lids and long curled lashes, at Cramer. All of us, including him, understood the situation perfectly. We knew he was a damn liar, and he knew we knew it. He had been in a hole up to his neck, and this was his try at scrambling out. He had had to cook up some explanation for his going to the garage, and especially for the pushbutton and his signaling with it, and on the whole it wasn't a bad job. Since Mrs. Fromm was dead he could quote her all he wanted to, and since Birch was dead too there was no risk in naming him. Egan had been his problem. He couldn't ignore him, since he was right there in the next room. He couldn't stick to him, since to act as attorney for a blackmailer whose racket was being exposed—and the exposure would hurt the Association, of which Horan was counsel—that was out of the question. So Egan had to be tossed to the wolves. That was it from where I sat; and, knowing the other three as well as I did, and seeing their faces as they looked at him, that was it from where they sat too.

Cramer turned to Wolfe with his brows raised in inquiry. Wolfe shook his head.

Cramer spoke. "Purley, bring Egan."

Purley got up and went. Horan adjusted himself in his chair, getting solider, and sat straight. This was going to be tough, but he had asked for it. "You realize," he told Cramer, "that this man is evidently a low criminal and he is in a desperate situation. He is scarcely a credible witness."

"Yeah," Cramer said and let it go at that. "Goodwin, how about a chair for him there near you, facing this way?"

I obliged. That would put Stebbins between Egan and Horan. Also it would give Wolfe Egan's profile, but since he offered no objection I placed the chair as requested. As I was doing so Stebbins returned with Egan. "Over here," I told him, and he steered Egan across. Sitting, the low criminal fastened his eyes on Dennis Horan, but they weren't met. Horan was watching Cramer.

"You're Lawrence Egan," Cramer said. "Known as Lips Egan?"

"That's me." It came out hoarse, and Egan cleared his throat.

"I'm a police inspector. This is Nero Wolfe. I'll soon have a report on you. Have you got a police record?"

Egan hesitated, then blurted, "The report will tell you, won't it?"

"Yes, but I'm asking you."

"Better go by the report. Maybe I've forgot."

Cramer passed it. "That man next to you, Archie Goodwin, has told me what happened yesterday, from the time you called on a man at a hotel on First Avenue—you thought his name was Leopold Heim—until you were brought here. I'll go over that with you later, but first I want to tell you where you stand. You may be thinking that you have an attorney present to protect your interests, but you haven't. Mr. Horan says he has told you that he can't represent you and doesn't intend to. Did he tell you that?"

"Yes."

"Don't mumble. Speak up. Did he tell you that?"

"Yes!"

"When?"

"About half an hour ago."

"Then you know you're not represented here. You're facing two charges, assault with a loaded gun and attempted extortion. On the first one there are two witnesses, Fred Durkin and Archie Goodwin, so that's all set. On the second one you may be thinking there's only one witness, Saul Panzer alias Leopold Heim, but you're wrong. We now have corroboration. Mr. Horan says that he was told last Friday evening, by a reliable person in a position to know, that you were involved in a blackmailing operation, extorting money from people who had entered the country illegally. He says that his agreement to represent you was given on an impulse which he now regrets. He says he wouldn't represent a low criminal like you. He—"

"That's not what I said!" Horan squeaked. "I merely—"

"Shut up!" Cramer barked. "One more interruption and out you go. Did you say you were told that Egan was in a blackmail racket? Yes or no!"

"Yes."

"Did you say you won't represent him?"

"Yes."

"Did you call him a low criminal?"

"Yes."

"Then shut up if you like it here." Cramer went to Egan. "I thought you had a right to know what Mr. Horan said, but we won't need that to make the extortion stick. Leopold Heim wasn't the first one, and don't think we can't find some of the others. That's not worrying me any. I want to ask you something in Mr. Horan's presence. Had you ever seen him before last night?"

Egan was chewing his tongue, or anyhow he was chewing something. Some saliva escaped at a corner of his mouth, and he wiped it away with the back of his hand. His jaws still working, he interlaced his fingers and locked them tight. He was having a hell of a time.

"Well?" Cramer demanded.

"I gotta think," Egan croaked.

"Think straight. Don't kid yourself. We've got you like that"—Cramer raised a fist—"on the assault and the extortion. It's a simple question: Had you ever seen Mr. Horan before last night?"

"Yeah. I guess so. Look, how about a deal?"

"No. No deal. If the DA and the judge want to show some appreciation for cooperation, that's up to them. They often do, you know that."

"Yeah, I know."

"Then answer the question."

Egan took a deep breath. "You're damn right I saw him before last night. Lots of times. Dozens of times." He leered at Horan. "Right, brother? You goddam lousy rat."

"It's a lie," Horan said calmly, meeting the leer. He turned to Cramer. "You invited this, Inspector. You led him into it."

"Then," Cramer retorted, "I'll lead him some more. What's Mr. Horan's first name?"

"Dennis."

"Where is his law office?"

"One-twenty-one East Forty-first Street."

"Where does he live?"

"Three-fifteen Gramercy Park."

"What kind of a car does he drive?"

"A fifty-one Chrysler sedan."

"What color?"

"Black."

"What's his office phone number?"

"Ridgway three, four-one-four-one."

"What's his home number?"

"Palace eight, six-three-oh-seven."

Cramer came to me. "Has this man had any chance to acquire all that information during the night?"

"He has not. No part of it."

"Then that will do for now. Mr. Horan, you are being detained as a material witness in a murder case. Purley, take him to the other room—who's in there?"

"Durkin and Panzer, with that Ervin."

"Tell them to hold Horan, and come back."

Horan stood up. He was calm and dignified. "I warn you, Inspector, this is a blunder you'll regret."

"We'll see, Mr. Horan. Take him, Purley."

The two left the room, Purley in the rear. Cramer got up and crossed to my wastebasket, dropped the remains of his cigar in it, and returned to the red leather chair. He started to say something to Wolfe, saw that he was leaning back with his eyes closed, and didn't say it. Instead he asked me if he could be heard in the next room, and I told him no, it was soundproofed. Purley came back and went to his chair.

Cramer addressed Egan. "Okay, let's have it. Is Horan in that racket?"

"I want a deal," Egan said stubbornly.

"For God's sake." Cramer was disgusted. "You're absolutely sewed up. If I had a pocketful of deals I wouldn't waste one on you. If you want a break, earn it, and earn it quick. Is Horan in the racket?"

"Yes."

"What's his tie-in?"

"He tells me how to handle things, like people that are trying to get from under. Hell, he's a lawyer. Sometimes he gives me leads. He gave me the lead on that Leopold Heim, goddam him."

"Do you deliver money to him?"

"No."

"Never?"

"No, he gets his cut from Birch. He did."

"How do you know that?"

"Birch told me."

"How did you get in it?"

"Birch. He propositioned me about two years ago, and I gave it a run. Three or four months later there was some trouble with a guy over in Brooklyn, and Birch fixed it for me to meet a lawyer at the garage to get a steer on it, and the lawyer was Horan. That was the first time I saw him. Since then I've seen him—I don't know, maybe twenty times."

"Always at the garage?"

"Yeah, always. I never met him anywhere but there, but I've talked with him on the phone."

"Have you got anything in Horan's handwriting? Anything he ever sent you or gave you?"

"No."

"Not a scrap? Nothing?"

"I said no. That cagey bastard?"

"Was anyone else present at any of your meetings with Horan?"

"Sure, lots of times Birch was there."

"He's dead. Anyone else?"

Egan had to think. "No."

"Never?"

"Not down in the basement with us, no. The night man at the garage, Bud Haskins, of course he saw him every time he came." Egan's eyes lit up. "Sure, Bud saw him!"

"No doubt." Cramer wasn't stirred. "Horan's ready for that, or thinks he is. He'll meet it by putting the word of a reputable member of the bar against the word of a low criminal like you backed up by a pal that he'll say you have primed. I'm not saying Haskins can't help. We'll get him, and we'll— where you going?"

Wolfe had pushed his chair back, got to his feet, and taken a step. He looked down at Cramer. "Upstairs. It's nine o'clock." He passed between his desk and Cramer and was on his way.

Cramer protested. "You actually—you walk out just when—"

"When what?" Wolfe demanded. Halfway to the door, he had turned. "You've got this wretch cornered, and you're clawing away at him for something to implicate another wretch, that unspeakable Horan, in the most contemptible enterprise on record. I admit it's necessary, indeed it is admirable, but I've contributed my share and you don't need me; and I'm not after blackmailers, I'm after a murderer. You know my schedule; I'll be available at eleven o'clock. I would appreciate it if you'll remove these miserable creatures from my premises. You can deal with them just as effectively elsewhere."

"You bet I can." Cramer was out of his chair. "I'm taking your men along, all four of them—Goodwin, Panzer, Durkin, and Cather—and I don't know when we'll be through with them."

"You may take the first three, but not Mr. Cather. He isn't here."

"I want him. Where is he?"

"You can't have him. He's on an errand. Haven't I given you enough for one morning? Archie, do you remember where Orrie has gone?"

"No, sir. Couldn't remember to save me."

"Good. Don't try." He turned and marched out.

Chapter 15

I have never seen as much top brass in one day as I did during the next eight hours, from nine in the morning to five in the afternoon that Tuesday, one week from the day Pete Drossos had called to consult Wolfe about his case. At the Tenth Precinct station house it was Deputy Police Commissioner Neary. At 240 Centre Street it was the Commissioner himself, Skinner. At 155 Leonard Street it was District Attorney Bowen in person, flanked by three assistants, including Mandelbaum.

It didn't go to my head because I knew it wasn't just my fascinating personality. In the first place, the murder of Mrs. Damon Fromm, linked as it was with two other murders, was still, after four days, good for a thousand barrels of ink per day, not to mention the air waves. In the second place, the preliminary jockeying for a mayoralty election had started, and Bowen and Skinner and Neary were all cleaning fish ready for the fry. A really tiptop murder offers some fine possibilities to a guy who is so devoted to public service that he is willing to take on additional burdens in a wider field.

At Manhattan Homicide West, at the Tenth Precinct, we were separated, but that was okay. The only items we were saving were the crisscross we had used on Egan and his notebook, and Saul and Fred knew all about that. I spent an hour in a little room with a stenographer, getting my statement typed and read and signed, and then was taken to Cramer's office for a session with Deputy Commissioner Neary. Neither Cramer nor Stebbins was there. Neary was gruff but chummy. His attitude implied that if they would just leave him and me alone for forty minutes we'd have it all wrapped up, but the trouble was that in less than half that time he got a phone call and had to let me go. As I was escorted along the corridor and downstairs and out to where a car was waiting, city employees I barely knew by sight, and others I didn't know from Adam, made a point of greeting me. Apparently the impression was around that I was going to get my picture in the paper, and who could tell, I might get drafted to run for mayor. I acknowledged the greetings as one who appreciated the spirit in which they were offered but was awful busy.

At Leonard Street, Bowen himself, the District Attorney, had a copy of my statement on his desk, and during our talk he kept stopping me, referring to the statement, finding the place he wanted and frowning at it, and then nodding at me as if to say, "Yep, maybe you're not lying after all." He didn't congratulate me on collaring Ervin and Egan and tricking Horan in. On the contrary, he hinted that my taking them to Wolfe's house instead of inviting cops to the garage was probably good for five years in the coop if only he had time to read up on it. Knowing him as I did, I overlooked it and tried not to upset him. The poor guy had enough to contend with that day without me. His weekend had certainly been bollixed up, his eyes were red from lack of sleep, his phone kept ringing, his assistants kept coming and going, and a morning paper had put him fourth on the list of favored candidates for mayor. Added to all that, the FBI would now be horning in on the Fromm-Birch-Drossos case, on account of the racket Saul and Fred and I had removed the lid from, with the painful possibility that the FBI might crack the murders. So it was no wonder the DA didn't ask me out to lunch.

In fact nobody did. It didn't seem to occur to anyone that I ever ate. I had had an early breakfast. By the time the session in Bowen's room broke up, a little after twelve, I had in mind a place around the corner I knew of that specialized in pigs' knuckles and sauerkraut, but Mandelbaum said he wanted to ask me something and took me down the hall to his room. He got behind his desk and invited me to sit, and started in.

"About that offer you made yesterday to Miss Estey."

"My God. Again?"

"It looks different now. My colleague Roy Bonino is up at Wolfe's place now, inquiring about it. Let's cut the comedy and go on the basis that Wolfe sent you to make her that offer. You say yourself that there was nothing improper about it, so why not?"

I was hungry. "Okay, if that's the basis, then what?"

"Then the presumption is that Wolfe knew about this blackmail racket before he sent you to make that offer. He was assuming that Miss Estey would be vitally interested in knowing whether Mrs. Fromm had told Wolfe about it. I don't expect you to admit that; we'll see what Wolfe tells Bonino. But I want to know what Miss Estey's reaction was—exactly what she said."

I shook my head. "It would give you a wrong impression if I discussed it on that basis. Let me suggest a basis."

"Go ahead."

"Let's say that Mr. Wolfe knew nothing about any racket but merely wanted to stir them up. Say he didn't single out Miss Estey, she was just first on the list. Say I made the offer not only to her, but also to Mrs. Horan, Angela Wright, and Vincent Lipscomb, and would have gone on if Mr. Wolfe hadn't called me in because Paul Kuffner was at the office accusing me of putting the bee on Miss Wright. Wouldn't that be a more interesting basis?"

"It certainly would. Uh-huh. I see. In that case I want to know what they all said. Start with Miss Estey."

"I'd have to invent it."

"Sure, you're good at that. Go ahead."

So there went the best part of another hour. When I was all through inventing, including answers to a lot of bright questions, Mandelbaum got up to leave and asked me to wait there. I said I would go get something to eat, but he said no, he wanted me on hand. I agreed to wait, and there went another twenty minutes. When he finally returned he said Bowen wanted to see me again, and would I kindly go to his room. He, Mandelbaum, had something else on.

When I got to Bowen's room there was no one there. More waiting. I had been sitting awhile, thinking of pigs' knuckles, when the door opened to admit a young man with a tray, and I thought hooray,

someone in this joint is human after all; but without
even glancing at me he went to Bowen's desk, put
the tray down on the desk blotter, and departed.
When the door had closed behind him I stepped to
the desk and lifted the napkin, and saw and smelled
an attractive hot corned-beef sandwich and a slab of
cherry pie. There was also a pint bottle of milk. The
situation required presence of mind, and I had it. It
took me maybe eighteen seconds to get back to my
chair, settle the tray in my lap, and bite off a healthy
segment from the sandwich. It was barely ready for
swallowing when the door opened and the District
Attorney entered.

To save him any embarrassment, I spoke up immediately. "It was darned thoughtful of you to have
this sent in, Mr. Bowen. Not that I was hungry, but
you know the old saying, we must keep the body up
with the boy. Bowen for mayor!"

He showed the stuff he was made of. A lesser
man would either have grabbed the tray from me or
gone to his desk and phoned that a punk had swiped
his lunch and he wanted another one, but he merely
gave me a dirty look and turned and went. In three
minutes he was back with another tray, which he
took to his desk. I don't know whose he confiscated.

What he wanted was to clear up eighty-five or
ninety points about the report Mandelbaum had just
given him.

So it was nearly three o'clock when I arrived, escorted, at 240 Centre Street, and going on four when
I was ushered into the private office of Police Commissioner Skinner. The next hour was a little
choppy. You might have thought that, with a citizen
as important as me to talk with, Skinner would have
passed the order that he wasn't to be disturbed for

anything less than a riot, but no. Between interruptions he did manage to ask me a few vital questions, such as was it raining when I got to the garage, and had any glances of recognition been exchanged by Horan and Egan, but mostly, when he wasn't answering one of the four phones on his desk, or making a call himself, or speaking with some intruder, or taking a look at papers just brought in, he was pacing up and down the room, which is spacious, high-ceilinged, and handsomely furnished.

Around five, District Attorney Bowen walked in, accompanied by two underlings with bulging briefcases. Apparently there was to be a high-level conference. That might be educational, if I didn't get bounced, so I unobtrusively left my chair near Skinner's desk and went to a modest one over by the wall. Skinner was too occupied to notice me, and the others evidently thought he was saving me for dessert. They gathered chairs around the big desk and went to it. I have a good natural memory, and it has been well trained in the years I have been with Nero Wolfe, so I could give a full and accurate report of what I heard in the next half-hour, but I'm not going to. If I did I would go sailing out the next time I tried being a wallflower at a meeting of the big brains, and anyway who am I to destroy the confidence of the people in their highly placed public servants?

But something did happen that must be reported. They were in the middle of a hot discussion of what should and what should not be told to the FBI when an interruption came. First a phone rang and Skinner spoke into it briefly, and then a door opened to admit a visitor. It was Inspector Cramer. As he strode across to the desk he darted a glance at me, but his mind was on higher things. He confronted them and blurted, "That man Witmer that thought he could identify the driver of the car that killed the Drossos boy. He just picked Horan out of a line. He thinks he'd swear to it."

They stared at him. Bowen muttered, "I'll be damned."

"Well?" Skinner demanded crossly.

Cramer frowned down at him. "I don't know, I just this minute got it. If we take it, it twists us around again. It couldn't have been Horan in the car with the woman Tuesday. We couldn't budge his Tuesday alibi with a bulldozer, and anyway we're assuming it was Birch. Then why did Horan kill the boy? Now that we've got that racket glued to him, of course we can work on him, but if he's got murder on his mind we'll never crack him. We've got to take this and dig at it, but it balls it up worse than ever. I tell you, Commissioner, there ought to be a law against eyewitnesses."

Skinner stayed cross. "I think that's overstating it, Inspector. Eyewitnesses are often extremely helpful. This may prove to be the break we've all been hoping for. Sit down and we'll discuss it."

As Cramer was pulling up a chair a phone rang. Skinner got it—the red one, first on the left—talked to it a little, and then looked up at Cramer.

"Nero Wolfe for you. He says it's important."

"I'll take it outside."

"No, take it here. He sounds smug."

Cramer circled around the desk to Skinner's elbow and got it, "Wolfe? Cramer speaking. What do you want?"

From there on it was mostly listening at his end. The others sat and watched his face, and so did I.

When I saw its red slowly deepening, and his eyes getting narrower and narrower, I wanted to bounce out of my chair and beat it straight for Thirty-fifth Street, but thought it unwise to call attention to myself. I sat it out. When he finally hung up he stood with his jaw clamped and his nose twitching.

"That fat sonofabitch," he said. He backed off a step. "He's smug all right. He says he's ready to earn the money Mrs. Fromm paid him. He wants Sergeant Stebbins and me. He wants the six people chiefly involved. He wants Goodwin and Panzer and Durkin. He wants three or four policewomen, not in uniform, between thirty-five and forty years old. He wants Goodwin immediately. He wants Egan. That's all he wants."

Cramer glared around at them. "He says we'll be bringing the murderer away with us. *The* murderer, he says."

"He's a maniac," Bowen said bitterly.

"How in the name of God?" Skinner demanded.

"It's insufferable," Bowen said. "Get him down here."

"He won't come."

"Bring him!"

"Not without a warrant."

"I'll get one!"

"He wouldn't open his mouth. He'd get bail. Then he'd go home and do his own inviting, not including us."

They looked at one another, and each saw on the others' faces what I was seeing. There was no alternative.

I left my chair, called to them cheerily, "See you later, gentlemen!" and walked out.

Chapter 16

I have never been on intimate terms with a policewoman but have seen a few here and there, and I must say that whoever picked the three to attend Wolfe's party that afternoon had a good eye. Not that they were knockouts, but I would have been perfectly willing to take any one of the trio to the corner drugstore and buy her a Coke. The only thing was their professional eyes, but you couldn't hold that against them, because they were on duty in the presence of an inspector and so naturally had to look alert, competent, and tough. They were all dressed like people, and one of them wore a blue number with fine white stripes that was quite neat.

I had got there enough in advance of the mob to give Wolfe a brief report of my day, which didn't seem to interest him much, and to help Fritz and Orrie collect chairs and arrange them. When the first arrivals rang the bell Orrie disappeared into the front room and shut the door. Having been in there for chairs, I had seen what he was safeguarding—a middle-aged round-shouldered guy wearing glasses, with his belt buckled too tight. Orrie had introduced us, so I knew his name was Bernard Levine, but that was all.

The seating arrangement had been dictated by Wolfe. The six females were in a row in front, with the policewomen alternating with Angela Wright, Claire Horan, and Jean Estey. Inspector Cramer was in the red leather chair, with Purley Stebbins at his left, next to Jean Estey. Back of Jean Estey was Lips Egan, within reach of Stebbins in case he got nervous and started using pliers on someone, and to Egan's left, in the second row, were Horan, Lipscomb, and Kuffner. Saul Panzer and Fred Durkin were in the rear.

I said Cramer was in the red leather chair, but actually it was being saved for him. He had insisted on speaking privately with Wolfe, and they were in the dining room. I don't know what it was he wanted, but I doubted if he got it, judging from the expression on his face as he marched into the office ahead of Wolfe. His jaw was set, his lips were tight, and his color was red. He stood, facing the gathering, until Wolfe had passed to his chair and got into it, and then he spoke.

"I want it understood," he said, "that this is official only up to a point. You were brought here by the Police Department with the approval of the District Attorney, and that makes it official, but now Nero Wolfe will proceed on his own responsibility, and he has no authority to insist on answers to any questions he may ask. You all understand that?"

There were murmurs. Cramer said, "Go ahead, Wolfe," and sat down.

Wolfe's eyes moved left to right and back again. "This is a little awkward," he said conversationally. "I've seen only two of you before, Mr. Horan and Mr.

Kuffner. Mr. Goodwin has provided me with a chart, but I'd like to check. You're Miss Jean Estey?"

"Yes."

"Miss Angela Wright?"

She nodded.

"Mrs. Dennis Horan?"

"That's my name. I don't think—"

"Please, Mrs. Horan." He was brusque. "Later, if you must. You're Mr. Vincent Lipscomb?"

"Right."

Wolfe's eyes went back and forth again. "Thank you. I believe this is the first time I have ever undertaken to single out a murderer from a group of mostly strangers. It seems a little presumptuous, but let's see. Mr. Cramer told you I have no authority to insist on answers to questions, but I'll relieve your minds on that score. I have no questions to ask. Not one. As I go along an occasion for one may arise, but I doubt it."

Cramer let out a low growl. Eyes went to him, but he didn't know it. He was fastened on Wolfe.

"I shall indeed ask questions," Wolfe said, "but of myself, and answer them. This affair is so complex that they could run into the hundreds, but I'll constrain myself to the minimum. For instance, I know why Mrs. Fromm wore those golden spiders on her ears when she came to see me Friday noon, they were a part of her attempted imposture; but why did she wear them Friday evening to the dinner party at Horan's? Obviously in the hope of surprising a reaction from someone. Again for instance, why did Mr. Horan go to the garage last night? Because he knew his greed had impelled him to a foolish action, giving Leopold Heim's name and address to Egan at this juncture, and he was alarmed—as it turned out, with reason. I suppose—"

"I protest!" Horan's tenor was squeaking. "That's slander! Inspector Cramer, you say Wolfe speaks on his own responsibility, but you're responsible for getting us here!"

"You can sue him," Cramer snapped.

"Mr. Horan." Wolfe aimed a finger at him. "If I were you I'd stop lathering about your implication in blackmail. On that you're sunk, and you know it, and now you're confronted with a much greater danger, identification as the murderer of Peter Drossos. You can't possibly escape a term in jail, but with my help you may go on living. When we finish here you're going to owe me something."

"You're damned right I am!"

"Good. Don't try to pay it, either in your sense or in mine. I was about to say, I suppose most of you know nothing about the extortion enterprise that has resulted in the death of three people, so you can't follow me throughout, but that can wait. One of you will assuredly be able to follow me."

He leaned forward a little, with his elbows on the chair arms and his ten fingertips resting on the desk. "Now. I don't pretend that I can do the pointing un-aided, but I have had intimations. The other day one of you was at pains to tell Mr. Goodwin of your movements Friday evening and Tuesday afternoon, though there was no earthly reason why you should have bothered. The same one made a strange re-mark, that it had been fifty-nine hours since Mrs. Fromm had been killed—extraordinary exactitude! Those were worth filing as intimations, but no more."

He clasped his hands in front of his middle

mound. "However, there were two major indications. First, the earrings. Mrs. Fromm bought them on May eleventh. Another woman was wearing them on May nineteenth. She must have got them as a gift or loan from Mrs. Fromm, or obtained them surreptitiously. In any case, Mrs. Fromm had them back and wore them three days later, Friday the twenty-second—and why? To try to impersonate the woman who had been wearing them on Tuesday! Then she knew who that woman was, she had some kind of suspicion about her, and, most important as an indication, she was able to retrieve the earrings, either openly or by stealth, for the purpose of the impersonation."

"Indication of what?" Cramer demanded.

"Of the woman's identity. By no means conclusive, but suggestive. She must have been one whose person and belongings were easily accessible, whether Mrs. Fromm retrieved the earrings overtly or covertly. Certainly that was in your calculations, Mr. Cramer, and you explored it to the utmost, but without result. Your formidable accumulation of negatives in this affair has been invaluable to me. Your ability to add two and two is unquestioned. You knew that my newspaper advertisement about a woman wearing spider earrings appeared Friday morning, and that Mrs. Fromm came here Friday noon wearing them, and that it was a good working hypothesis that she had retrieved them in that brief interval—two or three hours at the most. If she had had to go afar to get them you would have discovered it and exploited the discovery, and you wouldn't be here now. Isn't that true?"

"You're telling it," Cramer growled. "I didn't

know they were bought by Mrs. Fromm until this morning."

"Even so, you knew they were probably unique. By the way, an interesting speculation as to why Mrs. Fromm bought them when they caught her eye in a window. Mr. Egan has said that in phoning to him a woman used a password, 'Said a spider to a fly.' Possibly, even probably, Mrs. Fromm had over-heard that peculiar password used, and indeed that may have been a factor in her suspicion; and when she saw the spider earrings the impulse struck her to play a game with them."

Wolfe took in a chestful of air, with him at least a peck, and let it out audibly. "To get on. The man who ran the car over the boy, Pete Drossos, was a strange creature, hard to swallow and impossible to digest. The simplest theory, that he was the man who had been in the car with the woman the day before, and was afraid that the boy could and would identify him, was invalidated when I learned that the man in the car with the woman had been Matthew Birch, who was killed Tuesday night; but in any case his conduct was peculiar. I put myself in his place. For whatever reason, I decide to kill that boy by driving to that corner in broad daylight, and, if and when he appears and offers an opportunity, run the car over him. I can't expect the rare luck of having the opportunity at my first try; certainly I can't count on it; I must anticipate the necessity of driving through that intersection several times, perhaps many times. There will be people around. There will be no reason for any of them to note me particularly until my opportunity comes and I run over the boy, but I will be casually seen by many eyes."

He turned a palm up. "So what do I do? I can't wear a mask, of course, but there are other expedients. A false beard would be excellent. I scorn them all and make no effort to disguise myself. Wearing my brown suit and felt hat, I proceed with the hazardous and mortal adventure. Then manifestly I am either a peerless dunce, or I am a woman. I prefer it that I'm a woman, at least as a trial hypothesis.

"For if I'm a woman many of the complexities disappear, since most of the roles are mine. I am involved in the blackmailing project; it may be that I direct it. Mrs. Fromm gets wind of it—not enough to act on, but enough to make her suspicious. She asks me guarded questions. She gives me the spider earrings. Tuesday afternoon I meet Matthew Birch, one of my accomplices. He has me drive his car, which is unusual, and suddenly produces a gun and presses its muzzle against me. Whatever the cause of his hostility, I know his character and I fear for my life. He orders me to drive somewhere. At a corner where we stop for a red light a boy approaches to wipe my window, and to his face, there so close to me, I say with my lips, 'Help, get a cop.' The light changes, Birch prods me, and we go. I recover from my panic, for I too have a character. Wherever we go, somewhere, sometime, I catch him off guard and attack. My weapon is a hammer, a wrench, a club, his own gun—but I don't shoot him. I have him in the car, helpless, unconscious, and late at night I drive to a secluded alley, dump him out, run the car over him, park the car somewhere, and go home."

Cramer rasped, "I could do this well myself. Show something."

"I intend to. The next day I decide that the boy is a threat not to be tolerated. If Mrs. Fromm should somehow verify her suspicions and my connection with Birch is exposed, the boy could identify me as Birch's companion in the car. I bitterly regret my moment of weakness when I told him to get a cop, startling him into staring at us, and I cannot endure the threat. So that afternoon, dressed as a man, I get the car from where it was parked and proceed as already described. This time I park the car far uptown and take the subway home.

"By now of course I am a moral idiot, an egomaniacal sow with boar's tusks. Friday morning Mrs. Fromm gets the spider earrings and leaves the house wearing them. When she came home late that afternoon she talked with me, and told me among other things that she had hired Nero Wolfe to investigate. That was very imprudent; she should at least have suspected how dangerous I was. That night she got proof of it, though she never knew it. I went and found her car parked not far from the Horan apartment and hid behind the front seat, armed with a tire wrench. Horan came down with her, but—"

"Hold it!" Cramer snapped. "You're charging Jean Estey with murder, with no evidence. I said you're responsible for what you say, but I got them here, and there's a limit. Give me a fact, or you're through."

Wolfe made a face. "I have only one fact, Mr. Cramer, and that hasn't been established."

"Let's hear it."

"Very well, Archie, get them."

As I got up to go to the connecting door to the front room I saw Purley Stebbins pay Wolfe one of the biggest tributes he ever got. He turned his head and dropped his eyes to Jean Estey's hands. All Wolfe had done was make a speech. As Cramer had said, he hadn't produced a sliver of evidence. And Jean Estey's face showed no sign of funk. But Purley, next to her, fastened his eyes on her hands.

I pulled the door open and called, "Okay, Orrie!"

Some heads turned and some didn't as they entered. Orrie stayed in the rear, and I conducted Levine through the crowd to a chair that was waiting for him at the corner of my desk, from which he had an unobstructed view of the front row. He was trying not to show how nervous he was, but when he sat he barely got onto the edge of the chair, and I had to tell him to get more comfortable.

Wolfe addressed him. "Your name is Bernard Levine?"

"Yes, sir." He licked his lips.

"This gentleman near the end of my desk is Inspector Cramer of the New York Police Department. He is here on duty, but as an observer. My questions are my own, and you answer at your discretion. Is that clear?"

"Yes, sir."

"My name is Nero Wolfe. Have you ever seen me before this moment?"

"No, sir. Of course I've heard of you—"

"What is your business, Mr. Levine?"

"I'm a partner in B. and S. Levine. My brother and I have a men's clothing store at Five-fourteen Fillmore Street in Newark."

"Why are you here? How did it happen? Just tell us."

"Why, there was a phone call at the store, and a man said—"

"Please. When?"

"This afternoon about four o'clock. He said his wife had bought a felt hat and a brown suit at our store last week, last Wednesday, and did we remember about it. I said sure I remembered, I waited on her. Then he said so there wouldn't be any mistake would I describe her, and I did. Then he—"

"Please. Did he describe his wife or ask you to describe the customer?"

"Like I said. He didn't do any describing. He asked me to, and I did."

"Go ahead."

"Then he said he wanted to come and maybe exchange the hat and would I be there and I said yes. In about half an hour, maybe a little more, in he came. He showed me a New York detective license with his picture on it and his name, Orvald Cather, and he said it wasn't his wife that bought the suit, he was investigating something. He said he was working for Nero Wolfe, the great detective, and something had come up about the suit and hat, and he wanted me to come to New York with him. Well, that was a problem. My brother and I don't like any trouble. We're no Brooks Brothers, but we try to run a nice honest little business—"

"Yes. But you decided to come?"

"My brother and I decided. We decide everything together."

"Did Mr. Cather give you any inducement? Did he offer to pay you?"

"No, he just talked us into it. He's a good talker, that man. He'd make a good salesman. So we came together on the tube, and he brought me here."

"Do you know what for?"

"No, he didn't say exactly. He just said it was something very important about the suit and hat."

"He didn't give you any hint that you were going to be asked to identify the woman who bought the suit and hat?"

"No, sir."

"He hasn't shown you any photographs, any kind of pictures, of anyone?"

"No, sir."

"Or described anyone?"

"No, sir."

"Then you should have an open mind, Mr. Levine. I'm asking you about the woman who bought a brown suit and a felt hat at your store last Wednesday. Is there anyone in this room who resembles her?"

"Sure, I saw her as soon as I sat down. The woman there on the end." He pointed at Jean Estey. "That's her."

"Are you positive?"

"One hundred percent."

Wolfe's head swiveled. "Will that do for a fact, Mr. Cramer?"

Of course Jean Estey, sitting there between the sergeant and the policewoman, had had four or five minutes to chew on it. The instant she saw Levine she knew she was cooked on buying the outfit, since S. Levine would certainly corroborate B. Levine. So she was ready, and she didn't wait for Cramer to answer Wolfe's question, but answered it herself.

"All right," she said, "it's a fact. I was an utter fool. I bought the suit and hat for Claire Horan. She asked me to, and I did it. I took the package—"

The seating arrangement worked out fine, with

the policewomen sandwiched among the civilian females. When Mrs. Horan shot out of her chair to go
for Jean Estey, she got stopped so promptly and
rudely that she was tossed clear to the lap of the
policewoman on the other side, who made an expert
catch. In the row behind them some of the males
were on their feet, and several voices were raised,
among them Inspector Cramer's. Purley Stebbins,
now naturally a little confused, left Jean Estey to his
female colleague and concentrated on Dennis Horan,
who was out of his chair to rescue his wife from the
clutches of the lady official who had caught her on
the fly. Horan, feeling Purley's heavy hand on his
shoulder, jerked away, drew himself up, and spoke to
whom it might concern.

"That's a lie," he squeaked. He pointed a shaking
finger at Jean Estey. "She's a liar and a murderer."
He turned to direct the finger at Lips Egan. "You
know it, Egan. You know Birch found out she was
hogging it, she was giving him the short end, and
you know what Birch meant when he said he would
handle her. He was a damn fool to think he could.
Now she's trying to hang a murder on me, and she'll
suck you in too. Are you going to take it?"

"I am not," Egan croaked. "I've been sucked in
enough. She can fry, the crazy bitch."

Horan turned. "You've got me, Wolfe, damn you.
I know when I'm through. My wife knew nothing
about this, absolutely nothing, and I knew nothing
about the murders. I may have suspected, but I
didn't know. Now you can have all I do know."

"I don't want it," Wolfe said grimly. "I'm through
too. Mr. Cramer? Will you get these vermin out of
my house?" He turned to the assemblage and

changed his tone. "That applies, ladies and gentlemen, only to those who have earned it."

I was opening the bottom drawer of my desk to get out a camera; Lon Cohen of the *Gazette* had earned, I thought, a good shot of Bernard Levine sitting in Nero Wolfe's office.

Chapter 17

At eleven in the morning three days later, a Friday, I was at my desk typing a letter to an orchid collector when Wolfe came down from the plant rooms and entered. But instead of proceeding to his desk he went to the safe, opened it, and took something out. I swiveled to look because I don't like to have him monkeying with things. What he took was Lips Egan's notebook. He closed the safe door and started out.

I got up to follow, but he turned on me. "No, Archie. I don't want to make you accessory to a felony—or is it a misdemeanor?"

"Nuts. I'd love to share a cell with you."

He went to the kitchen, got the big roasting pan from the cupboard, put it on the table, and lined it neatly with aluminum foil. I sat on a stool and watched. He opened the looseleaf notebook, removed a sheet, crumpled it, and dropped it into the pan. When a dozen or more sheets were in the pile he applied a match, and then went on adding fuel to the flame, sheet after sheet, until the book was empty.

"There," he said in a satisfied tone, and went to

the sink to wash his hands. I tossed the book cover in the trash basket.

I thought at the time he was rushing things a little, since it was still possible they would need some extra evidence. But that was many weeks ago, and now that Horan and Egan had been duly tried, convicted, and sentenced, and it took a jury of seven men and five women only four hours to hang the big one on Jean Estey—what the hell.

Rex Stout

REX STOUT, the creator of Nero Wolfe, was born in Noblesville, Indiana, in 1886, the sixth of nine children of John and Lucetta Todhunter Stout, both Quakers. Shortly after his birth the family moved to Wakarusa, Kansas. He was educated in a country school, but by the age of nine he was recognized throughout the state as a prodigy in arithmetic. Mr. Stout briefly attended the University of Kansas, but he left to enlist in the Navy and spent the next two years as a warrant officer on board President Theodore Roosevelt's yacht. When he left the Navy in 1908, Rex Stout began to write freelance articles and worked as a sightseeing guide and an itinerant bookkeeper. Later he devised and implemented a school banking system which was installed in four hundred cities and towns throughout the country. In 1927 Mr. Stout retired from the world of finance and, with the proceeds of his banking scheme, left for Paris to write serious fiction. He wrote three novels that received favorable reviews before turning to detective fiction. His first Nero Wolfe novel, *Fer-de-Lance*, appeared in 1934. It was followed by many others, among them, *Too Many Cooks*, *The Silent Speaker*, *If Death Ever Slept*, *The Doorbell Rang*, and *Please Pass the Guilt*, which established Nero Wolfe as a leading character on a par with Erle Stanley Gardner's famous protagonist, Perry Mason. During World War II Rex Stout waged a personal campaign against Nazism as chairman of the War Writers' Board, master of ceremonies of the radio program "Speaking of Liberty," and member of several national committees. After the war he turned his attention to mobilizing public opinion against the wartime use of thermonuclear devices, was an active leader in the Authors' Guild, and resumed writing his Nero Wolfe novels. Rex Stout died in 1975 at the age of eighty-eight. A month before his death he published his seventy-second Nero Wolfe mystery, *A Family Affair*. Ten years later, a seventy-third Nero Wolfe mystery was discovered and published in *Death Times Three*.

Not for publication
Confidential Memo
From Rex Stout
September 15 1949

DESCRIPTION OF NERO WOLFE

Height 5 ft. 11 in. Weight 272 lbs. Age 56.
Mass of dark brown hair, very little greying, is not
parted but sweeps off to the right because he brushes
with his right hand. Dark brown eyes are average in
size, but look smaller because they are mostly half
closed. They always are aimed straight at the person
he is talking to. Forehead is high. Head and face
are big but do not seem so in proportion to the whole.
Ears rather small. Nose long and narrow, slightly
aquiline. Mouth mobile and extremely variable; lips
when pursed are full and thick, but in tense moments
they are thin and their line is long. Cheeks full but
not pudgy; the high point of the cheekbone can be seen
from straight front. Complexion varies from some
floridity after meals to an ivory pallor late at night
when he has spent six hard hours working on someone.
He breathes smoothly and without sound except when he
is eating; then he takes in and lets out great gusts of
air. His massive shoulders never slump; when he stands
up at all he stands straight. He shaves every day. He
has a small brown mole just above his right jawbone,
halfway between the chin and the ear.

DESCRIPTION OF ARCHIE GOODWIN

Height 6 feet. Weight 180 lbs. Age 32. Hair is
light rather than dark, but just barely decided not to
be red; he gets it cut every two weeks, rather short,
and brushes it straight back, but it keeps standing up.
He shaves four times a week and grasps at every excuse
to make it only three times. His features are all regular, well-modeled and well-proportioned, except the
nose. He escapes the curse of being the movie actor
type only through the nose. It is not a true pug and
is by no means a deformity, but it is a little short
and the ridge is broad, and the tip has continued on
its own, beyond the cartilage, giving the impression
of startling and quite independent initiative. The eyes
are grey, and are inquisitive and quick to move. He is
muscular both in appearance and in movement, and upright
in posture, but his shoulders stoop a little in unconscious
reaction to Wolfe's repeated criticism that he is too
self-assertive.

DESCRIPTION OF WOLFE'S OFFICE

The old brownstone on West 35th Street is a double-
width house. Entering at the front door, which is seven
steps up from the sidewalk, you are facing the length of

a wide carpeted hall. At the right is an enormous coat
rack, eight feet wide, then the stairs, and beyond the
stairs the door to the dining room. There were originally two rooms òn that side of the hall, but Wolfe had
the partition removed and turned it into a dining room
forty feet long, with a table large enough for six (but
extensible) square in the middle. It (and all other
rooms) are carpeted; Wolfe hates bare floors. At the
far end of the big hall is the kitchen. At the left of the
bìg hall are two doors; the first one is to what Archie calls
the front room, and the second is to the office. The front
room is used chiefly as an anteroom; Nero and Archie do
no living there. It is rather small, and the furniture
is a random mixture without any special character.

The office is large and nearly square. In the far
corner to the left (as you enter from the hall) a small
rectangle has been walled off to make a place for a
john and a washbowl — to save steps for Wolfe. The door
leading to it faces you, and around the corner, along its
other wall, is a wide and well-cushioned couch.

SKETCH OF OFFICE

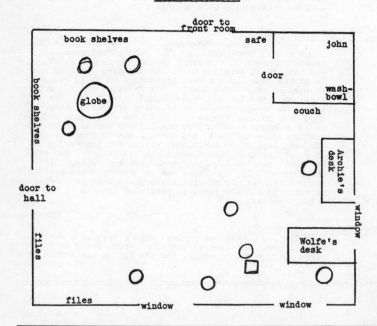

In furnishings the room has no apparent unity
but it has plenty of character. Wolfe permits nothing
to be in it that he doesn't enjoy looking at, and that
has been the only criterion for admission. The globe
is three feet in diameter. Wolfe's chair was made by
Meyer of cardato. His desk is of cherry, which of
course clashes with the cardato, but Wolfe likes it.
The couch is upholstered in bright yellow material
which has to go to the cleaners every three months.
The carpet was woven in Montenegro in the early nineteenth century and has been extensively patched. The
only wall decorations are three pictures: a Manet, a
copy of a Corregio, and a genuine Leonardo sketch. The
chairs are all shapes, colors, materials, and sizes.
The total effect makes you blink with bewilderment at
the first visit, but if you had Archie's job and lived
there you would probably learn to like it.

P. G. Wodehouse
Remsenburg
New York 11960
June 3.1969

Dear Den.

Thanks for the Ellery Queen and the two
paperbacks.   What a good story Buried Caesar is.
I had read it before, of course, but had completely
forgotten what happened after the adventure with the
bull.   I find I can re-read Rex Stout indefinitely,
which shows the importance of atmosphere. I am looking
forward to getting the Emma Lathen.

Good luck to the musical. What there was of it
in Ellery was most promising.

Yours ever

Plum

ජේෂ්ස්ටවුරගේ
රත් මතුවිම

අනුවාදය
ජ.ඒ.දැන්සකොවිරත්ත